SPEED

Also by BB Easton

Sex/Life: 44 Chapters About 4 Men (A Memoir)

The Sex/Life Novels

Skin

Star

Suit

SPEED

BB Easton

FOREVER

NEW YORK   BOSTON

Forever
Hachette Book Group
1290 Avenue of the Americas, New York, NY 10104
read-forever.com
twitter.com/readforeverpub

First trade paperback edition: August 2021

Forever is an imprint of Grand Central Publishing. The Forever name and logo are trademarks of Hachette Book Group, Inc.

The publisher is not responsible for websites (or their content) that are not owned by the publisher.

The Hachette Speakers Bureau provides a wide range of authors for speaking events. To find out more, go to www.hachettespeakersbureau.com or call (866) 376-6591.

Library of Congress Control Number: 2021939244

ISBNs: 978-1-5387-1838-4 (trade paperback), 978-1-5387-1837-7 (ebook)

Printed in the United States of America

LSC-C

Printing 1, 2021

This book is dedicated to my parents. Consider it my apology for bringing a twenty-two-year-old ex-con with a tattoo on his head home for dinner . . . when I was only sixteen.

An apology that you are never, ever allowed to read—ever.

AUTHOR'S NOTE

Speed is a work of fiction based on characters and events introduced in my memoir, *Sex/Life: 44 Chapters About 4 Men*. While many of the situations portrayed in this book are true to life, many others were added, exaggerated, or altered to enhance the story. I also changed the names and identifying characteristics of every character (and most locations) to protect the identities of everyone involved.

Due to excessive profanity, violence, graphic sexual content, and themes of juvenile delinquency, this book is not intended for—and should probably be completely hidden from—anyone under the age of eighteen.

GEORGIA
INTRODUCTION
19 PEACH STATE 99

There are two types of people in this world—those who've read my memoir, *Sex/Life: 44 Chapters About 4 Men*, and those who have not. Both types are welcome here. Unless, of course, you belong to one of those groups *and* your last name also happens to be Bradley or Easton. In that case, the odds of us being related by blood or marriage are simply too high for me to allow you to proceed. Please, Ms. Bradley, put the book down and back away slowly. Trust me on this, Mr. Easton. It's for your own good.

If your last name is *not* Bradley or Easton and this is your first dose of Harley James, hold on to your ass. He is the ultimate baby-faced bad boy, and he took me on the ride of my life. Pun not intended. Harley's character is loosely based on an actual ex-boyfriend of mine, but his name, identifying characteristics, and personality traits have been altered and/or exaggerated to the point that not even his mama would recognize him. I mean, she'd have her suspicions, but she couldn't prove a damn thing.

If you belong to the former group, then you've already been introduced to Mr. Harley James—two versions of him actually. You saw him portrayed as a lovable moron in my real-life journal entries *and* as a fictionalized lothario in the ones I left out for Ken to stumble upon. Well, I am happy to report that the fictionalized-lothario Harley is the one starring in this book while the plot, setting, and timeline are based on mostly true events. I tried to give you guys the best of both worlds—the sexy, dangerous, tattooed hero *and* a gritty, raw, true-life story.

Like I said in *Skin*, this book is *my* truth—it's just not one hundred percent *the* truth.

(In this case, it's more like sixty-five percent. Seventy-five, tops.)

Enjoy the ride!

SPEED

GEORGIA
GLOSSARY
19 PEACH STATE 99

ATV (abbr.)—All-Terrain Vehicle.

AWOL (abbr.)—Absent Without Leave. A military term used in reference to soldiers who have left their posts without proper clearance.

Bajillion (noun)—a made-up number somewhere between one billion and a shitload.

Benzo (noun)—Slang. An illicitly used anti-anxiety pill belonging to the benzodiazepine classification. Examples include Xanax, Valium, Ativan, and Klonopin.

Crotch Rocket (noun)—Slang. A specific type of imported motorcycle, characterized by a lightweight, aerodynamic body and favored by street racers.

Cumtrillionth (adj.)—a person's bajillionth orgasm.

Dip (noun)—Slang. Chewing tobacco.

DMV (abbr.)—Department of Motor Vehicles.

Doobie (noun)—Slang. A term hippies use in reference to a hand-rolled marijuana cigarette.

Factory/Stock (adj.)—a vehicle with no aftermarket modifications.

Fastback (adj.)—the sexiest muscle car body style ever made, characterized by a roofline that slopes in one continuous line down the back of the car to the rear spoiler.

Five-oh (noun)—Slang. A Ford Mustang with a five-liter V8 engine, produced from 1979–1993. The term refers to a small silver emblem affixed behind the front-wheel wells on this particular model that reads 5.0.

Fishtail (verb)—Slang. When the back end of a vehicle slides from side to side due to a handling or traction problem.

Flophouse (noun)—Slang. Cheap or free lodging with minimal amenities, often inhabited by several people at once and used as a place to hide from the police and/or do drugs.

Four twenty-nine (noun)—Slang. A vintage Mustang with a 429 cubic-inch engine.

Gutter punk (noun)—Slang. A homeless or transient youth whose appearance and lifestyle choices are associated with the punk subculture.

Head Shop (noun)—a retail store specializing in marijuana and tobacco paraphernalia.

Hooptie (noun)—Slang. A large, older model American sedan, often in poor condition but equipped with flashy after-market modifications.

Jarhead (noun)—Slang. A derogatory term used to describe a member of the United States Marine Corps. It is in reference to the flattop-style haircut that many Marines have, which makes their heads appear to be jar-shaped.

Jackalope (noun)—a mythical creature of North American folklore, created when deer antlers are affixed to a taxidermic jackrabbit.

Juvie (noun)—Slang. Juvenile Detention Center. A prison-like institution for minors.

Kegger (noun)—Slang. Keg party. A social gathering of teens and young adults centered around a metal barrel full of cheap, piss-colored beer.

MDMA (abbr.)—the street drug methylenedioxymethamphetamine, commonly referred to as ecstasy.

Motorhead (noun)—Slang. A car/racing enthusiast who has a wealth of knowledge about auto mechanics.

Mudding (verb)—Slang. Driving an all-terrain or four-wheel-drive vehicle off-road in muddy areas, such as creek beds or fields after a hard rain. The objective of this recreational activity is to get one's vehicle as filthy as possible without getting it stuck.

Narced (verb, past tense)—Slang. To inform the police or authorities that someone is in the possession of illegal drugs. Derived from the word narcotics.

Natty Ice (noun)—Slang. Natural Ice, an inexpensive brand of American beer, favored by rednecks.

Nine-eleven (noun)—Slang. A Porsche 911 model.

Peater (noun)—Slang. A made-up word for a passive cheater.

P.O.S. (abbr.)—Piece Of Shit.

Priors (noun, plural)—Slang. Prior convictions.

Racing slicks (noun, plural)—Special racing tires that are extra wide and have a smooth surface rather than tread.

Rager (noun)—See Kegger.

RBF (abbr.)—Resting Bitch Face.

Redneck (noun)—Slang. A derogatory term used to describe a rural, working-class white person from the southeastern

United States. The term refers to the tendency for men from these backgrounds to have sunburns on the backs of their necks due to working manual labor jobs outside.

Rolling (verb)—Slang. To be high on MDMA/ecstasy.

RPM (abv.)—Revolutions Per Minute.

Shittastic (adj.)—the polar opposite of fantastic.

SoCo (abbr.)—Slang. Southern Comfort, a brand of whiskey.

Spoiler (noun)—a flap or arch on the back of a car, designed to reduce drag and improve aerodynamics.

Skin (noun)—Slang. A member of the skinhead subculture.

Torque (noun)—an automotive measurement of how quickly a vehicle will accelerate, considered more important than horsepower in short-distance street racing.

Twenty-twos (noun)—Slang. Twenty-two-inch wheels.

Wifebeater (noun)—Slang. A fitted, ribbed white cotton tank top designed to be worn by men as an undergarment. The term refers to the abusive, working-class male characters who tend to wear these garments in classic American films.

Winch (noun)—a motorized rotating drum designed to reel in a length of cable attached to something very heavy. For example, a truck that has gotten stuck in the mud, like a little bitch.

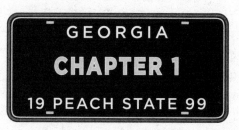

GEORGIA
CHAPTER 1
19 PEACH STATE 99

June 1998

When I woke up on my sixteenth birthday, I didn't leap out of bed to go get my driver's license. I wasn't thinking about the appointment I had to buy my first car that afternoon—a car that I'd been saving for since the day I turned fifteen and was legally able to work. I didn't give two shits about going to the mall, or opening presents, or eating a fucking piece of fucking cake. All I wanted for my birthday was to sleep through it, because whenever I was awake, so was my gnawing, soul-crushing pain. I could feel it chewing through the lining of my stomach, devouring my once-bubbly personality, sucking the energy from my bone marrow, swallowing my will to live. Being eaten alive hurt. Being awake hurt. Being asleep didn't.

I reluctantly opened my eyes and glanced over at the nightstand. The red numbers on the clock announced that I'd slept past noon again. The blueberry muffin sitting next to it with a candle shoved haphazardly in the top told me that my mom must have come in and tried to wake me up. My wide-open blinds, which were letting in an obscene amount of summer sun, let me know that she'd tried more than once. And that little white pill and glass of water on my nightstand? Well, they just pissed me off.

I sat up and squinted at the assorted bullshit on the table until I spotted my pack of Camel Lights. Swinging my spindly legs over the edge of the mattress, I reached past the food and water, opting for poison instead. I lit a cigarette and waited for that comforting, calming first inhalation to do its thing, but even smoking had become joyless. Just like everything else, I was going through the motions.

Hand to mouth.

Inhale.

Exhale.

Repeat.

I ashed my cigarette in an empty Altoids tin on the nightstand and stared at the pill my mother had left for me—the tiny white hope that had turned out to be just another disappointment. I picked it up and inspected it. If it hadn't had the word PROZAC stamped on the side of it, I would have assumed they'd just been giving me Tic Tacs.

That shit did nothing. Nothing but mute the vibrant colors of my world to a dirty, dull gray. Instead of my feelings being a violent riot of bitter, angry crimsons, churning, crashing ceruleans, and blinking, cautionary yellows, my inner world was now as gray as the cloud of smoke that hung four feet above the floor and three feet below the ceiling in my bedroom. As gray as my skin, which now draped between my ribs and puddled in the hollows of my cheeks and eye sockets.

As gray as the fading knight tattoo on the inside of my wedding ring finger.

I threw the glorified breath mint across the room and listened to the *plink, plink, plink* sound it made as it bounced off the wall, onto my "desk"—which was just two filing cabinets and an old door that my mom had scrounged up at Goodwill and spray-painted black—and landed in a heap of shiny Army-green nylon on the floor.

My chest felt as if someone had come up behind me and yanked the laces on an invisible corset. Tears stabbed at the corners of my eyes as images began flashing, unbidden, behind them. Images of a skinhead standing behind me at my locker, sliding a tiny green flight jacket up my arms and over my shoulders to warm my perma-chilled skin. Images of his smile when he turned me around to admire the fit. I'd never seen him smile before. Not like that. I'd wanted to make him smile again, but instead, I made him scowl when I told him I couldn't keep his gift. When I rejected him, just like everyone else had.

I squeezed my eyes shut and pressed the heels of my palms into them, trying to rid myself of the memory. The flashbacks were only getting worse. The doctor had acted like this was a simple case of normal teenage depression. Like all I needed was a little Prozac and some R&R to clear it up. Like watching your psychopathic, steroid-fueled skinhead boyfriend beat a man to death was normal. Like losing your childhood best friend to suicide and helping your hemorrhaging best friend deliver a baby in the same day was normal. Like having your first love suddenly join the Marines right before you found out that he might have cheated on you with a guy was normal.

Well, it didn't fucking feel normal. It felt heavy. The gravity of those compounded traumas was pulling me under, and I was too weak to swim to the surface. Too tired. Instead, I just sat on the bottom of the deep end and wondered how long I could hold my breath. Although my eyes stung from peering through nicotine instead of chlorine, my slowed, effortful movements, the weight pressing down on me, the alternating bouts of panic and resignation were all the same.

I was drowning.

Just not fast enough.

Without thinking, I stamped out my cigarette and stood up. Stars danced before my teary eyes, and tunnel vision threatened, but I pushed through the dizziness, fueled by my pain. Grabbing the vile baked good on my nightstand, I headed toward my parents' master bathroom in search of relief.

Out of habit, I crumbled the muffin into the toilet and flushed, destroying the evidence. I used to not eat because I wanted to be skinnier, prettier, Kate Mossier. Now, I didn't eat because I couldn't fucking eat.

Because I was the one being eaten.

In a frenzy, I threw open my mom's medicine cabinet, fully prepared to swallow the contents of anything and everything I could get my hands on just to make the ache go away.

But it was empty.

I yanked the mirror on my dad's side of the double vanity away from the wall as well. Empty. The stash of prescription opioids, antianxiety medications, and muscle relaxers I had known I would find there was just *gone*. Even the over-the-counter painkillers and cough syrups had vanished into thin air.

Rummaging through their drawers, cabinets, closets, dressers, I found nothing but toiletries, makeup, and clothes.

No.

No.

No!

My heart raced as the room began to tilt on its axis. I'd rushed in there, expecting to find the exit from my worst nightmare, but instead, I'd found myself trapped inside. There was no escape, and the walls were closing in.

Struggling to breathe, I clutched the edge of the bathroom counter and screamed, "Mom! Moooooom!"

My knees gave out before I heard her footsteps make it to the top of our squeaky stairs.

"Jesus Christ, BB," my mother said as she walked in on her emaciated daughter kneeling in front of her vanity with her forehead pressed to the cabinet door. "What's wrong?"

Everything. Every-fucking-thing.

"I can't find the Tylenol," I choked out.

"Do you have a headache, honey?" she said in that sweet, sympathetic voice that always made me want to curl up into her lap and cry.

I squeezed my eyes shut and nodded into the knotty wood.

"I'm sorry, baby. Must be a migraine, huh? Let me get you some Excedrin."

Instead of opening a cabinet or a drawer, my mom opened her closet door, right behind me. I turned and watched as she slid an armful of hanging tie-dyed sundresses aside and began turning the silver knob on a small black safe left and right. I couldn't see what she was doing once the door to the safe was opened, but I heard the familiar rattle of pill bottles as she rummaged around, looking for what she thought I needed.

When my mom reemerged from the closet with two little white pills in hand, I asked with betrayal in my voice, "Why is all the medicine in *there*?"

My mom looked around the bathroom and twirled a lock of long red hair around her finger, like she always did whenever she was uncomfortable. "Well, honey," she said, mustering a sad smile as her soft, earthy green eyes finally landed back on me, "that psychologist we took you to said that it might be a good idea for us to lock up all the pills in the house... and the weapons. You know, until you're feeling better."

The slap of those words knocked what little air I'd been able to swallow right back out of my lungs. Twin tears rolled down my pale, gaunt cheeks as I stared into my mother's face. Her small, reassuring smile did little to mask the pain in her exhausted eyes. Then, I broke the fuck down. Sobs shook free of my bony frame as the gravity of the situation sank in.

My mother had just saved my life.

Sitting next to me on the floor, my mom pulled me into her side and shushed me as I cried. "You know," she said, smoothing a hand weathered from decades of drawing and painting and sculpting down my freckled arm, "I think you should stop taking those pills. I did some research, and one of the side effects of antidepressants in teenagers is suicidal thoughts."

"Really?" I said, pulling the neck of my oversize T-shirt over my face to wipe my eyes and nose. I hoped she was right. Blaming the drugs for what I had almost done made me feel like less of a monster.

"Really. Honey, I think you just need to get your feelings

out. Do you want to talk to a counselor? Or paint? You used to love to paint. Or maybe you could write? You know, I read that writing letters to people and then ripping them up can be really therapeutic. Or maybe I saw that on *Oprah*."

Sitting with my back against the cabinet doors, my knees and face tucked inside the T-shirt I'd worn to bed the last few nights, I nodded. "Maybe I'll try that," I mumbled into the tear-soaked cotton. Then, taking a deep breath, I lifted my head and forced a smile for my mom's benefit. "After we go get my car."

Of course, before I could pick up my car, I had to stand in line at the DMV for two hours, try—and fail—to parallel park my mom's Taurus station wagon for a woman with a clipboard and a gratuitous amount of apathy, and then stand in line again to get my sunken-eyed, shaved-headed, skeletal picture taken.

Nobody likes their driver's license picture, but mine was physically hard to look at. I looked like a cancer patient. Or a drug addict. I looked like I was dying.

Because I was.

Over a boy.

In fact, everything I'd ever done up to that point had been in the name of a boy. One of my earliest memories is of me letting my kindergarten crush cut off one of my pigtails. Appropriate, considering that I'd been handing chunks and pieces of myself to boys ever since. Maybe that's why I was almost thirty pounds underweight. I'd finally given too much away.

Driver's license in hand, I went to see a man about a Mustang. I was a muscle car girl on a Ford Escort budget, but I managed to find a '93 Mustang hatchback with a five-liter engine and, much to my dismay, a stick shift transmission for pretty cheap. I didn't have enough money saved to buy it on my own yet, but my mom agreed to loan me what little savings she had to make it work. I think she was more excited about me not having to rely on boys for rides than I was.

I should have been elated. I'd wanted a car—a *Mustang*—for as long as I could remember. But as I sat in my new/used car in the driveway of my parents' house and pictured the faces of all the people who *wouldn't* be sitting in those passenger seats, the gaping holes in my life only became more apparent.

Knight? Boot camp.

Juliet? Baby duty.

August? Dead.

Lance? Dead to me.

Before my pity party had a chance to bust out the keg and throw on a mix tape, a dusty old Toyota Tercel with a glowing pizza delivery sign on top came barreling up our quarter-mile-long driveway. My parents and I lived in a little gray house out in the middle of the Georgian wilderness. My mom liked it because she could hide her pot habit out there, and my dad liked it because he was under the impression that the government was tapping the phones and itching to take his guns away. I fucking hated it because I lived at least half an hour away from all my friends. Back when I had friends, that was.

I sighed and slid down in the driver's seat to avoid having to interact with anyone else in my broken condition.

I listened for the sound of Pizza Guy's car leaving, but instead heard my mom yell, "BB...Bee Beeeeee...Come eat, baby!" totally blowing my fucking cover.

I sighed and got out of the car, ducking my head to avoid

Pizza Guy's gaze when we crossed paths. I didn't want to see his reaction to the tiny, frail, pale, boy/girl-looking thing that had just emerged from a parked car with rolled-up windows in the middle of June. I already knew that I looked like Gollum crawling out of his cave for the first time. I didn't need to see it written all over some stranger's face.

Instead of our usual TV trays in the living room, my parents and I sat at the kitchen "island"—a cheap high-top table and a couple of stools my mom had scored at Walmart—to endure all of the obligatory birthday things. After the pizza, which I'd barely touched, my mom presented me with one of her signature misshapen, slightly burned, homemade cakes. True to form, my pothead parents couldn't find any candles, so my mom lit a match and shoved it into the frosting. She and my dad sang me "Happy Birthday," and I smiled politely, counting the minutes until I could run up to my room and smoke a cigarette.

When I was done pushing crumbling cake around on my plate and feeding covert forkfuls of it to our golden retriever, my dad handed me a piece of paper. "Happy birthday, kiddo," he said with a smile.

The man had been unemployed for years, so I knew the gift was actually from my mother, but the fact that he was beaming from ear to ear as he handed it to me told me that he was definitely the one who'd picked it out—whatever it was.

As I unfolded the page, the curious wrinkle in my brow smoothed and lifted all the way up to my hairline. It was a picture of four shiny five-spoke alloy pony wheels. The Mustang I'd bought came equipped with the most embarrassing set of plastic hubcaps—the tires were pretty damn worn, too—but it never occurred to me to ask to have them replaced.

"Your mother just wanted to get you some safer tires, but I talked her into a little upgrade," he said with a wink. "You've got an appointment to get them installed at A&J Auto Body on Monday."

Whoever said money can't buy happiness never gave a set of pony wheels to a muscle-car-loving girl from a working-class family on her sixteenth birthday. I think it was the first time I'd smiled in weeks. Smiled? Hell, I screamed. I hugged. I jumped up and down.

Then, I ran upstairs, popped a Camel Light in my mouth, and called my last remaining friend to tell her the news. When Juliet asked, over the sound of a crying infant, if I'd had a good birthday, I told her yes. And, much to my surprise, I think I almost meant it.

Evidently, A&J Auto Body was the cheapest shop in town—and for good reason. The place was grimy as hell and appeared to have been decorated by a blind person in the 1970s. A squat, furry, troll-like man who looked like he had a dark brown toupee stuffed in the collar of his shirt greeted me with a grunt, then took my keys and left me standing at the front desk.

Not knowing where to go, I wandered through a door to what I assumed would be a nicotine-colored waiting area but instead found myself in the main garage. I normally would have just turned around and gone back in, but the car on the lift closest to me refused to let me leave.

It was love at first sight—a late '60s Mustang fastback body style, matte black paint job, matte black rims, blacked-out windows, and a massive open-air scoop on the hood. It looked like something straight out of *Mad Max*.

"Can I help you with somethin'?"

I turned and met the amused stare of a broad-shouldered, baby-faced, blue-eyed mechanic. His dirty-blond hair was pushed back in a messy pompadour. His forearms were covered in hot-rod tattoos. His pouty bottom lip was pierced. And his name was embroidered on the A&J Auto Body shirt hugging his hard chest.

Hellooo, Harley.

"Sorry," I sputtered. "I know I'm probably not supposed to be back here, but I..." I looked back up at the beast on the lift, and a deep longing seized my chest. "I can't leave her."

Harley—if that was even his real name—chuckled and said, "So, you like the ladies, huh?"

"What? No!" I snapped.

"Good." The mechanic smiled, and the twinkle in his mischievous blue eyes reminded me just *how much* I liked boys.

Trying to bring the subject back to cars and away from my sexual orientation, I looked around the garage and pointed to my faded black hatchback on the farthest lift. "I drive the baby version of this."

Harley glanced over at my most prized possession and nodded in approval. "Five-oh, huh? Not bad. Manual or automatic?"

"Manual," I groaned.

"No shit? Your boyfriend teach you how to drive that thing?"

"No," I said, letting my mouth hang open in pretend offense.

"Ah." Harley nodded. "You met him *after* you got the car."

"I don't *have* a boyfriend," I said, rolling my eyes.

God, he was cute. The guy had a face like James Dean and a body like Dean Cain. And that accent. Living in the South, southern accents are a dime a dozen, but Harley's was just subtle enough to be cute. Cute, cute, cute.

Harley smirked at me and asked, "Your old man must be a car guy then, huh?"

"You got me." I smiled. "I've been hoarding all his old *Muscle*

Car magazines since I was a kid. I used to cut out all the Mustang pictures and tape them to my bedroom walls, but the tape fucked up the Sheetrock, so my mom bought one of those clear plastic shower curtains with the photo pockets and—"

Harley held up a hand to silence me. "I'm gonna have to stop you right there"—he beamed— "'cause right now all I can picture is you in the shower, and I'm pretty sure I'm not gonna be able to process another word you say."

Oh my God!

I could feel the prickly heat of a blush creeping up my neck. I bit the insides of my cheeks to keep my face from splitting open into a blotchy, big-toothed grin caused by his sexy little comment. This guy, *Harley*, had to be in his early twenties, he was fiiiine as hell, and he was flirting with *me*.

Having no idea how to respond to that, I tried *again* to change the subject. "So, what do *you* drive?"

"Hmm…" Harley tilted his head and smirked. "Why don't you take a guess?"

Oh, we're playing games now. Okay…

I tapped my lips with my fingertips and eyed him, thinking hard.

"You strike me as a…Volkswagen Beetle kinda guy."

Harley almost laughed, then quickly scowled, trying to look offended.

"Wood-paneled Pinto?"

Harley pursed his ample lips, fighting back a grin.

"No? Hmm. Oh, I got it. Geo Metro."

That one had him wrinkling his nose in genuine horror.

"I know! It's a trick question! You drive a Vespa!"

Snort.

I was running out of ideas, so I looked around the shop and spotted a '64 Impala lowrider. "Ooh! I found it. Right there," I said, pointing to the hooptie. "The gold rims were a nice touch. I bet you even put hydraulics on it, didn't you?"

Harley finally let out the laugh he'd been biting back. It was deep and raspy and made my insides tingle.

"You're getting warmer," he said. "It's actually on hydraulics right now." Harley lifted an oil-smudged finger and pointed to the matte black sex machine above my head.

"No!" I screamed and smacked him in the chest with the back of my hand. "No fucking way!"

"Yep. That's my old lady." Harley beamed.

"Oh my God! That's *yours*? *Yours*? Like you *own* it? And you get to *drive* it? Holy shit! What year is it? A '69? What engine does it have? Is it all original?"

Harley cocked his head to one side and said, "You said you're a muscle car girl—you tell me."

"Oh, shit." I rubbed my hands together, accepting his challenge. "Let's see... if it's a '69, which I think it is, then it could be a GT, a Mach One, or a Boss. Or an E, but those are super rare. The GTs had different hood scoops than this one, and I'm pretty sure the Mach Ones had cable and pin tie-downs. So, this has got to be a Boss, right? But is it a Boss 302 or a Boss 429? Ugh!"

Harley let out a low whistle and clapped his oil- and tattoo-covered hands together a few times. "Damn, girl. If you weren't so young, I'd ask you to marry me."

I laughed on the outside, but on the inside I was doing fucking round-off back handsprings. The owner of *that* car, and *that* face, and *that* body, and *those* tattoos was flirting with *me*!

Unable to filter my big fucking mouth, I said, "You know,

sixteen-year-olds can get married in the state of Georgia as long as they have a note from their parents."

Harley laughed and said, "Well, hell. I guess I'd better scrounge up a ring quick 'cause I'm not lettin' you get away."

My stomach did a double salto with a full twist and stuck the fucking landing.

I decided to change the subject from our impending engagement back to the car, if only to help me regain my composure.

"So, is it a 302 or a 429?" I asked, nudging my head toward the matte black orgasm on wheels above us.

"Guess you're just gonna have to wait to find out."

"Ah, man!" I whined. "Wait until when?"

"Tonight." Harley grinned at me like the devil himself, about to convert another sinner. "I'm taking you to the track, lady."

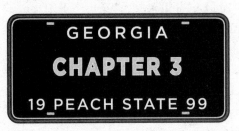

Lady? Lady. Lay-DEE? LAY-dee.

On the way home from the shop, I replayed my conversation with Harley—the hunky, tattooed, baby-faced mechanic—over and over in my head. Not only was I smiling for the second day in a row, but I also couldn't fucking stop. I was driving my very own Mustang—with shiny new pony wheels, thankyouverymuch—and I had a date that night with the sexiest motherfucker I'd ever seen in my life.

And he'd called me *lady*.

Lady. I liked it. It sounded so grown-up. Strong. A lady was somebody who deserved respect. All Knight had ever called me was *punk*.

Punk—noun. *Slang.*

1. something or someone worthless or unimportant.

2. a young ruffian; hoodlum.

3. an inexperienced youth.

4. a young male partner of a homosexual.

5. *Prison slang.* A boy.

How appropriate, considering that, the day Knight had left for the Marines, Lance Hightower—the punk rock object of my obsession since sixth grade—told me that he gave Knight a blow job while we were dating. As in, Knight had cheated on me with a *guy*. And not just any guy. The guy I had been in love with until Knight drop-kicked his way into my heart.

Lance had *also* told me that the only reason Knight was attracted to me at all was because I looked like a little boy.

Like a *punk*.

I glanced in the rearview mirror and sighed audibly when I realized that my hair hadn't miraculously grown eighteen inches since that conversation. I'd shaved almost all of it off last fall, except for my bangs and two longer side pieces, in an attempt to get Lance Hightower to notice me. Obviously, my plan hadn't exactly worked out.

Ronald "Knight" McKnight, our school's only skinhead, noticed me instead. He'd spent months pursuing me, wearing me down, isolating me from my friends, and eventually, making me love him. When I fell, I fell hard. And, right as I was about to serve him my forever on a fucking platter, Knight pushed me away. With the slam of one door, he'd gone from being my true love to my tormentor. He'd ignored me, bullied me, even gotten physically aggressive with me. Then, he'd upped and joined the Marines to protect me from his lack of self-control.

It'd been three weeks since Knight left for basic training. Three weeks that had somehow felt like three days and three decades all at the same time. I'd accepted that it was over. It had been over long before Knight left for boot camp. But what I hadn't been able to accept, what kept gnawing at me from the recesses of my mind, was the question of whether or not he'd cheated.

I wanted to know how to feel. Was I supposed to miss Knight or hate him? Had he really cheated on me, or had Lance made the whole thing up? Lance wasn't exactly trustworthy—okay, he was a vindictive little drama queen—but honestly, I kind of hoped that he'd been telling the truth. Then I could feel angry for a change.

I was so fucking sick of feeling sad.

I pulled to a stop next to a blue metal mailbox in front of the post office, then pulled a crinkled envelope addressed to Recruit Ronald McKnight out of my shapeless, furry, leopard-print purse. I stared at the letter in my lap, immobilized by indecision. Should I rip it up, like my mom had suggested, or should I just say *fuck it*?

As much as I wanted closure, I was terrified to mail that letter. I knew my words were going to make Knight mad. Like, *really* mad.

And when Ronald McKnight got really mad, people got hurt. People went missing.

People got their heads bashed in with a baseball bat.

The blast of a waiting car horn startled me, causing my body to respond mindlessly. My left arm shot out of the open driver-side window and dropped the ticking time bomb into the mail slot. My left foot popped the clutch. My right foot stabbed at the gas pedal, and my coordination was so off that the car lurched forward and stalled out with a violent shudder.

Much like my heart when I realized what the fuck I'd just done.

Rct. Ronald McKnight
Marine Corps Recruit Depot
283 Blvd De France
Parris Island, SC 29905

June 22, 1998

Dear Knight,

Peg gave me your address. I hope you don't mind. Actually, I don't give a shit if you mind or not. I'm not afraid of you anymore because you're not fucking here. You went off and joined the Marines so that you could serve your country and keep me from spending the rest of my life with a psycho. Right? Isn't that what you told me?

Well, Lance Hightower told me a different story-a story that began with you letting him suck your dick in the student parking lot and ended with you beating his ass to a pulp and getting him expelled from school the next day. I always suspected that you were the one who narced on him. I thought it was because you were pissed about him offering me meth, but it didn't have anything to do with me, did it? You wanted Lance gone so that you wouldn't have to face what you'd done.

I didn't want to believe him at first, but the more I think about it, the more it all makes sense. Why you always insisted that Lance was gay, even before he came out. Why I saw you two together in the parking lot that day. Why you attacked him that afternoon. Why you took steroids and drove a monster truck and dressed like a fucking skinhead. Why you joined the Marines.

You were fighting who you really are, covering it up with every tough-guy thing you could think of. And when that didn't work, you ran away from it.

I don't care if you're gay or bi or just fucking confused. That's not the fucking point. The point is that, whatever you are, you hid it from me. You allowed me to believe that what we had was real. But it was all an illusion, wasn't it? You never loved me. You lied to me. You manipulated me. You made my life a living hell. And now I find out that you fucking cheated on me too?

I don't expect an explanation from you. I don't even want one. I'm sure whatever you have to say will be another fucking lie anyway. I just want you to know that I finally know the truth.

Maybe now it will stop hurting so goddamn much.

Have a nice life.

BB

"Jules, I have a fucking date in two hours, and I don't know what the hell to wear! I need you!" I held my glittery plastic Nokia between my cheek and shoulder while hopping up and down, trying to shimmy into a skintight pair of python-print vinyl pants.

"A date? For the past two weeks you've been too depressed to leave the house and now, all of a sudden, you have a date? Who's taking you out? The mailman? 'Cause I'm pretty sure that's the only guy you've seen since school let out."

Juliet was sassy, even on a good day, but now that her boyfriend was in jail and she was stuck at home with a newborn, she was a raging hormonal bitch. I didn't mind though. Talking to her reminded me that shit could always be worse.

"You're one to talk. I'm pretty sure you haven't left the house either," I teased.

"I just had a fucking baby! My tits are leaking everywhere, I'm still in maternity clothes, and I haven't taken a shower in four days."

I laughed as I shoved my feet back into my well-worn black

combat boots. "Excuses, excuses. So, back to my thing. I'm thinking python pants, boots—of course—and maybe a plain black tank top. I want to be casual but sexy. This guy is, like, in his twenties."

"First of all, you know it's June, right? It's, like, a million degrees outside. I don't know how the fuck you think you're going to survive out there in pleather pants and those shitkickers you wear."

"I get cold in shorts!" I whined, pulling the phone away from my ear so that I could push my spindly arm beneath the spaghetti strap of a black lacy camisole.

"And second, does this grown-ass man know how old you are?"

"What does it matter? I'm old enough. Sixteen is the legal age of consent in Georgia. Besides, your boyfriend is, like, twenty-six," I said with a little more salt than I intended.

"*Ex*-boyfriend. And, Jesus, calm down, Judge Judy. I was only curious."

"Sorry. Ugh. I'm just freaking out. I don't want him to see me as some little kid, you know?" I stepped in front of my full-length mirror and turned sideways. With my thick black liquid eyeliner and red liquid-filled Wonderbra, I almost looked seventeen. Almost.

"So who's the lucky asshole?" Juliet deadpanned.

"Oh my God, Jules, he's so fucking cute!" I squealed. "His name is Harley and he's a mechanic at the garage where I got my tires today and he has two full tattoo sleeves and this big, fat pierced bottom lip and he's super fucking flirty and he has this sexy blond sex hair and oh my God"—I sucked in a breath—"he drives a fucking 1969 Boss 429! Or it could be a 302, but

I'm pretty sure it's a 429. And I think he's going to let me drive it to—"

"Harley *James*?" Juliet cut me off, her tone significantly less enthusiastic than mine.

"Yeah!" That was the name he'd put into my cell phone before I left the shop anyway. "You know him?"

"Everybody knows him! He was, like, the original Peach State High punk. Don't you remember? He had spiky blond hair, like Billy Idol, and got kicked out of school in eleventh grade for clocking the principal in the face! Oh, *and* I heard that he'd already slept with over a hundred girls by then, too."

I did kind of remember rumors about somebody like that, but we were still in middle school, so they hadn't really made an impression. Plus, I'd been too busy obsessing over a certain gorgeous punk rock god in my own grade—Lance Hightower.

"Oh yeah," I said, pretending to know who she was talking about while I dug around in my makeup bag.

"Girl, you better use protection," Juliet warned. "That guy is a *whore*."

"Okay, *Mom*," I whined. "So, do man-whores like nude lipstick or red lipstick better?"

"Better go with nude, seeing as how it's probably going to be smeared all over his dick later."

"Ew!" I shrieked, causing Jules to burst into an evil belly laugh. It felt so good to hear her do that even if it was at my expense.

"Fuck, I think I just woke up the baby," Juliet said once her cackle died down. "Ugh. There's another reason why you need to use protection tonight. These things are the worst."

"Girl, I watched you push him out. Trust me, I'm poppin' birth control pills like Tic Tacs now."

Juliet giggled a little bit, but I could hear the sadness creeping back in at the end.

"Have fun," she said as the wailing in the background suddenly changed to coos and grunts. "Be safe."

"You have your boob in that kid's mouth right now, don't you?" I said, trying to lighten the mood.

"Oh yeah," Juliet said. "Don't think you're the only one getting action around here."

GEORGIA
CHAPTER 5
19 PEACH STATE 99

Even though I followed the directions scrawled on the back of my A&J Auto Body receipt to the letter, I still missed my turn at least three times. Harley had warned me that there wouldn't be a sign, but he'd failed to mention the fact that the street was in the process of being reclaimed by the fucking forest.

Oh, this feels safe, I thought as I crept at five miles per hour down what was probably the driveway of a rape shack. *A grown-ass man you've never met asks you to meet him somewhere with no signs and no address in the middle of the fucking woods, and you say yes because he told you he might let you drive his car. You might as well have climbed into a panel van with a stranger for a piece of candy, dumbass.*

My annoyingly persistent optimism refused to hear it though, snapping back, *Yeah, but I saw the candy, and I saw the stranger. And they're* totally *worth climbing into a panel van for.*

Just then the narrow street crested a hill, and I was temporarily blinded by the six o'clock summer sun. Flipping the red heart-shaped sunglasses from the top of my head back down onto my face, I slowed almost to a stop and peered into a crater the size of a stadium below. It looked like it had been clear-cut by developers in preparation to build a neighborhood. The main street had been paved—just a large oval with a few driveways jutting off here and there—but there were no houses. There were no diggers. There were no Porta Potties, trailers, or evidence that anyone had been working on anything at all. The only thing down there was mud, pavement, and the sexiest car mankind had ever produced.

The Boss was parked at the bottom of the hill, and even though the June sun was blazing down on it without mercy, it didn't sparkle, and it damn sure didn't shine. That matte black finish took the sunlight and fucking swallowed it up, like a matte black hole on matte black wheels. And leaning against it—smoking a cigarette and wearing a pair of black Dickies, black boots, a chain wallet, and a NOFX T-shirt—was the only man sexy enough to drive it.

Harley fucking James.

When he heard me coming down the hill, Harley lifted his head and flashed me a sideways smile that made me feel a little less nervous. Or more nervous? Maybe less nervous and more excited? Whatever it did, it scrambled my brain because, as soon as I pulled up next to him, I threw the car into first, pulled up the emergency brake, and took my foot off the clutch...all before cutting the engine. My car shook, sputtered, and stalled out in spectacular fashion.

I shrieked and buried my face in my hands as Harley made his way over to my side of the car.

Be cool, BB. Be cool. You're a badass. Right? So be a badass. What would a badass do if she stalled out in front of a super-hot grown-ass man?

I pried my hands off my face and looked around frantically for my cigarettes. Lighting one with shaking fingers, I exhaled and said a silent prayer before pushing open my car door.

I was swathed in thick, humid air and the rumbling sound of Harley's gravelly laughter. I swung my ten-pound steel-toed combat boots out, sitting sideways in the driver's seat, and looked up the length of Harley's long, lean body. My heart was pounding, and my cheeks were on fire, but I exhaled a slow, steady stream of smoke and tried to pretend like I hadn't just stalled the fuck out in front of a legendary bad boy.

"Hey," I said, forcing myself to look him in the eye and thanking God for the advent of big plastic sunglasses.

He was even hotter than I remembered. It had only been a few hours, but the fact that he dressed like a laid-back punk rocker had my tits in a tizzy. He was the coolest fucking person I'd ever met, and he wasn't even trying. And that face? *Fuck me.*

"Hey." Harley chuckled, holding out both palms.

I stuck my cigarette between my teeth and put my hands in his, letting him pull me out of the car. Harley ran his callused thumbs over the backs of my hands before dropping them. The sensation made my insides quiver.

"You know, there's a better way to kill your engine," he teased.

I rolled my eyes behind my sunglasses and exhaled a puff of smoke out of the side of my mouth. "I know," I said. "I just like to make a big entrance."

I forced myself to meet Harley's gaze, and my breath hitched. Goddamn. Even when he smiled, it looked like a pout with those bright blue puppy-dog eyes and that puffy, pierced bottom lip.

"Mustang clutches are a bitch," he said in a voice that sounded like both sugar and sandpaper. "Maybe you should have started with a Vespa."

I scoffed in pretend offense and smacked him in the chest with the back of my hand.

"Damn, woman! You said it first." Harley laughed, shielding himself with his hands, as if I might attack again.

"Yeah, but you drive *that*." I motioned over my shoulder with my thumb. "Somebody could probably call your mama a Vespa, and you'd be like, *I'm sorry. I can't hear you over the sound of my Boss 429.*"

I shut my door and leaned against it, needing more than just gravity to hold me and my shaky knees up.

Harley smirked at me. "I thought you couldn't tell if it was a 302 or a 429," he said with mischief in his pretty blue eyes.

"Let's just say, if you made me come all the way out here for a puny little 302, I'm gonna be pretty fucking disappointed."

Harley smiled all the way, and I noticed for the first time that he had a gap between his front teeth. Just a sliver of space, but it was enough to put me at ease. I had a gap between my front teeth, too. Even after two years of braces, it still never closed all the way. But I liked it. People said it made me look like Madonna. A boobless, ninety-one-pound, shaved-headed Madonna.

"Well, let's get your disappointment over with then."

Harley held out his elbow for me to take and walked me around to the driver's side of his matte black orgasm on wheels. As if I were just going to hop in. As if it were a fucking Honda Accord or some shit. I let go of his elbow and kept walking, circling the car one, two, fifteen times. It was like being in the presence of the *Mona Lisa*. Or the Hope Diamond. How was there not an interconnected laser system protecting this priceless piece of art?

I glanced up at Harley, who was obviously enjoying my reverie. I'm sure, out there in the suburbs of Atlanta, nobody had a fucking clue just how amazing that car really was. On the classic car auctions my dad and I watched on TV, the Boss 429s always went for over a hundred thousand dollars. How the fuck was a high school dropout driving around in *that* car?

He is *a mechanic,* the optimistic voice in my head insisted. *Maybe he built it himself, from the ground up. Maybe he pieced it together from found parts, and now it's worth six figures. Maybe he's an entrepreneur with earning potential.*

Or maybe he's a drug dealer, my rational side chimed in.

Harley cocked his head to one side, squinting through the blazing sun, and said, "Are you gonna fire her up or just make her feel like a piece of meat?"

"Harley James, are you a feminist?" I asked with a smirk as he opened the driver's side door for me.

"Sure. We'll go with that," he said as I made my way over to him.

I flicked my cigarette onto the pavement before climbing in—*ooh, I'll bet that looked super badass*—and fought the inexplicable urge to wrap my arms around his waist and just inhale him as I ducked under his arm. I told myself he probably just smelled like sweat and motor oil. I *know* I smelled like sweat. My skintight, rubbery python pants were soaked on the inside.

As soon as my vinyl-wrapped ass hit his leather-wrapped seat, I let out a little moan. I couldn't help it. I was sitting in my dream car, and it smelled like leather and testosterone. If there is a heaven, I'm pretty sure I was sitting in it.

Harley came around and sat in the passenger seat, leaving both of our doors wide open so that we wouldn't die of heatstroke.

I ran my hands over the wooden steering wheel and looked at him in awe. "You kept it all original," I said, marveling at the walnut dash.

"'Cept for the gauges, seat belts, pedals, and gearshift." He chuckled. "But, yeah, I kept the steering wheel. That thing is too fuckin' cool to replace. When was the last time you saw a wooden steering wheel?"

"I think my grandma's Buick had one," I blurted.

Harley's hand shot out, pointing toward my open door. "Get the fuck out," he said, scowling for about half a second before his wicked little smile slid back into place.

I exhaled and gave his veiny, tattooed arm a little shove. "Don't do that, fucker!"

Harley smiled so big I thought his bottom lip was going to burst through the silver hoop restraining it.

He reached into his pocket and pulled out a set of keys. Then, he jammed one into the ignition. "Well, if you're not gonna get out, let's see what you got," he said, raising his eyebrows and locking those pretty puppy-dog eyes on mine. "Crank her up and tell me what she's working with."

Jesus, did I even know how to turn on a car? I'd only had one for a little over twenty-four hours.

Um, okay... left foot, clutch. Right foot, brake. Uh... first gear? First gear. Parking brake...

I looked at the center console where the hand brake was in my car and saw nothing but smooth wood grain and a pack of Camel Lights.

Fuck.

I looked at Harley, who was watching me in amusement, and said, "Sorry, man. I think your car's broken. Somebody forgot to install the parking brake."

A laugh burst out of him that changed the bubbly feeling in my chest from anxiety to adoration. It had been so hard to get Knight to laugh. Just making that grumpy asshole smile had been my singular reason for getting up in the morning. It had been a challenge and, at times, the only way to keep him from fucking killing someone. But Harley smiled for free. He laughed. He teased. He played. He flirted. Hell, I think he was fucking happy. I used to be happy, too, before everything turned to shit. Being around Harley helped me remember what that felt like.

I was starting to think that Harley and I might be the same person. He and I were as similar as Knight and I were different. And I liked it.

Harley leaned over so that his face was mere inches from mine. Then, he reached for a handle under the steering wheel. Tapping it with two fingers, he said, "Step on the clutch and brake at the same time, and then push this in."

I did as I was told, leaving nothing left but to turn the key. I took a deep breath and cranked her up. The engine screamed to life, the entire car rumbled around us, and my panties were suddenly soaked.

"Now, give it a little gas, but *don't* take your foot off the clutch," Harley yelled over the sound of his purring sex machine.

I gingerly tapped the gas pedal with one steel-covered toe and watched the RPM needle lift as a deafening roar filled the cabin. That was no 302. My mouth fell open, and my wide eyes cut to Harley's. He reached over and lifted my heart-shaped sun-glasses, placing them on top of my shaved head, and smiled.

"So? Did you drive all the way out here for nothing?" he asked, cocking his head to one side.

I shook my head with my mouth still agape, unable to form a witty retort. My cool, completely shattered.

"Now, this time"—Harley gestured toward the pedals—"give it just a little gas, and hold it steady as you ease off the clutch."

I shook my head again.

"You don't want to drive it?" Harley furrowed his brow.

More head shaking.

"Lady, shut your door, put your hands on the wheel, and get your foot off that clutch."

Oh my God, oh my God, oh my God, oh my God…

How was I supposed to operate a fucking jet on wheels when I could barely operate my own limbs at that moment?

I awkwardly pulled my door shut and grabbed the wheel at ten and two—just like I had at the Department of Motor Vehicles during my driving test—and gave her a little gas. As the roar built, I swallowed hard, squared my shoulders, and eased off the clutch.

Please don't stall out. Please don't stall out. Please don't—

The car shot off like a rocket, slamming my head back into the headrest. I let off the gas to slow down, but evidently that was the wrong thing to do because the car started jerking and hopping like the fucking wild stallion it was named after.

"More gas!" Harley yelled.

I slammed my foot back on the gas, much harder than I'd

intended, and the Boss raged full speed ahead into the first turn on the oval street.

"Shift!"

Fuck.

I shifted into second, and it actually wasn't hard. That part felt familiar.

"Now, ease off the gas *a little* as you turn."

I did it and let out a sigh of relief when the car didn't do that hopping thing again.

"That's it. Now, once you get the hang of it, you can get up to third gear on the straights. Then, just pop it into neutral during the turns, tap the brake, and shift back into second."

Through my adrenaline-fogged ears, it all sounded like Greek, but Harley coached me through every turn.

After about ten laps, I was doing it on my own, and I had finally released my death grip on the steering wheel enough to be able to feel my fingers again. After fifteen laps, I was actually getting the hang of it. And after twenty laps, I felt like I needed a post-sex cigarette.

I pulled to a stop next to the poor man's version of the beast I'd just tamed and...stalled the fuck out.

"Oh my God!" I screamed, clamping a hand over my mouth. "I'm so sorry!"

I expected Harley to bite my head off, but instead he just laughed and said, "You know, you should really try turning the key to the left sometime. That works too."

I loved him. That was it. I loved him.

I locked eyes with the baby-faced bad boy and was surprised to discover that I didn't want to look away. Holding Knight's gaze had always felt like staring into the eyes of a zombie. His irises were so pale. So cold. Focused and unflinching. Murderous and remorseless. Harley's eyes, on the other hand, were bright. Playful. *Alive.* When he looked at me, I didn't feel like I was being studied or psychoanalyzed. I felt like I was sharing an inside joke with a friend.

As I drank in his messy dirty-blond hair, his mischievous blue eyes, his pouty, pierced lip, his aura of fun, I realized that Harley James had just become my favorite person on the planet. So what if I'd only known him for six hours? Harley James was going to be my new BFF.

Hopefully, with benefits.

The inside of a black car with a black interior parked in the full sun is no place to try to get to know someone in the middle of summer. Harley cranked up the AC to full blast, but it simply couldn't compete with the heat coming off that big block engine, the Georgia sun, and my raging hormones. He asked if I wanted to go somewhere cooler to hang out, maybe grab dinner, and at the mention of food my stomach growled about as loud as his 429 cubic-inch engine.

I hadn't eaten yet that day, and it was already almost seven o'clock. I'd been hospitalized for anorexia the month before when I fainted in the delivery room after Juliet gave birth to Romeo, and it had been a wake-up call. A wake-up call that had lasted all of about two days.

I knew I needed to eat. I just didn't want to. Ever. That acidic churning in my stomach made me feel so accomplished. So in control. And it was also a welcome distraction from the emotional pain I'd been drowning in after losing almost everyone I cared about within the span of just a few weeks.

But being near Harley was an even better distraction—one that I was willing to eat a dozen cronuts injected with cheesecake, dipped in bacon grease, and rolled in powdered calories to prolong.

Harley laughed at my gastrointestinal theatrics and told me to follow him to the Waffle House up the street.

Fucking Waffle House.

My first date with Knight had been at the Waffle House, too. Goddamn, I had a type.

I was heartbroken to have to turn the keys to that beautiful beast back over to Harley, but driving my own car felt about a million times easier after wrestling the Boss for twenty minutes. I didn't even stall out when I parked next to Harley at the diner. He noticed and did a slow clap as I got out of the car.

"You tried the key trick that time, huh?" Harley teased, lighting a cigarette as he walked over to me.

"Yeah, but I like my way better," I said, fishing around in my cavernous bag for my own smokes. "It's much more dramatic."

Harley stopped right in front of me, his shadow blocking out the abusive sun, and placed the butt of his cigarette within an inch of my mouth. The cigarette that had just been in *his* mouth. My gaze jumped from my purse to Harley's oil-stained fingers to the flames and hot rods on his forearm to his eyes, which were hooded yet challenging. Harley's offering felt intimate, like foreplay. He wanted to see how I felt about swapping saliva with him. Well, I felt just great about it, and I let him know by wrapping my lips around the filter, biting down, and snatching the entire thing out of his hand.

I grinned at him with the cigarette still between my teeth and said, "Thanks."

Harley smiled in approval. "Anytime."

There was a promise in his reply, and it made my pussy clench.

He shook another cigarette out for himself and escorted me into the diner. Waffle House is a seat-yourself kind of establishment, and Harley chose to sit in a booth by the window. I'm pretty sure it was just so that he could keep an eye on the Boss. If I drove a hundred-thousand-dollar car in this part of town, I'd probably want to keep an eye on it too.

"So, what *was* that place?" I asked, gesturing with my thumb in the direction we'd just come from.

"The track?" Harley slid a plastic ashtray into the center of the table and ashed into it. "It was gonna be a neighborhood, but the developer stopped construction after the roads were built. Technically, all that land is still private property, but since the dude who owns it skipped town, there's nobody around to report us for trespassing. The cops can't bust anybody for street racing on it."

"So people race there?"

"Fuck yeah. Almost every weekend." Harley looked at me as if he were considering something, then bit the corner of his mouth and cocked his head to one side. Pointing two fingers at me, his cigarette pinched between them, Harley said, "You're gonna race there too."

I snorted and shook my head. "Fuuuuuck no I'm not," I said, holding my hands up in the universal sign for *fuck no*. "I literally *just* got my license."

I cringed inwardly at my admission as a bedraggled waitress

yelled from behind the counter that she'd be with us in a minute. Harley ignored her.

"*That's* why you're gonna win," he said with a smug smile. "Nobody's gonna bet on a little girl in a factory-model five-oh."

Little girl.

His words stung. I wasn't a little girl. I mean, I *was*, but I didn't want *him* to see me that way.

"You bring your car to my shop," he continued, "and I bet I can get that thing up to four hundred horsepower in no time. Not that you'll even need it. Five-ohs have some serious fucking torque." Harley gestured out the window toward our matching black Mustangs. "You could make a shitload of money with that thing, lady."

"Then you race it," I said, stamping out my cigarette.

"Can't," Harley said, shrugging his wide shoulders. "Nobody'll bet against me anymore. If I don't start throwing some races soon, I'm gonna have to find a new track to work."

"Is that how you can afford to drive such a badass car? Racing?" The second the question was out of my mouth, I squeezed my eyes shut in regret. *Shit.* That was *so* none of my business.

Harley pursed his pretty mouth. "Sure," he finally answered. "We'll go with that."

The waitress barreled over and took our order without even trying to hide her annoyance at our presence. Harley and I each asked for the same thing—their famous greasy hash browns and coffee. I fucking hated coffee, but that's what grownups drink. Right?

Grown-ups = coffee

Little girls ≠coffee

Therefore, BB + coffee = grown-up

As I doctored my mug of steaming black filth with at least five containers of creamer, all the ice from my glass of water, and at least fourteen packets of sugar, I looked up and noticed Harley smirking at me from behind his mug.

"What?" I snapped, a little too self-conscious about my lack of coffee skills.

"Nothing," he said, taking a sip of what looked like squid ink.

"Are you drinking that shit black?" I asked.

Harley shrugged. "You get used to it, workin' at the shop. Those assholes never have cream or sugar."

Jesus. Harley might be even older than I thought.

That face made him look eighteen, but his faded tattoos, grease-stained hands, broad shoulders, laid-back style, expensive-ass car, and super-mature coffee preferences screamed otherwise.

"How old are you?" I blurted out, stirring my Frankendrink for the millionth time.

"Twenty-one," Harley said, watching me with amusement as he took another sip of his putrid black beverage.

I almost choked.

Twenty-one?

Harley James was officially fucking perfect.

"If you're twenty-one"—I coughed—"then why the fuck are we drinking *coffee*?"

Harley laughed as he reached for his wallet. "That's an excellent fuckin' question, lady." He stood up and tossed a few bills on the table, then extended a big, blackened hand in my direction. "I got some beer back at the house. You wanna get outta here?"

The second my hand slipped into Harley's, every muscle in

my body tensed in anticipation. I felt like a motor that had just been turned on—vibrating, idling, just waiting for Harley to give me a green light. My gaze landed on the shiny silver hoop barely containing his full bottom lip as he pulled me out of the booth, and I nodded. It didn't even matter what the question had been. If Harley was doing the asking, my answer was going to be *yes*.

Yes, yes, yes, yes, yes.

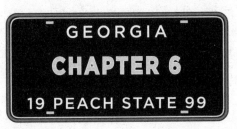

GEORGIA

CHAPTER 6

19 PEACH STATE 99

As I followed my dream car and my dream guy down a dozen twisty, tree-lined back roads to God knows where, the reality of my situation began to settle in. Not only was I going home with a man—like, a grown-ass man, whom I'd just met that day—but I was doing it less than a month after saying good-bye to my first love. It felt wrong. It felt slutty and shitty and wrong.

But Knight left, my ever-present sense of positivity chimed in, dousing my guilt with cold water. *He broke your heart, hollowed it out, used it as an ashtray, and then he fucking left. He said he wanted you to find somebody better, right? Well, here he is. What could be better than a tattooed hottie who makes you smile, drives a Boss 429, and is old enough to buy alcohol? I'll tell you what. A tattooed hottie who makes you smile, drives a Boss 429, is old enough to buy alcohol,* and *has his own place.*

As soon as my persuasive, optimistic side won me over, I followed the Boss into the gravel driveway of an adorable little bungalow on the outskirts of Atlanta. The drive sloped down a hill next to the house and out to a freestanding shed at the back

of the property. Harley parked inside the weathered tin struc-
ture, and I parked in a patch of overgrown grass next to it—
concentrating really hard on not taking my foot off the clutch
until *after* I shut off the ignition.

I glanced at my reflection in the rearview mirror, fluffed my
bangs, took a deep breath, and stepped into the glow of the setting sun.

I heard a loud clang as Harley pulled the garage's sliding
metal door closed and secured it with a padlock. He looked at
me and smiled. The sunlight had turned orange and was coming
in sideways, illuminating all the tiny specks of pollen and dan-
delion fuzz floating in the air between us.

"This is it," he said, gesturing around the unkempt yard with
an unlit cigarette between two fingers.

"I love it," I replied. It reminded me of my house. Small.
Secluded. Overgrown. Wild.

Harley lit his cigarette and offered it to me again. I accepted
it with my hand instead of my teeth that time, suddenly feeling
shy in the face of potential fuckery. I was at his house. I mean,
I wanted to be at his house, but now, I was actually at *his house*.
Where his *bed* was. Where he had sex with silly little girls who
followed him home pretending to just want beer.

We walked together through the knee-high grass, up the
wooden back steps, across the weathered porch, through the
back door, and into what will forever hold the title of Nastiest
Bachelor Pad I've Ever Seen in My Entire Fucking Life.

We entered through the kitchen, which was all mustard-
colored 1950s-era appliances, ripped linoleum, dirty dishes,
empty beer cans, dented aluminum furniture, exposed light
bulbs, and random holes in the Sheetrock, each about the size of

a human head. I stood with my mouth hanging open as Harley headed straight for the fridge.

Pulling out two cans of Natural Ice, Harley handed one to me and said, "Sorry the place is a fuckin' mess. My brother and his redneck friends had a party a few nights ago and shit got rowdy."

I laughed, looking around at the destruction. "Shit got rowdy, huh?"

"The living room is still in one piece—sort of." Harley led me through the entryway into a very sparsely furnished living room.

In the center was a well-worn leather sectional and coffee table—definite thrift store finds—facing a big-screen TV that had so many wires, controllers, game systems, DVD players, speakers, and stereo head units sprouting from it that it looked like an electronic octopus. The only decor to be seen was a collection of neon beer signs hanging on the left wall, their plugs all jammed into a single power strip on the floor.

As I walked toward the wall of neon, Harley flipped a switch on the other side of the room, almost blinding me.

"Jesus!" I cried, shielding my eyes from the multicolored assault. "Where did you get all these?"

"I stole 'em from the liquor store I used to work at," Harley said without a shred of shame. "Vendors used to send 'em to us all the time, but sometimes, they got *damaged* and had to be *thrown away*, you know?"

"Oh, I know," I said, turning away from the wall of wattage to face him. "That shit happens all the time at Pier One. Funny how the *damaged* stuff seems to wind up *behind* the dumpster instead of *in* the dumpster." I smiled.

"You work at Pier One?" Harley asked, flopping onto the sectional and downing about half of his beer in one gulp.

"Yeah," I said, taking a sip of mine as I walked around the couch to where he was sitting. "Until they fire me. I'm pretty much the worst employee ever. I just show up and rearrange all their displays. I don't even ring people up because one of the managers said my shaved head might 'intimidate' the customers." I rolled my eyes and used finger quotes around the word *intimidate*. I was so *not* intimidating.

"I like your hair," Harley said with a smile. "It's fuckin' badass."

Badass?

No.

What?

Did Harley James just call me a badass?

I sat on the couch next to him and just stared at his sweet puppy-dog face for a second. Who the fuck was this guy? And where had he been all my life? He was so...nice. And hot. And fun. And funny. Harley might have looked bad, bad, bad with those tattoos and muscles and lip ring that I just wanted to bite, but he was a good guy. I could tell.

And when his brother walked in the back door, carrying a big flat box and a grocery bag, I found out that Harley might just be too good to be true.

"Motherfucker, you owe me thirty bucks!" the younger James brother yelled into the living room as he set everything down on the wobbly kitchen table.

Harley chuckled. "That's my little brother, Davidson."

"Davidson?" I whispered back, trying to suppress my laughter. "Your mom named you guys Harley and Davidson?"

The redneck version of Harley grabbed a beer out of the

fridge and leaned against the entryway between the kitchen and living room. "Technically, we're the same age, and you know I go by Dave, asshole."

"Are you twins?" I asked, glancing quickly back and forth between them.

If they were, they weren't identical. Both cute. Both had the same mischievous blue eyes, but Dave had short brown hair stuffed under a baseball cap with a fishing hook stuck in the bill, and he wasn't quite as tall.

"Irish twins," Dave said. "I'm ten months younger."

"It took you fuckin' long enough," Harley said, standing up. "We're starvin'." Holding his hand out to me, Harley added, "I called *Davidson* here when we left Waffle House and told him to pick some stuff up for us on his way home from work." Turning his head toward the kitchen, he raised his voice. "Now he's being a little bitch about it."

Dave held up his middle finger as he chugged his beer.

When we walked into the kitchen, I saw what Harley was talking about. There, on the table, was a pizza box and a store-bought chocolate cake that said *Happy Birthday* on top in red icing. My breath caught as I swung my head around to stare at Harley in disbelief.

My eyes stung. Why did my eyes sting? Oh my God. Was I going to cry? I should know. I was used to crying after the shittastic few months I'd been having but never because of something happy. The utter sweetness of it caught me completely off guard.

Harley shrugged and said, "You said you just got your license. Figured you just had a birthday, too."

Cool be damned. I launched myself at him. Harley caught me and stumbled back a step or two as I wrapped my legs around his waist and my arms around his neck, squealing, "Thank you, thank you, thank you," before planting a chaste kiss on his cheek.

Or at least I *tried* to give him a peck on the cheek. Before my lips could make contact, Harley gripped my ass a little tighter and intercepted my innocent kiss with his sly, smiling mouth. The energy shifted. The ground shifted. And my pulse shifted into fucking overdrive as I held my breath and let him kiss me. Harley's expert lips parted mine. His graceful tongue slid across and around my own. His lip ring teased me, and when my scattered wits finally came back together, I captured that damn thing between my teeth and gave it a gentle tug—just like I'd been dying to do all day.

"You were right, bro," Dave's voice, muffled by pizza, said from somewhere behind me. "Bitches *love* birthday cakes."

Harley broke our kiss just long enough to grab an empty beer can off the counter and throw it at his brother.

Dave blocked the projectile and laughed. "Are y'all gonna eat or just fuck right here in the kitchen? 'Cause, if y'all are gonna fuck, I should probably make some popcorn."

Oh my God.

I buried my beet-red face in Harley's neck and held on for dear life as he hurled another half-dozen cans at his brother. I inhaled him shamelessly from my hiding place. He didn't smell like sweat and motor oil like I'd thought he would—he smelled like gasoline and leather seats. The combination made my thighs tighten around his narrow hips involuntarily.

Giving my ass one last squeeze, Harley took a step forward

and set me down in one of the rickety aluminum chairs at the kitchen table. The pizza box was open, and two slices were already missing, thanks to Dave. Harley pulled a couple more beers out of the fridge and handed me one, taking the seat to my left. There, we ate and drank and smoked and talked and laughed and laughed and laughed for hours.

The guys said they were renting the house from their uncle and had been living there for a couple of months. They had three younger half-sisters who still lived at home with their mom and stepdad. I learned that Dave worked at the Army/Navy surplus store and had had the same job since he graduated from Peach State High. I also learned that Harley had been on his own since he was seventeen.

"This motherfucker got kicked out of school *and* kicked out of the house on the same damn day!" Dave slapped his knee and coughed out a laugh as he passed the blunt he'd just lit to Harley.

Harley took a drag and shrugged. Exhaling, he said, "She didn't even care that I got expelled. Mom just wanted me outta the house because she had so many goddamn kids."

"Oh, I heard about that!" I said, shaking my head when Harley offered me the blunt. Pot was about the only drug I ever turned down. That shit made me sleepy as hell. I don't know how my parents smoked so much of it. "Didn't you get kicked out of school for punching the principal in the face?"

Harley and Davidson looked at each other, then burst out laughing in unison.

I took another swig of Natty Ice and watched them with a tipsy smile on my face. They were so fucking cute. Dave had this boyish smart-ass Southern charm while Harley was all tattooed, muscle-car-driving, motor-oil-in-his-blood man, but when they joked around, they were almost the same person. And, since Harley and *I* were almost the same person, that made the three of us a set of peas in a fucking pod.

Dave leaned over and clutched my forearm. "Get this shit... get this shit..." he cried through his giggles. "Harley didn't punch Principal Jenner. Principal Jenner fucking *punched Harley*!" Dave pointed at his brother and erupted into another bout of laughter. "Jacked him right in the fuckin' jaw!"

Both guys were practically crying, but I didn't get the joke.

Looking at Harley in shock, I said, "He punched you? You could have fucking sued him! You could have gotten him fired!"

"Nah," Harley said, waving me off. "After what I said I did to his mama the night before, I had it comin'."

"So after he got expelled, *I* told everybody *Harley* punched *Principal Jenner*! Now he's fuckin' famous!" Dave said, shoving Harley in the shoulder. "He got so much pussy after that, it was insane!"

I'd heard about all the pussy he'd gotten, but I didn't ask about that. I didn't want to know.

Harley just looked at me with those puppy-dog eyes and shrugged. He didn't deny it. And, with a face that cute and a body that hard, he didn't need to.

Glancing over at the clock on the microwave, I realized that it hadn't changed since the last three times I'd peeked at it. Still said *9:05*. And it was still blinking.

Fuuuuuck.

A sinking feeling washed over me as I tore through my purse, looking for my phone. I found it within seconds and illuminated the screen. It read *10:28.*

"Shit! I have to go!" I chucked my phone back in my bag and scrambled to find my car keys. Glancing across the table at Harley and Dave, who obviously didn't understand the sudden urgency of the situation, I said, "I have to be home in thirty minutes or my dad's gonna fuckin' kill me."

I stood up, but Harley immediately wrapped his thick hands around my waist and pulled me down onto his lap.

"Don't go," he whispered into my ear, nuzzling the sensitive skin just below it.

My body melted into his on contact. God, it felt good to be held by a man. I'd missed that, more than I'd realized. I wanted so badly to stay and explore every ounce of promise held in those two words, but instead, I said, "Harley, I have to. I have a curfew," pressing on his chest to help my tipsy ass stand back up.

Harley snaked his bulging, colorful arms around my body and held me tighter. "Nope. Sorry. You're just gonna have to tell him that I'm your daddy now."

"Harley, for real!" I said, slapping him on the chest. "I have to go!"

Dave laughed. "If she's calling anybody *Daddy* around here, it's gonna be me. I mean, I *am* the one who bought her that birthday cake."

"Ugh!" I wriggled out of Harley's embrace and sprinted for the back door like Cinderella at the stroke of midnight.

As I scampered down the splintered stairs and into the pitch-black night, I realized that Harley and Dave had probably never had a curfew growing up. Nobody had been waiting up to make sure they got home safe. From the sound of it, the only thing their mom had been waiting around for was a good excuse to kick them both out. The thought made me sad and also explained why they were acting so nonchalant about me being late.

As I fumbled to unlock my door in the darkness, I heard the back door slam shut and heavy footsteps, taking the stairs two at a time, behind me.

Fuck. I don't have time for this.

I turned around to see the outline of Harley jogging across the yard toward me, backlit by the glow of the house. Even his run was sexy. Long strides. One hand holding the waist of his low-hanging Dickies. The chain attached to his wallet catching the moonlight as it bounced.

"Sorry I ran out like that. I just really have to—"

Harley closed the distance between us and caught the rest of my apologetic words in his mouth. He kissed me fervently. His hands were everywhere. My breathing, erratic. I wanted to wrap my legs around his waist again. Let him take me right there, out in the open. I wanted nothing in between us but the humid summer air and the sheen of sweat on our skin. I wanted *him*. The man who, in a single day, had breathed life back into my deflated soul. But if I didn't get the fuck home, I wasn't going to be seeing him again for a very, very long time.

"Harley," I rasped into his welcoming mouth. "Harley. I have to go. Please."

Harley released my bottom lip with a pop and furrowed his brow. "Can I call you?" he asked, breathless. "I have your number on file at the shop."

I nodded, fumbling behind me for the door handle. "Thanks for today. It was the best day I've had in a really long time."

It might have been the best day of my life, but I wasn't going to tell him that. Not yet at least.

"Me too," Harley said, giving me one last lingering peck as I pulled my door open. "Drive safe, lady."

As I peeled out of there, I looked at the clock on my dashboard—*10:42. Fuck my life.*

I had eighteen minutes to figure out where I was and how to get home, which I estimated was at least half an hour away. I managed to retrace my steps back to the Waffle House, and from there, I followed signs to the only highway I knew—the one that led due east out of Atlanta and straight through my town.

I raced home, tipsy on beer and high on Harley, going fifteen to twenty miles per hour over the speed limit the entire way. I didn't even turn on the radio. I just replayed the last ten minutes of my life over and over in my head with a big, dumb smile on my face. Once I was out of the city, I switched to back roads, downshifting in the middle of the turns, just like Harley had taught me that afternoon.

I pulled into my parents' driveway with one minute to spare, stalled out in my designated parking spot, and practically dived across the threshold as the clock struck eleven. Gasping for air, I poked my head into the living room where my paranoid, insomniac, conspiracy-theorist father spent his nights smoking cigarettes, polishing his guns, and watching CNN.

"Hi, Dad! Night, Dad!" I chirped before running up the stairs and locking myself in the bathroom.

The old me would have spent the next half hour in there,

throwing up all the pizza, birthday cake, and beer she'd consumed. She wouldn't have been able to rest until the damage had been undone. The new me, however, had other reasons for locking herself in the bathroom. Reasons that involved thoughts of Harley's oil-stained hands on her pale, freckled skin and a showerhead with a massage setting.

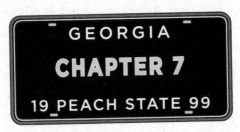

GEORGIA

CHAPTER 7

19 PEACH STATE 99

I needed something to do. I was going out of my mind checking my phone every five seconds waiting for Harley to call.

I'd bitten off all my fingernails, applied and reapplied my makeup, worn a path into the carpet next to my bed from pacing, and smoked at least a pack of cigarettes—and I'd only been awake for an hour. I'd even called in to work to see if I could pick up some extra shifts. I knew they'd say no, but it was worth a shot.

I was so restless. I'd gone from going to school full-time, working part-time, and spending every other minute with Knight to working twenty hours per week and spending the other hundred and forty-eight staring at a TV screen and wondering if I'd ever be able to feel again.

Well, I was feeling again. Feeling like I wanted to jump out of my fucking skin.

The night before had been more fun than I'd ever had. Don't get me wrong; I'd had *plenty* of fun in my sixteen years, but it was always the bad kind of fun. The kind of fun that ended with somebody getting hurt. Or getting into a fight. Or brandishing a weapon. Or getting pregnant. Or vandalizing a drug dealer's car. Or dying. Or getting arrested. Or going to the hospital. Or having a bad trip. Or puking up malt liquor all night. Or running from Latin gangsters. Or having to walk three miles to Juliet's house at two a.m. with no jacket. That was how my nights of "fun" usually ended. And I guess my night with Harley could have ended the same way if I'd gotten busted going twenty miles over the speed limit with beer on my breath. But I hadn't.

Because Harley was an angel.

That was the only explanation. Harley was a golden-haired angel delivered to me from the universe to apologize for the utter shitshow my life had become after Knight kicked his way into it.

The gods must have been like, *Damn, that really went sideways fast. Our bad. Here's a tattooed, muscle-bound, baby-faced sex machine to make up for it. Oh, and we'll even gift wrap him in a vintage Mustang. Our treat.*

But if he were really a gift from the cosmos, then why hadn't he fucking call—

"Hello?" I almost dropped the glittery Nokia that hadn't left my hand all morning as I scrambled to answer it. "Hello!"

"Hey, lady." The gravelly sound of Harley's voice and the lazy smile I could almost see on his face had me squeezing my eyes shut and pressing my lips together in an attempt to suppress the girlie squeal that was about to burst out of me.

"You called," I squeaked in disbelief.

Harley chuckled. "Of course I fucking called. I can't stop thinking about you."

Blink, blink.

"BB?"

"Huh?" I cleared my throat. "I'm sorry. You'll have to leave a message. BB is dead right now."

Harley's laugh danced through my head and into my heart and tickled my fucking soul.

"Is she alive yet?" he asked.

"Let me check...nope. You killed her pretty good."

"What about now?"

I smiled so big my face hurt. "Um..."

"I was really hoping she'd come see me at work today."

"What time?" I blurted out.

Shit. Lost my cool again.

"Around four? I get off at five, and this afternoon is looking pretty slow."

"Okay," I said. "I mean, I'll see if I can reanimate BB by then. She might want to eat your brains though, so just be prepared."

Oh, good save, I thought, rolling my eyes at myself.

Harley chuckled and said, "Tell BB she can eat any part of my body she wants."

I blushed crimson at the innuendo in his voice.

"See you at four, little zombie," he said before hanging up.

As soon as I finished writhing on the floor, I decided to go to Juliet's house. I could help out with the baby and kill a few hours before I got to see the man of my dreams again. Maybe Jules could even take a nap while I was there. Her bitchy ass needed one.

I threw on a pair of ripped jeans, shoved my feet into my combat boots, and reached for the Dead Kennedys tank top hanging in my closet. Then, I immediately snatched my hand back as unwanted memories began flashing like a slideshow behind my eyes. Holding Knight's hand. Wearing his jacket. Walking from his tattoo shop in Little Five Points, where we'd spent the night, over to Boots & Braces, the store where he bought all his imported skinhead clothes. The sketchiest warehouse I'd ever seen. The one rack of punk T-shirts that the owner said was there for "profiling purposes." The tank top in my hands and my lips on Knight's cheek when he dropped me off at work.

I slammed my closet door and stared at the wooden surface, breathing hard. "No," I said aloud to no one but myself. "Not today."

I stood there until my heart rate returned to normal and the unshed tears receded. Then I picked my favorite Dropkick Murphys tank top off the floor, shrugged it on, and got the fuck out of there.

Going to Juliet's house had been the perfect distraction. It's hard to be a spiraling nervous wreck when you're holding a sleeping newborn. I even took it upon myself to give Romeo a bottle— with help from Juliet's little brother—so that his exhausted mama could nap longer.

Evidently, that had been the wrong choice.

Juliet woke up an hour later, refreshed but practically drowning in her own milk. She was leaking like a faucet from missing Romeo's scheduled feeding. Too bad the little guy was still in a milk coma from the bottle I'd given him and couldn't help her out. The time had finally come—time to figure out how to use the goddamn breast pump.

I read the instructions out loud and tried to stifle my giggles as Juliet mashed her giant boobs into the suction cups. When she was finally ready, I flipped the switch...and the loud, cartoonlike pumping sound had us both laughing our asses off. It was all so fucking ridiculous. So ridiculous in fact that I was almost late getting over to the garage.

I saw him the second I pulled into the A&J Auto Body entrance. Harley was standing out front, smoking a cigarette, and *goddamn* did he look good. Dirty good. Oil-smudged-wifebeater-and-a-pair-of-dark-gray-Dickies good. The sight of him had my stomach doing backflips. I couldn't believe that superhumanly sexy thing had kissed me. *Twice.*

When Harley saw me pull in, he smiled and gestured into one of the bays with two fingers. I followed his lead and entered the garage, concentrating hard on not stalling out again.

As soon as I killed the engine, Harley came around and opened my door. He was sweaty and filthy, and I didn't give a single fuck.

"Hey, lady," he said, leaning into the car and pressing a lingering kiss to my lips.

The second the cool metal of his lip ring touched my skin, my eyes slammed shut and my core tightened like a coil. I wanted to suck his tongue into my mouth and run my fingers through his wild blond hair, but he was at work, and I was too chickenshit.

As he pulled away with a smile, Harley popped my hood by pulling a lever under my steering wheel that I hadn't even known was there. Walking around to the front of my car, he propped up the hood and looked inside.

"Hell yeah," he said as I came around to see what all the fuss was about. "I found a cold air intake in the back, and it looks like it'll fit."

"In English, please," I said, still smiling from that kiss.

Harley grabbed something off the tool chest behind him

and turned back toward me. "This thing. Your engine. More horsepower."

"Ah, gotcha," I said. "Is that why you wanted me to come see you? So you could stick your doohickey under my hood?"

"I love it when you talk dirty to me," Harley said with a smile, snaking one arm around my waist and pulling me toward him.

"You're the dirty one," I said, pushing him away and wrinkling my nose in mock disgust. "Where is your shirt?"

Because I want to steal it and take it home and use it as a pillowcase.

Harley shrugged. "It's hot as balls in here. You're lucky I still have pants on."

I disagreed but kept that to myself.

For the next forty-five minutes, Harley and I talked while *he* tinkered and *I* periodically slurped the drool back into my face. When he was done, Harley tried to scrub the grease off his hands with this special gooey orange stuff, but I'm pretty sure no amount of soap would ever be enough to get those things squeaky clean again.

While he washed up, Harley said he wanted to test out the new *blah, blah intake car thingy* he'd just installed at the track, and I nodded. Because that was what I did when Harley asked me questions. I said *yes*.

Harley clocked out, and I followed him back to the track. Watching him drive that matte black beast for ten minutes was like horrible, torturous foreplay. I was dying to get my hands on everything in front of me, but it was all just beyond my reach. Harley could have just left his car at the garage and ridden with me while we tested out the flux capacitor or whatever he'd just installed, but I got the sense that he didn't let that car out of his sight any longer than he had to. Not that I blamed him. Hell, even I would probably consider committing a little grand theft auto if I saw that thing sitting in an empty parking lot.

Once we got to the track, Harley had me scoot over so that he could drive. He slid my seat all the way back to accommodate his long legs and flashed me a knowing grin as he cranked her up. Revving the engine a little bit, Harley whistled. "Damn, lady. You're sitting on a fuckin' gold mine here. A little girl in a stock five-oh." He shook his head. "It's too fuckin' easy."

I wanted to argue with him, tell him I wasn't racing, but the words *little girl* were sticking out of my chest like a knife. It was hard to breathe, let alone form a coherent counterargument.

My abilities were even further obliterated when Harley popped the clutch and gunned the engine at the same time. My head slammed back into my seat as Harley jammed the shifter into second, somehow *accelerated* through the first turn, then threw her into third on the straightaway. I white-knuckled the center console and armrest as Harley cut the next corner, going way faster than I'd thought was fucking possible.

"Fuck yeah!" Harley shouted as we came out of the turn, smacking the steering wheel with the butt of his hand. "Those all-weathers I put on yesterday are grippy as shit. Dumb fucks come in here with racing slicks, thinkin' they're Billy Badass, and they fishtail through the turns every time. I can't fuckin' wait to see you smoke their asses in a set of all-weathers." Harley practically cackled as he slammed it into fourth.

"Harley, I told you—"

"You just need some practice, that's all," he said, giving my thigh a reassuring squeeze. Like it was no big deal. Like he had all the confidence in me in the world.

I liked that Harley saw me as someone with ass-kicking potential. Someone capable of beating grown men at their own game. Somebody worthy of the nickname *Lady*. He was wrong, of course—so very wrong—but I wanted to keep the charade going as long as I could.

"Fine," I huffed. "I'll practice, but that's it. And if I wrap this thing around a tree, you're buying me a new one."

"Deal," Harley said, pulling over so that I could switch places with him.

I climbed back into the driver's seat and had to slide it forward at least ten inches before my feet could even touch the pedals again.

Harley leaned across the center console and wrapped his left hand around my right thigh. "I got you," he breathed into my ear.

The warmth from his mouth disappeared in an instant, carried away by the blasting AC. Gently pressing down on my leg, Harley made my foot compress the accelerator. The volume of the engine and the needle on my RPM gauge began to rise.

Sliding his hand over to my left thigh, Harley spoke louder over the growing roar. His voice rumbled across my skin, leaving a path of goosebumps in its wake. "Good. That's perfect. Now, let the clutch out. Slowly. The second you feel it catch... stomp the gas."

Harley gripped my thigh harder and pulled up, easing my foot off the clutch. Just as I began to feel the car engage, Harley's hot breath in my ear said, "Now."

I slammed my right foot down, just like he'd said, and was forced backward in my seat as the car bolted forward like a bullet. The first turn came way faster than I'd expected, but Harley was right there, in my ear.

He put his right hand over mine on the shifter and pressed down on my left thigh with his left hand. "Push in the clutch, and shift into neutral."

I did it with Harley guiding me like a marionette.

"Now, shift into second, and give it just enough gas to catch."

Harley's hand slid up my thigh, and two of his thick fingers stroked my bare skin through one of the holes in my jeans. The proximity of his hand to the place that had been soaking fucking wet since I first laid eyes on him was such a distraction that I stabbed the gas instead of tapping it and watched in horror as my RPM needle fell like a lead balloon. The car slowed to a stop all by itself, and I looked at Harley with my mouth hanging open in horror.

"What did I do?"

Harley chuckled and reached forward to pull the hood latch. Kissing me on the cheek, he said, "Probably just needs a new valve to go with that cold air intake. This ole girl's got more torque than she knows what to do with."

Harley and I hopped out and peered into the engine. It all looked pretty engine-y to me, but Harley immediately spotted the problem. He said I'd thrown a belt, whatever that meant, and called his coworker buddy to bring him one on his way home from the shop.

Harley and I stood in the shade next to the Boss while we waited, smoking cigarettes and finding excuses to touch each other. I didn't even care that my brand-new/used car was broken. I knew Harley would fix it. All I could think about was the fact that his fingers were hooked through my belt loops.

Harley leaned against his back fender and spread his feet apart, pulling me to stand between his legs. My heart was beating a mile a minute as he smiled at me, his eyes dropping to my lips. Then it stopped altogether when I registered the sound of an engine rumbling through the trees. I couldn't breathe. Couldn't blink. Couldn't move as images of Knight's giant white monster truck came to mind.

No. That's impossible, I thought, listening with perked ears, like a bunny on high alert.

Sensing my apprehension, Harley wrapped his big, reassuring hands around my waist and smiled. "Sounds like Bubba called in the cavalry."

I turned and looked at the opening in the trees where the road emerged from the woods just as a caravan of jacked-up trucks and racing trucks and ATVs came barreling into the clearing. I sighed in relief, then giggled as I noticed a fucking tractor bringing up the rear of the redneck brigade.

"All this for a thrown belt?"

Harley laughed as the parade descended upon us. "They live for this shit."

The head truck and the one behind it—a pair of Chevys caked in dried Georgia clay—parked next to us while a few other trucks drove past us, halfway around the track, and straight into the woods through a tiny opening between two trees.

A short, beefy-looking dude in a fisherman's hat hopped out of the bigger Chevy and walked over to us, holding a black strip of rubber and a wrench. "Got yer belt, man. That it over there?" he said, gesturing toward the track where my car was parked with the hood up.

"Yeah." Harley didn't bother to let go of me as he addressed his buddy. I liked that. "What's with the posse? Y'all that excited about watching me change a drive belt?"

"Nah, we're goin' muddin'." Raising his voice and turning his head toward the other truck, Elmer Fudd yelled, "Brought the tractor just in case JR's dumb ass gets stuck as bad as last time." Leaning in and grinning, he said in a quieter voice, "I coulda got him out with the winch. We just like bustin' his balls."

"I heard that, motherfucker," a skinny guy wearing Wranglers and cowboy boots said as he walked over to us. "Hey, I know you," he said, gesturing to me with the soda can he'd been using as a spittoon. "You're Punk, Knight's girlfriend, right?"

Harley bristled, his fingertips digging into my waist.

"I heard he left for the service. How's he doin'?"

"I-I don't know," I stammered, acutely aware that Harley was behind me, breathing through his nose about as loud as a bull. "We broke up before he left."

"Ah, man," JR said. "That's too bad. I had weight trainin' with that sum'bitch. Motherfucker put up over three hundred pounds one time. Craziest shit I ever saw." Looking over my shoulder at Harley, JR's eyes went wide. "I mean, uh...good to see you, Punk."

"BB," Harley said in a voice deep as hell and laced with malice. "Her name is BB."

"Uh, okay," JR said, spitting brown tobacco juice into his can and walking backward toward his truck. "Bubba, I'm goin' in. Good to see y'all. Harley," he said, tipping the bill of his ball cap before turning and half-sprinting toward his vehicle.

"I'll be in there to pull ya out in a second," Bubba called after him with a chuckle. "Dumbass."

Harley took the drive belt and wrench from him with a quick "Thanks," then headed straight for my car.

I hustled after him, trying to keep up. Everything about his posture had changed. His shoulders were tense. His hands were balled into fists at his sides. Something JR had said seriously pissed him off, and I didn't want to make it worse.

I watched silently over Harley's shoulder as he turned something with the wrench, popped the old belt off, wove the new one onto a half-dozen pulley-turny thingies, and then tightened it back up with the wrench—all in under five minutes. I had to admit, watching him work was a major turn-on, and the thought that he might be jealous had me a little hot under the collar, too.

The fact that it was ninety degrees outside had me just plain ole hot.

When he was finished, he wiped his hands on his gray work pants and turned toward me. "All done. You wanna give her another spin?"

"Why'd you get so pissed off back there?" I blurted.

Harley's jaw flexed, and his sparkly blue eyes hardened.

"Harley?"

He walked around to the passenger door and opened it. "Can we talk about it in the car? It's too fuckin' hot out here."

I hopped into the driver's seat and turned on the AC. Harley closed his eyes as the cold air hit his face.

"Okay, spill it."

Taking a deep breath, Harley turned toward me with all traces of humor wiped from his pretty face. "What did he do to you?"

I laughed. I couldn't help it. How was I supposed to even answer that? Knight had done *everything* to me. Everything that one person could do to another person. Good, bad, or fucking psycho—he'd done it all... to me.

"Did he hurt you?" Harley asked.

"Yeah." The word came out of my mouth with more attitude than I'd intended. I'd said it the way you might say *Duh*, or, *What the fuck do you think?*

Harley's jaw clenched, and he cracked two knuckles on his right hand. "Did he...cut you?" he asked, his voice quiet but deadly.

Images of the butterfly knife Knight kept in his pocket glinted behind my eyelids. Images of him teaching me to flip it open and shut in the back of his truck. Him slicing my inner thigh with it as I came in his mouth. Him sucking the blood from the wound as I pulsed around his fingers.

"Yeah," I said, looking straight ahead, seeing nothing. "He did."

Snapping out of my past and back into the present, I turned to face Harley. "How do you know about that?" I asked, the air conditioning doing little to cool my flushed cheeks.

"I used to live in a house in Little Five Points with a bunch of punks and skins," Harley said. "One of my roommates was a skin chick named Darla. She used to hang out at Spirit of Sixty-Nine."

My hand immediately flew to my mouth, covering my silent gasp. I knew how this story ended. Knight had told me himself. The only girls he'd been with before me were skin chicks he'd met at Spirit of Sixty-Nine—a bar in Atlanta where he used to help clean up after-hours. When I'd asked if he'd dated any of them, Knight had said no, not after what he'd done to them. He confessed to me that he'd hurt those girls. He admitted that he liked to "make people bleed." Knight had stood in front of me and told me exactly what kind of monster he was, and I'd looked the other way because of another confession he'd made during that same conversation. The part where he told me he loved me.

"You know her?" Harley asked, his jaw muscles flexed.

I blinked and shook my head.

"Well, your little boyfriend carved her ass up. I had to take her to the hospital to get stitches and a fuckin' tetanus shot after what he did to her."

I squeezed my eyes shut and willed away the tears.

Poor Darla.

Poor sick, psychotic Knight.

"He ever cut you like *that*?" Harley asked, his voice getting louder.

I shook my head.

"He ever lay a hand on you?"

I hesitated. I wanted to shake my head again, but Harley already knew the answer. And I was a terrible liar.

"Fuck!" Harley yelled as he hit my dashboard with the side of his fist. "I swear to God, if I ever see that motherfucker again, he's a dead man."

Thanks to the catlike reflexes I'd developed after months of being Knight's girlfriend, Harley's sudden outburst caused me to jump back in my seat. Harley noticed my exaggerated reaction and reached for me with a crumpled brow.

"Hey," he said, pulling my hand away from my body, puppy-dog eyes in full effect. "I'm not like him, okay? I promise. I would never fucking hurt a woman. *Ever.* I don't care if you punch me in the fucking face. Here. See?" Harley lifted my hand and used it to hit himself in the cheek over and over, making little punching sound effects every time. He didn't stop until I was giggling hysterically.

"What if I punched you in the balls?" I asked through my tears.

"Let's find out," Harley said, moving my hand from his face to his crotch.

I screamed and yanked my hand away. "Asshole!" I giggled, swatting him on the arm.

"I think you missed. My balls are down *here*," Harley said, lifting his hips and pointing to his junk with a smirk.

I laughed even harder, wondering what I'd done to get so fucking lucky. I'd spent the last three months praying for someone to protect me from the wrath of Ronald McKnight. Someone who would *stand up* to him instead of *serving me up* to him on a fucking platter the second he flexed his steroid-enhanced muscles. Someone who was willing to throw down with the devil himself. And there he was—sitting in my passenger seat, making me laugh and trying to get me to touch his Johnson.

Harley James really was a gift from the gods.

I'd been trying to pick up extra shifts at work for weeks, and they chose *that* moment to call and take me up on my offer.

One of my coworkers was sick, and they needed me to pick up the evening shift for the next few days. I probably could have just told my manager no, made up some excuse, but A) I was a terrible liar, B) I needed the money, and C) I was seconds away from ripping Harley's grease-stained clothes off in my passenger seat with my teeth when she called, and I kind of panicked.

I had only known the guy for two days—*two days*—and I was fucking gone over him. I remembered what Juliet had said about him being a man-whore in high school. And what his brother had said about him being a man-whore *after* high school. As badly as I wanted to see him again, I knew I needed to slow things down. Harley had become the light at the end of a long, dark tunnel for me, and even though I had a feeling that light might very well belong to an oncoming train, I was sprinting toward it nonetheless.

Pulling into Harley's driveway on Thursday, I concentrated hard on *not* taking my foot off the clutch until after the ignition was off just in case he was watching. I checked my reflection in the rearview mirror as inconspicuously as possible. Then I gathered my keys and sunglasses with shaking hands. As soon as I stepped into the high-noon sun, my heart wedged itself into my throat tighter than my ass had been wedged into the fuzzy, tiger-striped velour pants I was wearing.

I told myself I'd chosen those pants because all my other clothes were dirty, but I couldn't even lie to *myself*. I'd known when I stepped into those stretchy, stripy, slutty things that morning that I wanted Harley to take them right back off. In fact, I had to hear my Catholic-upbringing-induced guilt give me shit about it the whole way over.

You know this is a booty call, right? my guilt whispered.

No, it's not, I countered. *We're just two people who both happen to have the day off, hanging out.*

My guilt rolled its eyes. *Yeah, hanging out in an empty house while Harley's brother is at work. What do you think you're gonna do over there? Play pinochle?*

Maybe, I thought. *Maybe we'll play video games. I don't know.*

Those don't look like video-game-playing pants to me.

Fuck you, Guilt.

Oh, I think I'm gonna have to take a number for that. Looks like you've already got a wait-list.

Ugh!

Taking a deep breath, the way someone would right before walking barefoot over hot coals, I made my way across Harley's patchy, pine-needle-covered front lawn and didn't exhale until I pressed his doorbell. When the door opened, I sucked in another deep breath—that time, in the form of a gasp. Harley's usually messy blond pompadour was extra disheveled, his jaw had a hint of scruff peppering it, and he was wearing nothing but a pair of plaid boxer shorts.

Fuck me.

"Hey, pretty lady," Harley said, his voice gruff and his eyes squinty as he pulled a white Minor Threat T-shirt on over his head and opened his front door wider to let me in.

"Hey," I said, stepping into his living room. "Did I wake you up?"

"Mmhmm," he said, closing the door behind us and pulling me in for a hug.

I was sad there was a shirt between us. I wanted to feel his skin against my cheek and under my hands where they came to rest on his back.

"I'm sorry," I said into the soft white cotton. "You did tell me to come around noon, right?"

"Mmhmm," Harley hummed again.

I could feel his smile against the top of my head. I didn't think it was possible, but sleepy Harley might have been even sexier than confident mechanic Harley. All I wanted to do was steer him back into whatever bed he'd just crawled out of and roll around in it with him for the next two to three *days*.

Keeping one arm around my shoulders, Harley walked me into the house and over to the couch. The coffee table was littered with beer cans and lighters and rolling papers and ashtrays made from random car parts and at least one bong.

"Gimme a sec," Harley said, releasing me to sit. "You wanna smoke?" he asked, probably noticing the way I was eyeing all the paraphernalia on the coffee table.

"Oh. No. Thanks. Weed makes me super sleepy," I said, wiping my shaky, sweaty palms on my skintight fuzzy pants.

The movement caused Harley's heavy-lidded gaze to land on my tiger-striped thighs. He curled his big, fat bottom lip into his mouth and tongued his lip ring as he stared.

"I'd take a beer though," I blurted, desperately needing something to calm my nerves. "Do you mind if I grab one?"

Harley gave me an indignant look and said, "Pssh," before heading toward the kitchen with the sleepy swagger of a sated lion.

I watched him move with my thighs pressed together and my lip between my teeth. All the beer in the world wasn't going to help me get my shit together in the presence of that...*man*. He exuded sex unlike anyone I'd ever met, and he didn't even seem to be trying. Unlike me in my animal-print pants, cropped Operation Ivy tank top, and visible red bra straps. I was definitely trying. I might as well have shown up wearing a sandwich board that said *Down to fuck*.

On his way back into the living room, Harley drank me in and gave me a slow, appreciative smile. "Can't let a pretty lady get her own beer," he said, handing me a can of Natural Ice.

"You should never let a beautiful woman light her own cigarette."

Knight's voice in my head sounded as clear as the day he'd uttered those words. For a split second, I wasn't in Harley's living room anymore. I was sitting on the tailgate of Knight's Frankentruck, wearing his hoodie and watching him light my cigarette with swollen, bleeding knuckles.

"I'm sorry. What?" I shook my head and blinked.

Harley wasn't standing in front of me anymore. I turned my head toward the sound of a toilet flushing and saw Harley in the bathroom just down the hall. His back was toward me, but I could see his reflection in the vanity mirror as he began brushing his teeth.

Did he just pee with the door wide open?

I don't know why, but the idea made me smile.

When Harley returned to the living room, he'd thrown on his signature Dickies and chain wallet, but he was still sporting some serious bedhead and facial scruff. I smiled at him like a goddamn fool. Partly because I'd chugged half of my beer and was already feeling tipsy, but also because he was just so damn cute.

"What?" he asked, giving me the side eye.

"You peed with the door open," I said, beaming as I pulled my feet underneath me on the couch.

"I didn't know you were into that kinda thing." Harley smirked as he plopped down on the couch next to me. "I can give you a golden shower later if you want."

I shoved his arm, and he made a show of flopping over on the couch, as if I had the strength of a hundred men.

I fucking loved Harley.

When he sat up, Harley reached for a lighter and the bong on the table. It was already packed. He took a hit and held the air in his lungs as long as he could. Exhaling with a tiny cough, Harley pointed to the plastic tube and said, "You mind?"

"Oh no. Go ahead," I said. "I actually really like the smell. It smells like my house."

Harley gave me a puzzled look.

"My parents smoke. All the time. They're total hippies. My mom wears Birkenstocks and tie-dye and shit."

Harley smiled. "My parents smoke, too, but they're bikers."

"Uh, yeah. I figured that out the second you introduced me to your brother. Harley and Davidson? Really?"

Harley chuckled. "Dave fucking hates it."

"So, if you guys are the same age and he's only ten months younger, that means you must have a birthday soon, huh?" I'd given it a lot of thought—obviously.

Harley exhaled a stream of smoke and choked out, "Yeah. August ninth."

"Oh, you're a Leo," I said, finishing off my beer. "I love Leos. Super compatible with Geminis." I felt a blush begin to crawl up my neck. Had I really just said the words *love* and *compatible* in the same sentence? Oh my God. How cheesy.

Harley coughed out a laugh. "You really were raised by hippies."

I helped myself to another beer, and while I drank it, Harley and I talked for what felt like hours. He was just so relaxed and funny and flirty that I got high simply by being near him. His aura wrapped around me like a mink shawl—soft and warm and sexy. I committed all his mannerisms to memory. The way his eyes narrowed when he was about to tease me and drooped like a cartoon basset hound when he was trying to be cute. The way he ran his fingers through his hair when he was talking and sucked on his lip ring when he was listening. But when his hand found my fuzzy velour-covered thigh and began stroking it absentmindedly, my ability to form new thoughts and memories went completely out the window.

My ability to filter my fucking mouth disappeared too, because the words "Can I see your room?" tumbled from it completely unchecked.

Harley gave me a knowing smile and stood up, offering his hand. I took it and let him lead me down the hallway, a little embarrassed but not ashamed. My panties were soaked from the heat of his gaze, the warmth in his words, and the trail of fire left by his fingertips. Harley's touch—his attention—kept the darkness at bay. It made me feel like myself again. I wanted him, and with my guilty conscience passed out from day drinking, I couldn't think of a single reason to deny myself what I wanted.

I might have only been sixteen, but after the twisted, kinky, bloody fuckery Knight had subjected me to, I was about as far from virginal as a person could get. I wasn't just experienced; I was a veteran. And I had the scars and piercings to prove it. Harley might have brought out the giddy schoolgirl in me, but in the bedroom, I planned on showing him just how grown-up I really was.

That is, until I actually saw his bedroom.

"Harley! Where's all your furniture?" I cackled in the doorway, pulling him to a stop.

His room consisted of a mattress on the floor, and...well, that was about it.

Harley turned around and shrugged. "What? You don't like how I decorated?"

"This place feels like a flophouse. Are you running from the cops?" Yep, my filter was definitely off duty.

After a pause, Harley asked, "What if I am?" His expression was completely unreadable.

Was he being serious? Harley didn't do serious. No, he had to be fucking with me.

"Just because you're on the lam doesn't mean you can't

at least tack up a poster here and there. Jesus!" Dropping his hand, I walked to the opposite wall to open the blinds and let in some light. "Didn't you say you've been living here a couple of months? It looks like you just moved in yesterday. Were you robbed?"

Harley leaned against the doorframe and smirked as I made a drunken fuss over his lack of decor. When I walked back over to him, the mood sufficiently crushed, Harley took my hand and said, "C'mon," tugging me back out into the hallway behind him.

"Where are we going?" I asked as we crossed the living room and headed through the kitchen, toward the back door.

"We're gonna fuckin' decorate."

Between the growl of Harley's 429 cubic-inch engine, the delicious vibration of my seat, the way the muscles and veins under his tattoos flexed and bulged with every shift, and Harley's hand stroking my fuzzy thigh, the drive to Trash—my favorite store in Little Five Points—almost brought me to orgasm.

The ride also helped me realize a few things. The first thing I discovered was that, if you pour two beers into the empty stomach of a ninety-something-pound girl in the span of one hour and then put her in a bouncy, rumbly car for fifteen minutes, she *will* be fucking wasted by the time you get to your destination. The second thing I discovered was that telling Harley to take me to a store in Little Five Points had been a very, very bad idea.

Little Five Points had always been my happy place. It was a tiny neighborhood on the east side of Atlanta full of funky novelty shops, vintage clothing outlets, record stores, tattoo parlors, dive bars, head shops, and more graffiti than you could shake an incense stick at. It was where any self-respecting punk, skin, goth, hippie, Rastafarian, or skater shopped, and until Harley pulled the Boss into a back corner parking spot in a lot behind Terminus City Tattoo, I had always kind of thought of it as home.

Before he even killed the engine, I could feel my heart pounding in my chest. Out of my chest. Could practically see it trying to claw through my rib cage. My wide eyes landed on the alley that separated Terminus City Tattoo from the fetish club next door, and I couldn't breathe. That was *our* alley. The place where Knight had found me sick from ecstasy and alcohol and taken me into his work to care for me. The stairs where I'd spent dozens of Friday nights sitting and smoking and talking with him after the tattoo shop closed. The same shop where he'd pierced me, tattooed me, fucked me, loved me, opened up to me, and shown me exactly what kinds of demons dwelled inside him.

The kind that cut.

The kind that killed.

Invisible hands wound around my neck and squeezed as I relived the night everything had fallen apart. The night an innocent man had lost his life. The night that Knight had put his hands on me in anger for the first time. The night he'd shoved me down those fire escape stairs and locked me out of his life forever. Stars danced behind my eyes as the interior of the car closed in around me, swallowing me whole, taking me prisoner.

"Hey." Harley's gentle yet rough voice floated into my consciousness on some faraway breeze, rousing me from my nightmare.

I felt pressure on my thigh. Rubbing maybe?

"Hey. You okay? What's wrong, babe?"

Babe. Did he just call me babe?

A warmth spread through me as my basic bodily functions suddenly decided to start working again. I sucked in lungfuls of life, almost hyperventilating on the bliss of being able to breathe again. Harley *was* rubbing my thigh, and it felt amazing. He made me feel safe. Knight was gone, and Harley was here. I was safe. I was safe.

I'm safe.

I blinked rapidly at Harley. His brows were pulled together in concern as he reached up and cupped my jaw.

"Sorry," I said, clearing my throat, expecting it to be sore from the invisible choking I'd just received. "I haven't eaten all day. I think I blacked out for a minute."

"Shit, lady. Let's get you some food. Where do you want to go?"

"Not the Yacht Club," I said a little too quickly, remembering that a *Knight Loves BB* heart was carved into one of the tables there.

Harley took me to a funky Mexican place that had been established in an old auto body shop.

Fitting, I thought.

They'd kept the giant metal garage doors and huge industrial ceiling fans. They'd suspended paintings from the ceiling at random heights, and all the tables and chairs were mismatched vintage patio furniture fully equipped with equally mismatched outdoor umbrellas. It was rugged and fucking adorable. Just like Harley.

After getting a good five pounds of chips and cheese dip in me, I felt about five hundred percent better. When we were ready to go, Harley dropped a few bills on the table, and we left—just like he'd done at Waffle House. It was so weird. He drove this crazy expensive car and overpaid for all his meals like money was no object, but then he lived in this tiny little house with his brother and slept on a mattress on the floor. It didn't add up, but over the last few months, I'd learned that nobody made any fucking sense. People were liars. They were impostors. They were shady as fuck. Even the good ones. If you were lucky enough to find someone who made you feel good, you were lucky enough.

As Harley and I crossed the street and headed toward Trash, I clutched his hand to stay grounded. I didn't look at the spot in the middle of the street where Knight and I had gotten into our first fight. I didn't look at the bench where we'd sat on Valentine's Day and planned our future. And I damn sure didn't look at the old Victorian mansion he'd said he wanted to live in with me and fix up on the weekends.

But I still couldn't shake the feeling that I was being watched. That my worst nightmare was lurking in the shadows, foaming at the mouth with rage as I paraded a new man around on his turf. As I desecrated everything we'd experienced there.

No, I thought. *Stop it. Knight is gone. He's gone, and you're safe.*

The words seemed to bring me comfort, so I repeated them over and over in my head.

He's gone.

You're safe.

He's gone.

You're safe.

He's gone.

I squeezed Harley's hand and was met with a reassuring smile.

You're safe.

Once we entered the store, I was transported into a world of whimsy that brought some much-needed distraction. Trash was like Disneyland for freaks and drag queens. Novelties, sex toys, drug paraphernalia, stripper shoes in men's sizes, clothes for every kind of subculture, counterculture, and gender bender under the sun, and the kitschiest home décor money could buy.

Harley gave me a peck on the lips that made my heart swell before we split up—him disappearing into the head shop in the back of the store and me falling down the rabbit hole of possibilities over in housewares.

I needed a theme. Cars seemed too obvious. Harley had kind of a punk, rockabilly look, but band posters seemed too juvenile. Then I passed a rack of black T-shirts with white skulls screen-printed on them and got an idea. Grabbing four of them, I decided I would turn them into throw pillows using my mom's sewing machine. I might even add some fringe to give them little Mohawks.

Then, I zeroed in on a framed pen-and-ink drawing of an anatomically correct heart. Bingo. I had a theme—body parts. The second I picked the drawing up, however, the store fell away. I found myself sitting at my desk in Mr. Kampfer's AP chemistry class, holding an unfolded piece of notebook paper covered in psychotic all-caps handwriting with a huge pencil-and-ink drawing of an anatomically correct heart in the middle. Blinking the image away, I slammed the framed art back onto the shelf, as if it were teeming with spiders.

He's gone.

You're safe.

I continued to wander around the housewares department, wondering what Harley would like. I didn't know him all that well, but I knew him well enough to know that I was probably trying way too hard. I could have picked out a fish tank full of rubber mice or a mannequin wearing a top hat and a strap-on, and Harley would have had the same reaction. He'd smile. He'd buy it. And he'd proudly display it without giving a single, solitary fuck.

Reason number nine hundred eighty-eight why I was totally gone over Harley James.

Eventually, I just settled on a taxidermic jackalope bust. Everybody loves jackalopes. Sticking the antlered freak of nature under my arm, I made my way to the back of the housewares department where something stopped me dead in my tracks.

There, in the corner of the store, half-tucked behind a beaded curtain, was the coolest chair in the history of sitting. It was a simple wooden dining room chair with off-white upholstery, but the back cushion had been screen-printed with the image of a realistic-looking rib cage and spine, and the seat cushion had been screen-printed with a pelvis and thighbones. It was brilliant. It was ridiculous. And, most importantly, it fit my theme.

Harley walked up behind me as I ogled the work of art. Wrapping his arms around my waist and resting his scratchy chin on my bare shoulder, he and I studied the chair in silence.

"I love it," I said barely above a whisper.

"Then get it," he replied, placing a soft kiss on my freckled skin. Followed by another, a little higher up, and another.

As Harley trailed kisses from my shoulder to my earlobe, a tingly heat danced over my skin and caused my vag to contract around nothing. If I affected Harley half as much as he affected me, I knew he had to be sporting a killer hard-on, but he didn't press it into me. Didn't pressure me for more. He waited for my lead.

Reason number nine hundred eighty-nine why I was totally fucking gone over Harley James.

As we made our way to the checkout stand—me holding a jackalope and an armful of T-shirts and Harley carrying the chair—he stopped in front of a collection of four-foot-tall hollow metal statues of medieval knights in full armor.

Picking one up with his free hand, Harley turned to me and asked, "What about—"

"No!" I yelled, loud enough to turn heads.

Harley's eyes went wide, and he slowly put the knight back down, as if I'd threatened him at gunpoint. "Okay, okay. The lady doesn't like the knights. Good to know."

At the register, Harley pulled two hundred-dollar bills out of his fat wallet to pay for the assorted bullshit I'd picked out. I watched to see if he would wait around for the change. He did, but he immediately dropped it into my cavernous purse. I cursed at him and tried to dig the money out, but my hands were full of stuffed jackrabbit, and Harley was already out the door with his new chair.

Drug dealer, my guilty conscience whispered.

Fuck you, Guilt. He has a job, I snapped back. *Maybe mechanics make good money.*

You just keep telling yourself that, honey, my guilt whispered in a patronizing tone.

When Harley and I got back to his car, we looked at the shit in our hands, then at the Boss, then at each other, and then burst out laughing. Harley set his new chair down in an empty parking spot, lit a cigarette, and had himself a seat. He casually draped one arm over the back of the chair and rested one ankle on the opposite knee. Something about his posture reminded me of a king on a throne—a scruffy, tattooed king in his crumbling inner-city kingdom.

Always up for a good challenge, I eyeballed the car, doing all kinds of mental calculations. "Do you have any space in your trunk?" I asked.

Harley's faced morphed from smug to severe in the blink of an eye. "Nope," he said flatly. "Trunk's full."

That was it. *"Trunk's full."*

He didn't offer any explanation. Didn't volunteer to move some things around to make space. The trunk was off-limits, and so was that conversation.

"Okaaaay…" I said, furrowing my brow at his sudden change in demeanor. "Let me try something else."

I wrestled the jackalope and T-shirts into the tiny backseat area behind the driver's seat, then slid the passenger seat as far back as it would go. I flicked my fingers at Harley, gesturing for him to bring me the chair. He carried it over to me, and I was able to flip it upside down and nestle it into the passenger seat like a puzzle piece.

"Ha!" I exclaimed, turning around and poking Harley in the chest with my finger. "I fucking did it!"

Harley looked over my shoulder, eyeing my handiwork. "Good job," he said with a smirk. "So, where are *you* gonna sit?"

"Fuck," I muttered, turning around to recalculate.

With both front seats pushed all the way back—one to accommodate the chair and one to accommodate Harley's long legs—there was no way I was going to fit back there without losing an eye to a jackalope antler.

While the wheels in my head were still spinning with alternate configurations, Harley walked around and sat in the driver's seat. Looking at me through the open passenger door with bright eyes and a dark expression, he said, "Looks like you're ridin' bitch."

I raised a confused eyebrow at him. "I thought *riding bitch* was when somebody sat in the middle seat."

"Not the way I do it," he said, patting his lap.

Unable and suddenly unwilling to figure out another way, I slammed the passenger door shut and practically pole-vaulted over to Harley's side of the car. I climbed into his lap and sat sideways, sticking my feet in an open space under the chair on the passenger seat. Afraid that I was blocking his view, I ducked my head into the crook of Harley's neck and pressed a little kiss into the scruff below his jaw.

"Fuck," Harley hissed, pulling his door shut with one hand and gripping my hip with the other. His cock swelled and hardened against my ass as he claimed my mouth with those full fucking lips. Harley's left hand gripped the back of my fuzzy shaved head while his right kneaded the flesh beneath my fuzzy tiger-striped pants.

The cold steel of Harley's lip ring warmed quickly against my mouth. I couldn't wait to hear it clink against the barbell in my clit. *Or* the ones in my nipples.

Shit.

The thought of my piercings brought me back to the present. Knight had done those piercings himself, not even a hundred feet away. And now I was making out with another guy, another *man*, in his fucking parking spot. We had to get out of there. We had to get the fuck out *now.*

"Let's go home," I whispered into Harley's parted lips.

Harley cranked the engine, turned the AC on full blast, and

pulled out of the parking lot with one eye on the road and his tongue still tangled with mine. I pulled away so that he could drive, but it wasn't easy. My mouth continued to nip and suck at his neck and stubbled jaw. Between shifts, Harley's right hand slipped between my legs, causing my breath to become ragged against his skin. He slid his fingers along my seam, over my clothes, sending a jolt of electricity through me every time his pressure passed over my piercing.

Turning his head toward mine, Harley growled, "Shift. Into fourth. Now."

I fumbled with my left hand until I found the gearshift. As soon as I felt Harley step on the clutch, I pulled it down into the fourth position.

The car accelerated as Harley's hand slid beneath the waistband of my pants and into my ruined panties. The second his finger found steel, Harley groaned, "Fuck me," and pressed his soda can of an erection into my hip even harder. He rubbed the jewelry in small circles, then said, "I want to see it," in a voice so gruff, I didn't recognize it as his.

"Watch the road," I panted back.

Harley slid his hand out and gripped the stretchy material in his fist, yanking my pants and cotton panties down in one motion so that he could see what he'd felt. "Goddamn," he muttered. "Pierced *and* fucking bald. Who *are* you?" Harley released my clothes to downshift and turn onto a side street.

"I've been wondering the same thing about you," I admitted, latching on to his neck and sucking until the capillaries burst.

I could tell we were getting close to the house because Harley was doing a lot more shifting and making a lot more turns.

"I'm the guy who's gonna lick that pussy in about thirty

seconds," he growled, just as I felt the car go over a bump and down a steep hill.

The interior went dark as Harley pulled into the garage behind his house. He popped the parking brake and threw open his door, not bothering to turn off the motor or air-conditioning, before sliding out from under me. Kneeling on the cement floor of the garage, Harley grabbed my hips and rotated me so that I was sitting sideways in the driver's seat. He tugged my tiger-striped pants and sopping-wet panties to my ankles with both hands. Then, he sat back on his heels and pushed my knees apart with the callused hands of a man who knew his way around a machine.

The air in the garage was stiflingly hot, but the way Harley wet his lips as he stared at my exposed flesh gave me chills. His hands slid further up the insides of my thighs as his head dipped forward, and suddenly, slick heat collided with slick heat. Harley dragged his tongue up the length of my pussy like an ice cream cone. Like something he'd been waiting to savor. I leaned back with my elbows on the center console and my head on the wooden chair taking up the passenger seat as Harley pushed my thighs even further apart. Spreading me open with his thumbs, he licked me again. And again.

The car growled and vibrated underneath me, only heightening the experience. When Harley slid a thick finger inside me, my body gratefully clenched around it. When he curled it forward and stroked a spot I hadn't even known existed, I arched my back and groaned without shame. And when he switched from long, torturous licks to quick flicks of his tongue over my barbell, I gripped the console with both hands, threw my head back, and screamed.

By the time I fell back to earth, Harley had shut off the engine, scooped me up in his arms, and was carrying me up the back stairs with my pants still around my ankles. He unlocked the back door and kicked it open, then set my bare ass on the kitchen counter and kissed me, hard.

"Get these off," Harley growled, tapping my ankle.

I bent forward just enough to wrestle my combat boots, pants, and panties off, but didn't relinquish Harley's mouth until he lifted my tank top over my head. As he removed his own shirt, I quickly unclasped my bra and tossed it aside, not wanting him to discover that it weighed five pounds and was full of water.

At the sight of his dick, my eyes went wide, and my mouth fell open. I wasn't built to take dicks the size of Pringles cans, yet there I was, face-to-face with another one.

My shock was quelled when Harley reached out with both hands and ran the pads of his thumbs over my nipples.

"They're wings?" he asked with awe in his voice.

For once, I forgot to be insecure about my complete and total lack of breasts. The barbells through my nipples had tiny silver wings on each side instead of beads. Knight had picked the jewelry out for me—a fact that I tried desperately to push out of my mind the second Harley's hand palmed my tiny breast and his mouth closed around my own. Taking a step forward, Harley pressed his thick erection against my trembling core. He slid it up and down as we kissed, bathing himself in my cum, which I could taste all over his lips.

"What do you want to do?" he rasped into my mouth.

"I want to fuck you," I said.

It was the truth. Good, bad, or ugly, I wanted to fuck Harley

James, and I had since the moment I laid eyes on him. I didn't care if it was right or wrong. It was my choice, and I was choosing to feel good again. I was choosing happiness over despair. I was choosing Harley over a ghost.

Harley groaned and gripped my ass harder. "Fuck," he hissed, grinding against me. "Say that again."

"I want to fuck you," I said, pulling his bottom lip into my mouth.

Harley pressed his forehead to mine and poised his manhood against my entrance.

Just before he surged forward, a bitchy, monotone voice inside my head whispered, *Whore.*

It was Juliet's warning, echoing in my ears like a broken record.

"Girl, you'd better use protection. That guy is a whore."

A whore…whore…whore…

As ready as I was for the sweet oblivion Harley was offering, I knew there was only one way to get Juliet to shut the fuck up.

Placing my hands on Harley's taut stomach to stop his advance, I swallowed hard and whispered, "Condom?" I had some in my purse, but it was all the way out in the car.

Harley bent over and dug around in his pants pockets until he found a little foil packet tucked away in his wallet. Flashing me a wicked smirk, he ripped the square wrapper off and flicked it across the room without looking. Watching him slide his fist down the length of his shaft as he sheathed himself had me spreading my legs wider and gripping the edges of the kitchen counter with both hands.

When Harley stepped between my legs again, instead of claiming me right there on the kitchen counter, he grabbed my ass with both hands and picked me up. I squealed and wrapped my arms around his neck as he turned and laid me on my back on the kitchen table.

Smiling down at me, Harley pulled my knees up so that they were bracketing his rib cage and propped himself up on his forearms. I squeezed my eyes shut, bracing myself for the pain, but Harley entered gently. He swept his tongue into my open mouth as he pressed forward, inch by inch, allowing me time to adjust. He waited until I lifted my hips to urge him in deeper and didn't fill me completely until I was digging my heels into his lower back, begging for more.

It didn't hurt, and that was when I realized, for the first time in my life, that it didn't have to. With Knight, it had always hurt. If not from his size, then from his teeth or his blade or his piercing needle. I'd learned that pleasure and pain just went hand in hand, but with Harley, there was only pleasure. He made sure of it.

"You okay?" Harley whispered once he was fully seated inside me. "You're so fucking tight."

I nodded, pressing my pelvis into his for encouragement.

Harley slid his forearms under my upper back and gripped my shoulders with his hands. Withdrawing slowly, he filled me again—that time, not quite as deep. I could tell he was being careful with me, and while I appreciated his thoughtfulness, it wasn't what I was used to.

I was used to bloodshed.

"Harley," I whispered, digging my heels into his back and lifting my hips to meet him.

"Fuck," he growled. "You keep that up, I'm not gonna be able to hold out."

"Don't hold out," I pleaded.

Eat me alive.

Harley's grip on my back and shoulders tightened as he picked up the pace. The push and pull was delicious. The creaking of the table with every thrust was music to my ears. The taste of myself on Harley's tongue was intoxicating. But when I captured his bottom lip with my teeth and sucked on his lip ring, Harley's reserve finally crumbled. He used his upper body strength to pull my entire body down onto his thrusts, filling me to the hilt with every needy advance. I wrapped my forearms around his neck and held on for dear life, which was good because the table's creaks suddenly turned into snaps and cracks.

Just before the entire thing collapsed beneath us.

With my limbs already wrapped around him and his arms cradling my back, Harley was able to stand up just before the bottom fell out, keeping us from ending up impaled on a pile of twisted aluminum. I screamed and squeezed him tighter as we both looked down at the wreckage.

With him still deep inside me, Harley's gaze met mine.

"You just saved my life," I said, kissing his sex-swollen lips.

"How will you ever repay me?" Harley gave me a sideways grin as he pressed my back against the kitchen wall.

"Oh, I can think of a few ways," I said, my eyes rolling up into my head as he filled me again.

"Mmhmm...me, too," Harley murmured into the crook of my neck.

Keeping me pinned to the wall with his hips, Harley suddenly let go of my back and grabbed my inner thighs with both hands. "I got you," he reassured me when I clutched his neck and shoulders tighter.

He spread my legs as far apart as they would go with his hands. My thighs, which had been clamped around his waist, were now pressed against either side of my body by Harley's strong palms. He cursed through his teeth as he watched himself enter me, quickly resuming the frantic pace he'd established on the kitchen table.

"Fuck, you're tight," he hissed into my ear, filling me until his balls slapped my ass with each thrust. "Fuck." Harley squeezed my thighs harder, pumped faster, and kissed the shit out of me until his cock stiffened and a moan ripped from his chest.

It was the sexiest sound I'd ever heard.

Breathing heavily, Harley slowly lowered my legs to the floor. He didn't pull out of me though. Instead, he dropped his forehead to mine and asked, "What do you want to do?"

There was that question again. *What do you want to do?* I liked it.

"What do you mean?" I panted, squeezing my thighs around his already-recovering cock.

"I mean," he breathed, "how do you like to get off?"

My cheeks heated. After what we'd just done, I shouldn't have been embarrassed, but for some reason, saying what I liked *sexually* out loud made me feel shy. Nobody'd ever asked me before.

Swallowing hard, I looked up at him and admitted, "I like to be on top."

Harley furrowed his brow as he met my demure gaze. Still catching his breath, he repeated my words indignantly, "You like to be on top?" He gestured behind himself at the pile of rubble in the middle of the floor. "You mean, I did all that work for nothin'?"

I burst into nervous laughter, and Harley watched my giggle fit with a self-satisfied grin on his face.

"Woman," he said, wrapping my legs around his waist again, "you can ride my cock anytime, anyplace, anywhere."

Reason number nine million forty bajillion why I was totally, irreparably, and hopelessly falling for Harley James.

Harley carried me into his bedroom and managed to sit in the middle of his mattress—I couldn't even call that thing a bed—without ever pulling out of me. I clung to him with my arms and legs as he flopped onto his back, his head landing on the pillow. His sheets were navy blue and surprisingly soft. With the sunlight coming in from the blinds I'd opened earlier, it didn't feel like an opium den at all anymore. It felt like the only place I wanted to be.

The jolt of our landing caused Harley's dick to surge inside me. Our eyes locked, and suddenly, we were back. Starving for each other, as if the car and the kitchen had never happened.

I propped myself up with my hands on his chest and ground into him, taking the opportunity to look down and admire his body. Harley was beautiful. Filled out and muscular but in a natural way—like a man who worked for a living, not like the 'roided-out weight lifter I was used to. His defined arms were decorated with hot rods and flames from shoulder to wrist, and his strong hands—stained black in the creases from working on cars—touched me with appreciation and reverence. Not with anger. Not with the intention of making me bleed.

As I hovered over him, Harley slid his rough hands up my bony ribs, palmed my petite breasts, and stroked my pierced nipples with both thumbs. The sensation sent a tingly bolt of electricity directly to my clit. I moaned and ground the bundle of nerves into him harder. God, I was so close.

Harley cursed as I rolled my hips. Then he sat up, taking me by surprise. Wrapping his meaty hands around my waist, Harley drove my body up and down along his shaft as he pulled one straining pink nipple into his mouth. When he grazed it with his teeth, the electric current I'd felt moments before exploded into a lightning storm. I grabbed his face and whimpered into his mouth as my pussy contracted violently around him.

"Fuck, woman," Harley groaned, digging his thick fingers into my hips.

He lifted my body up at least half a foot and held me there, thrusting into me hard and fast from underneath. His increased tempo and desperation only heightened my orgasm. I clung to him with all my strength as my inner walls gripped him like a vise, wave after wave of pleasure racking my body.

Harley came with a guttural, primal grunt as he pulled me down onto his straining cock one last time. We tumbled backward onto the mattress—spent and, for the time being, sated. With my restless mind silenced, I snuggled into Harley's warm chest, lulled to sleep by the drifting of his fingertips along my spine and the throbbing of his pulse where we were still joined.

I woke to the sound of Dave banging around in the kitchen and yelling about a table. It must have woken Harley up too, because he snorted and pulled me closer, completely unconcerned. The movement reminded me that he was still inside me, and evidently, his little nap had given him a brand-new boner.

"What the fuck, man?" Dave's voice was much closer now. Like in-the-room close.

I scrambled to grab the sheet and pull it over us, but it was too late. He'd seen everything. Not that he or Harley seemed to mind.

"Y'all fucked in the kitchen, didn't you?"

My cheeks heated, and I pulled the sweat-soaked sheet over my mortified face.

"Right there on the kitchen table, and y'all didn't even have the decency to wait for me to get home from work first."

I giggled under the sheet.

Jesus, Dave.

"Sorry, bro." Harley chuckled, trying to sound remorseful. "I tried to wait, but BB jumped me. She couldn't keep her hands off me, man. What was I supposed to do?"

I tickled him, then stifled a moan as his laughter caused his dick to throb inside me.

I heard Dave mutter something about us being assholes and peeked my head out from under the sheet just in time to see him walking out the door with his middle finger in the air. As soon as he was gone, Harley threw the sheet completely off the bed and thrust into me with his fully awakened cock. I should have been worried about the fact that we were going on round three with the same condom, but I was too fuck-drunk to care.

My brain had been sitting on a month's worth of unused endorphins, and in one afternoon with Harley, I think I'd blown through all of them. I was high on stockpiled serotonin, high from the smell of pot wafting in from the living room, and high on Harley as he fucked me slowly and sweetly in the late-afternoon sun. Nothing could possibly bring me down.

Not even Dave when he appeared in the doorway again, wearing a headlamp and offering to "shine some light on the subject."

After the cumtrillionth orgasm of the afternoon, I dragged Harley by the hand into the house's only bathroom so that we could shower off. We were sweaty and sticky and disgusting. The bathroom was at the entrance of the hallway, which was in full view of the couch, so I sprinted in the hopes that Dave wouldn't see us.

Just as I scurried through the door, yanking a very naked man in behind me, I heard Dave yell, "Wait, are those titty rings? Goddamn it, Harley!"

I slammed *and* locked the door.

"You guys have a fucked-up relationship." I laughed, turning to face Harley.

He leaned against the vanity in all his long, lean, tattooed glory and smiled. That hard body combined with that baby face had me squeezing my cum-covered thighs together.

"He's just mad I'm not sharing."

My jaw fell open. "You guys *share*? Like, *girls*?"

Harley's mouth pulled up on one side. "If they're into it."

My eyes went wide. *Holy shit.*

Harley shrugged. "When you're only ten months apart, you get used to sharing."

"Well, I'm an only child," I said with a haughty huff. "I don't *do* sharing."

"That's good," Harley said as he laced his fingers through mine and pulled me toward him, "because I'm keeping you all to myself." He leaned down and kissed me. Then, he gave my ass a little smack as he pushed off the vanity to start the shower.

I wanted to ask him what that meant. I wanted to over-analyze every word of that sentence for proof that Harley and I were boyfriend and girlfriend—that he loved me and we were getting married—but the possibility that I might be wrong was just too real. I needed the fantasy. Holding on to the idea that a virile sex god like *that* might actually be satisfied with a boyish, flat-chested *child* like me was the only thing keeping me going.

I wasn't about to throw away my newfound will to live by doing something stupid, like asking questions.

Harley and I ended up spending, like, forty-five minutes in the shower... talking. He asked me if I still wanted that golden shower. I asked him about his tattoos. In addition to his sleeves, he had a few random ones that piqued my interest. Like the one that just said *ARM*... on his chest. And the one that just looked like a pointy letter *Y* on his shoulder. He also told me that he had one on his head, but I couldn't see it through his adorable mop of blond hair.

Every badly drawn, unfinished, jailhouse-looking tattoo I could find had a story behind it. Through them, I got a glimpse into Harley's past as an impulsive, reckless teenage gutter punk, squatting with a band of misfits and runaways in Little Five Points. Even though his stories were hilarious, they also made my heart ache. After his mom had kicked him out, Harley had basically been homeless—a street kid doing whatever the fuck he wanted and whatever it took to survive. No wonder he'd looked so at home while sitting in that chair in the Terminus City parking lot earlier. He *was* home.

Just as the hot water ran out, Dave banged on the door like the fucking FBI, yelling, "Dinner, bitches!"

Evidently, he'd gotten so stoned that, when the munchies struck, he just ordered one of everything on the menu from the local Chinese takeout place. For the second time that week, Harley, Dave, and I ate, drank, smoked, and laughed as the earth slowly rotated away from the sun.

Of course, we had to eat while leaning over the coffee table because Harley and I had reduced the kitchen table to scrap metal that afternoon, but it was pretty obvious that furniture wasn't exactly a priority for the James brothers.

I made sure to start the good-bye process at least twenty minutes before I actually needed to leave, knowing that Harley would probably try to thwart my efforts to escape again. And he did. He gave me the puppy-dog eyes. He begged me to spend the night. He offered me another beer. He told Dave to hide my purse. And, eventually, shoulders slumped in defeat, he walked me out to my car.

But he did talk me into smoking one last cigarette.

I hopped up onto the lid of my trunk, and Harley stood between my dangling legs, idly rubbing the fuzzy material covering my thighs with his free hand. I was physically uncomfortable being that close to him with all of our clothes on. It felt wrong. Unnatural. I was full of holes, literally and figuratively, and Harley was the one holding all the pegs.

"God, I wish you could stay," he said, sincerity shining out of his heavy-lidded eyes in the moonlight.

"Me too," I admitted.

"You should probably just move in." The corner of his mouth pulled up just a hint as he took a drag from his cigarette.

I laughed. "We'd never get anything done."

"Oh, we'd get plenty done." Harley slid his hand up to my hip as he exhaled a stream of smoke away from my face.

I blushed, thinking back over the afternoon. "Dude. We broke a table."

Harley gave me a sideways glance. "Good thing I don't have a bed, or you probably woulda broken that too, you savage."

I thought back to sleeping with him inside me. Tickling

him. Cuddling with him. The desperate, needy sex. The sweet, slow sex. Nothing and no one had ever made me feel that good before. Since meeting Harley, I'd gone from wanting to die to feeling as though I could fly. He'd done what my psychologist couldn't do. What my antidepressants couldn't do. What my best friend, mom, and one angry letter to Knight hadn't been able to do. He gave me back my happy. With zero adverse side effects.

"Are you working tomorrow night?" Harley's voice snapped me out of my reverie.

"I get off at six," I said, excitement blooming in my tiny bosom.

Harley beamed. "Good. There's gonna be a race tomorrow night, at the track. I want you to come with me."

My excitement deflated like a balloon. "Harley, I told you. I don't wanna—"

"Not to race. Just to hang out. I…" Harley paused. His Adam's apple bobbed in his throat. "I want you to meet everybody."

It didn't seem like a big deal to me—meeting a bunch of rednecks and motorheads—but the way Harley hesitated made me realize that it *was* a big deal to him.

My face erupted into a huge grin.

"What?" he asked.

"Nothing." I beamed.

"What?" Harley growled.

I shook my head and pressed my lips together with my teeth, trying to squelch my smile. It didn't work.

"Fuck this." Harley flicked his cigarette butt into the street, turned around, and tickled the shit out of me with both hands.

I shrieked and squealed and tried to push him away until I finally blurted out, "You like me! Okay? You fuckin' like me! Now stop it!"

Harley stopped tickling me. He practically stopped breathing. His eyes locked on to mine, shiny in the dark, his playful expression suddenly unreadable.

Fuck. Why did I have to say that? We had the perfect day, and I fucking ruined it.

Regret washed over me as I waited for him to deliver the blow. To shatter my fantasy and send me home just as damaged as he'd found me. Harley was a whore. He didn't do relationships. He didn't do serious.

But his face suggested otherwise. I held on to my hope as Harley gripped the edge of my spoiler and bent forward until our faces were completely aligned.

"Lady," he said in a voice thick with sincerity, "you have no fucking idea."

Then, he kissed me.

And then I died.

When I pulled onto the unmarked road that led to the track, my headlights cutting through the low-hanging tree branches and illuminating the pine-needle-covered pavement, I could feel a kind of kinetic energy in the air. I could hear the rumble of engines, even over the sound of my cassette player and blasting AC, and I could see the gauzy glow of artificial light up ahead, emanating from the crater just beyond the tree line.

When the woods parted and the road plunged down into the makeshift stadium, I couldn't believe my eyes. The place was overflowing with people and cars and trucks and ATVs and motorcycles, and, I swear to God, I think I even saw a couple of riding lawnmowers. They were all parked in the center of the oval-shaped track, all surrounded by girls with their tits hanging out and guys with their chests puffed up, and they were each playing a completely different type of music at full volume.

As I circled the oval, searching with giddy anticipation for a certain matte black fastback, I noticed that the cars seemed to be grouped by type. There was the Japanese import crew with their colorful paint jobs and neon ground effects. There was the redneck crew, huddled around a bunch of racing trucks with nets for tailgates. There was the ride-or-die crew, hanging out by a collection of crotch rockets blasting DMX. And there was a crew of retro-looking rockabillies clustered around an impressive collection of vintage American muscle. I assumed Harley belonged to the muscle car crew, but really, he would fit in with any of them. He had the style of a rockabilly, the subtle twang of a good ole boy, and the swagger of a gangster.

I began to wonder if I would ever find him out there. His car would be impossible to spot in the dark—that thing was basically a shadow on wheels—but thankfully, its owner shone so bright I spotted him the moment I rounded the first turn.

Harley had parked outside the oval track instead of inside where everyone else was partying. He stood next to the Boss with his arms folded across his chest, talking to a semicircle of people gathered in front of him. It reminded me of a NASCAR driver taking questions from the media after winning a big race. I remembered Harley saying something about people not wanting to race him anymore, but seeing him in that environment really drove it home. Harley was fucking famous.

I parked about fifteen feet away from the Boss, which was as close as I could get without hitting a member of his entourage. After work, I'd changed into fishnets, cutoff jean shorts, and a white wifebeater with a black bra underneath. It was skimpy, but looking around, I still felt a little overdressed. I fluffed my bleached bangs in the rearview mirror, wiped the smudged mascara from under my eyes, and took a deep breath.

Harley had left his spot by the Boss and was waiting at my door when I opened it. I don't know what happened. One second, I'd been anxiously primping in my car, and the next, I was wrapped around Harley's torso with my fingers in his hair and his tongue in my mouth. It was as if our bodies had become magnetically charged during the hours we spent pressed against each other the day before. The moment the obstacle between us was removed, we collided.

Finally finding my wits, I pulled away enough to make eye contact. "Hi," I said breathlessly.

Harley smiled at me with swollen lips. "Hey, lady."

"I missed you." The words tumbled off my tongue so easily, I almost forgot to cringe.

"I missed you, too."

I closed my eyes and let my head fall to the right, my tongue sticking out to the left.

Harley chuckled. "Did I kill you *again*?"

I nodded, my tongue still hanging out of my mouth.

"Good thing I know CPR," Harley said just before sliding a hand up my bony side and wiggling his fingertips between my ribs.

As I screamed and swatted his hand away, a thick Southern accent interrupted our little reunion.

"Uh, Harley, looks like we got comp'ny."

I looked over Harley's shoulder to see his coworker, Bubba—the guy who'd delivered my drive belt—standing behind him, gesturing toward the track with his chin. I turned my head in the opposite direction and saw a half-dozen German sports cars coming down the hill. BMWs, Mercedes, a Porsche, maybe an Audi. Luxury cars.

"Who are they?" I asked, guessing from everyone's reaction that they weren't welcome.

"Just some Buckhead prep-school douche bags," Harley

readjusted my tank top which had bunched up during his tickle assault. "We call 'em *tourists*. They only come down here during summer break. Everybody fuckin' hates 'em 'cause they roll up in cars their rich daddies paid for, actin' like their shit don't stink, but I love 'em."

"Why?" I asked, kind of hating them already.

"'Cause they practically beg me to take their money. Just watch."

The imports parked on the other side of Harley's car in a cute little row, each one at a perfect forty-five-degree angle. Six doors opened and shut, almost in unison, and six frat-boy D-bags walked up like they thought they fucking owned the place. Considering the wide berth everybody else gave Harley, they obviously weren't showing him the same level of respect as the rest of the community.

Harley didn't seem to care though. He kept one arm loosely draped around my shoulders and didn't even puff up his chest when they approached.

"Oh, shit. Y'all musta got your allowance today, huh?" he asked with a lopsided grin.

The pink-Polo–wearing asshole in front sneered, his reply dripping with classic Ivy League condescension, "Real cute, Harley. My boy Preston here just got a new Porsche, so *your crew* is going to be paying our allowance today. That thing can beat any P.O.S. on this field."

"Why doesn't your boy *Preston* step up then?" Harley asked.

Polo shirt number two stepped forward and said, "'Sup?" with a flick of his chin.

I rolled my eyes. I couldn't help it.

"So, you think you can smoke anybody here?" Harley asked,

stroking my shoulder with his fingertips, bored indifference in his voice.

"Fuck yeah," Tweedledum answered. "Got the nine-eleven Turbo model."

The way Harley's back muscles contracted under my hand told me he was trying not to laugh. "How about me?" he asked, tilting his head toward the Boss. "Think you can handle a four twenty-nine?"

"Dude. C'mon. That's a ten-second car," Fratty McDoucherton replied, eating his words.

"You said you could beat anybody. I'm anybody."

Then Harley gave my shoulder a little squeeze—so tiny, I almost missed it—and added, "How 'bout this? I'll race your nine-eleven . . . in any car you want."

Preston's mouth fell open.

Pink Polo's mouth fell open.

My mouth fell open.

"What?" Preston asked.

"Any car?" Pink Polo asked.

"Any car on the field," Harley replied. "That's what you said, right? You can smoke any piece of shit here? Well, prove it. Pick one."

I watched in horror as all twelve douche-bag eyeballs scanned the sea of race cars and then all came to rest on something behind me.

No.

No, no, no, no.

Preston's lip curled into a sneer as he pointed over my shoulder. "That one. The five-oh."

Fuck.

I stared at the side of Harley's face, trying to telepathically tell him that he was a fucking idiot.

He shrugged, ignoring the invisible daggers shooting out of my eyes, and said, "You sure? I know my way around a Mustang, man. This might not be pretty."

The wannabe Abercrombie models all burst into laughter, making my cheeks flush with shame.

"Dude, I hate to break it to you, but there is no way you're going to beat a nine-eleven Turbo with a *base model* Mustang." Pink Polo's tone was so fucking haughty, I prayed to every god ever invented to help Harley win.

I prayed even harder when I heard Harley say, "Two *G*s says I can."

Shit! Two grand? Is he out of his fucking mind?

As all six trust-fund babies laughed in unison, Harley dropped his arm from around my shoulders, reached into my front pocket, and stole my goddamn keys.

"Harley, what the fuck are you doing?" I whispered. "My car can't beat a Turbo."

Glancing behind me at the hatchback that was about to lose him two thousand dollars, Harley put his finger to his lips and said, "Shh…she's gonna hear you. You don't want to hurt her feelings."

Crazy bastard.

Turning back toward the crowd of Ken dolls, Harley said, "Do I need to make it two *hundred*? I forgot y'all didn't get your allowance today."

Preston shook his head, still snickering. "It's your future bail money, bro. You can give me as much of it as you want."

Harley pointed two fingers at Preston and shot back, "I'm

gonna need bail money if you keep runnin' your fuckin' mouth." His tone was surprisingly threatening, but in the blink of an eye, he dropped his finger gun and resumed his cool composure. Jingling my keys, Harley said, "Let's do this. The lady's gonna call it." Harley didn't wait for confirmation. He simply turned and walked toward my car with long, determined strides.

Hustling to catch up to him, I huffed, "What do you mean, *the lady's gonna call it*? Call what? What do I do?"

Harley opened my door and turned to me with a smile. "You just stand on the *X* and put your hands in the air and when we signal that we're ready...you drop 'em." Giving me a quick kiss, he added, "Then, get the fuck outta there 'cause I'm gonna be back around before you even know I'm gone."

Before I could protest, Harley slid my seat all the way back and climbed into my car. When he cranked the engine, Björk's "Army of Me" came blaring out of my speakers. He didn't even change it. Just gave me a wink and slammed the door.

As Harley pulled onto the track, the crowd of motorheads, rednecks, rockabillies, and thugs went wild. They screamed, clapped, hollered, and honked as he took what felt like a victory lap before the race even began. Meanwhile, I was having a minor panic attack trying to figure out where this mythical *X* was that I was supposed to be standing upon. I scanned the poorly lit pavement on my side of the track but couldn't see shit.

Fuck, fuck, fuck.

"Hey, Punk," a twangy voice said from behind me. "I'll take you to the starting line."

I turned to find JR standing a few feet away, fiddling with his dip can, an apologetic look on his face.

"Sorry. I meant BB. Please don't tell Harley I said that."

I laughed and gratefully gripped his skinny bicep as he led me right through the center of the field. The crowd parted for us, but the attention didn't feel good. It felt appraising. Judging. Questioning. The guys stared and elbowed each other. Their girlfriends glared and covered their mouths as they whispered. It was as if the entire crowd wanted to know who the little boy/girl with the shaved head was and what the hell their king had been doing with his tongue in her mouth.

When JR and I got to the other side of the track, both cars were idling at the starting line, which I could now see was just a white stripe spray-painted across the pavement. JR walked me a few paces in front of them and pointed to a tiny white *X* on the ground.

I squeezed his arm and mouthed, *Thank you*, as I stepped with knocking knees onto the mark...and into the blinding rays of four headlights.

I raised one hand to shield my eyes, thankful that the light had rendered me temporarily unable to see the hundreds of judgmental faces watching me. I knew they were there though, waiting for me to fuck up. They were about to get their wish, too, because the anxiety of literally being put on the spot had me dangerously close to barfing all over my combat boots.

What did Harley say? Raise my hands?

I swallowed hard and lifted my hands into the air. The action elicited an overwhelming cheer from the crowd. I turned and squinted out into the sea of people, my eyes adjusting to the glare, and saw...smiles. Fist-pumping. Beer cans and red plastic cups sloshing in the air. These were the people Harley had brought me here to meet. *His* people. They weren't against me; they were with me. But more importantly, they were against the douche bag in the Porsche.

The douche bag who needed to go down.

Cupping my hands around my mouth, I yelled into the deafening crowd, "Har-ley!"

I wasn't sure if they'd even be able to hear me until the entire crowd answered back in unison, "HAR-LEY!"

My mouth spread into a face-splitting grin in response.

"Har-ley!" I yelled again.

"HAR-LEY! HAR-LEY! HAR-LEY!" the crowd began to chant.

I beamed as the chorus of support for my man bounced off the surrounding trees and drowned out the sound of the racers' engines. It was so loud, I knew Preston had to be able to hear it.

Fuck you, frat boy, I thought as I turned to face the racers again.

Harley flashed my headlights, the Porsche followed suit, and everything that happened next occurred in the span of one breath.

I squeezed my eyes shut.

I dropped my hands.

A wind tunnel's worth of air pressure, heat, and noise blasted me from all sides.

Two hands clamped down on my biceps and pulled me out of the street.

Another blast of hot air and screaming engine noise blew past me.

A symphony of "Woohoo" and "Fuck yeah" erupted behind me.

I opened my eyes and looked around. JR and Bubba were literally jumping up and down behind me, as was basically the entire crowd on the field.

No fucking way.

I scanned the track for The Little Mustang That Could and spotted it rounding the nearest curve, going significantly slower than before. Harley pulled to a stop on the pavement right next to me with Preston following close behind.

As soon as his door was open, we were colliding magnets again.

"How the fuck did you do that?" I whisper-yelled into Harley's ear, my fingers diving into his wild blond hair and my thighs reclaiming their rightful place around his waist.

Harley's smug voice against my neck rumbled through me. "Turbos don't kick in until you hit higher RPMs. They're worthless on a short, round track. Fucking dumbass." He chuckled, and the vibration sent a current of need straight to the place where I was split open and pressed against his taut abs. "To win here, you just need shit-tons of torque and grippy tires."

The layers of clothing between us scorched my skin. I thought I was in awe of him before—his sense of humor, his attitude, that deadly baby-face-and-hard-body combo, the way he handled a car, the way he handled me—but I had no idea who the fuck I was dealing with. Harley James was a living legend, a working-class hero, and looking over my shoulder at the sea of adoring rebels cheering for him, I realized that I was the last one to know. As usual.

Preston approached us with a pouty fucking scowl on his pretty-boy face as the rest of the German import crew pulled up, single file, behind his precious nine-eleven Turbo. Harley gave me a quick kiss and set me down, flicking his chin toward JR and Bubba. I took that as my cue to let him handle his business, but it made me nervous. I gnawed on my fingernails as I stood by his friends and watched the pissing contest unfold. I couldn't hear what they said to each other over the deafening heckles coming from the crowd, but Preston eventually shoved a wad of cash into Harley's hand and stormed off, squealing his tires on the way out.

I swear, I could almost hear the sound of Nickelback floating on the breeze as those douche bags disappeared into the night. As soon as they were gone, the crowd swelled, swallowing Harley completely. I wanted him all to myself, but it looked like I was going to have to get in line. Literally. I stood on my tiptoes and craned my neck, trying to catch a glimpse of him over the shoulders of full-grown fanboys and girls in high heels.

Engines rumbled as two lightweight trucks pulled up to the line, ready to race.

Shit! My car's in the way!

I stayed low and pushed through the crowd, weaseling my way back over to Harley. I wasn't going to interrupt him—just pat him down for my keys so that I could move my car—but as soon as my fingertips slipped into his pocket, Harley grabbed my wrist and pressed my palm against his package instead.

I squealed and yanked my hand away in shock, using it to punch Harley in the thigh. But as soon as my brain registered the heat and thickness of what I'd been palming, I immediately regretted my reaction. I'd been dying to touch him all day. I could still feel his phantom member in my palm as I stood up and gave Harley a playfully angry glare. I could still feel it when he wrapped his arm around my waist and pulled me into his side. And I was seriously considering reaching down and feeling it again when the sound of my name filtered through the excited blood pumping in my ears. I looked up at Harley, who smirked down at me as if he could read my mind.

"BB...this is everybody."

Oh shit.

He'd introduced me, and I'd been too busy salivating over his dick to notice. A painful tingle flooded my neck and cheeks as I turned and gave about a dozen greasers a mortified smile.

"Hey," I said, my voice rising an octave, as if I'd been caught with my hand in the cookie jar.

Harley's fan club mumbled their greetings, gawking at me, as if I were a freak-show exhibit that they'd just paid five dollars to see. I was used to being stared at by strangers. I had a shaved head. I wore too much eye makeup. I was shockingly under-weight, and I dressed like a wannabe rock star trying to sleep her way to the top. I gave people plenty of reasons to stare. Usually, I ignored the unwanted attention, chalked it up to natural human curiosity, but these stares felt different. The rockabillies weren't interested in my look. They were interested in figuring out what the fuck made me worthy of their king. Their scrutiny made me want to bury my face in Harley's T-shirt, but I squared my shoulders and smiled extra big instead.

Crack a joke, BB. For the love of God, this is awkward.

"So"—I rolled my eyes up toward Harley, feigning annoyance—"will one of you please tell this asshole that he owes me half of that money?"

I was rewarded with a collective symphony of deep, manly laughter.

Thank God, I thought as I sighed and relaxed into Harley's side.

"She has a point, man." A dark-haired *Jailhouse Rock*–era Elvis lookalike chuckled. "I mean, it *was* her car."

"Your little five-oh smoked that motherfucker," an extra from the movie *Grease* added, his eyebrows raised almost to his hairline in surprise.

"Pssh, that was all Harley," I said, glancing up at him with a dreamy grin on my face.

"Don't listen to her," Harley said, clamping his free hand down over my mouth. "This little girl knows fucking everything about muscle cars. She's gonna beat all your asses one day."

I swatted Harley's hand away as the guys all laughed and elbowed each other over his joke. But I knew he wasn't joking. Harley really thought I could do this—race grown men in my little Mustang hatchback. The idea was both incredibly flattering and incredibly frightening. And altogether insane.

A horn blared from the starting line, causing me to jump and cling to Harley even tighter.

Goddamn catlike reflexes.

Harley rubbed my bare arm and said, "We better move the 'Stang before Jimbo and Cal Junior start their bitchin'."

Before we could get away, the guys all had to take turns slapping Harley on the shoulder and clapping him on the back in a masculine show of congratulations.

"Hang on to this one," they said.

"Keep an eye on her."

"You better watch out, man. This one's trouble."

I took their sarcastic sentiments as a show of acceptance, and beamed as Harley steered me toward the little black hatchback's passenger door and opened it for me. Sliding into the driver's seat, Harley cranked the engine and was met with a fresh blast of AC and a fresh round of cheers from the crowd as he pulled away.

"Jesus," I said, sitting sideways so that I could admire him. "They fucking love you, man."

Harley smiled. "They only love me 'cause I'm not takin' their money every weekend anymore."

He steered my car into the grass next to his and killed the engine. That corner of the track was empty now that everyone had gathered around the starting line, and once my headlights were off it was dark too.

"Speakin' of money," Harley said, reaching into his front pocket, "I do believe I owe you half of Preston's college fund."

"What? No!" I yelled, grabbing Harley's forearm to keep his hand buried in his pocket. "I was totally kidding! I can't take your money!"

Harley smiled, his lip ring glinting in the dark. "I love how you think you have a say in this."

I couldn't respond. The words *I love* coming out of *that* mouth rendered me temporarily paralyzed. Had I really thought he was going to say *I love you*? That was ridiculous. We'd only known each other for four days.

Get a grip, BB. Christ.

Ignoring my slack-jawed stupor, Harley graciously changed the subject. "Hey, I put your chair and that antler bunny in my room. Wanna come see?"

The wicked gleam in his eye and the quirk in his eyebrow made it apparent that Harley was as eager as I was to resume our activities from the day before.

My body screamed yes, but based on how long it had been dark outside, I knew my curfew was rapidly approaching.

"I wish I could, but I have to get home," I pouted. "And, for your information, that *antler bunny* is called a *jackalope*."

Harley smiled. "Well, I'm gonna start calling him Dave because that motherfucker totally watched me jerk off this morning."

Swallow.

Blink.

Breathe.

I had guy friends. I knew how they talked. But hearing *this guy* talk like that, after the hours I'd spent wrapped around his talented dick the day before, opened a chasm of lust and longing inside my chest. *Among other places.*

"Oh, really?" I asked, my voice husky and my pulse racing as I tucked one of my longer side pieces of hair behind my ear.

"Mmhmm," Harley said, reaching over and tucking the matching chin-length lock of hair behind my other ear. "I was thinking about you."

I held my breath, confident that my heart was beating fast enough to keep me alive without air.

"Were you thinking about me too?" Harley asked, sliding his index finger down the side of my neck and under my jaw.

"Mmhmm." I nodded slightly, caught in his stare.

"Did you touch yourself while you thought about me?" Harley asked, his finger poised under my chin.

I swallowed hard, then nodded again.

Harley closed his eyes and cursed under his breath. When he opened them again, they were puppy-dogified. Brows pulled together in the middle, eyes wide, bottom lip full and pouty. Harley didn't just take whatever he wanted from me, like Knight had. He used his pretty face and begged for it.

"Will you *show me?*" he asked, knowing good and goddamn well that I was going to fulfill any request that came out of that pretty, pierced mouth.

Emboldened by my raging hormones and the cover of darkness, I obediently unbuttoned my ratty jean shorts and slid them down my legs and over my combat boots. Knowing there was no way I could gracefully take off a pair of pantyhose in a car while wearing boots, I simply propped my left foot up on the center console, hooked a finger into one of the holes of my fishnets, and used it to pull my black cotton thong over to one side, exposing myself to him through the mesh. There wasn't much light in the car, but the way Harley stared and tongued his lip ring told me that he could see plenty.

He groaned as I massaged my clit in slow circles, sucking his lip and sliding his right hand up my left leg. When he reached the apex of my thighs, Harley stuck his middle finger through the fishnet material and used it to circle the perimeter of my entrance. "Fuck, you're wet," he whispered just before sliding that finger all the way inside me, all the way to the last knuckle.

When his fist met my sex, I whimpered.

Harley withdrew, leaving me achingly empty. Then he wrapped both hands around my waist and pulled me onto his lap. My surprised squeal turned into a shameless moan as soon as my ass pressed against the rock-hard bulge in Harley's pants. He wrapped his hands around my thighs and shifted my body so that my back was against his front, my legs were spread open, and my knees were being held apart by his.

Then Harley laced his fingertips into the stretchy mesh covering my bald, pierced pussy and ripped that shit wide open.

Harley looked down over my shoulder as he plunged his

finger into me again. I rolled my hips and ground my ass into his straining cock, praying that he would read my mind and fill me with it like he had the day before. Like I needed him to.

"What do you want?" Harley rasped into my ear before trailing kisses down the side of my neck.

"You," I whispered into the thick, humid air.

"You have me, lady," Harley growled into my shoulder. "Now tell me what you wanna do with me."

"I want to fuck you." My words from the day before. I hadn't meant to sound so needy, but that was exactly what I was. I needed Harley to fill the void more than I needed air in my lungs or blood in my veins. I needed him to patch my holes. I needed him to make my brain make the chemicals that would keep me afloat.

"Goddamn, I love it when you say that."

I was glad it was dark outside so that Harley couldn't see me blush. I rolled off his lap and dug through my purse on the floorboard until I found a condom, which gave Harley just enough room to shimmy his pants and boxers down below his ass. After sheathing himself, Harley pulled me back onto his lap, lined himself up with my emptiness, and then, I sank.

"Fuck," Harley groaned as we reconnected, wrapping his hard arms around my torso and dropping his chin to my shoulder.

The way he held me felt intimate. Loving. He felt the magic, too. There was just something so *right* about us like that.

Harley held me tight and kissed whatever exposed flesh his mouth had access to as he slowly thrust into me from underneath. The pleasure was perfect. *We* were perfect. I threw my head back onto his shoulder and gripped his thighs with both hands, content to live in that moment forever.

As Harley's pace quickened, I turned my face toward his and captured his mouth with my own. The combination of his pillow-soft lips, unyielding steel jewelry, and warm, determined tongue made me even more desperate than before. I didn't want to come. I didn't want that perfection to end. But when Harley's fingers found the place where *I* was soft and wet and pierced with steel, my need took over completely.

The fingertips digging into Harley's thighs were replaced with fingernails. The lip I was sucking was met with teeth. My mews and purrs were replaced by growls. And Harley only stoked the fire. He drove harder, rubbed faster, and kissed deeper until I was afraid to come. Not because I would lose our connection, but because I might not survive it.

My fear lost the battle, however, when Harley thrust into me fully, lifting both of our bodies off the seat, and stilled. I felt his cock buck inside me as he came, and the image of him pouring himself into me caused my core to spasm and contract, as if on cue. Immaculate pleasure washed over me—lifting my burdens, drowning my pain, and flooding my fears—until my body went limp against Harley's chest. I rode the wave of relief until it receded, leaving me right back where I began—on the rocky shore of reality.

Reaching for the ignition, I turned my key one click to the right, just enough to illuminate the dashboard. The clock read *10:36.*

"Fuck! Harley, I have to go!" I said, shimmying my thong back into place and diving over to the passenger side to put my shorts back on.

Pulling off the condom and tying it in a knot, Harley watched me flail in amusement.

"What are you doing tomorrow night?" he asked, raising his voice over the din of the crowd and the engines behind us.

"I have to work." I pouted, buttoning my fly and adjusting my tank top.

"Is it okay if I come by?"

I glanced up and met his gaze. Harley wanted to see me at *work*?

I smiled bigger than I'd intended and nodded.

Tomorrow would make five days that week that Harley had found a way to see me. I couldn't believe it. He seemed like the kind of guy who would wait five days just to call a girl back, but here he was, making plans with me again.

I leaned over the center console and kissed him. Hard. Kissed him in a way that said, *I want to see you again, too*, and *Everything sucks when you're not around*, and *We should probably just go ahead and move in together*.

Then, remembering the time, I shoved Harley's shoulder toward the door and said, "Now, go, goddamn it!"

Harley chuckled and gave me one last little peck on the lips before opening my car door. He turned around to tell me *Goodbye*, or *Good night*, or *Drive safe*, but I slammed the door in his face before he could get the words out and cranked the engine.

As much as I would have loved to cuddle and whisper sweet nothings with Harley for the rest of eternity, if I didn't get my ass home, I was going to be spending that eternity grounded in my tiny bedroom.

I slid the driver's seat all the way forward and flipped on my headlights, ready to tear out of there...only to discover that I couldn't see shit through my sex-fogged windshield.

Son of a bitch.

I tried to wipe a patch of the moisture away with my hand, but that only smeared the fogginess around. I turned my defroster on, but that thing would take several minutes to do its job. I even flipped on my windshield wipers in desperation, but that did nothing, considering that the fog was on the *inside* of the glass. There was no way around it. I was going to have to do the *drive of shame*.

Instead of walking home after a one-night stand with mascara under my eyes and high heels in my hand, I got to drive past at least a hundred of Harley's admirers, going about five miles per hour with a post-sex cigarette hanging out of my mouth and my mostly-shaved head sticking out of my open window because I couldn't see through my fogged-up windshield. It wasn't exactly my finest moment, but I can't say that I was embarrassed either. In all honesty, after seeing the way those people revered Harley, I might have even felt a tinge of pride as I drove past the field of skanks shooting daggers at me with their eyes. Harley could have plowed any girl there that night, but he'd chosen me.

And now, everybody knew it.

A thousand dollars.

It had taken me a full year of working nights and weekends at Pier One Imports to save up that much money, and there I was, staring at the same amount, earned in less than one minute at the track.

I'd found the sweaty wad of cash stuffed in my purse when I got home that night. Ten hundred-dollar bills crammed between my cell phone and wallet. I laid each one out flat on my bedspread, then I arranged them into different designs. A sun. A star. A house with Benjamin Franklin peeking out the window.

I stared at the artwork on the front, on the back, trying to commit every line and detail to memory. I knew I'd have to give the pretty little pieces of paper back the next day, but until then I was going to enjoy them. Hell, I might even tape them to my skin and wear them as pajamas. The fact that they were currency was completely irrelevant. They were gifts from Harley, and to me, that meant more.

My hands arranged and rearranged the faded green parchment as my mind replayed the events of the night. I smiled, thinking about how easily Harley had hustled those douche bags. I smiled, remembering how I'd made his friends laugh.

I thought about the way he'd ripped my fishnets open in the front seat of my car and how he'd said, "You have me, lady."

I wondered what that meant. Like, I had him in my car, or I had his heart?

I smiled some more. Then, I looked down at my absent-minded creation and almost screamed.

I threw the paper rose to the floor and covered my mouth with both hands. My eyes shot over to a plastic cup on my desk where a bouquet of similar-looking flowers sat, collecting dust. Flowers made from notebook paper. Flowers that had been intended to cheer me up.

I could see Knight's face, as if it were right in front of me, glaring at me with those glacial-blue zombie eyes from behind a fistful of notebook-paper flowers. Knight, my high school's only skinhead, had followed me to detention that day. He could have gone home, let me find my own ride, but he hadn't. He sat in detention right next to me, drawing me pictures and making me flowers to pass the time. No one had ever given me flowers before.

That afternoon we got drunk together. We laughed. We teased each other. Then, Knight wrestled me to the ground and kissed me. I hadn't wanted him to kiss me then, and after the way he'd treated me before he left, I didn't want him to kiss me ever again. But in between our first kiss and our last existed a chunk of time when my whole world revolved around Knight's lips. Making them smile. Trying to get them to open up and talk to me. Counting the minutes until they'd be back on my body.

Looking down at the hundred-dollar bills on the ground, twisted and folded into an exact replica of one of Knight's paper roses, I felt his presence in the room. I got still. My ears perked up, listening for the rumble of his truck in the distance. My nose twitched, searching for traces of his musky, cinnamony cologne in the air. The tiny hairs on the back of my neck shot up violently. My breathing all but ceased.

You're safe.

He's gone.

You're safe.

He's gone.

You're safe.

He's gone.

But he wasn't. The ghost of Knight remained, imprinted somewhere deep in my psyche, and it was haunting me from the inside out.

I couldn't focus at work. I had ten hundred-dollar bills in one pocket and a cell phone that hadn't rung all day in the other. The battery was almost dead from my incessant checking. I only fluffed and organized the displays in the front of the store, making sure to face the main entrance at all times. We weren't very busy for a Saturday, which was good, because every time the doorbell chimed I had a little heart attack.

It was almost time for my break when I noticed a woman standing at the checkout counter. Looking around and realizing that nobody else was available to ring her up, I huffed and headed over. She was buying at least twenty-seven candles, and of course, she wanted each of them gift-wrapped *separately*. I usually loved gift-wrapping, but it forced me to stand with my back to the door, which was the last thing I wanted to do while waiting for Harley fucking James to make his appearance.

After bagging the last gift box, I turned around and handed my bedazzled works of art to the customer with a huge smile on my face. Not because I was that awesome at customer service, but because a living fucking legend was standing right behind her.

I'd never seen Harley in the wild before. Only at his work, at his house, and at places we'd gone to together. Standing in the middle of Pier One Imports, he looked as beautiful and dangerous and out of place as a full-grown Bengal tiger.

My customer thanked me, then turned and walked around the tattooed Pegasus standing between her and the door.

"How can I help you?" I coyly asked the disheveled blond standing with his fists in his pockets and a smirk on his face.

Pulling something out of his pocket, Harley dropped to one knee and said, "You can start by marryin' me."

Scrambling up onto the cash stand, I peered over the edge to see Harley opening a black velvety ring box. Inside was a tiny white gold ring with a strip of tiny square-cut diamonds embedded within the band.

I froze as my brain spun and sputtered, trying to process this fucked-up scene.

He can't be fucking serious. You should laugh. Obviously, he's just messing with you. I mean, it hasn't even been a full week!

No! Jesus, don't laugh at him! What if he's serious? You'll crush him!

He's not serious. Harley doesn't do serious.

But those sure do look like real diamonds. People don't just go around handing out diamond rings as gag gifts, BB.

Harley might. He gave me a thousand dollars yesterday just because I cracked a joke about it.

You do have a point.

Fuck.

Say something!

A small crowd had gathered around the cash register where I was perched on all fours, staring at a man on bended knee down below me.

My manager cleared her throat from somewhere behind me and said, "Um, BB? Why don't you go ahead and take your break now?"

Great idea.

"You got it!" I chirped, leaping off the cash stand and grabbing Harley by his outstretched hand.

He flashed me a megawatt smile, obviously amused with himself and the little spectacle he'd caused, and allowed me to drag him out the front door and around to the side of the building.

Once we were away from prying eyes, I turned and faced him. "What are you doing?" I whisper-yelled, afraid that I would actually scream the words if I tried to use my regular voice.

Harley grinned. "I told you the day you came into my shop that I was gonna ask you to marry me."

"No, you said you *would* ask me to marry you if I wasn't so young."

"Well...you're older now."

"By like a week," I giggled. "Where did you get that?"

Harley pulled the ring out of the fuzzy black box and held it up. "The pawnshop next door to Dave's work. The owner owes us...some favors." Harley's smile faded and his eyes narrowed, but he recovered quickly. "I saw this little guy and thought it might actually fit your skinny-ass finger."

While I stood with my mouth hanging open, Harley slid the tiny band onto my wedding ring finger. He was right. It fit perfectly.

I stared down at my hand, still unable to tell whether or not Harley was kidding. He hadn't told me he loved me or even called me his girlfriend yet, which were kind of prerequisite steps before proposing marriage, but he *had* asked me to move in with him. Although I was pretty sure he'd been kidding about that, too. Now he was giving me a diamond ring simply because a shady pawnshop owner owed him something?

It was all beginning to add up. Harley was just a big, impulsive kid who liked to play with really expensive toys.

"Harley, do you even know my name?" I asked, looking up at him with a sideways smile.

"Yes, *BB*," he said, mischievous blue eyes sparkling.

I rolled my eyes. "No, my *real* name."

"It doesn't matter what your real name is"—Harley bent down so that we were nose-to-nose—"because pretty soon, it's gonna be BB *James*." He wagged his head from side to side a little and gave me a peck on the lips before standing back up.

"*Brooke Bradley* James," I corrected, flipping my hand over to see if the diamonds went all the way around. They did, and they sliced right across the faded tattoo that I had almost forgotten about underneath.

"That sounds like three people." Harley chuckled, pocketing the velvet ring box and digging around for his cigarettes and lighter.

"Yeah," I quietly agreed, staring at the gray smudge that had once resembled the silhouette of a knight on horseback.

Five months ago, when Knight had given me that tattoo—branded my wedding ring finger with his name—I'd been one hundred percent sure that he and I would be together forever. That our relationship was as permanent as the ink on my skin.

Well, I'd been right about that part. Knight had put my tattoo in the one place he knew wouldn't last, and just as it began to fade, he disappeared too.

Now there I was, wearing another man's ring before Knight's mark had fully left my skin. Or my soul. It felt wrong. Knight had no right to have that kind of hold on me—not after the way he'd treated me, broken me—but he did just the same.

Before I realized what I was doing, I pulled the trinket off my finger. Handing it back to Harley with a fake smile, I said, "You're gonna have to do better than that if you want to get with *all this*," motioning down the length of my skeletal body with my free hand.

Harley laughed and took the ring from me, completely unfazed by my rejection. Dropping it into his pocket, he pulled me close and smiled against my mouth. "You're right," he said, his voice lowered. "And I'm gonna keep askin' till you say *yes*."

Not knowing what to say, I kissed him. I kissed him for thinking of me and for making me smile. I kissed him to say I was sorry and to thank him for putting me *somewhat* back together. And I kissed him to distract him from the lit cigarette I was about to snatch out of his hand.

Harley and I smoked and laughed and lazily made out on the side of the building until it was time for me to go back in.

"Hey, next time, you can park behind the building in the employee lot if you want. That way, you won't have to worry about the Boss getting dented by a runaway shopping cart or something," I said, hinting that I hoped there would be a next time.

Harley smiled. "Smart *and* beautiful. I knew you were perfect. C'mon." He turned and pulled me by the hand toward the front of the building.

"Where are we going?" I giggled, digging in my heels.

"To the courthouse," Harley said, casting a devilish smile over his shoulder at me.

"Harley, it's seven o'clock on a Saturday. I'm pretty sure the courthouse is closed."

Turning to face me with a look of triumph on his face, Harley pointed the butt of his Camel Light at me and said, "That's not a no."

Goddamn, he was cute. I was beginning to regret giving that ring back. Being Mrs. Brooke Bradley James was sounding better and better by the minute.

"Harley, I have to go back to work," I said, tugging him toward me and changing the subject.

Harley wrapped his big hands around my bony shoulders, dropped his forehead to mine, and said, "Nope."

"Yep."

"Nuh-uh."

"'Fraid so, buddy."

Harley shook his head, causing my head to shake back and forth, too. "Never."

"Are *you* gonna pay my car payment and insurance when I get fired?" I asked, immediately regretting my question.

I remembered what had happened the last time I made a joke about money. The consequences were burning a hole in my back pocket. I covertly slipped the wad of cash out of my jeans and slid both hands into Harley's front pockets, depositing the money along with them.

"That car will pay for itself, lady."

I pushed up onto my tiptoes and kissed Harley, effectively

ending the conversation. "Thanks for coming to see me," I whispered against his mouth.

"Anytime," he said, giving my ass a squeeze before releasing me to sprint toward the store's front entrance.

When the sliding doors opened, I could see on one of the decorative wall clocks that I was ten minutes late getting back from break—a fact that was not lost on my manager, who was giving me the stink eye from behind the register.

Shit.

I smiled at her innocently and began busying myself with some bullshit by the front door so that I could watch Harley walking away. He was all long legs, tattooed arms, smooth swagger, and blond sex hair, and I was sending him away with a pocketful of my rejected gifts. What the fuck was wrong with me?

My question was answered a moment later when the throaty rumble of an approaching diesel engine caused my body to freeze—along with all of its basic functions. I watched the parking lot in horror, screaming at Harley from inside my fleshy prison to get the fuck out of there. As he cranked up the Boss and pulled out of the parking lot, a delivery truck pulled in and drove around to the back of the building, taking the sound I'd thought belonged to Knight's monster truck along with it.

He's gone.
You're safe.
He's gone.
You're safe.
He's gone.
You're safe.
I'm fucked.

For the remaining two hours of my shift, I floated around Pier One Imports in a giddy fog. I accomplished next to nothing, which was nothing new, but at least I did it with a smile on my face for a change.

"Looks like somebody finally got laid."

Craig, the only Pier One employee less productive than me, plopped down on a wicker settee next to where I was in the process of rearranging the entire Mountain Mist candle collection. He crossed his long, slender legs and leaned forward, studying me with eyelashes that went on forever. His Afro was cut short and bleached blond, just like Sisqo's. Based on the number of times I had to hear him sing the "Thong Song" per shift, I'd guess he was a pretty big fan.

I looked at Craig, and a smile split my face in two.

"I knew it! You been mopin' around this place for months, girl! Then today you come in here wit' a little pep in yo step"— he snapped his fingers in the air for emphasis—"and I just knew. That girl got herself some D." Craig stood up and placed his splayed hand over his heart. Then he leaned in so that no one else would hear. "But when that man showed up wit' a *got*damn diamond ring, I was like, *Shiiiiiit. B must ha' dat bomb-ass pussy.* Good for *you*, baby."

He draped an arm over my shoulders as we both doubled over in laughter. Just like the good old days—before everything in my life had gone to shit. God, it felt good to laugh again. As our giggles died down, we heard the metallic clicking sound of the front door being locked.

Craig looked at me with wide eyes. "It's nine o'clock, bitch! You know what that means!"

I groaned and rolled my eyes as Craig grabbed my hand and pulled me over to the cash stand. He threw open one of the cabinets, swapped out the corporate-approved CD in the store sound system for one of his own, then treated all of us to his favorite closing-time ritual. A storewide performance of the "Thong Song."

I sighed and twerked in amused defeat as Craig danced circles around me. Throughout the song he gyrated around my ass like it was something special, which was absolutely ridiculous. The girl in the song had "dumps like a truck." All I had were dump*lings*.

When I walked out to my car ten minutes later I was still smiling from ear to ear and singing about a girl with "thighs like what." When I sat inside my little Mustang and cranked the engine, I felt a newfound confidence behind the wheel, thanks to Harley. And when I looked in the rearview mirror before backing out of my parking spot I screamed and slammed on the brakes.

Zombie eyes held my wide-eyed stare in the mirror.

Musky, cinnamony cologne seized my lungs.

Adrenaline flooded my bloodstream.

Pins and needles stabbed my every hair follicle.

My heart slammed against my rib cage.

My brain sent panicked signals out to every extremity—*Door handle! Open! Run!*—but they went unreceived. I was paralyzed. Frozen to the spot by his icy stare.

The shadow man in my backseat spoke. "I got your letter." His clear, deep voice sounded like controlled chaos. Syllables sliding through clenched teeth with restrained rage. Heavy, hot breaths being pulled and pushed through flared nostrils.

Meanwhile, I couldn't breathe at all. Couldn't blink. Couldn't tear my gaze away from the rearview mirror. I was caught in the eye of an F5 tornado. One wrong move, and I'd be annihilated.

"I wanted you to look me in the fucking face and tell me you believe him. That you think I'm a fucking cocksucker."

I couldn't see anything but his cold, calculating eyes, but I could hear his breaths and feel the heat he was radiating. It filled the already-sweltering car, causing droplets of sweat to roll down my sides.

"What do you think I saw when I got here, Punk?" Knight's voice dropped an octave as his hand shot out from the darkness and wrapped around my mouth, pulling my face to the right. Toward him. Forcing me to confront my own personal nightmare.

"Harley James. Harley fucking James!" Knight squeezed my cheeks so hard, my mouth folded into a reluctant kiss against his rough palm. He leaned forward so that our eyes were mere inches apart—his angular lips curled into a snarl—just before the word *no* tore from his chest in a burst of anger.

I flinched and tried to pull away, but his hold on me only

tightened. Clenching my eyes shut, I willed myself not to cry, but my breaths came out as whimpers.

When Knight spoke again, he'd resumed his controlled snarl. "What did I say when I left, Punk? Huh? What the fuck did I say?" He jerked my face in his hand, pulling a high-pitched shriek from my lungs. "I told you I loved you. I told you I was doing this for *you*. I told you to find somebody fucking *better*! And this is what you do? A month later, you're fucking *Harley James* and telling me that *I'm* the piece of shit? That *I'm* the liar? That *I'm* the cheater? That *I'm* some fucking faggot who never let you all the way in?" Knight let out a menacing laugh that made my adrenal glands shudder and constrict. "Oh, you're *alllll* the fucking way in, Punk. You're in my goddamn guts. You've seen my shit-stained soul. You're the only fucking person who knows what I am inside, but it seems like you need a little reminder."

Knight wrapped his hands around my rib cage and dragged me into the backseat while I was still struggling to process his seething words. My ass landed on his thighs, the back of my head landed against the passenger window, and my heavy boots got stuck between the driver's seat and the center console, immobilizing my legs. Knight gripped my face again, pressing my head harder into the glass.

"If you had stopped and used your *fucking* brain for one second," Knight growled, his chest heaving, "you would have realized that you and I weren't even together when Lance said he sucked my cock. We didn't start dating until *after* he got expelled, did we?" Knight forced my head to move from side to side against the glass, silently answering his own question. "But you didn't want to use your brain, did you? You wanted a reason to hate me. You wanted an excuse to fuck that piece of shit guilt-free."

Tears pooled behind my closed lids as I realized that Knight was right. About everything. We *hadn't* been together when Lance said Knight cheated on me. And I *did* want a reason to hate him. I'd needed one. Because if I didn't hate him, that meant that I still loved him. And if I still loved him, then I was fucking doomed to spend eternity in the darkness I'd been living in before Harley showed up. Doomed to sit idly by while a piece of my heart used himself as target practice overseas. Doomed to miss him forever.

"Well that doesn't fucking work for me," Knight said, removing his hand and replacing it with his lips. He kissed me hard, unleashing every ounce of anger he'd been holding back. He kissed me like he wanted to hit me. Like he wanted me to hit him back.

My hands instinctively found their way back into his velvety-soft white-blond buzz cut as I accepted his rage. His madness. His love. My body cried out for his, longing for the pleasure-pain he'd taught it to crave.

"You are *mine*," Knight growled against my mouth, gripping the back of my neck. "Do you fucking understand? You're mine until *I* say you're not."

His words terrified and elated me at the same time. After the way he'd cast me aside, I'd felt like a crazy person—like I'd imagined this great love, made it all up in my own head. I'd felt insignificant and insane. But here he was, with my lip between his teeth, telling me what my heart had known all along—that not only had he let me in, he'd locked the door behind me and thrown away the key.

I pulled my feet free from the center console and shifted so that I was straddling him. Knight must have pushed the passenger seat all the way forward when he climbed into the back because there was more room than I'd expected. His huge arms wrapped around my body, pulling me even closer, as he dropped his face to my neck. For a split second, I saw the sweet boy underneath all the muscles, the tattoos, the hate. I saw Ronald, and he was clutching me to his chest as if I were a teddy bear during a lightning storm. Then he was gone along with my T-shirt as Knight tore it off over my head. Followed by his own.

I unclasped my bra as he unbuttoned my jeans, longing to be skin-to-skin with him again. Memories of sleeping with him late into the afternoon on an itchy brown couch surfaced. The way our breathing lungs and beating hearts would synchronize automatically. How hard and heavy his body felt on top of mine, yet soft. Touchable. How much younger he looked when the monster in him was asleep and his zombie eyes were hidden by lids lined with long blond lashes.

As Knight looked down, concentrating on relieving me of my boots and jeans, those same long lashes glinted in the light from the adjacent parking lot. He was really there. Every one of my senses confirmed it. Knight had come back.

Once I was in nothing but my socks, Knight freed himself from his camouflage pants and pulled me to him. The sparks that flew when our flesh collided were blinding. Scorching. Fire licked between my legs where his cock throbbed against me and spread up my torso where our chests heaved in unison. Knight's fingers dug into my bony hips and slid my waifish body up and down against his. I gripped his fuzzy head again—my favorite thing to touch in the world—and panted into his mouth.

Knight broke our kiss and bit down on my earlobe as his thrusts became harder. "Am I gonna get that piece of shit's cum on my dick?" he hissed through his clamped teeth.

"Fuck you," I spat before my brain had time to catch up to my mouth.

"Fuck me?" A laugh rumbled like thunder from his chest. "Fuck *me*? Do you have any fucking idea what it does to me, thinking somebody else has touched you?"

"Yeah, I do!" I yelled. "Because that's exactly how I fucking felt every time I saw you and Angel Alvarez together before you left!" I began to shake just thinking about it. "She answered the door when I came looking for you. She followed me around school, talking shit and telling me you never loved me. She and her little hood-rat friends even said she might be pregnant with your baby! And you stood by and let her do it because you thought it would help me 'move on.'" I made air quotes around the words with my fingers for emphasis. "So you don't get to fucking judge me for trying to *move on* when all you've done for the last three months is push me away!"

I shoved his chest with shaking hands, but it did nothing to satisfy my rage. I smacked his hard torso and upper arms with my open palms, but the slapping sounds couldn't quell my hurt. Knight just took it, staring at me like a laser scope as I pounded away at his flesh.

"Fuck you!" I cried, lifting a hand to slap him across the face.

Knight caught my skeletal wrist mid-swing and held it in the air next to my face, never blinking. "You didn't answer my question," he said. His voice was eerily calm.

"Yes, I did! I *do* fucking know how it feels!"

"Not *that* question," Knight said, cocking his head to one side.

I huffed, trying in vain to pull my restrained hand away from him. "No, you're not gonna get his cum on your dick, if that's what you're asking. Fucking asshole."

Knight raised an eyebrow. "No?" he asked, continuing to study me.

"No, goddamn it!" I shouted, finally yanking my wrist free.

It wasn't a lie. It wasn't the whole truth either, but if Knight had wanted the whole truth, he would have asked a different question. He heard what he wanted to hear, and before I could suck in my next breath, we were joined.

Electricity coursed through my veins at the contact, as if Knight were the plug and I were the socket. He lit me up from the inside out, turning feelings back on that I'd thought would be forever dark. Igniting the pleasure-pain sensation that I thought I'd never experience again.

I rode his body, as familiar as my own, as he nipped and sucked his way down my neck. The last time I'd seen him we were fucking good-bye in his truck in the exact same parking lot. Now we were fucking good-bye again as well as *I'm sorry*, *I missed you*, *I love you*, and *Don't leave me*. Knight used sex as a way to inject me with all the words and thoughts and emotions that he didn't know how to express any other way. It wasn't pretty. It wasn't fun. It hurt and it healed, all at the same time.

With my hands cupping the sides of his fuzzy head and his gripping the back of my neck and one bony hip, we breathed the same air and beat to the same rhythm and prayed to the same universe to make it last forever. But the gods didn't listen, or maybe our bodies were the rebels. Either way, the moment didn't last. It exploded in an electrical fire of teeth and nails, bleeding skin and broken capillaries.

We stayed pressed together for a long time. Long enough for our breathing to even out and our heartbeats to synchronize, the way they always did. Long enough for my brain to start working again. Long enough for me to realize that, twenty-four hours ago, I was fucking a different man in the front seat.

My empty stomach roiled.

Knight still had a grip on the back of my neck, but he was using his rough touch to massage it, rubbing slow circles with his firm fingers.

Eventually, Knight broke the silence. Placing a kiss on the top of my head, he asked, "What time do you need to be home?"

That simple question made my eyes sting and my chest constrict. Knight might have been a psychopath with a rage disorder, but I couldn't deny the fact that he cared. That he thought about me before he thought about himself. That even when he was hurting me, he was really trying to love me.

"Eleven o'clock," I whispered, forcing my words out around the lump in my throat.

Knight released my hip and looked at his wrist. He was wearing a simple watch with a dark green canvas band. I'd never known him to wear a watch before.

"It's ten fifteen," he said, dropping his chin to the top of my head and pulling me closer. "We've got thirty more minutes."

"Knight?" I asked, hardly able to hear my own thoughts over the sound of his heart thumping beneath my cheek. "How did you get here? Aren't you supposed to be at boot camp for two more months?" Sitting up, I looked at him with a bowling ball

in my gut. "You didn't, like, go AWOL just to come see me...
did you?"

Knight's face gave nothing away. His clothes didn't either. He
was wearing a pair of camo pants, but those might have been
ones that he already owned. I hadn't really gotten to see his
T-shirt before he tossed it on the floorboard, but it was pretty
generic too—a solid color, maybe black or dark green. It definitely wasn't the skinhead band T-shirt with tight Levi's rolled
up at the bottom and skinny suspenders—braces—that I was
used to. That's for sure. Had he come straight from boot camp,
or was he just dressing differently now?

"There are ways to get leave," Knight said, his tone sending
chills up my spine. "Family emergencies come up. Shit happens."

I didn't want to know what kind of family emergency he was
talking about because, whatever it was, I had a feeling he had
something to do with it. The last time I'd been in the same room
as him and his "family," Knight had smashed out the glass doors
on every built-in cabinet in the living room with a fireplace poker,
beaten his stepfather's face to a pulp, and had a gun pulled on him
by his own mother. Knight could instigate a "family emergency,"
no problem.

"Knight...what did you do?" I asked, my voice barely above
a whisper.

Knight ran his thick hands up my bare thighs and stared
directly into my eyes in warning. "I did what I had to do. It'll
take a hell of a lot more than a few miles and a few Marines to
keep me from you, Punk."

His indirect answers made me nervous, but I swallowed and
asked the question gnawing away at me anyway, "Did you hurt
someone?"

"No," Knight snapped. Then his tone softened. "One of my clients does medical billing for Emory Hospital. You'd be surprised how easy it is to get forged admission paperwork when free tattoos are on the line."

"But you don't have a car on base. How did you—"

"I took the bus."

"Jesus, Knight. You did all of that just because of my letter? You could have just written me back, you know."

Knight smiled. Really smiled. Smiled the smile that I had bent over backward to elicit from him every day since the first time I saw it. The smile that had tricked me into thinking he was sane. That I was safe.

"Maybe I'll try that next time," he said, all sparkly white teeth and sparkly white eyes.

I touched his beautiful grin with two fingers just to make sure I wasn't imagining it. Then, I kissed his smiling mouth with everything that I had. We had twenty minutes left, and we spent them doing what we did best. What Knight had taught me how to do. What I wished I'd never done with anybody but him. We made love—violent, passionate, miserable love.

Then we did what we did worst and said good-bye.

I hadn't slept. I'd spent the entire night with my T-shirt pressed to my face, trying to extract a hint of Knight's scent from the overpowering odors that my shift at Pier One had left behind. It was there, beneath the blaring notes of patchouli and eucalyptus and lavender and vanilla. If I shut my eyes and concentrated hard enough, I could smell it—just a whisper of cinnamony musk. The scent strangled me with longing and made my heart race.

The fact that Knight's feelings for me were every bit as real as I'd once imagined—that he hadn't cheated on me with Lance, hadn't lied about who he was—made things both better and worse. The sting of unrequited love was gone, but it had been replaced by the ache of loss. Somewhere, out there in the night, a broken, dangerous man moved through the shadows, carrying pieces of me in his pocket—a chunk of my heart, a sliver of my soul, the blood he'd drawn, the flesh ejected when he'd pierced me, a lock of hair from my shaved head, a jar of my tears, my hymen, my innocence.

But there was one thing that he didn't have despite the number of times I'd thrust it into his murderous hands. Knight refused to take my future. He left it shiny and new, still in the wrapper. So what would I do with it? Put it on a shelf and waste it pining over him, or give it to someone else to open and play with?

And would anyone even want it once they realized how many pieces were missing?

"You. Little. Slut," Juliet said, tucking her boob away and handing Romeo to me.

With his curly black hair and almond-shaped eyes, he looked just like his half-Japanese, half-African-American mama. Thank God. His piece-of-shit daddy, Tony, who was doing hard time for selling drugs, was far from a looker. Or a thinker. Or a father for that matter.

I draped a burp cloth over my shoulder and accepted the sleepy-eyed, milk-drunk newborn. I'd made the mistake of criticizing Juliet's heavy-handed burping style once, so now it had become my job.

"Shut up and tell me what to do," I pleaded. "I'm freaking out."

"I can't shut up *and* tell you what to do, dumbass," Juliet said, rolling her eyes.

"Ugh! You know what I mean," I huffed.

Standing up with a burp cloth and a baby draped over my shoulder, I paced back and forth across Juliet's new basement bedroom, rubbing Romeo's back instead of smacking it. Juliet's mom had moved her and the baby down there so that they'd "have more room," which I suspected was code for, *so that I can get some fucking sleep.*

"Listen," Juliet said, raising a nonexistent eyebrow, "you know how I feel about . . . Skeletor."

We locked eyes, and a year's worth of history passed between us. Juliet hated Knight. Hated him so much she couldn't even bring herself to say his name. Maybe that was why I'd come to her for advice. Because I needed someone to give me permission to let him go.

"I know," I said, wiping the spit-up off Romeo's chin with the cloth.

Satisfied with his burp, I cradled the sleepy guy to my chest and resumed my pacing. Having something heavy and warm to hold on to was surprisingly comforting. The quiet snoring didn't hurt either.

"He's the fucking devil," Juliet continued. "Let's see. He stalked you for months until he finally manipulated you into being his girlfriend. Then, as soon as he'd brainwashed you into caring about him, he completely shut you out of his life. He let Angel bully you because he wanted you to think they were fucking. He *choked you* when you confronted him at school about the steroids; don't think I forgot about that shit. Then, when you still didn't give up—because you're an idiot—he joined the Marines and told you to find somebody better."

Juliet's voice rose as she pointed at me in anger. "So you spend a month moping in your room, depressed as fuck, with no word from him, and when you finally do what he said and find somebody better he shows up and tries to take that away from you too. What in the actual fuck, B? I can't believe we're even having this conversation. That guy is a psycho who has done nothing but hurt you and scare you and fuck with your head. That's it. End of story. Move on."

Yeah, there was definitely a reason why I wanted Juliet's opinion.

"Well, when you put it like that…" I said, cringing from her brutally honest blow-by-blow.

"You know I'm right. And you're trying to decide between *him* and Harley? Harley's fucking *nice* to you. Like super nice. And from what you've told me, it sounds like he's got a pretty face and a big ole dick, too. So, I'm sorry, but I don't see what the fuck the problem is."

The image of Harley's face, and his dick, made me smile. "He's got a badass car, too," I added wistfully.

"And a badass car. See? There's literally no contest. Harley wins, and Skeletor can go back to hell where he came from."

I laughed and tried to push the guilt of what I was considering into the deepest recesses of my mind. She was right, right? It didn't matter how I felt about Knight. He was bad for me. He'd hurt me. And we weren't even technically together. I wasn't cheating on him if I kept seeing Harley. He didn't even have to know. Harley made me happy. And, now that I'd seen how low I was capable of getting, giving up the one thing that made me high was too big a risk to take.

Just then my purse erupted into a crescendo of robotic beeps and tones.

Doodleoodleoodleoodleoo.

Juliet's face lit up with the triumph of an argument won as she pointed to it and yelled, "And he *calls* you when he wants to talk instead of hiding in the backseat of your car like a fucking serial killer!"

I ignored her comment. I was too busy tossing a sleeping

baby at her, diving into my purse to find my phone, and sprinting into the bathroom to take the call.

I answered on the last ring, totally out of breath.

The sound of smoke being exhaled greeted me on the other line, followed by the warm, raspy words, "Hey, lady."

My adrenaline instantly evaporated into a puddle of swoon juice.

"Hey, Harley."

I smiled into my phone and felt my cheeks get hot. Oh my God, was I seriously blushing over two little words? I looked in the mirror to check the extent of my blotchiness and gasped when I saw something way more colorful than my pink face—a stage five hickey, right on the front left side of my neck.

"Shit."

"You okay?" Harley asked.

"Uh, yeah," I said, yanking up my Bauhaus T-shirt to see what other damage had been done. "I just ... saw a spider."

As Harley laughed and made fun of me for being a pussy, I stared at the purple-and-red Jackson Pollock painting that had once been my torso. Hickeys, finger-shaped bruises, and bloody scabbed-over bite marks marred the landscape of my pale, freckled flesh. I looked like I'd been attacked. By a wolverine. And a vacuum hose attachment. At the same time.

"BB?"

"Huh? Sorry, I ... I didn't hear you. This thing is staring at me with at least six of its eight eyes. I think it wants to eat me."

"It's not the only one."

I blinked and replayed his words in my head to be sure I'd heard him correctly. "Harley!"

He chuckled in that deep gravelly voice that made my insides clench and said, "Come over."

"I can't." The words shot from my mouth before I had a chance to formulate a solid excuse.

I wanted nothing more than to let Harley do exactly what he was offering, but there was no way I could let him see me looking like that. Jesus, I might as well have had a blinking neon sign on my chest that said, *Knight wuz here*. I was going to need at least a week to heal up.

"What about tomorrow?" Harley asked.

"Uh...I'm going out of town!"

Goddamn, I was a terrible liar.

"Really?" Harley sounded genuinely surprised. "Where you goin'?"

"Um..." I looked around the bathroom, desperate for inspiration. My eyes landed on Juliet's little brother's swim trunks, which were hanging up to dry in the shower. They had a picture of Snoopy on them and his little yellow friend—

"Woodstock!" I blurted.

"You're going to Woodstock?" Harley asked, incredulous.

"Yep. My parents, man. Total hippies. They're taking me on a road trip to the place where Woodstock was held so that I can experience the majesty or some shit."

"You guys are driving all the way to New York?"

Woodstock was in New York?

"Uh-huh," I lied. "It's totally gonna suck."

Harley bought my bullshit, or at least pretended to, and made me promise to call him as soon as I got back. He said he was going to miss me.

I was going to miss him more.

Walking out of the bathroom with my phone dangling from my dejected hand, I met Juliet's hopeful gaze and lifted my shirt.

Her mouth fell open, and her eyes narrowed to slits. "That motherfucker."

GEORGIA
CHAPTER 14
19 PEACH STATE 99

July 1998

"Harley, get up!"

"Not until you answer me."

My eyes flicked from Harley, who was kneeling before me in the middle of his living room, holding a tiny diamond band in his outstretched hand, to Dave, who was standing in the doorway of the kitchen with an amused smirk on his face.

Lowering my voice, I whispered, "Are you really going to make me tell you no in front of your brother?"

"Ha!" Dave laughed and clapped his hands together once. "She fucking said no!" Pointing at me, he added, "I love this girl! Hell, *I* kinda wanna marry her now."

Harley stood up, completely undaunted, and smirked at me. Tucking the ring back into his pocket, he pulled me in for a hello kiss while simultaneously flipping Dave off over his shoulder.

"Fuck me?" his little brother called from the kitchen. "I'm not the one who just *served* your ass, son!"

I felt Harley smile against my mouth as his tongue teased

mine. He smelled like gasoline and cigarettes—an explosive combination that I'd missed every minute of every day that I'd pretended to be away.

I had healed up pretty well with some help from a vial of vitamin E oil I'd found in my mom's collection of homeopathic bullshit. As long as Harley didn't rub the concealer off the fading hickey on my neck, I should be okay.

The thought of how I'd gotten that hickey made my guilt flare back up, but when Harley told his brother to "Shut the fuck up and bring my woman a beer," it erupted into a three-alarm inferno of remorse.

His woman. God, I felt like an asshole.

With a beer in one hand and a Camel Light in the other, I settled into the couch and listened as Harley and Dave regaled me with stories from our week spent apart. Harley took my boots and socks off, but instead of rubbing my feet like I hoped he would, he stuck his lit cigarette between two of my toes so that he could hit the bong that Dave had just passed to him. It was fucking adorable. *He* was adorable, and when he exhaled and tipped the bong to me in a silent offer, I couldn't say no.

The previous week had been hell. I'd spent every moment either racked with guilt or shaking in fear. Every creak, every beep, every bump in the night had me practically jumping out of my skin. I was convinced that Knight was there somewhere, watching me. Positive. He'd become the monster under my bed, the *Skeletor* in my closet. And when I hadn't been busy worrying about Knight, I'd been worrying about Harley finding out about Knight.

But now that we were finally together again, I was feeling a whole new level of anxious. I was desperately trying to play it cool—in my coochie-cutter shorts and my Andrew W.K. T-shirt with the sleeves cut off—while on the inside I was literally willing myself not to have a panic attack. Maybe it was time to give pot another shot. I'd take feeling sleepy over having a coronary on Harley's filthy brown carpet any day.

I sat up and flicked my fingers at Harley, gesturing for him to pass me the bong without looking too eager. I might not have been a pothead, but I knew how all the accessories worked. Hell, I'd probably drunk bong water as a baby the way thirsty pets drink out of the toilet, but I let Harley light it for me anyway.

The smoke smelled comforting but burned like fire in my lungs, causing me to cough like a son of a bitch. Harley and Dave laughed, already half-baked themselves, and I couldn't help but chime in. Laughing felt amazing. So did Harley's arm around my shoulders when he passed the bong back to Dave and pulled me in close. I relaxed into his side instantly.

All the tension I'd been carrying around melted like ice and slid from my bones, forming a puddle of bullshit I was done worrying about on the floor, thanks to Harley. The man was better than therapy. Better than Prozac. I stepped into his aura, and all was right with the world. The difference between how I'd felt during our week apart and how I felt after spending only thirty minutes in his presence made it abundantly clear. I needed him. Regardless of how I felt about Knight. Whether I loved him or loathed him, it didn't matter.

Harley = happy.

No Harley = fucking miserable.

"Hey, you wanna come by the shop tomorrow?" Harley managed to ask while still holding in the hit he'd just taken. Exhaling without so much as a cough, he added, "I got a valve in that

I think will work with your new cold air intake. Then we can go test it out and grab some dinner."

I nodded up at him dreamily, my gaze drifting from his sparkly blue eyes to the silver ring hugging his big, fat bottom lip. Just as I was about to crane my neck up to kiss him, Harley covered his mouth with the bong and took another hit. My disappointment quickly turned to elation, however, when Harley's lips found mine a moment later. He exhaled a slow stream of smoke directly into my open mouth and then sealed it shut with a lingering kiss.

My head spun, both from the weed and from the giddy, effervescent feeling I got anytime that beautiful, baby-faced bad boy touched me.

As soon as Harley pulled away, I exhaled with a cough, then a giggle when Dave raised his hand and said, "My turn! My turn!"

Harley smacked him in the face with an open hand, which led to Dave grabbing his arm and twisting it backward, which caused Harley to punch him in the shoulder with his free hand, which caused Dave to pull him to the ground like a crazy redneck spider monkey. I laughed my ass off and held the bong over my head to keep it safe while Harley and Dave rolled around on the living room floor for the next five minutes. They'd obviously been raised on WWF because those two knew every WrestleMania move and term ever invented.

At one point, Dave stood up, patted his elbow twice, and yelled "Atomic Elbow Drop!" before throwing himself at Harley, who rolled out of the way at the last minute.

As soon as Dave slid to a stop on the carpet, Harley rolled back, locked Dave's arm behind his back, and wrapped his other arm around his neck in some kind of a modified sleeper hold.

"Cross-Face Chicken Wing, motherfucker," Harley muttered, exerting himself while trying to contain Dave's thrashing body. "You done yet?"

Dave, whose face was turning purple, reluctantly nodded. As soon as Harley let go, Dave gasped for air and motioned toward me with an outstretched arm. "BB," he croaked. "Please, I"—*cough*—"I think I need CPR."

Harley chuckled and grabbed him by the wrist, pulling him to his feet. The guys did that thing where they hug and pound on each other's backs at the same time, then they flopped back onto the couch like nothing had even happened.

Chugging the rest of his beer, Harley belched and assessed what was left in my can, which wasn't much. He kissed me on the temple and got up to get us two more. On his way back into the living room, Harley flipped a light switch, illuminating the wall of neon signs behind me. The sun was beginning to set, and the room had gotten darker.

"Y'all wanna watch a movie?" Harley asked, grabbing a remote control off the coffee table.

In a few clicks, the giant TV boomed to life, and *The* motherfucking *Fifth Element* began playing. I stared at Harley in disbelief.

"Shut the fuck up," I deadpanned.

"What?"

I gestured at the TV. "Harley, this is my favorite movie."

"No, it's not." He smirked.

"Why?" I snapped back.

"Because it's *my* favorite movie. I called dibs. You can ask Dave." Harley turned and flicked his chin at his brother. "Hey, *Davidson?*"

"What, asshole?"

"What's my favorite movie?"

Without taking his eyes off the screen, Dave said, "*Steel Magnolias*. Duh."

I laughed and grabbed Harley's arm before he could smack the poor guy in the face again.

"Hey, Dave?" I asked, peeking around Harley's body.

"Yeah, princess?"

Making searing eye contact with Harley, I asked, "What's *my* favorite movie?"

"*Debbie Does Dallas*. Or at least it was when we watched it together last night." Looking at Harley, Dave added, "Your girl loves a full bush, man."

I totally let Harley smack him in the face that time.

Remembering what was in my trunk, I ran outside and came back carrying four little skull pillows that I'd sewn during my week in "Woodstock" and a gray chenille blanket that had gotten "damaged" and accidentally fell behind the dumpster at work. I dropped all the pillows onto Dave's head, who immediately grabbed one and curled up with it. Then I snuggled under the blanket with Harley on the other side of the L-shaped sectional.

After two beers and too many bong hits the room was a little spinny, so I lay down with my head on the armrest. Harley did the same, spooning me from behind. His big, strong arms were the only things keeping me tethered to the couch. I was floating. Worries, gone. It was just me and my favorite guy and my favorite movie and soft chenille on my bare legs and the lingering smell of marijuana in the air. I was safe and warm and fuzzyheaded.

"Thanks for the blanket, lady," Harley whispered in my ear just as his fingers slid under the waistband of my denim cutoff shorts.

"Mmhmm," I mumbled in response.

The neon beer signs and glow of the TV were the only light in the room—and Dave seemed to be pretty focused on Milla Jovovich in that little rubber suit—so I didn't mind one bit when Harley's fingers roamed even lower.

I could feel his erection swell against my ass, and I pressed against it in need as he teased my clit under the blanket. Harley's breath was hot on the back of my neck as he dipped a finger inside me, then, it was gone. An explosion went off on the TV, followed by machine gunfire, providing the perfect distraction for Harley to stealthily unzip his pants.

Welcome rigid heat slid between my thighs and against the thin crotch of my teeny, tiny shorts.

Fuck me.

I reached between my legs and touched the smooth head of Harley's cock, wishing like hell that I could grind against it the way I wanted to.

At the next explosion, Harley unzipped my shorts. More machine gunfire, he inched them below my ass. And, when the police sirens blared, Harley's cock was back between my legs—only that time, there was nothing between us.

"Fuck, you're wet," Harley whispered, his face buried in the curve of my neck.

His big, warm arm squeezed my waifish body tighter, so I pressed my thighs together and squeezed him right back.

Harley fucked my thigh gap slowly, using small movements and long pauses to keep from drawing any unwanted attention.

With every pass, the head of his cock grazed my slick entrance with a little more pressure.

Harley was begging for an invitation. And my body was ready to roll out the welcome mat.

If Dave hadn't decided to get up and take a piss right then, my stoned, beer-logged brain probably would have just fucked Harley without protection.

As soon as Dave was out of the room, I rallied every one of my remaining brain cells and dug a condom out of my purse. I passed it back to Harley, then slid my shorts down around my ankles under the blanket. When Harley pressed against me again, I let him in. The connection was immediate. Overwhelming. I gasped as we clicked into place and relished in the feeling of being whole again.

Just then I heard the toilet flush, and the bathroom door opened. When Dave walked across the living room he eyed us warily, but said nothing as he sat back down on his side of the couch. I closed my eyes and breathed a sigh of relief as Harley began to move again. Slowly. Discreetly. And at torturously random intervals.

I stifled a moan and peeked at Dave's side of the couch. He wasn't watching the movie. He was sitting with his back against the armrest, taking deliberate sips of his beer, watching *us*.

Somewhere in the rational part of my brain I knew I should feel weird about it, but I didn't. I couldn't. My inhibitions had been tranquilized. Besides, Dave had walked in on us before, right? He'd seen me naked. So, this was actually *less* weird because this time we were covered by a—

Before I could finish my rationalization, Dave leaned forward, grabbed the bottom edge of the blanket, made direct eye contact with me, and yanked it the fuck off. I gasped as cool air bathed my exposed flesh. I expected Harley to be pissed, but instead, he kicked my shorts the rest of the way off with his foot, wrapped a hand around my thigh, spread my legs open, and gave Dave a better view.

I squeezed my eyes shut as Harley began thrusting into me with abandon, no longer holding back for the sake of modesty. If I kept my eyes closed, I could pretend like Dave wasn't watching. I could focus on the delicious pressure building in my core. But I couldn't shut out the unmistakable sound of a zipper going down or the sickening smack of flesh against flesh. I knew without looking that Dave was jerking off. I didn't dare open my eyes. Not because I was afraid to see it, but because I was afraid I wouldn't be able to look away.

Harley spread my legs wider and reached down to tease my clit piercing.

"Fuck, that's hot," Dave mumbled. "Can I touch it?"

"Fuck no," Harley snapped.

"Let me see those titty rings then."

Oh my God! Are they seriously having a fucking conversation right now?

Harley gripped the bottom of my T-shirt and pulled it up to my chin. Then, he grabbed the front of my bra and yanked it up and over the top of my tiny breasts.

"Fuckin' A," Dave hissed just as Harley gently tugged on one of my nipples.

It sent a bolt of electricity straight to my clit, and I involuntarily clenched around Harley's cock. With my eyes still squeezed shut, I could hear Dave's breathing, and beating off, accelerate. It was so erotic, the sound of him pleasuring himself while watching us, that I decided to take a peek.

I opened my eyes and saw Dave sitting with his back against the opposite armrest, casually fisting his cock. I'd never seen a guy masturbate before. It was freeing, in a weird way. Dave and Harley's complete lack of inhibition, their love of life and all its pleasures, their trust in me, the lack of fucks they gave about what anybody thought—it made me feel like a sexy badass too. Like one of them.

Dave's eyes locked on to mine. There was no shame in them. Only heat. Scorching blue heat. Dave and Harley had the same eyes, but Dave's were rimmed in dark lashes and hooded by darker brows. They were beautiful. I wondered what he would have done to me if Harley had let him participate. Wondered if I would've liked it.

Our eye contact was broken when Harley wrapped his arms around my ribs tighter and rolled onto his back. I instinctively planted my feet on either side of his thighs for stability, which gave Dave a front row seat to Harley thrusting in and out of me from underneath. I let my head fall back against his shoulder as I gripped his rock-hard forearms for dear life. My orgasm was so close. I was so turned on, but that last little bit of shyness in the back of my brain refused to let me come in front of Dave.

Just then I felt a hesitant finger stroke the barbell between my legs. I didn't have to open my eyes to know that it didn't belong to Harley—his arms were still wound around my torso. It was Dave, touching me after Harley told him not to.

And I loved him for it.

I decided not to look. If I didn't look, then I could pretend like it was Harley. If I didn't look, then—

Shit, I looked.

Dave was on his knees, straddling Harley's long legs, jerking his dick with one hand and stroking my pussy with his other. His biceps strained against his tight white T-shirt, which glowed orange in the light of the neon signs. When he saw me watching him, Dave lifted his finger to his lips, silently telling me to keep quiet. Then he turned his baseball cap around backward.

I immediately discovered why when he bent forward and flicked my clit with his tongue.

My body detonated at once. Fireworks went off behind my eyes, and sparks coursed through my blood. Dave sat back up just before my thighs clamped shut, narrowly missing his head, as I tried to contain the tiny explosions rocking my core. Harley cursed as I contracted around him, thrusting into me harder until he followed me over the edge.

As I lay panting, my back to Harley's front, naked aside from my bra and T-shirt—which were still hiked up to my armpits—I didn't feel dirty.

I didn't feel dirty when Harley pulled out of me, gave me a kiss, and headed to the bathroom to clean up.

I didn't feel dirty until he was gone—when I discovered that my boyfriend's brother had come all over my stomach.

I looked at Dave, who had already tucked his junk away and was sipping his now-warm beer on the other side of the couch as if nothing had even happened.

"You're gonna clean this up, asshole," I said with a pointed stare.

"Want me to lick it off?" Dave said, flicking his talented tongue at me.

"Ugh," I huffed, pretending to be offended as I grabbed my clothes and stomped off to join Harley in the bathroom. In reality, I was running away to keep from taking him up on his offer. Who even was I?

"Harley, Dave came on meeee," I whined once I got to the bathroom.

Harley laughed and said, "Better on you than on the couch. C'mere."

He wet a washcloth in the sink and turned around to wipe me off. I watched his face as he worked.

Even though he was three years older than Knight, almost four, Harley's face looked younger somehow. He didn't have an angry *V* creased into his forehead or fine lines around the corners of his eyes from a lifetime of scowling. His cheekbones were rounded where Knight's were angular, and his mouth was full and pursed where Knight's was drawn and sharp. While Knight carried the weight of the world on his shoulders, Harley let it roll right off his back. I loved that about him.

Sure, Knight'd had a shitty childhood—I didn't exactly know how shitty because he refused to talk about it—but Harley hadn't exactly had a perfect life either. He just didn't let it bring him down. Maybe it was because he was high all the time. Maybe that was the secret. My mom was high all the time, and she was pretty fucking happy, too. Knight fucking hated drugs, and look at how angry he was. Maybe that was it. Maybe Knight just needed to smoke some weed and relax. I giggled, picturing him sparking up a fatty, and realized that I was obviously still high.

Harley looked up. "Did that tickle?"

"Mmhmm," I said, pinching my closed lips between my teeth to keep from cracking up.

Harley threw the washcloth into the sink and asked, "Does

this tickle?" He grabbed my ribs and wiggled his fingertips in between my bones.

I screamed and wriggled away from him, only to find that there was nowhere to go. Harley grabbed me again, but instead of tickling me, he pulled me in for a hug. I molded into his body and sighed in relief.

Wrapping his colorful arms around me, Harley rocked me from side to side with his face buried in my neck.

"Hey, lady?" he mumbled against my skin.

"Mmhmm?" I mumbled back.

"Does this tickle?"

Then, he snorted like a pig against the sensitive skin just below my ear.

I squealed and pushed his face away, laughing even harder than before.

"Hey! What the fuck are you doing to my girlfriend in there?" Dave yelled from the living room.

Harley looked at me and smiled, disarming me with his pretty blue gaze and his mop of sunny sexy hair. Then he yelled back, "She's *my* girlfriend, motherfucker!"

And then I died.

JULY 15, 1998

DEAR BB,

I SWORE I WASN'T GOING TO WRITE YOU, BUT I CAN'T GET YOU THE FUCK OUT OF MY HEAD.

KINDA LIKE HOW I SWORE I WAS GOING TO STAY AWAY FROM YOU, TOO. I'M SORRY I CAME TO SEE YOU. IT PROBABLY MADE SHIT HARDER ON YOU, BUT I CAN PROMISE YOU, IT'S BEEN A THOUSAND TIMES HARDER ON ME. IT'S LIKE I'M NOT EVEN HERE. MY BODY IS HERE, BUT IN MY MIND I'M STILL IN THE BACKSEAT OF

YOUR CAR, OR I'M WATCHING THAT
MOTHERFUCKER MAKE OUT WITH
YOU IN THE PARKING LOT.

KNOWING THAT I'M STUCK HERE
WHILE THAT PIECE OF SHIT IS OUT
THERE TRYING TO FUCK YOU IS
DRIVING ME CRAZY. I CAN'T STAND
THE THOUGHT OF YOU BEING WITH
SOMEONE ELSE, BUT AT THE SAME
TIME, I CAN'T STAND THE THOUGHT OF
YOU ENDING UP WITH ME EITHER. SO
I DON'T KNOW WHERE WE GO FROM
HERE.

ALL I KNOW IS THAT I MISS YOU. I
THOUGHT I COULD GO BACK TO BEING
MISERABLE AND ALONE, BUT NOW
THAT I KNOW WHAT BEING HAPPY
FEELS LIKE, IT'S NOT THAT FUCKING
EASY.

ESPECIALLY WHEN I KNOW THAT
ALL I HAVE TO DO TO FEEL THAT WAY
AGAIN IS FIND YOU.

I JUST WANT YOU TO KNOW THAT
I STILL LOVE YOU. I'LL ALWAYS
FUCKING LOVE YOU, PUNK. EVEN

WHEN I'M BEING A FUCKING
ASSHOLE.

LOVE,
KNIGHT

I stared at the piece of paper in my hands and waited to see which emotion, which thought would emerge first. But nothing came. I leaned back against the headboard of my bed and blinked at the psychotic, all-caps handwriting—handwriting that used to find its way into my pockets every day at school, handwriting as familiar to me as my own—but still…nothing. Was I broken? Was I a horrible person? Had I felt so much in such a short amount of time that I straight up ran out of feelings?

I grabbed my pack of cigarettes from my nightstand and shook a Camel Light and a lighter into my palm. As I smoked, I read and reread Knight's words. He loved me. He missed me. He was sorry. Harley is a piece of shit. And he wants me to be celibate for the rest of my life.

Maybe *that's* why I couldn't feel anything. Because how do you feel grief, guilt, longing, and outrage all at the same time? I was going to have to pick one because my sixteen-year-old amygdala was not equipped to process that many contradictory emotions at once. The gears had simply jammed up. Nothing was getting through.

I remembered my mom saying that writing things down could help me express my feelings, so I slid my cigarette and lighter back into the pack and yanked my giant, fuzzy animal-print chasm of a purse off the floor. I was sure I had a piece of paper and a pen in there somewhere. I wasn't going to write Knight back. I just wanted to figure out how to feel about what the fuck I'd just read.

I found a pen, but more importantly, I found some paper. Lots of it. Green rectangular pieces of paper with pictures of Benjamin Franklin on them to be exact. As I pulled fistful after fistful of hundred-dollar bills out from the recesses of my bag, one emotion finally burst free from the traffic jam in my mind. Delight. Giddy, mad, magical delight. Harley, that mother-fucker, had snuck all the prize money back into my purse!

I giggled and squealed and kicked my feet, causing wads of cash to scatter across the bed like tumbleweeds. I loved Harley's surprises. They were always crazy and fun and over-the-top. Knight was full of surprises, too. Surprises that ended in blood and/or tears being shed.

Suddenly feeling inspired to write, I grabbed one of the bills and smoothed it over the back of my thigh. Pulling the cap of the pen off with my teeth and spitting it across the room, I wrote in my own all-caps handwriting, right across the front, *FUCK YOU, KNIGHT.*

And *I LOVE HARLEY* across the back.

GEORGIA
CHAPTER 16
19 PEACH STATE 99

August 1998

When I'd decided to transfer to the local community college for eleventh grade so that I could double my credits and graduate from high school a year early, it sounded like a great idea. When I'd toured the campus and filled out my admission paperwork, it'd seemed new and exciting. I'd felt like a goddamn grown-up. But standing in the middle of the East Atlanta College parking lot, turning a map with at least fourteen different buildings on it upside down and right side up, trying to figure out where the Humanities department was, I began to have my doubts.

What the fuck even is *the Humanities department?* I thought as I stomped off in what I hoped was the right direction. *Aren't we all members of humanity? Are some of us more human than others? Do you have to be, like, extra human to get in? Are they gonna take a blood sample to check my DNA at the door?*

The first building I passed was labeled JULIUS C. WILCOX DEPARTMENT OF MATHEMATICS.

If math were my first period, I'd already be in class by now.

But it was too late to switch my schedule. For one, courses available to high schoolers were limited, so you kinda had to take what you could get. But I'd also kinda forced Juliet to enroll, and I might have sorta signed her up for all the same classes as me.

By the time I found my Psychology 101 classroom, I was one of the last people in the door. I spotted Juliet right away—in the back of the auditorium, where I'd known she would be. And she looked *incredible*. Her hair had been woven into dozens of long braids, Janet Jackson style, and her signature black eyeliner and penciled-on black eyebrows were back. She looked like her old self again. Only better somehow.

I made my way up the stairs and sat down in the seat she'd saved for me. Giving her a sympathetic smile, I asked, "How you doin', hon?"

Juliet had left Romeo in the college's on-site daycare that morning. It was her first time being away from him since he was born, which was going on three months. I'd expected her to be a little emotional. I had *not* expected her face to split open in a megawatt grin.

"I'm fucking awesome. I feel like a person again, BB. Like an actual human, not just some disgusting, smooshy milk machine."

"But do you feel *extra* human?" I grinned, beyond relieved that she was having a great first day. "I have this theory that to get into the Humanities department you have to be, like, extra human."

"Oh yeah," she said with that classic Juliet sarcasm. "I'm *sooo* extra."

Just then a girl about our age sat next to me in the one remaining seat on our row. She looked like a Caucasian version of Juliet. Long black hair, eyes rimmed in black liner, but alabaster skin, like she hadn't seen the sun all summer. And the black baby-doll dress she was wearing made her look like Wednesday Addams.

"Hey," she said, her voice as monotone as Juliet's was sarcastic.

"Hey," I chirped. "I'm BB. This is Juliet."

Juliet gave a half-smile and a chin nod, trying to look like a badass. She was terrible at making girl friends. Or guy friends, for that matter.

"I'm Victoria," Goth Girl said.

"Which high school did you transfer from?" I flicked my thumb back and forth between myself and Juliet. "We're from Peach State. Couldn't get out of that hellhole fast enough."

"Central."

Juliet and I both recoiled and gasped in unison. Central High had a reputation for being even worse than Peach State. The joke was that you didn't graduate from Central; you got paroled.

"Do you guys know where I can buy some weed around here?" Goth Girl asked.

I liked her. She didn't beat around the bush.

"No, but my boyfriend would probably sell you some," I said. *Considering that he might, in fact, be a drug dealer,* I added in my head.

"I'm going over to his house after school if you want to come. It's his birthday, so I'm sure there will be plenty of weed to go around."

Goth Girl shrugged and kind of nodded, so I took that as a yes.

Turning to Juliet, I asked, "You wanna come, too, now that you're a person again?"

"Nah, I probably shouldn't take my baby to a drug deal, but thanks anyway." Juliet smiled and rolled her eyes, but I could hear a hint of bitterness in her voice. She totally wanted to come. Poor thing.

The day went by in a blur of syllabi, scribbled notes, and the sound of my own voice chanting, *I can't believe I'm in college. I can't believe I'm in fucking college*, over and over in my head.

I'd been dying to go to college since middle school. No tardy bells. No bullies. No bullshit. You choose your own schedule, show up wearing whatever the fuck you want, do the work, and go home. For somebody who loved school but hated rules, college was a dream come true.

Juliet, Goth Girl, and I made a pretty good team, too. Juliet's bossy ass took over map and time management duties. I listened and took notes during class. And Goth Girl scoped out the social scene, determining who the cool kids were and where they hung out between classes. We looked like a bad joke—*So a goth chick, a punk chick, and Janet Jackson circa* Poetic Justice *walk into a bar…stop me if you've heard this one before*—but we felt like rock stars.

With my first day of college under my belt and a new friend following me in her hand-me-down Buick LeSabre, I sped over to the birthday boy's house to celebrate.

Instead of pulling around to the backyard, like I'd intended, I slammed it into park the second I spotted Harley and Dave in the front yard. Goth Girl almost rear-ended me, but I had to stop. The scene was just too fucking ridiculous.

The James brothers were sitting in a couple of rusty old lawn chairs under a pine tree with their bare feet submerged in a kiddie pool. They had on matching spring-break-style airbrushed T-shirts that said, *Picture Me Rolling*, with a pair of dice on the front. Matching cheap plastic sunglasses. And they were each holding a beer in one hand and a tiny battery-powered fan in the other. But the best part was the patch of sand haphazardly dumped on the grass with an inflatable palm tree sticking out of it a few feet away from Harley.

Yanking my key out of the ignition, I threw open my car door and ran out into the yard. "What the fuck are you guys doing?" I cackled.

"It's my birthday present." Harley beamed, spreading his arms and sloshing his Natty Ice as he gestured at the fever dream before me.

Dave smiled and chimed in, "I figured, if we can't go to the beach, we'll just bring the beach to us."

"Why can't you go to the beach?" Goth Girl's deadpan drawl came from somewhere to my right.

I turned to look at her and had to shield my eyes. The sun reflected off her pallid skin worse than a *Twilight* vampire.

Harley and Dave traded glances as some silent understanding passed between them. I didn't like it. It felt like they were speaking in some kind of telepathic twin language that I didn't comprehend. Dave eventually gestured toward Harley, inviting him to answer Goth Girl's question.

I expected Harley to drop some bomb, based on the way they were acting, but instead he just quipped, "Because *Davidson* here is too fuckin' poor."

"Fuck you," Dave spat, splashing his brother with baby-pool water.

Harley laughed and shook the shit out of his beer, spraying foamy Natural Ice at Dave like a fire hose.

Turning to Goth Girl, I smiled and said, "Victoria, meet Harley and Davidson."

I expected Goth Girl to arch an eyebrow and act too cool for school, but instead she half-smiled and looked at Dave, whom I noticed was half-smiling right back.

"I go by Dave," he said, standing up and wiping the beer suds off his white wifebeater as he plastered on his best Southern charm.

Fucker even took off his hat as he walked over. He never took off his hat for me. Goth Girl tentatively accepted his out-stretched hand. Instead of shaking it, like a normal person, Dave lifted her hand to his lips and kissed the back of it. I rolled my eyes so hard I thought I might pop a blood vessel.

"It's nice to meet you, *Victoria*."

"I go by VV."

She didn't tell me that.

"No shit?" Dave turned around and shouted at Harley, "Hey man, we got a VV *and* a BB now."

Whatever. I am not *calling her that.*

Harley gestured for me to come over, so I went and sat on his lap, leaving the two lovebirds alone.

"How was school, lady?" Harley asked, planting a kiss on my temple.

I took a swig from his beer and told him all about it, using big hand gestures and zero pauses. Harley smiled as I rambled. I couldn't tell if he was just happy for me or if he was amused by my manic enthusiasm, but either way, that smile was sexy. My eyes dropped to Harley's lip ring. With my ass on his lap and his mouth that close to mine, I really wished we didn't have company.

When I was done telling my story, Harley clapped his big, oil-stained hand on my thigh and said, "That's it. We're having a party. *You* just started college, it's *my* motherfuckin' birthday, and hell, *Dave* might even get laid tonight."

We both laughed and glanced over at Dave and Goth Girl, who were smiling from ear to ear at each other. That was the first time I'd seen Goth Girl smile. She was actually really pretty. Great teeth. That black lipstick made them look super white. Even whiter than her skin, if that was possible.

"Hey, *Davidson*," Harley chided. He loved watching Dave bristle whenever he said his full name. *Especially* in front of a girl. "You wanna throw a rager tonight?"

"Hell yeah," Dave said, never taking his eyes off my new friend.

"Good, because I went ahead and picked up some party favors." Harley shifted my weight and reached into one of his front pockets, retrieving a tiny Ziploc baggie with half a dozen white pills inside.

"What are those?" I asked quietly, my eyes wide.

"Ecstasy," Harley replied. "You ever tried it?"

"Mmhmm," I mumbled as the memory pulled me backward in time, from the light of day to the dark, strobing bowels of Sin—a fetish club that I'd had no business being in at the age of fifteen.

I was right back there, crawling through a sea of leather-clad sadists and rubber-clad masochists again, frantically trying to escape their grabby hands and gyrating hips. My stomach churned, preparing to reject the white pill with the lightning bolt on it that Juliet's boyfriend had said would help me "stay awake." I remembered the smell of the dumpsters as I burst through an exit door and landed on my hands and knees in the alley. I remembered the skinhead who'd carried me into his tattoo shop and force-fed me and talked to me about art and smoked with me on the fire escape and took care of me while I came down from my high. I also remembered how badly I'd wanted to touch him even though I knew I should be afraid. How the white pill had made me want to dance and scream and strip off my clothes.

Harley's voice brought me back into the light. "It'll take a little while to kick in, so we should dose now. You in?"

I looked up at Harley, which was a mistake because he was giving me those goddamn puppy-dog eyes he knew I couldn't resist.

Leaning in closer, he whispered, "It'll be fun," as he slid his rough hand up my bare thigh.

There was no mistaking the innuendo in his voice or denying that I wanted whatever fun he was offering.

Nodding, I held out my hand, which was quickly joined by two others—Dave's and Goth Girl's. Harley dropped a Tylenol-shaped pill with a tiny *CK* logo stamped on the top into each of our palms.

"Calvin Klein is making ecstasy now?" I giggled, holding the pill up in front of my face. "Will it make me smell like CK One, too?"

"I fuckin' hope not," Dave said with a wink as he popped his into his mouth and chased it with a swig of beer.

He offered the can to Goth Girl, but she waved him off and swallowed it dry.

"Oh, shit! It's like *that* at Central High, huh?" I teased.

Goth Girl shrugged like it was no big deal, but that little half-smile told me she felt like a badass.

Harley and I took ours at the same time—me chasing the

bitter-tasting pill with what was left of Harley's equally disgusting Natty Ice.

"So," I said, clapping my hands together as soon as I was sure I wasn't going to barf, "what now?"

"Now," Harley said with a grin, "we prep."

———————

Prepping for a party at the James house involved Dave picking up a keg in his truck, Harley calling everybody in his phone, and Goth Girl and me going to buy luau supplies. We figured, with the inflatable palm tree in the front yard, we might as well keep the theme going. You'd be amazed at how many plastic leis, grass table skirts, and tiki torches you can buy for under twenty bucks at Walmart.

There was a moment, after Dave's redneck friends and the rockabilly crew from the track started showing up, that Goth Girl and I just looked at each other and burst out laughing. We were all grinding teeth and dilated pupils, having the time of our fucking lives.

I couldn't believe I'd just met her that day. Maybe it was the ecstasy talking, but I felt like I'd known Victoria my whole life. She didn't say much, but when she did talk, it was dry and ballsy and exactly what everybody else in the room was thinking. She was cool as hell, man.

I introduced her to the people I knew, which I'd expected to be like three dudes but turned out to be almost everyone at the party. My relationship with Harley was still pretty new, but between hanging out at the shop while he tuned up my car, going with him to a couple of races, and bumping into some of Dave's redneck buddies here and there, I'd managed to meet most of their friends in just under two months. That made me feel pretty fucking amazing. And I was already feeling pretty fucking amazing, thanks to Calvin Klein and his designer MDMA.

Once we'd made the rounds, Goth Girl and I headed to the back porch, where Harley and Dave were sharing a joint with Bubba and JR by the keg. Harley pulled me into his side, somehow maintaining his chill despite having a head full of ecstasy, beer, and weed. I, on the other hand, was practically jogging in place. A few other people trickled outside, and the next thing I knew Harley was bragging to the entire peanut gallery about how Goth Girl and I had just started college that day. I mean, technically, I was still a high schooler, at least for the next year, but I wasn't about to correct him. His version made me sound so much older.

"So, whadda you wanna be when you grow up?" Bubba asked, spitting a black loogie into a beer can.

"Well, I'm going to school for psychology," I said, trying to pick one of the three floating Bubbas to focus on, "but I kinda wanna be a showgirl, too."

"No shit? Like in Las Vegas? With the"—Bubba gestured above my head—"feathers and all?"

"Yep!"

"You got any moves?" Dave interrupted, pointing his red plastic cup at me. The side of it was mangled, like he'd been chewing on it, and his pupils were so big, it looked like he was wearing black contact lenses.

"Fuck yeah," I said, swaying on my feet as I listed my accomplishments on my fingers. "I can do the high kick. I can do the...hip roll. I can do the...bra-tassel-shimmy thing. I don't have the boobs to make the tassels go in two different directions at the same time, but once I get some implants, it's fucking *on*. Just you wait and see."

Harley's hand slipped under my tank top as his hot, beer-and-cigarette-scented breath hissed in my ear, "I don't wanna wait." His voice sounded rich, layered, as if someone had recorded him saying the same sentence three times then played all three tracks simultaneously.

My eyes closed as my skin ignited in desire. That simple touch felt like it sank through every layer of flesh and muscle and massaged my very bones. I felt completely enveloped by his aura—usually so cool, now warm as a crackling fire. If that man wanted a show, I'd give him a goddamn show. Hell, I would've sawed a bitch in half if he'd asked me to.

Looking up into Harley's blackened irises, I felt tethered to him somehow. Like our arms had wound around each other and into each other and through each other until there was no *other* anymore. There was only *us*.

"You're the birthday boy," I cooed, my voice husky and full of promise.

"Wait. What? BB's strippin'?!" Dave yelled, drawing the attention of everyone on the porch. "I'll get the black light ready!" As he took off for the door, Dave snatched up both me and Goth Girl and dragged us along.

"What the fuck, man?" Harley asked, sounding more amused than angry.

"BB's gotta rehearse, damn it!"

I heard a Solo cup crash into the sliding door just as Dave pulled it shut behind us. Goth Girl and I giggled and tripped over our own feet as Dave tugged us down the hall and into his bedroom. I'd never been in there before, but as soon as he flipped a switch on the wall, it all made sense. A black light, strobe light, disco ball, and boom box playing Ginuwine all roared to life, transforming the drab bachelor pad into a tiny little strip club. The only thing missing was a pole and a DJ booth.

"What kinda girls are you bringin' home, Dave?" I teased, poking him in the ribs.

When Dave glanced over at Goth Girl, I suddenly wanted to eat my words.

"None lately," he admitted, holding her gaze. Then, looking at me, he added, "I just do a shitload of drugs."

We laughed until Dave locked the door behind us and started digging in his closet.

"Uh, Dave?" I asked, dodging an adult-sized kangaroo costume as it went flying across the room. "Whatcha doing?"

"Lookin' for props, dummy. Here, wear this," Dave said, tossing a white feather boa at me.

In the black light, it looked like a fluorescent-purple man-eating caterpillar was flying toward me, so I screamed and karate-chopped it to the ground like a fucking ninja.

As I stomped on it to make sure it was dead, Goth Girl hooked a finger into the neck of my tank top and peeked inside. "She has on a white bra!"

Awesome. Now they're both playing costume designer.

"What color is her underwear?" Dave asked, rummaging through his dresser drawers.

Goth Girl tugged at the waistband of my cutoff shorts. "I don't know, but it has white hearts on it!"

"Good enough," Dave said, tossing condoms and rolling papers and sock balls over his shoulder. Then, slamming the last drawer shut, Dave turned around and grinned in triumph. His teeth glowed in the black light, then disappeared, then reappeared—twenty-four times per second, thanks to the strobe light. He thrust a yellow highlighter into the air above his head, as if it were fucking Excalibur. "Ladies, this shit just went to the next level."

Ten minutes later, I was hiding in the closet, wearing nothing but my bra and panties, a white feather boa, and a shitload of fluorescent body art. Neither Goth Girl nor Dave had any artistic ability, so I'd had to write *HAPPY BIRTHDAY, HARLEY* on my own stomach, backward, while rolling. It could have said *HAPPY HANUKKAH, GRANDMA*, for all anyone cared. We were all speaking the same fucked-up language at that point.

I heard the trippy, sultry sounds of Outkast's "ATLiens" come on just as Dave's Southern drawl boomed over the music.

"Laaaaadies and asshoooooles! It's the moment you've all been waiting for! Here, for your birthday pleasure, is the one, the only Baaaaambi Boooooty Clap!"

Bambi Booty Clap? Jesus, Dave. No pressure or anything.

As soon as André 3000 started rapping, I burst out of the closet to find Harley sitting on the end of Dave's bed, grinning like a damn fool, and Dave and Goth Girl sitting with their backs against his headboard, totally making out. I actually appreciated the fact that two-thirds of my audience weren't even paying attention. It helped me loosen up and focus on the one audience member who really mattered. My guy. My hero. My motherfucking savior, Harley James.

We might as well have been the only two people on Neptune. Nothing was familiar, except the connection I felt to the man staring at me with glowing eyes and teeth. The light made things look otherworldly. The rapid blinking made time feel like it was moving in slow motion. The bass in the song made the ground feel like it might crumble beneath us. So why not fucking dance?

I held Harley's gaze as I rocked my hips from side to side and slid my hands over the places where curves should have been. Unclasping my five-pound water bra, I let it slide down my arms, then playfully tossed it at Harley's face. Luckily, my aim was shit; otherwise, he probably would have ended up with a black eye.

I stepped toward him as I swayed to the beat, looping my boa around his neck once he was within arm's reach. Giving him a chaste kiss, I quickly spun around and rubbed my ass on his crotch, like I'd seen Elizabeth Berkley do in the movie *Showgirls* when it came on HBO late at night.

Harley's hands grazed my thighs as his fingers tugged at the sides of my panties. I swatted them away and took a step forward, watching him over my shoulder as I bent at the waist and slid my last remaining article of clothing down my legs.

Completely naked, I twerked a little—popping my hips like Craig had shown me how to do during our closing-time dance parties. When I turned back around, I propped one foot up on the bed next to Harley and rolled my hips like nobody was watching. It was just me, the beat, and the man blinking in and out of existence before me. The man whose big hands were pulling me closer. The man whose lap I was climbing onto. The man who was unbuckling his belt.

When I felt flesh against my flesh, my eyes popped open. We weren't alone on Neptune. We were in Dave's bedroom. I was naked, Harley had his cock out, and we had an audience.

Over Harley's shoulder, I saw Dave and Goth Girl watching us with hooded lids and gaping, hungry mouths. I froze and clung to Harley's shoulders, suddenly feeling all-too-exposed. Letting Dave watch was one thing, but Goth Girl?

Three is a party. Four is a crowd.

Harley must have sensed my apprehension because he stood up—with me still wrapped around him like a spider monkey—and growled, "Show's over."

Carrying me out the door and across the hall to his room, Harley kicked the door shut and tossed me onto his mattress, which is where we remained for the next few hours while Harley showed me *exactly* why they called that little white pill *ecstasy*.

When I finally stumbled out of that room—on shaky legs, cloaked in one of Harley's A&J Auto Body shirts with his name embroidered on the front—I crept over to Dave's room to get my clothes. I listened with my ear against the door to see if the coast was clear and heard the unmistakable sounds of skin slapping against skin and names being moaned, even over the thumping of Outkast, which was playing for the hundredth time in a row.

Laughing to myself, I made my way to the bathroom, not giving two fucks who saw me in Harley's shirt and no pants. As I peed, I realized that the laws of physics had returned. The lights behaved like normal lights. Nothing was strobing. The floor wasn't tilting. My brain wasn't being scrambled by booming bass and mind-blowing orgasms. It was just me, on the toilet, in a regular old bathroom, realizing that it was probably late as *fuuuuck*.

Like *late*, late. Like wherever-my-phone-was-it-probably-had-forty-seven-missed-calls-from-my-paranoid-father-and-one-from-the-local-police-station late.

I flushed and flew out of there, ignoring all the drunk rockabillies and rednecks between me and my purse.

When I pulled my phone out and mashed the buttons, nothing happened. No lights. No sounds. Dead.

Fuck!

Throwing my bag over my shoulder, I dashed over into the kitchen and peeked at the microwave, which I'd made sure was set to the correct time after my first little curfew fiasco at the James house. The red numbers didn't even make sense.

12:02, they said.

12:02.

No.

What?

No.

No, no, no, no, no, no, no.

Flying into Dave's room, not even bothering to knock, I scooped up all my clothes while simultaneously trying not to see, breathe, hear, or touch anything in the direction of the bed. I dashed back into Harley's room, where he was lounging on his back in all his naked male glory, puffing on a cigarette and blowing smoke rings into the air. I shimmied back into my shorts and tank top. Then I shoved my feet into my unlaced boots. I didn't have time to admire him. I didn't even have time to explain why I was fleeing—not that I needed to. Harley knew. He sat up and watched me prepare to meet my doom with sad, droopy blue eyes and arched brows—not because I was going to get in trouble, but because he didn't want me to go.

"I'm so fucked," I choked out, just before planting a quick good-bye kiss on his sex-swollen lips.

"Yeah you are," he teased.

His little joke didn't exactly lighten my mood. When was Harley going to realize that it wasn't fucking funny? That some people had fucking consequences when they broke the rules. That my ass was going to get straight-up handed to me in less than thirty minutes—that was, *if* I didn't wrap my car around a tree on the way home.

"Happy birthday," I grumbled on my way out the door.

It was nice knowing ya.

I thought I'd sobered up enough to drive home—until I hit the back roads. Every twist and turn had my empty stomach in upheaval. I remembered that particular brand of nausea. I'd felt the same exact way at Sin just before I fled the ocean of gyrating dominants and submissives and ended up on all fours, barfing in the alley.

As soon as I pulled into my driveway, I could feel the bile beginning to rise. The second my car was in park, I threw open my door, leaned out, and spewed a vile combination of keg beer and stomach acid all over the driveway. No skinheads came to my rescue that time. I was going to have to do this on my own.

As soon as my dad's shadow fell over me, I burst into a fit of tears and hiccups. What was he going to do to me? Would I be grounded forever? Would he take away my car? Public shaming? Tar and feathers?

"Shit, Scooter. Not you too," he said, in a voice that was the opposite of wrathful.

Huh?

I sat up and wiped my mouth on the back of my hand. Looking at my dad, all I saw was concern in his tired, bloodshot eyes.

"Your mother's been throwing up for hours. Must be food poisoning. I'll bet the mayo went bad. I don't know how you two eat that shit."

I just stared at him, unable to process what was happening. Was I not in trouble? Did I actually have food poisoning? No, that was ridiculous. You had to eat food to get food poisoning.

"Come on. Let's get you inside before the next wave hits," he said, extending a hand to help me out of the car. "You think you can handle Gatorade? I have the orange kind. You don't want to get dehydrated."

And that was it. Either my dad had been too busy tending to my legitimately sick mom to realize how late I was or he'd forgotten to care. Either way, my punishment never came.

At least, not that night.

It's amazing how common interests can bring people from different walks of life together. Like fast cars. And starting fires.

I don't know whose bright idea it was to build a bonfire in the middle of the track, but I'll be damned if every single faction didn't pitch in to help make that shit happen. The girls—gangsta, chola, rockabilly, and redneck—all gathered rocks from the edge of the woods to line the pit while the guys found tree branches to break over their knees and use as kindling. Bubba got a little too excited and yanked a pine tree right out of the fucking ground with his truck's winch.

Show-off.

Once the fire was ablaze, the truck owners all backed their tailgates up to the fire pit for people to sit on. Beers were drunk. Mosquitoes were slapped. The sun went down. The music—a different genre blaring out of every aftermarket stereo—grew louder, and engines began to rev. It was race time.

Harley and I were sitting on Bubba's tailgate, happy as a couple of pigs in shit, when he gave me a peck on the lips and said he'd be right back. I'd been to enough races by then to know what that meant. Harley was going to go hustle.

So I lit a cigarette—my favorite go-to behavior whenever I had to be somewhere by myself—and tried my best to look cool yet approachable.

I'm not sitting here by myself like a loser. I'm smoking. It's a totally different thing.

Just as I was considering lighting a new cigarette with the butt of my current one, a girl walked over and hopped up next to me—which was no small feat, given the lift kit on Bubba's truck.

This chick looked like an old-school calendar girl. Her blonde hair was pinned in victory rolls and tied with a cute little blue-and-white bandana. Her curves were accentuated by a blue-and-white-checkered halter top and pair of red high-waisted shorts. And she was wearing bright-red lipstick. Bitch looked like the Fourth of July, and sitting next to her made me feel like April 15—fucking Tax Day.

"Hey," she said, giving me the smile of a spokesmodel. "This is going to sound really weird, but did you used to date a tattoo artist named Knight?"

I glanced around to make sure Harley wasn't within earshot. Knight wasn't exactly his favorite subject. Or mine. Happily, the insanity of starting a new school, keeping up with a college-level course load, working part-time, and seeing Harley every chance I got had kept my mind pretty busy. Until Miss July showed up, I probably hadn't thought about Knight for, like, five whole minutes.

"Yep, that's me," I answered hesitantly. "Why do you ask?"

Miss July's face brightened, if that was possible. "I knew it! I rec-ognized you from the photo on his tattoo station. I stared at that damn thing for, like, three hours while he did my thigh piece."

She laughed, shifting her weight so that I could get a better look at the outline of skulls and roses etched onto her leg. It was definitely Knight's work.

"I'm Tracey." She beamed, offering me her red-tipped fingers.

I accepted her outstretched hand and cringed inwardly, knowing exactly what was going to come next.

"Damn, honey! Your hand feels like a little ice cube!"

There it is.

I gave her a lackluster smile and snatched my cadaverous hand back. "Yeah, I get that a lot."

"You are sittin' by a fire in the middle of August, girl! You need to put some meat on your bones!"

I rolled my eyes. "I get that a lot, too." I didn't mean to be rude, but my weight was yet another subject that I didn't exactly feel like discussing with a stranger.

So far, Miss July was batting oh for two.

"Sorry, hon. I didn't mean—"

"No, it's fine. That's a beautiful tattoo," I interrupted, point-ing at her thigh and successfully changing the subject.

It really was. Just like him, Knight's art had a very distinctive style—intense, complex, and dangerous.

"Right? He drew it himself. I had an appointment set up for him to fill in the color, but the shop owner called and canceled it. All she said was that he joined the service." Tracey gave me a sad, sympathetic smile. "I hate to ask—I mean, you're obvi-ously with Harley now—but . . . do you know when Knight will be back? I don't want somebody else to touch his work, but at the same time, I don't want to walk around with a half-finished tattoo forever either."

I sighed as I stared back at yet another girl left in the lurch when Knight disappeared. Another girl left incomplete. Searching for answers. Wondering whether or not to move on.

"If I were you," I said, plucking another cigarette out of my pack, "I'd move on."

Tracey's perfectly penciled eyebrows shot up. That was not the answer she wanted to hear.

"Sorry," I said, lighting my Camel Light and blowing the smoke toward the fire. Smoking wasn't just my favorite sitting-alone behavior; it was my favorite difficult-conversation behavior as well. "But I don't think he's coming back. At least, not for good. Knight told me he was shipping off to Iraq right after basic training, and knowing his stubborn ass, he'll probably stay there until they kick him out."

"Really?"

I nodded and watched as the delicate stream of smoke I'd just exhaled floated over and joined forces with the gray cloud billowing up from the bonfire. Looking back at Tracey, I offered her my open pack. With slumped shoulders, she helped herself to a cigarette.

"You could have Bobbi do it," I offered, not wanting to be such a buzzkill. "She does incredible work. She did a back piece for Knight that looks just like his style."

"Yeah, maybe I'll do that," she said.

"Sorry." I shrugged. "Getting fucked over is just part of the Ronald McKnight experience."

"Don't be sorry," Tracey said, pulling her Miss July smile

back on. "You're the only person who's been able to tell me what the hell is going on. Thank you."

I faked a smile right back.

I saw Harley approaching from the other side of the bonfire. God, I loved to watch that man walk. Purposeful strides, long legs, chain wallet glinting in the glow of the fire. Harley's mischievous blue eyes were glued to me as he advanced, and his pursed, pierced lips were pulled into a smirk.

Uh-oh.

As soon as Harley rounded the bonfire, he pointed at me, then jerked his thumb over his shoulder. "You're up."

I blinked. "What do you mean, *I'm up*?"

Harley kept the serious act going, but the tug at the corner of his mouth told me there was a joke that I wasn't in on quite yet.

"I mean, you're up next, woman. You're racing tonight. Go get the 'Stang and meet me at the starting line."

My surprised exhale came out as a laugh. "No. What? No. I'm not *racing*. Here," I said, digging my keys out of my front pocket and holding them out as far away from me as possible, "you do it."

Harley shook his head at me. "Nope. Not tonight, pretty lady. We've got a newbie here who needs a warm welcome."

I gave Harley the side eye. "Are you trying to say you want me to lose?"

"I want you to make sure he leaves with a smile on his face." Stepping between my legs, Harley placed his hands on my hips and dropped his forehead to mine. "I *know* you can do that."

Rolling my eyes, I looked over at Tracey, who was absolutely no help. She simply grimaced and shrugged in the universal sign for, *I can't help you.*

Harley took advantage of my head turn by forging a trail of kisses from my earlobe to my collarbone.

Groaning, I acquiesced. "Okay, fine. But only because I get to lose."

"You don't *get to lose*," Harley whispered in my ear. "Between the mods I made and the way you've been practicing, you could easily take this guy. He's in a Turbo, so I'm gonna need you to back off the gas in the turns enough to let him stay ahead. Homeboy has deep pockets, so if we play this right we'll be able to take him for twice as much later."

I hated the idea of *playing* someone, but that was the game. Everybody on the field was either winning, losing, or watching, and they loved every second of it. Who was I to judge?

Hopping off Bubba's tailgate, I told Tracey to wish me luck and headed over to my car with a bowling ball in my gut. I drove about two miles per hour as I made my way around the track to the starting line, stalling as long as humanly possible. I don't know why I was so anxious. Harley hadn't just given me permission to lose; he'd commissioned it. The pressure was off. But pulling up next to a tricked-out Toyota Supra Turbo with a spoiler the same size and shape as the Golden Gate Bridge didn't exactly calm my nerves.

Harley was waiting for me, just like he'd said he would be. I rolled down my window to talk to him and was immediately assaulted by the roar of the crowd. Who were they cheering for? Probably not the new guy, so that only left me. But I was there to lose. The idea of disappointing Harley's people, *my* people, made me feel even more nauseous.

Harley leaned in through my open window and gave me a kiss. "Now don't you go winning on me, okay?"

That one made me laugh out loud. "Yeah, okay. I'll try."

Yeah fucking right.

"I'm calling this one, so as soon as you see my hands drop, stomp on it. You'll probably get the jump on him, so remember what I said, and take it easy through the turns to let him stay ahead."

I nodded and tried not to roll my eyes. The fact that Harley thought I needed encouragement to *take it easy through the turns* was adorable. I needed encouragement not to get completely fucking lapped.

As soon as Harley took his spot on the white *X*, my stomach churned out a fresh batch of stomach acid.

Oh fuck. Here we go.

Harley squinted into our headlights and held up two fingers.

Two laps.

I lowered my parking brake.

Harley put his hands up.

I took my left foot off the brake and gave the gas pedal a tiny bit of pressure while the clutch was still pushed in, watching the RPMs rise slowly, just like he'd taught me.

When Harley's hands dropped, I stomped the gas the rest of the way down and popped my left foot off the clutch at the same time. Harley was right. I definitely got the jump on him. In fact, I think I went fucking airborne for a second.

My head slammed back into the headrest as I struggled to maintain control of The Little Five-Oh That Could. I don't know what the fuck Harley had done to my car, but whatever it was, that shit worked. I was already entering the first turn.

With my adrenaline surging and my brain doing nothing but repeating, *Oh shit, oh shit, oh shit,* on a loop, my body reverted to muscle memory. Without thinking, I did exactly what Harley and I had been practicing. What I'd done a thousand times on that same track, only in the daylight and with an audience of one. I eased off the gas through the turn, prayed to Jesus that my tires didn't skid or spin out, resisted the urge to downshift, and gassed it once the straightaway was in sight.

Elated that I'd made it through the first turn alive, I punched it and threw it into third before the realization of what I'd just done hit home. Glancing in my rearview mirror, I saw the shiny white Supra—a good four to five car lengths behind me.

Fucking hell.

There was no coming back from that. Not when I was already pulling into the second turn. The way I saw it, I had three choices.

1. Fake a mechanical problem, which would require lying skills that I did not possess.
2. Slow down enough to let him pass me, in which case I might as well hire a skywriter to fly overhead and write, BB THREW THE RACE, in smoky cursive.
3. Win and fuck up Harley's master plan.

Looking in my rearview mirror again, it became more evident that I didn't really have a choice. I was already back on the straights, and Homeboy was just pulling into the second turn.

I eased off the gas a little, just to keep it from being a landslide, but as soon as Supra Man started to catch up, I lost him again in the third turn.

"Goddamn it!" I screamed at him from inside my car. "It's like you're not even trying! Do better, asshole!"

Before I knew it, I'd rounded curve number four and crossed the finish line. Just like that. Boom. Failure. I had one job to do, and I'd fucked it up. I mean, seriously, how hard is it to *not* win at something? Especially something that you're not even good at.

I did the saddest victory lap in history and pulled up next to Harley, who was waiting for me at the starting line—looking positively pissed off.

Shit. Shit, shit, shit.

The only other time I'd seen him that pissed off was when he'd found out that I used to date Knight, but this was scarier because, this time, he was mad at *me*. I had no idea what the ripple effect would be from my fuckup, but I was sure it would be pretty bad. Harley always had these little hustles planned out so that every domino would fall exactly the way he wanted. Well, my domino didn't fucking fall at all, so now what?

I took a deep breath and opened my car door, but Harley was gone. When I stood up, the noises coming from the crowd were an odd mixture of excited and infuriated. Unless Supra Man had a cheering section I didn't know about, those jeers were for me. From *my* people.

A thick hand grabbed me by the elbow and spun me around. It was Harley, and he was staring at me with an unreadable expression.

Holding up two fingers with a wad of cash pinched between them, Harley said, "Here's your winnings, Speed Racer."

When I didn't take the money, Harley shoved it into the front pocket of my ripped jeans, then turned toward the crowd and waved a cluster of rednecks over. When he faced me again, his scowl had been replaced by my favorite twinkly-eyed, naughty grin.

"And here's *my* winnings."

One by one, the hillbilly truck enthusiasts lined up to smack their bitter dollar bills—tens, twenties, even a few hundreds—down on Harley's open palm.

He chuckled and talked shit the whole time, calling them "sexist assholes" and telling them, "That's what y'all get for betting against a lady."

Bubba was last in line.

Harley tsk-tsked him with a smile and said, "I think you owe BB an apology."

Bubba looked at me with shame and sincerity in his dark brown eyes. "I'm sorry. You won the shit outta that race, girl. You oughta be real proud."

As Bubba walked off with his floppy fishing hat in his hands, I stared at Harley with my mouth hanging open and my eyebrows pulled together.

"What...the fuck...just happened?"

"You just made us a shitload of money; that's what happened." Harley smiled and bopped me on the end of my scrunched-up nose with his index finger.

"You *wanted* me to win?" I didn't know whether to be pissed off or impressed.

"No, I *knew* you'd win. Especially against that dumbass." Harley flicked his chin in the direction of the highway, which was the direction Supra Man had run off in after his loss. "Not only was that thing an *automatic*," Harley said the word as if it personally offended him, "but it also had a couple of heavy-ass subwoofers in the back. That motherfucker was just beggin' to give somebody his money. Might as well be you."

Harley's smile was infectious. I couldn't be mad at him when he looked at me like that.

"You fucking played me!" I laughed, jabbing a finger into his chest.

"Nah, I just didn't want you to be nervous."

"You took side bets against me!" I smacked him on the chest that time.

"Hey!" Harley grinned and held his hands up in surrender. "I was the one who bet *on* you, okay?"

It was the truth. Time stood still for a moment while the weight of that statement sank in. Harley was the only one who had bet on me. He'd believed in me when no one else had. He'd believed in me more than I believed in myself. He'd believed in me enough to risk losing hundreds, possibly thousands, of dollars.

And he also believed in me enough to risk looking like a jackass in front of the very people who worshipped him, which is exactly what happened when he dropped to one knee and asked me to marry him right there on the track.

And I said, "No," with a smile on my face, a stack of hundreds in my pocket, and my first win under my belt.

It was the first cool, overcast day in what felt like years. Harley had come to see me on my lunch break, and he was wearing a busted old leather motorcycle jacket that conformed to his firm body like a layer of molten sex. It was so effortlessly chic that I wanted to kiss him and throw paint on him, all at the same time. It wasn't fair. How did he always look so fucking James Dean with literally zero effort?

I, on the other hand, had on a shiny new maroon flight jacket that I'd bought at Trash the night before—basically, the second the cold snap had hit. Of course, I did have a much cooler, much more authentic Army-green one at home, but considering that I couldn't even look at it without hyperventilating, shiny new maroon would have to do.

As the wind whipped through the Pier One Imports parking lot, I shivered and zipped my new frock up to my neck.

"Goddamn, it's cold." I stamped out my cigarette and wriggled into Harley's arms. "It's fucking August. What the shit?"

Rubbing my back over the slick surface of my jacket, Harley rested his chin on the top of my head and chuckled. "It's not cold; *you're* cold. I'm starting to think you only love me for my body heat."

" 'You only love me when you want punani,' " I teased back, quoting an old reggae song.

Harley had tossed the *L* word around here and there, but until he said it for real—with an *I* before it and a *you* after it—it didn't count. I'd accepted the fact that Harley James didn't take anything seriously. I was actually great with it. I'd had enough serious for one lifetime.

But, evidently, *serious* hadn't had enough of me.

My soul registered the vibration before the rumble was even audible. My breathing ceased. My ears perked up. My back went rigid in Harley's embrace. And then I heard it, on the wind.

The sound of my doom.

I looked up at Harley with pleading eyes as the growl built in the distance. I don't even know what I wanted him to do. Run? Save himself? Save me? Get angry and morph into The Incredible Hulk? Whatever it was, he was going to have to do it soon because the roar of Knight's engine was only getting louder.

When Harley's eyes broke away from mine and darted over my shoulder, I knew it was too late. We'd been spotted. And we were all gonna die.

I stood, bolted to the ground, and watched in horror as Harley casually flicked his cigarette butt into the middle of the parking lot. Then he turned around, seemingly unconcerned that we had but seconds to live, and unlocked his trunk. When the lid opened, I realized exactly why Harley was so goddamn relaxed. I also finally found out what the fuck he'd been hiding in his trunk all that time.

Harley had been driving around with a motherfucking

arsenal back there—handguns, sawed-off shotguns, rifles, revolvers, laser scopes, and boxes upon boxes of ammo.

I wasn't dating a mechanic. I was dating motherfucking Batman.

My head swiveled from left to right as I alternated between watching Knight barrel down on us at a speed that made me think he might just run us over and be done with it and watching Harley as he picked up an oil-stained rag and used it to grip the handle of a small black handgun. Careful not to leave fingerprints, Harley ejected the clip, checked to make sure that it was loaded, then popped it back in with a bloodcurdling *click*.

Knight lurched his Frankentruck up onto a flowerbed a few feet away just as Harley shoved the handgun into the pocket of his leather jacket—cool as a motherfucking cucumber—and closed the lid on what looked like a zombie apocalypse survival kit.

When Knight rounded the back of his truck, he looked ready to go full-on Skeletor. His undead eyes were almost clear in the overcast light. His nostrils flared. His teeth gnashed. And his camo pants and plain black T-shirt were stretched taut over muscles swollen from grueling daily boot camp workouts.

I waited for the fear to kick in—the physiological response that always gripped me whenever I was in Knight's presence. The tightness that seized my throat and squeezed my lungs, the sweating, the racing heart. But it wasn't there.

I wasn't there.

Harley tucked me into his side and thrust the gun in his pocket toward Knight. "That's close enough, jarhead."

Knight stopped, curling his lip into a sneer and tilting his head to one side, appraising Harley. "You think you're the only one here with a piece?" His voice was deep and clear and almost sounded amused.

I should definitely feel scared right now. This is weird.

"Doesn't matter. Whatever you got, it's prob'ly government-issued. Fingerprints and serial numbers *all* up on that shit." Harley sucked his teeth, making a *tsk* sound. "Be a pity for you to get dishonorably discharged before you even got to kill your first A-rab, wouldn't it, you fuckin' racist?"

Why can't I feel my feelings? Am I broken?

Knight's eyes flared. "Be a pity for you to go back to being somebody's bitch in jail, wouldn't it? Shooting a Marine in broad daylight?" Knight shook his head. "With your priors, you'd get fuckin' life."

Shit. It's starting to sprinkle. If I don't go inside soon, my bangs are gonna curl up.

Harley shrugged. "Like I said, doesn't matter because you're gonna turn around, get back in your redneck mobile, and go the fuck back to wherever you came from." Harley gestured toward the white monstrosity before us with the barrel of his pocketed gun. "But know this. If you come around my lady again, I *will* fucking end you. I'd be doing the whole fuckin' world a favor. I know what you are, what you do to girls. I know how you like to carve 'em up for kicks, you sick fuck."

I wonder what time it is. I bet my break is almost over.

Knight took two strides forward and jammed a finger into Harley's chest. "You don't know shit about me! Or her!" His finger swung from Harley to me. "If you did, then you'd know that she fucking likes it!"

Huh? What did I miss? Why is Knight pointing at me?

Harley let go of my shoulders and took a step forward so that he was nose-to-nose with Knight. "Say that shit again."

Knight sneered. "If you knew shit about her, you'd know she has *my* fucking name tattooed on her finger."

Actually, it's almost gone now.

Harley puffed up his chest, breathing audibly through his nose and holding Knight's stare.

Knight grinned and poked Harley one more time. "If you knew shit about BB, you'd know that she's still fucking *me*."

Um, what now?

Harley's hand flew, smashing Knight across the face with the side of the gun. As his head pivoted to the side on impact, red droplets sprayed out, dancing with the clear ones falling from the sky. Knight turned his face back to Harley and smiled, blood coating his perfect white teeth. He looked like a madman, especially when he tilted his head a few degrees to the left, which was when I knew shit was about to go sideways. Fast.

I watched from the safety of my disassociation bubble as Knight reared back and head-butted Harley directly between the eyes. Harley stumbled backward, bumping into me where I was still leaning against the back of his car.

That's weird. I can't feel my body either.

They were practically on top of me. All I could see were the crazed whites of Knight's eyes and the red smears across his teeth as he pulled his fist back and cocked Harley square in the jaw. Harley's body slumped against mine for just a moment, just long enough for me—and Knight—to think he was unconscious. Then he swung a nasty right hook and caught Knight directly in the temple.

Harley was still holding the gun, but he'd turned it around backward, gripping it like a roll of quarters to fortify his punch.

Man, Harley fights dirty.

Knight shook off the blow and grabbed Harley's gun arm, twisting it until I thought it was going to snap right off. Harley's face contorted into a grimace, and his knees buckled. As he sank toward the ground, Harley suddenly wrapped his free arm around Knight's thigh, yanked his leg off the ground, and used his body weight to pile-drive Knight backward into the asphalt.

Harley immediately pulled Knight into one of the Wrestle-Mania moves I'd seen him use on Dave—an Anaconda Vise or maybe a Killswitch?—but Knight got a hand between his neck and Harley's elbow, blocking the choke hold.

I wonder how much longer this is going to last. I don't want to get written up for being late. Again.

A guttural yell, followed by the sound of something clattering to the ground, caught my attention.

Harley.

Harley needed me. But I was gone. Where was I?

Focus, BB! What the fuck is wrong with you? Do something!

Through the rain, I could see Knight and Harley rolling around on the asphalt. At first, it looked like Harley had Knight in some kind of choke hold, but on second glance, I realized that Harley's forearm was over Knight's mouth, not his throat, and Knight was biting the shit out of it.

Harley grunted in pain and repeatedly slugged Knight in the side of the head with his free hand, but it didn't matter. Knight was a human pit bull. Once he locked on to something, it took an act of God to make him let go.

Or maybe a gun.

Like the one at my feet.

I leaned over and picked up the black 9mm, as if it were some alien apparatus that I had to figure out how to activate. I knew how to shoot it. I'd shot cans off the fence post in our backyard with my dad a million times. I needed to figure out how to use it *without* shooting it.

I could wave it around in the air. Fire a warning shot. I could hit Knight with it, but that didn't exactly work out for Harley. Maybe I could just throw it at his head from here?

While I wrestled with the jammed gears in my head, I found out exactly what would make Knight let go of my boyfriend.

It wasn't a gun.

It was police sirens.

By the time I registered what was happening, Harley and Knight had just...vanished. One second, they were locked up like a human pretzel in the middle of the parking lot, and the next, I was being blasted from both sides by the exhaust from their massive V8 engines. When the toxic cloud lifted, I realized that I was alone, in a public place, in the rain, holding a Glock with the serial numbers filed off.

That now had my fingerprints on it.

In my mind, there was only one choice—shove that fucker in my pocket and get my ass back inside. The only problem with that plan was that my pockets weren't as big as Harley's, so the entire black handle stuck out like a neon sign that read, *PLEASE COME ARREST ME.*

As the police cruiser pulled into the parking lot behind me, I did what any outlaw in the movies would have done. I stuck a *loaded gun* into the waistband of my jeans, pulled my jacket down over it, and kept moving.

I held my breath and walked on eggshells toward the front of the store, terrified that I was going to accidentally blow off a foot or a kneecap or one of my labia. I could see my reflection in the floor-to-ceiling windows before me, but more importantly, I could see the reflection of the police cruiser as it pulled up behind me and slowed to a crawl. The officer had turned the siren off but kept his blue lights flashing.

What the fuck did that mean? Was I being pulled over?

I played dumb and kept walking. I was almost there. The sidewalk in front of the store would be mine in three, two...

As soon as I stepped up onto the curb, the police cruiser turned and slithered down the next lane over.

Oh thank motherfucking God.

Exhaling a strangled breath, I pulled open the front door and headed back into work—with a loaded 9mm in my pants.

I clocked back in at the cash register—eleven minutes late—grabbed my purse from one of the cabinets, and headed straight for the restroom.

I have no idea how long I sat on that toilet. Maybe five minutes? Maybe an hour? It was long enough for me to stash a loaded handgun in my bag, replay my distorted version of what had just happened a few hundred times, and begin to experience the return of my feelings.

Unfortunately, they decided to come back all at once.

When my manager came looking for me, I told her I wasn't feeling well. It wasn't a lie, but of course, she automatically assumed food poisoning. Why did everyone always jump to food poisoning? What the fuck were these people eating? Anyway, she let me spend the remainder of my shift sorting the new fall napkin rings into their respective bins—a cush job by any standards.

As I sorted the pumpkin rings from the dried cranberry coils, I tried to sort my feelings into nice little boxes, too. Boxes labeled Anger, Sadness, Security, Betrayal, Lust, and Love. I selected the galvanized silver napkin rings to represent Harley; they looked like they'd been smudged with oil, like his hands. And I chose the black lacquer ones for Knight; they reminded me of black holes, like his pupils. Also like Knight, they didn't seem to fit in with the others.

In my mind, I pictured a box labeled Anger and saw myself dropping a black ring inside with a *plink*. I couldn't fucking believe Knight had pulled that shit again. Why did he keep showing up? Just to force me to say good-bye to him all over again? I was so fucking sick of him leaving, and leaving, and leaving. I couldn't fucking take it anymore. I dropped another black napkin ring in the Anger box just for good measure, then tossed one into the box marked Sadness while I was at it.

Thinking of Harley, I dropped a silver napkin ring into the box labeled Security. I wasn't mad at him for starting that fight even though he'd left me holding the bag—or the gun, in this case. In fact, I was proud. I'd been praying for someone to protect me from Ronald McKnight since the day we met, but no one had been up to the challenge until Harley. And talk about being up to the challenge. Motherfucker didn't even sweat. Didn't even flinch. *And* he'd thrown the first punch.

Was that something he'd learned in jail?

I vaguely remembered Knight saying something about Harley being in jail. Whatever. It was probably for shoplifting or some stupid teenage bullshit. I probably needed to talk to him about why the fuck he'd been driving around with a cache of firearms in his trunk, but honestly, I was too turned on by his badassery to care.

Plink into the Lust box.

There were only two boxes left—Betrayal and Love. Looking back and forth from black to silver, I eventually selected a third napkin ring—one with a stupid-looking turkey on it—and dropped it in. That napkin ring represented *me*. *I* was the betrayer. I'd betrayed Harley by sleeping with Knight, and now he knew it. And there had been betrayal in Knight's eyes when he saw Harley with his arm around me. Knight had obviously thought things had changed between us since our last encounter, and I hadn't told him otherwise. I'd moved on, or tried to, and Knight's surprise upon discovering that fact twisted in my gut like a knife.

The only box still empty was Love.

And that's exactly how I left it.

I peeled out of my parents' driveway the next morning with a black-market Glock under my seat and a crumpled piece of paper smashed between my hand and the steering wheel—two separate issues that needed to be addressed. Immediately.

I tried to avoid looking in the rearview mirror as I flew down the highway. I was operating on zero sleep and even less food, I'd applied new eyeliner over old, and my hair was a fucking train wreck. After being caught in the rain the day before, my inch-long, grown-out strawberry-blonde buzz cut had curled into little Betty Boop-style flips all over my head, and my overgrown bangs were so damn wavy I'd just pulled them to one side and pinned them with a barrette.

I shivered inside my new jacket and debated whether or not to turn on the heater. I didn't want to. By turning on my heater, I would basically be admitting that something was seriously wrong with me. Normal, healthy people don't wear down jackets and run their heaters in Georgia in August—cold snap or not.

But I had more pressing matters to worry about than my

dwindling body mass index, so I said, "Fuck it," and cranked that shit up.

For starters, I had to figure out where to go first. To a sane person, ditching the handgun would probably seem like priority number one, but sanity and I weren't exactly on speaking terms right then. I was being pulled by a force more powerful than logic. It was as if the letter in my hand was steering itself straight back to its author. And I went along for the ride, if only to give that motherfucker a piece of my pissed-off mind.

I let the letter lead my feet up those rickety wooden stairs and guide my fist to pound on that all-too-familiar weather-beaten door. I'd been coming to that house since my very first boy-friend, Colton Hart, lived there with his sad, bedraggled single mom, Peg. When Colton moved out, Peg took Knight in. He could have afforded his own place with what he made at the tat-too parlor alone, but for some reason he preferred Peg's nasty old house. I think it was because being there made him feel useful. He was always fixing things around the house and taking care of her geriatric German Shepherd. At Peg's, Knight had a purpose. At his step-dad's house, he had a restraining order.

When the door swung open, what I saw standing on the other side of that threshold made me feel as though I was look-ing through a portal into my past. Everything in Peg's house was exactly as I remembered it—itchy brown '70s decor, the smell of cigarette smoke thick in the air. Even the boy standing before me looked exactly the way I remembered him looking first thing in the morning—bare feet, tight Levi's rolled up at the bottom, white Agnostic Front T-shirt, half-untucked, red braces hanging from his waist instead of stretching over his shoulders.

I thought for a moment that I could just step across the plane of the open door and into the past. Into Knight's waiting arms. Into a time when my only worry had been keeping my mom from finding out that I wasn't actually spending my Friday nights at Juliet's house. But as soon as my eyes made it up to Knight's face, my fantasy popped like a delicate, beautiful bubble, revealing the harshest of realities behind it.

The left side of Knight's face was purple. And blue. And greenish. And yellow. His eye was almost swollen shut, and there was a nasty gash just below his eyebrow that looked like it could use a few stitches.

Knight looked tired. Beaten. And, for possibly the first time in his life, utterly defeated.

"Why the fuck are you crying?"

"I'm not cry—" As soon as I heard my voice break, I realized he was right.

Holy shit. I am *crying.*

Wiping my nose on the back of my hand, I remembered the wad of paper still tucked inside my fist. "I got your fucking letter."

Knight stared at me, his usually crystalline eyes cloudy from exhaustion.

"And..."

"And? And you're fucking *here*! Again!" I waved the folded piece of paper in the air. "You said you were staying in North Carolina! You said you had nothing to come back to!"

Knight didn't yell back. He simply took a deep breath and replied, "I changed my mind."

"Yeah? No shit! Funny how you keep doing that!"

"Why are you here, Punk? Shouldn't you be off blowing your boyfriend somewhere?"

"Why are *you* here, Knight? Why the fuck do you keep coming back? You're not going to stay! All you do is tell me that we can't be together, so why the fuck do you keep showing up? Why are you doing this to me?"

Knight took a step forward and braced his hands on the doorframe. "Because I fucking need you! Okay? Because you're all I fucking think about! Because you're the only person I can fucking stand on this planet, and I fucking miss you. Okay? I miss every-goddamn-thing about you!"

Knight reached across the invisible plane separating us and jammed a finger into the side of my nose, causing me to wince and turn my head. "I miss that fucking heart-shaped freckle on your nose."

Then he stepped across the plane completely, crowding me in.

I took a step back but found myself teetering on the edge of the top stair. With nowhere to go but down, I stood there and let Knight cup my cheek in his blazing hot hand.

He swiped a thumb over the imperfection he found there. "I miss that fucking dog-bite scar that looks like a dimple when you smile." Sliding his rough hand from my cheek to my neck, Knight grasped the zipper he found at the base of my throat and tugged. "And I miss the way you looked in *my* fucking jacket. Not this bullshit." Pulling the zipper down, Knight yanked my new coat off over my shoulders and threw it down the stairs behind me.

The sound of my own sobs alerted me to the fact that I was still crying, even harder than before. Trying to get a grip on my erratic emotions, I concentrated on what I was feeling.

Why was I crying? Was it because I was afraid Knight was going to hurt me?

No.

Was it because Knight was touching me?

No.

Was it because I wanted him to touch me?

Yes.

Was it because he was hurting?

Yes.

Was it because I wanted to tell him that I missed him too, but that would make me a shitty person because I already had a new boyfriend?

Fuck yes.

When Knight grabbed me by the wrist and pulled me inside the house, I didn't fight him. When he led me upstairs to his room, I went willingly. And when he shut and locked the door, I felt the outside world disappear behind it.

That room had always been our safe place. Sure, I'd been cut, bitten, handcuffed, and painted with my own blood in there, but what Knight had said to Harley was true. I'd loved every minute of it. In that room, with its tiny, dated furniture and complete lack of decor, I'd been closer to Knight than I ever thought two humans were capable of being. In that room, Knight had shed his skinhead persona for me—only me—and turned into the fuzzy-headed, freckle-faced boy who stole my heart. The boy who had the smile of an angel, if only I could coax it out of him. For a moment, nothing beyond those four walls mattered.

We were home.

Knight stepped toward me, but that time, I didn't back away.

I reached up and gently touched his face. Gazing into the tiny sliver of glacier blue peeking out from beneath his swollen, blackened lid, I whispered, "We need to get some ice on this."

We.

Goddamn it.

Knight ignored my concern and pulled me close. When his mouth sealed over mine, I pictured his teeth smeared scarlet the day before.

I wonder if it hurts him to kiss me.

When he parted my lips and swept his tongue into my mouth, he didn't taste like cigarettes and Winterfresh gum, like he usually did. He tasted like coppery blood and brown liquor.

Has he been up all night, like me?

As Knight laid me down on the bed and pulled off my boots and jeans, I wondered how Harley was doing.

Has he been up all night, too?

As I lifted my arms to let Knight tug my Pixies T-shirt off, I was busy cataloging every injury Harley had sustained during their fight.

I wonder if his arm is okay. Knight bit him pretty bad. He might have a concussion from that head-butt, too.

And, as Knight stepped out of his jeans and boxers, all I could hear was the echo of his voice.

"If you knew shit about BB, you'd know that she's still fucking me."

Had Harley believed him? Was he mad at me? Did he think I was cheating on him?

Oh my God.

I am cheating on him.

I didn't realize the gravity of my situation until Knight's hard, naked body was hovering over me on the bed. The outside world *did* still exist. And there was a man out there in it who'd risked his life to defend me. And he was hurt. And, even worse, he might be mad at me.

When Knight kissed me, I froze. When his eager mouth moved down my neck to my breasts, to the nipples he'd pierced himself, I squeezed my eyes shut and held my breath. And when his fuzzy blond head disappeared between my legs, I felt twin tears roll down my cheeks.

I didn't have to check in with myself to know why I was crying that time.

I was crying because I was a selfish fucking asshole.

Even through my guilt-paralysis, Knight knew exactly how to get me off. He'd trained my body to like what he did to it, to bend when he pushed, to come when he wanted. And I did.

As the guiltgasm seized me, causing muscles I hadn't even known I had to tense and contract, Knight rolled onto his back next to me and jerked himself off. I watched in agonizing impotence as he forced an ending to our ill-fated reunion. Knight came with a strangled cry, spurting ribbons of cum all over his stomach and hand. Then, he sat up without a word, walked to the door, unlocked it, and left.

I was relieved that he hadn't expected me to reciprocate, but my lack of participation only added more rapids to the river of remorse I was drowning in. Somehow, I'd managed to cheat on Harley *and* reject the man I was cheating on him with, all at the same time.

When Knight didn't come back right away, I tiptoed over to the doorway and spotted him across the hall in the bathroom. He was standing in front of the still-running sink with his head down, gripping the edge of the counter with both hands. The sight of him stopped me dead in my tracks. His broad, muscular back bore the exquisitely detailed McKnight coat-of-arms tattoo that had taken Bobbi months to complete, but his posture was far from regal. Knight was a picture of both physical strength and emotional fragility.

I padded across the hall and wrapped my arms around his torso from behind, resting my cheek between his shoulder blades.

"I shouldn't have come back," Knight said, his voice sounding hoarse.

"No," I corrected, feeling his body relax in my arms and his heart rate slow beneath my cheek, "you shouldn't have left."

But he had.

And now it was my turn.

As I crossed over Peg's rotten, splintered threshold for what I suspected might be the last time, I found the wadded-up piece of paper that had dragged me there, lying faceup on the front porch.

AUGUST 18, 1998

PUNK,

I KNOW YOU PROBABLY DON'T WANT TO HEAR FROM ME SINCE YOU NEVER WROTE ME BACK, BUT I'M GRADUATING FROM BASIC TRAINING NEXT FRIDAY. I JUST THOUGHT YOU MIGHT WANT TO KNOW. YOU MIGHT FUCKING HATE

ME, BUT I KNOW YOU CARE ABOUT
SHIT LIKE THAT.

I GET TEN DAYS OF LEAVE AFTER
GRADUATION. THEN, I GO TO
INFANTRY SCHOOL AND SHIP OUT
TO IRAQ. I THOUGHT ABOUT COMING
HOME DURING MY LEAVE, BUT WHAT
WOULD BE THE FUCKING POINT?
THERE'S NOTHING WAITING FOR ME
THERE. YOU WON'T EVEN FUCKING
TALK TO ME.

I KNOW I'M AN ASSHOLE. I KNOW
THE ONLY THING I'M GOOD AT IS
HURTING PEOPLE. BUT I'M FUCKING
TRYING. I SPENT THE LAST TWELVE
WEEKS BEING SCREAMED AT, HAVING
MY IDENTITY TAKEN AWAY FROM
ME, EATING SHITTY FOOD, SLEEPING
ON A COT, AND WORKING MY ASS
OFF BECAUSE I THOUGHT IT WAS
THE RIGHT THING TO DO—FOR BOTH
OF US.

I'M SORRY I CAN'T FUCKING SHOW
IT LIKE A NORMAL PERSON, BUT I DO
LOVE YOU. MORE THAN ANYTHING IN

MY SHITTY FUCKING LIFE. I ALWAYS
WILL.

LOVE,
KNIGHT

P.S. IF YOU NEED ANYTHING, FUCKING
ANYTHING, THIS IS WHERE I'LL
BE TRAINING FOR THE NEXT TWO
MONTHS BEFORE I SHIP OUT.
PVT. RONALD MCKNIGHT
ALPHA CO. CLASS 10-98 4TH PLT.
ITB BN. SOI MCB
PSC BOX 20166
CAMP LEJEUNE, NC 28542-0166

"Fuck you, letter," I muttered, snatching it off the ground and tearing it to pieces. "This is all *your* fault."

I tossed the guilt-trip confetti into the air, then stomped down the stairs to pull my brand-new—but significantly less shiny—jacket out of the mud. As I shrugged it on, Knight's serial-killer handwriting flitted around me like Satan's snowflakes, sticking to every wet patch of fabric they could find. Mocking me. Telling me that, although I might be able to walk away from that house, pieces of the man inside were coming with me whether I liked it or not.

"I'm not fucking him!" The words shot from my mouth the moment Harley's battered face appeared in the doorway.

Really, BB? That's what you're going to lead with? Not a, Hey, how are you? *Or a,* Hey, here's your gun back. *Not even a,* Hey, thanks for taking on a bodybuilding skinhead Marine for me.

Evidently, my guilt was going to have to be absolved before any semblance of a normal conversation could take place.

The whole way over, I'd told myself it wasn't that bad. That I wasn't, like, a *cheater* cheater. I was just a passive cheater—a peater, if you will. A peater, peater pumpkin eater. It wasn't like I'd reverse-cowgirled Knight or anything. I'd just lain there and tried not to cry while his mouth was on me. That wasn't real cheating. Nope. No, sir. That was...peating. It's a totally different thing.

Harley gave me a sleepy-eyed smile and pulled me in for one of his all-is-right-with-the-world hugs.

Anytime I was worrying or obsessing about something, Harley would simply smash me into his chest, wrap his arms around my shoulders, and rest his chin on the top of my head. I think it was his way of shutting me up, but whatever, it fucking worked. It was like being back in the womb. If wombs smelled like marijuana and gasoline.

"You're not mad at me?" I squeaked, wrapping my arms around his waist and nuzzling my face into his bare chest.

"It's not your fault that motherfucker's psycho."

And that was it. Water under the bridge. Relief rushed through my body like a tsunami, relaxing my tensed muscles, washing the adrenaline out of my bloodstream, and overflowing from the corners of my eyes.

"Hey? Are you crying?" Harley tilted my chin up and looked at me.

I smiled at him and nodded, overcome by my feelings for that man. "Thank you"—I sniffled—"for believing me. And for standing up for me yesterday. I"—*love you*—"was so worried you were gonna be mad at me."

Harley's jaw was swollen on one side, and he had a nasty purple lump forming in the middle of his forehead, but his heavy-lidded azure eyes still sparkled like sapphires.

"You're my lady." He shrugged. "Somebody wants to fuck with you, they gotta go through me. Besides"—Harley lifted one hand and plucked at a few of my crescent-moon-shaped curls—"how could anybody be mad at somebody this cute?"

"Oh my God, don't even look at my hair," I squealed, shielding my eyes from his gaze with my hand.

"I like it. Makes you look like Drew Barrymore in *Mad Love*."

I giggled. "*You* saw *Mad Love*?"

"Saw it? Woman, I fuckin' own it."

And, with that, Harley popped the movie in and proceeded to do what he did best. He made me forget. As Drew Barrymore and Chris O'Donnell flew down the highway in a fit of young runaway love, Harley and I floated away on a cloud of pot and cigarette smoke, making lazy midday love on the sofa. Time ceased to exist. The previous twenty-four hours felt as far away as another lifetime. All I could process were happy hands and friendly fingers and smiling, sucking lips and generous, gyrating hips and fuzzy, light-headed bliss and that *click* of completeness once my empty places were finally full again.

Harley also made me forget the fact that he had a nasty bite wound on his forearm. The pained hiss he let out when I rolled over onto it made me remember.

Sitting up, I grabbed Harley's wrist and turned his right arm over. "Jesus Christ, Harley!"

His arm looked like it had been caught in a fucking bear trap. Two parentheses-shaped channels were laid open, oozing pus and coagulated blood, the skin red and raised all around.

"This is bad. I think you might need to go to the hospital, baby."

"Nah. Just needs a couple of stitches," Harley said, sitting up and reaching for his pack of smokes.

"You can't stitch bites. It traps the bacteria inside and causes infection. You have to clean it really well and just pull the skin shut with a butterfly bandage."

"How do you know so much, smarty-pants?" Harley teased, exhaling a stream of smoke out the side of his mouth.

I turned my face and pointed to my cheek. "Dog bite."

"No shit? I just thought that was a dimple."

The fact that Knight knew about my scar and not Harley made me even angrier with him for some reason. I didn't want him to know things about me that my own boyfriend didn't know. It wasn't fair.

I pulled Harley into the bathroom and rummaged through what limited storage they had. All I could find in terms of first aid was a half-empty box of Band-Aids. I wondered who had used the ones that were gone. Obviously, not Harley. Motherfucker would die of gangrene first.

As I washed out his wounds with soap and water—trying not to think about the fact that, just that morning, my tongue had grazed the teeth that had left those marks—I decided to bring up Harley's transgressions instead.

"So," I began, keeping my eyes on his forearm as I rinsed away the grime, "you never told me your trunk had a fucking arsenal in it."

"No, I didn't." Harley's tone was serious.

Harley didn't *do* serious.

I looked up and searched his face for that glimmer of mischief, but it wasn't there. All I found was the swollen purple, greenish evidence of what had transpired the day before, which had also been *very* serious.

"Harley, whatever it is, I don't care. Besides, if I wanted to turn you in, I think I would have by now."

Harley gazed at me with an unreadable expression. He was thinking—no, he was *deciding* whether or not I was trustworthy.

Based on my behavior that morning, even I had my doubts.

"This shit goes a lot deeper than just me, lady. If I tell you, I'm putting people I love at risk."

"Dave." His brother's name fell from my lips innocently—an answer to a riddle—but Harley's face told me he wasn't happy that I'd solved it.

"That's already more than you oughta know."

Patting his wounds dry with the one cleanish towel I could

find, I asked, "Does it have to do with the pawnshop owner? The guy you got my ring from?"

I was afraid I was overstepping, but for some reason, my question made Harley crack a smile.

"What?"

"You called it *your* ring."

"It will be my ring if you ever learn how to propose right," I teased. "And don't change the subject."

I don't know if Harley decided he could trust me or if he just realized that I already knew too much, but he finally started talking. "You remember when you first came over here, and we were jokin' about damaging stuff at work?"

I nodded, pulling a few Band-Aids out of the box.

"Well, Dave does that at the Army/Navy store...but with guns."

My jaw dropped open.

"He marks a couple here and there as being damaged, which takes them off the inventory. Then he files off their serial numbers and sells them to the pawnshop owner next door. *Larry.*" Harley sneered when he said his name. "That greasy motherfucker moves 'em quick. Usually, sells 'em under the table the same day."

"So why are *you* involved?" I asked, cutting notches out of the sides of a regular bandage to make it a butterfly shape—just like my mom had done all those years ago when our family dog tried to take a chunk out of my face.

"Let's just say, Dirty Larry is even shadier than we thought, so Dave has me moving this batch for him myself."

"So"—I pinched Harley's wound shut where it was gaping

open the most and applied one of my makeshift butterfly bandages to it, holding it shut—"you're a gunrunner."

Harley didn't respond, but I could feel his eyes boring into the top of my head as I put him back together. I could also feel the tension rolling off his body. It was as if he was readying himself to tackle me to the ground if I decided to run screaming to the authorities.

I shrugged, applying the last bandage, then finally met his worried stare with a small smile. "At least you're not a drug dealer."

Harley's battered baby face broke into a grin. "You think pushin' guns is better than drugs?"

"No." I laughed. "I just fucking hate drug dealers."

And with that, Harley dropped to one knee in the middle of his disgusting bachelor-pad bathroom, pulled the ring he'd extorted from a crooked pawnshop owner out of his pocket, smirked at me with a face swollen from my ex-boyfriend's fist, and asked me to marry him. Again.

My heart swelled.

I didn't care how bad he was. Bad felt a hell of a lot better than broken.

GEORGIA
CHAPTER 21
19 PEACH STATE 99

September 1998

> *Goddamn, this bitch is boring.*
> *Whose idea was it to take Calculus in the afternoon?*
> *Oh, yeah. Mine.*
> *Ugh.*
> *Juliet's not even pretending to be awake.*
> *Goth Girl's painting her fucking nails.*
> *Forty-two more minutes of this shit?*
> *What did I used to do when I was bored in class?*
> *I wrote notes! Yes! Duh!*

Completely abandoning the empty page of notes I was *supposed* to be taking, I flipped to the next blank page in my notebook and stared.

And stared.

And stared.

Who the fuck should I write to? My only two school friends were sitting on either side of me, and writing Harley a note just felt stupid. He was a full-grown man. What was I going to do, hand it to him at his house?

Who did I used to write to?

Oh. Right.

Him.

It had been almost a month since he, since we, since whatever happened at Peg's house happened. I hadn't spoken to him since.

At first, I'd used my anger as an excuse. But after the first few days, remorse started to settle in. Knight hadn't tried to contact me at all even though he was in town for another week after that *encounter.* An encounter where I'd rejected him, made him feel like shit, and then run straight into the arms of another man— the same man who'd attacked him the day before while I stood by and did nothing. Knight was just a few weeks away from heading into a war zone, and knowing him, there was a good chance he might not make it home. I didn't want what had gone down at Peg's house to be our last interaction.

Knight was also just a few days away from turning nineteen. The thought made me almost as sad as the idea of him going off to war. The year before I'd stolen him a chicken sandwich from the school cafeteria on his birthday, and I'll never forget the look on his face. It was heartbreaking. It was as if he'd never received a gift in his fucking life. His mom didn't acknowledge the day she'd given birth to him, and his dad didn't even acknowledge his existence. Why should he expect anyone else to give a shit? If I hadn't peeked at his driver's license, I wouldn't have even known it was his birthday at all.

That settled it. I was writing Knight a letter. It would give me a little closure before he went to Iraq, and Knight would know that somebody at least remembered his birthday. *And* I would keep it totally platonic so that I didn't feel like the world's shitti-est girlfriend. Again.

No. Big. Deal.

It was also totally normal that I'd been carrying around two scraps of mud-stained paper in my wallet that I maybe kind of saved after ripping Knight's letter up and that maybe kind of spelled out his new address when I taped them back together. Not weird at all.

Pvt. Ronald McKnight
Alpha Co. Class 10-98 4th Plt.
ITB BN. SOI MCB
PSC Box 20166
Camp Lejeune, NC 28542-0166

September 14, 1998

Dear Knight,

How is infantry camp? Or training? Or school? Or wherever you are? Better than boot camp, I hope. You never hear about infantry camp, so it must not be as bad.

East Atlanta College is waaaaay better than Peach State High. I'm so happy I transferred. There's no fucking drama here. Everybody just shows up, goes to class, and then goes the fuck home.

I met a girl named Victoria here who is cool as shit. She wants to go by VV, but I just call her

Goth Girl. Never to her face though. She kinda looks like she might cast a spell on me if I piss her off, but so far, she's been nice-ish. She and Juliet and I have all the same classes.

I'm in Calculus right now, and it fucking blows. This teacher is the worst. I basically have to teach myself everything when I get home because I can't concentrate on a word she says.

She literally just said, "A differential equation with no partial derivatives is an ordinary differential equation while the derivative with respect to a single variable is considered a partial derivative."

That shit just came out of her mouth, Knight. What the fuck does that even mean?

At least my Psychology class is amazing. I don't think I told you, but when you left, I decided that I wanted to become a psychologist. Not to get too heavy or anything, but I wish I could have helped you more. I don't know what all happened to you, and you don't ever have to tell me, but I wish you'd had somebody to talk to about it. Somebody trained to help you work through it. It would be cool if I could at least do that for other kids. Maybe even you one day, if you ever decide you want to talk.

Whatever. Sorry. That's not why I'm writing you. I really just wanted to say...

HAPPY BIRTHDAY!!!

I know you probably thought you could run back to North Carolina and avoid your birthday

altogether, but I couldn't let you get away with
that. Besides, I heard that in boot camp you're
not allowed to have junk food. I don't know how
it is in infantry camp (or wherever you are), but
just in case, I'm gonna hit up the vending machine
for you after class. If I recall correctly, you like
everything that ends in -tos.

I'm pretty sure they don't have Tostitos, and
there's no guarantee on the Fritos, but I can
probably scrounge up some Cheetos and Doritos no
problem.

   Well, my class is almost over, so I'd better go.
I really hope you have a good birthday. Stay safe,
okay?
   Love,
   BB

GEORGIA

CHAPTER 22

19 PEACH STATE 99

SEPTEMBER 18, 1998

YOU FUCKING BITCH,
   I CAN'T FUCKING BELIEVE YOU SENT
ME A BIRTHDAY PRESENT. ALL THE
GUYS FOUND OUT AND SANG ME
MOTHERFUCKING "HAPPY BIRTHDAY"
BEFORE LIGHTS OUT LAST NIGHT. I
WANTED TO THROAT-PUNCH EVERY
ONE OF THOSE ASSHOLES.
   THANKS FOR THE CHEETOS AND
DORITOS THOUGH. THE FOOD HERE IS
SHIT.
   I'M GLAD YOU'RE LIKING SCHOOL.
INFANTRY SCHOOL IS HEAVY ON
THE INFANTRY AND LIGHT ON THE

SCHOOL. WE TAKE SOME CLASSES, BUT MOSTLY WE'RE OUTSIDE HIKING WITH HEAVY-ASS PACKS ON AND SHOOTING SHIT ALL GODDAMN DAY. I LIKE IT THOUGH. FOR ONCE IN MY LIFE, I'M JUST LIKE EVERYBODY ELSE. EVERY ASSHOLE HERE HAS A SHAVED HEAD, ANGER ISSUES, WEARS COMBAT BOOTS, AND JUST WANTS TO FUCK SHIT UP. IT MAKES ME FEEL LIKE MAYBE I MADE THE RIGHT DECISION AFTER ALL.

IT'S TAKEN ME A WHILE TO GET TO THIS POINT THOUGH. HONESTLY, I THINK IT'S BECAUSE I'VE BEEN AWAY FROM YOU. EVERY TIME I SEE YOU I FEEL LIKE I'VE MADE THE BIGGEST MISTAKE OF MY LIFE. BUT SEEING YOU WITH HIM, SEEING YOU CHOOSE HIM, THAT SHIT FUCKING KILLED ME. I'LL NEVER FORGET THE WAY YOU LOOKED, JUST STANDING THERE, STARING AT ME WITH THOSE BIG, DUMB GREEN EYES, WHILE YOUR NEW FUCK BUDDY TRIED TO BEAT MY ASS. IT'S LIKE YOU WEREN'T EVEN THERE.

YOU WERE THE SAME WAY AT PEG'S HOUSE. JUST FUCKING GONE. THE BB I KNOW CAN'T SIT STILL OR SHUT THE FUCK UP FOR FIVE SECONDS. I GET THAT YOU'RE UPSET WITH ME, BUT THERE'S SOMETHING ELSE GOING ON. IF I FIND OUT HE'S GOT YOU ON DRUGS OR SOME SHIT, I SWEAR TO GOD, I WILL FUCKING FIND HIM AND I WILL FUCKING GOUGE HIS EYEBALLS OUT WITH MY THUMBS AND PISS INTO HIS FUCKING SKULL.

YOU ARE SO MUCH FUCKING BETTER THAN HIM. YOU HAVE NO IDEA WHAT YOU'RE WORTH, PUNK. NO FUCKING CLUE. YOU WERE TOO GOOD FOR ME, AND YOU'RE DAMN SURE TOO GOOD FOR THAT PIECE OF SHIT. YOU CAN'T TRUST HIM. HARLEY DOESN'T FUCKING CARE ABOUT YOU. I KNOW YOU THINK HE DOES, BUT HE ONLY CARES ABOUT WHAT YOU CAN DO FOR HIM. ALL THOSE STREET KIDS ARE THE SAME. THEY'RE FUCKING CON ARTISTS. HARLEY WILL FUCK YOU OVER THE SECOND HE GETS

A CHANCE, JUST WATCH. ONCE A GUTTER PUNK, ALWAYS A GUTTER PUNK.

SEE? THIS IS EXACTLY WHY IT'S BETTER WHEN I DON'T FUCKING TALK TO YOU. BECAUSE NOW I WANT TO PUT MY FUCKING FIST THROUGH A DOOR OR GO AWOL JUST SO THAT I CAN COME BACK DOWN THERE AND PUT MY FIST THROUGH HIS FUCKING FACE AGAIN. HARLEY SHOULDN'T BE ALLOWED TO BREATHE THE SAME AIR AS YOU, LET ALONE STICK HIS DICK IN YOU. HE'S FUCKING GUTTER SLIME.

IF YOU'RE GOING TO FUCK SOMEONE WHO DOESN'T DESERVE YOU, IT SHOULD BE ME. ME, NOT THAT PIECE OF SHIT. I FUCKING LOVE YOU. I'D FUCKING KILL FOR YOU. AND, WHETHER YOU WANT TO ADMIT IT OR NOT, YOU STILL LOVE ME TOO.

THAT BIRTHDAY LETTER FUCKING PROVED IT.

KNIGHT

GEORGIA

CHAPTER 23

19_PEACH STATE_99

October 1998

For somebody who hates cold weather, I fucking love the smell of fall.

Around here, fall smells like burning leaves. Georgia is basically one big forest with streets, homes, and businesses carved out of it, so when the trees begin to shed their summer foliage, the entire state finds itself knee-deep in crisp, crinkly russets and golds. There aren't enough places on earth to hide that many leaves, so every autumn, people take to their barrels and fire pits, filling the sky with the sweet-smelling souls of the leaves they'd been buried under.

On that particular October night, it smelled like the entire world was on fire. I had a nose full of cocaine and a pocketful of hundred-dollar bills as I flew down the dark, twisty back roads that led from the track to Harley's house. My windows were down. My heater was on full blast. And my steel-toed boot couldn't press the accelerator hard enough.

It had been a good night. Harley had convinced a customer at work—a white dude with a gold grill who was getting gold rims put on his Mitsubishi Eclipse—that he would slay at the track. Maybe even make enough to pay for those twenty-twos he'd just bought. By the end of the night, Gold Grill Guy and his buddies had *lost* enough money to buy each of us a set. One of them had even raced Harley. Harley! In the Boss! Fucking dumbasses had balls bigger than their brains.

Harley had suggested that Gold Grill Guy race *me*, which, of course, got his panties all twisted. Fucker acted like it was an insult to drive on the same track as me, let alone at the same *time* as me. I'd only wanted to put five hundred bucks on it, but Harley goaded him into seeing my five hundred and doubling it.

I believe his exact words were, "You afraid of a little girl in a five-oh, bro?"

It didn't bother me when Harley referred to me as a little girl anymore. He only said it at the track when he was trying to make me seem like an easy mark. As soon as the races were over, I was back to being *lady*. Or *woman*. Nicknames I didn't deserve but was trying desperately to live up to.

I'd beaten Gold Grill Guy by at least two car lengths. Honestly, I'd expected him to just keep on going—the dude had *flight risk* written all over him—but Harley'd had Bubba and JR block the exit road with their trucks during the race. That motherfucker was always one step ahead. Of *everybody*.

Even me.

I knew I wasn't talented. I never expected to win any of the races Harley set me up on, but he knew what he was doing. He'd trained me to drive exactly the way he would on *that particular track*. He'd done God knows what to my car to make it perform on *that particular track*. On a straightaway, I would lose. On a bigger NASCAR-style oval, I would lose. But on a track where torque and grip were everything, horsepower was secondary, and turbochargers got you nowhere, me and my unassuming little hatchback were Harley's perfect secret weapon.

"Harley doesn't fucking care about you. I know you think he does, but he only cares about what you can do for him."

Fuck you, Knight. You're just jealous.

Knight's voice would still creep into my consciousness and hijack my thoughts sometimes, but I'd gotten better at telling it to shut the fuck up.

The flashbacks didn't paralyze me the way they once had anymore either. They were simply memories. Intrusions. Besides, I knew that Harley wasn't using me. We were a team. Hell, we were BB and fucking Clyde.

As I inhaled another lungful of fall, my sinuses tingled, and my throat tasted like aspirin—remnants of the line I'd snorted off of Bubba's tailgate before we left the track. I'd done coke before but never before *driving*. It made the whole experience so much better. The smells, the deep rumble of the engine, the vibrations, the speed. I felt like I was going to lift right off the pavement and fly. I stuck my arm out the open window, like the wing of an airplane, cranked up the stereo, and sang my heart out to Blondie's "Heart of Glass" while I soared through the smoke-scented night.

When I finally landed at Harley's house, I couldn't feel my hand *or* my face, but I didn't care. I had more pressing needs.

Even though I'd been driving at least twenty over the speed limit, Harley had still beaten me home. I bounced up the steps to the back door and let myself in—no longer bothering with formalities where Harley was concerned—and found him and

Dave standing side by side with their backs toward me, hovering over their beige Formica kitchen counter.

I was just about to ask what they were doing when I saw Dave lean over and heard a loud snorting sound. Then he stood up and rubbed his nose.

"Fuuuck, that's some good shit."

Turning toward me with a huge smile, Harley waved me over. A flash of light glinted off the razor blade between his index and middle finger. "C'mere, woman. We're celebratin'."

Dave opened his eyes and focused on me. "I heard you kicked some ass at the track tonight, B. Get in here!" Taking a step toward me, Dave grabbed me by the back of the neck and gave me a fucking noogie.

Asshole.

He laughed hysterically as I pushed him off and tucked myself into Harley's side.

Harley chuckled and wrapped his free arm around me as he took the razor blade and divided a tiny pile of white powder into two skinny lines right on the countertop. He set down the blade, snatched a rolled-up hundred-dollar bill out of Dave's hand, then offered it to me. "Ladies first," he said with a grin.

I accepted the improvised straw without hesitation. Coke was fun—it was like snorting pure enthusiasm—but it wore off after about thirty minutes and always left me wanting more. Good thing I was too poor to buy it on my own. I could totally see how people got addicted to that shit.

While Harley and I inhaled our lines, Dave dug around in their cabinets until he found a bottle of Cuervo Gold. "Dude, dude, *dude*," he said, holding up the bottle and practically running in place. "Are you thinking what I'm thinking?"

Harley's eyes flicked to mine, glowing with the same bright blue mania as his brother's. "Fuck yeah, I am."

My head swiveled back and forth from one smirk to the other. "What? What's going on? Tell me. Are we doing shots? Because if we're doing shots I'm gonna need a chaser. And you can't let me do more than, like, three, or I'll puke. I've never done tequila shots though. Only Southern Comfort. That shit burns like hell. Wait, why do you need salt? Wait. Oh my God, is that a lime? You guys have a *fruit* in your house? No fucking way!"

I burst out laughing—mostly out of embarrassment over how quickly I was talking—as Dave chopped that lime up faster than Edward Scissorhands. While I was busy praying he didn't lose a finger and trying to keep my rambling mouth shut, Harley was behind me, unzipping my jacket. Once it was off, he tossed it onto their new kitchen table, then began kissing and suckling his way down my neck. My head rolled back onto his shoulder just as his tongue dipped into the hollow of my collarbone.

"You don't have to take any shots if you don't want to, lady." Harley's voice rumbling against my clavicle made other parts of me jealous. "All you have to do is stand there and look pretty."

Just as I opened my mouth to ask what he meant, Harley turned my body toward his and placed a wedge of lime between my teeth. Then he smiled. Fuck, he was cute. I just stood there with that damn hunk of lime in my mouth and stared at him— wishing it were his lip ring between my teeth—as he dusted my wet, protruding collarbone with salt. Then, accepting a minia- ture glass of amber liquid from his brother, Harley held it up in a tiny *cheers* motion before leaning forward and licking the salt from my skin. Stifling a moan, I bit down on the lime between my teeth a little harder. I tasted a burst of tart juice as Harley stood and knocked back his drink. Slamming his empty glass on the counter, Harley pinned me with a wild-eyed stare and came at me with teeth bared, clamping down on the other half of the lime in my mouth. Fiery, salty lips closed around my own as he sucked the juice that would have run down my chin.

As soon as Harley yanked the spent lime rind out of my mouth with his teeth and spit it into the sink next to us, Dave replaced it with a fresh one. I looked into his eyes—as blue and crazed as Harley's but hooded by darker lashes and eyebrows—and held my breath. Dave leaned forward, breaking our eye contact, and slid his tongue slowly across my collarbone.

I gasped at the contact—somehow managing to keep the lime in my mouth—and looked to Harley. His jaw was flexed, his nostrils flared, and his eyes were narrowed to slits. Was he jealous? *Harley?* I held his gaze and tilted my head, offering Dave better access as he salted my wet skin.

Harley's chest rose and fell in fury. He *was* pissed. And I fucking loved it.

As much as my body wanted to be the jelly in a Harley-Davidson sandwich, my heart was begging for Harley to stake his claim. I didn't want to be shared. Not really.

I wanted to be cherished.

I smirked at Harley around the lime in my mouth as his brother tucked his face into my neck and sucked the salt from my skin.

As soon as he pulled away and tipped his shot glass up, Harley growled, "Fuck this," and yanked me away from his brother by my upper arm. Grabbing the bottle of tequila in his other hand, Harley dragged me out of the kitchen.

"What the fuck, dude? I was just getting to the good part!" Dave called after us with a chuckle.

Harley didn't even respond. He stomped into his bedroom, kicked the door shut behind us, and tossed me onto his mattress. I flopped onto my back, lime still between my teeth, and tried to focus on him in the dark. Tiny blades of light sliced through the cracks between the door and the wall, turning Harley into a backlit shadow man. One of the slivers cut through the bottle of amber liquid in his hand just before he tipped it up to his mouth.

After a long chug, Harley's voice rumbled through the darkness. "You wanna fuck him, don't you? You were just gonna stand there and let him suck on your neck like a whore!"

Note to self: Cocaine and tequila make Harley a fucking asshole.

I pulled the lime out of my mouth and spat back, emboldened by the asshole powder coursing through my own bloodstream, "*I'm* a whore? *You're* the whore! You probably don't even know how many girls you've slept with. I bet it's in the hundreds. I'm just another one of your little fuck buddies, aren't I?"

Note to self: Cocaine makes you an asshole, too.

Harley set the bottle next to the mattress and crouched over me on all fours. I could feel his hot, tequila-and-lime-scented breath on my face just before five callused fingers wrapped around my jaw. "This is different, and you fucking know it."

"What's so goddamn different about it?"

Tell me! Tell me I'm special! Tell me you love me!

"Nobody fucking touches you but me!"

"Oh, you don't want *Dave* to touch me? Well, too fucking late," I chided, pointing to the side of my neck with the hand holding the lime.

I guess Harley's eyes had adjusted to the light enough to see my gesture because he snatched the lime out of my hand and rubbed the wet wedge along the same trail that Dave's tongue had traveled. Taking another swig of tequila, Harley then dragged his rough tongue over my salty, sour flesh, erasing any evidence that his brother had ever been there.

Shoving the lime wedge back between my teeth, Harley pulled the bottom of my *Boys Don't Cry* T-shirt up to my neck and unclasped the front of my heavily padded black bra. Grazing one of my winged nipples with his thumb, Harley asked, "He ever touch you here?"

I shook my head and held my breath as Harley splashed tequila into the hollow between my almost nonexistent breasts. He lapped it up, then found my mouth with his and sucked on the sour fruit between my lips. Excess alcohol slid down my rib cage and pooled in my belly button. Excess lime juice cascaded down my jaw and disappeared into the flips of wavy strawberry-blonde hair at the nape of my neck. And excess fluid of an entirely different kind pooled between my legs.

I didn't know who this person was. Harley had never been aggressive with me before. He'd never shown any sign of jealousy or possessiveness. Yet it felt familiar. I'd been spoken to that way before. I'd been handled roughly. And I'd liked it.

In fact, I'd missed it.

There, in the dark, high on cocaine and face-to-face with my demons, I let myself pretend. I let Harley tear at my clothes and grip me too tight and curse at me—all while picturing someone even rougher. Someone even needier. Someone who wasn't satisfied until he'd opened me up and sucked the blood from my veins.

Following the trail of tequila down my torso, Harley swirled his tongue inside my navel as he hastily unbuckled my studded belt. In yet another eerily familiar move, Harley yanked my jeans and panties down to my ankles and left them there, not bothering to take off my combat boots. Knight used to fuck me with my ankles bound the exact same way. He lived life as if he could hear the seconds ticking away. Every minute was precious, and he'd rather spend them buried between my legs than taking off my boots.

Harley spread my knees apart as far as they would go, considering my bindings, and grabbed the bottle off the floor next to him. As he leaned forward, I felt his warm, wet tongue first, followed by the burning trickle of tequila as it cascaded through my folds and into his waiting mouth. I squirmed and hissed and bit down on the lime harder as the stinging intensified. Harley licked and sucked the tender places until the singe dulled to a tingle. Then, climbing back up my body, he chomped down on the lime and tore it from my mouth. Dripping sour citrus onto my chin, Harley turned his head and spit the rind onto the carpet.

Flame-blue eyes found mine in the dark as Harley slid a finger inside me. I gasped at the unexpected burn. His hand must have been soaked in tequila from all the body shots. My eyes watered as he cupped my sex, stinging my delicate skin like salt in a wound. He probably had no idea that it hurt at all, but then again, it was Harley. That motherfucker always seemed to know *exactly* what he was doing.

"He ever touch you *here*?" Harley's tone was deep and smug.

He expected me to shake my head like a good little girl and say, *No, sir. Never.* Well, fuck that. Harley wasn't the only one who wanted to fuck and fight. I'd snorted the same powdered insanity that he had, and I was ready to throw down. Besides, coked-up, pissed-off Harley was the closest I'd ever get to having Knight back, and I realized that I wasn't ready to let him go just yet.

Licking the lime juice from my lips, I smiled and slowly nodded.

Harley's eyes narrowed and his nostrils flared. "*What?*" His voice was so deep it shook me to my core, but there was no going back. The crazy train had left the station.

I left him hanging while I slipped his wallet out of his back pocket and pulled out a condom. As I concentrated on unwrapping it, I finally said, "Dave licked my pussy while you fucked me on the couch. He's good, too. Made me come in five seconds flat."

Harley reared back. His fist flew. I squeezed my eyes shut just before a crunch sounded above my head, and something sprinkled all over my face. Drywall.

"That motherfucker!"

I brushed off my face, laughing like a goddamn lunatic.

"Why are you so mad? I thought you liked to share."

Eat me alive.

"I told him not to fucking touch you!" Harley growled, gripping a handful of splintered Sheetrock and ripping it away from the wall.

"Why don't you want to share with your brother, Harley?"

Make me bleed.

Harley snarled and hurled a chunk of drywall across the room.

"Why?"

Tell me you fucking love me! Tell me this means something! Knight fucking meant something! Who the fuck are you?

In less than ten seconds, Harley tore his shirt off over his head, unbuckled his belt, freed his punishing erection, snatched the condom out of my hand, and rolled it on. Closing my legs and pushing them over to one side, Harley pinned my bent knees together against the mattress and plunged into me as far as my unprepared body would allow. The sudden stretching caused the alcohol burn to intensify, and I cried out. Harley retreated and entered again and again, punctuating each thrust with a different word.

"Because.

You're.

Fucking.

Mine."

Mine.

Knight used to call me his.

I closed my eyes and let the pleasure-pain I never thought I'd feel again wash over me. It was almost the way I'd remembered it—the intensity, the mania, the passion. The pain. If I couldn't have Knight, at least I knew that Harley was just a few lines of blow, a few shots of tequila, and a lick from his brother away from playing him for the night.

I was a whopping three hours late getting home that night. I tiptoed in, hoping my dad had fallen asleep on the couch but no such luck. He was waiting up for me, polishing his guns at the kitchen table. Never a good sign. I apologized profusely and made up some stupid lie about falling asleep at Goth Girl's house, but it didn't matter. I was grounded as fuck.

I spent the next day hiding in my room from my parents' disapproval, smoking cigarettes and checking my phone every five minutes out of boredom. Harley never called to make sure I got home okay or to ask if I was in trouble for breaking curfew. He probably forgot that I had a curfew even though I reminded him literally every time we hung out. Or maybe he was sleeping off a hangover. He'd drunk *a lot* of tequila the night before. Maybe, if I were lucky, he wouldn't even remember what had happened.

Saturday afternoons were shit for TV, so I decided to listen to The Cure and draw. That would help pass the time until I had to go to work. But as Robert Smith crooned about a girl who was always falling down, I didn't doodle on the blank page I was staring at. I tumbled into it.

In my mind, I was back at Terminus City Tattoo, after-hours, flipping through the pages of a notebook filled with intricate sketches of dragons and knights and medieval iconography. Knight's breath was hot on my neck as he watched me admiring his work. His talent was far superior to mine. Always had been.

Knight and I had attended the same elementary school, only he was a few grades ahead of me. My mom had been the art teacher there, and I remembered her giving extra attention to a "special little boy" who didn't "get along with the other kids." I hadn't known him back then, but I'd seen his drawings on the bulletin board behind her desk, right next to mine. Our art was like night and day. Mine was every bit as colorful and happy as Knight's was dark and violent. But even still, his was more beautiful.

My Cure-induced flashback was shattered by the distinct metallic clanging of a mailbox being opened and shut. I stared out my second-story window at the simple black mailbox at the end of our long, wooded driveway, and I could almost hear the psychotic, all-caps handwriting shouting at me from inside.

I'd gotten a letter.

I could feel it.

OCTOBER 23, 1998

DEAR BB,

I JUST GOT TO IRAQ.

I'VE KNOWN MY WHOLE LIFE THAT I'M NOT GOING TO LIVE TO SEE THIRTY, BUT NOW THAT I'M HERE,

I'M STARTING TO THINK I MIGHT NOT EVEN MAKE IT TO TWENTY.

IT'S A FUCKING SHITSHOW. OUR CARAVAN WAS UNDER FIRE AS SOON AS WE LEFT THE FUCKING AIRPORT. OH, AND I SAW A FUCKING HAND ON THE SIDE OF THE ROAD. A HAND. I THINK IT WAS A WOMAN'S.

ANYWAY, IT MADE ME REALIZE THAT THE SHIT I NEED TO SAY TO YOU CAN'T WAIT. ESPECIALLY SINCE MAIL CAN SOMETIMES TAKE UP TO THREE WEEKS TO GET BACK AND FORTH FROM HERE.

I JUST WANT TO TELL YOU THAT I'M SORRY I WAS SUCH AN ASSHOLE IN MY LAST LETTER. I KNOW I SAID IT WAS BETTER WHEN I DIDN'T TALK TO YOU, BUT THAT WAS FUCKING BULLSHIT. NO MATTER WHAT THE FUCK I SAY, NO MATTER WHAT YOU DO, NO MATTER WHO YOU'RE FUCKING, I WILL NEVER NOT WANT TO TALK TO YOU. DON'T EVER QUESTION THAT. IF I DIE TOMORROW, YOU NEED TO KNOW

THAT THE ONLY DAYS THAT FUCKING
MATTERED IN MY WHOLE PATHETIC
FUCKING LIFE WERE THE ONES WHERE
I GOT TO TALK TO YOU.
 I LOVE YOU, PUNK. ALWAYS WILL.
  YOU CAN GO BACK TO MOVING
ON NOW.

                                          KNIGHT

I suddenly knew exactly what to put on that blank page I'd been staring at—the apology I should have written two months ago.

NOVEMBER 11, 1998

DEAR BB,

I JUST GOT YOUR LETTER. YOU DON'T NEED TO BE FUCKING SORRY. JUST KEEP WRITING ME, OKAY? YOUR LETTER WAS THE FIRST CONTACT I'VE HAD WITH MY OLD LIFE SINCE I GOT HERE.

TELL ME ABOUT SCHOOL. TELL ME ABOUT YOUR PARENTS. TELL ME WHAT COLOR YOUR HAIR IS NOW. ARE YOU STILL GROWING IT OUT?

BEING HERE IS SO FUCKING STRANGE. NOTHING IS THE SAME.

I DON'T EVEN FEEL LIKE I'M ON THE SAME PLANET. THIS PLACE LOOKS LIKE FUCKING MARS. AND ALL THE MARTIANS HAVE GUNS.

THE FOOD IS DIFFERENT. THE LANGUAGE IS DIFFERENT. MY CLOTHES ARE DIFFERENT. AND MY PROBLEMS ARE REAL FUCKING DIFFERENT. I USED TO HAVE TO SUPPRESS THE URGE TO KILL PEOPLE. NOW, IT'S HOW I EARN A FUCKING PAYCHECK.

I WANT TO REMEMBER WHAT IT'S LIKE TO HAVE AN IDENTITY. TO HAVE STUPID SHIT TO WORRY ABOUT THAT DOESN'T INVOLVE BEING BLOWN UP BY AN IED. I WANT TO REMEMBER WHAT IT'S LIKE TO FALL ASLEEP WITH YOU ON MY CHEST INSTEAD OF A TWENTY-POUND FLAK JACKET.

SHIT, I HAVE TO GO. PLEASE WRITE BACK.

I LOVE YOU.

KNIGHT

November 25, 1998

Dear Knight,

So, you just want to hear about my life? That seems pretty fucking boring, but okay. Um, let's see...I am still growing my hair out. My bangs are almost down to my nose now, and the shaved part is, like, two inches long. I just bleached it all platinum blonde, which it doesn't seem to be very happy about. The shit feels like pine straw now.

School is still going great. I'm out right now for Thanksgiving break. It looks like I'm going to get straight As again this semester, so I'm still on track to graduate early and get a scholarship to UGA or GSU. I'm leaning toward GSU. I don't even think UGA would let me in. I'm pretty sure you have to submit photographic evidence that you own at least five red-and-black dresses and shake a pom-pom while doing a keg stand as part of the entrance application process.

Let's see…what else? Juliet's baby's first word was BB! You have no idea how bad that shit pissed her off. I fucking love it. It's no wonder he likes me better. Juliet's a total bitch. Of course, I probably would be too if I had a fucking six-month-old. Better her than me, man.

My parents are fine. My dad still isn't working. He just moves from the couch to the kitchen table a few times a day and mutters about how the government is coming to take his guns away. My mom is still teaching art at Peach State Elementary and trying to stay high every minute that she's not there. I'm still working at Pier One, and they're still threatening to fire me at least once a week. Same old, same old.

That's about it. I'm sure you don't want to hear about the rest.

I probably shouldn't say this, but…I miss you. I don't even know why. You're such an asshole. Hey, there's some of your old identity for you. You're an asshole named Knight. Ronald McKnight actually. You have no middle name. You're nineteen years old. Your mom is a fucking cunt. Your dad is some big-shot businessman in Chicago who knocked her up and never looked back. You used to dress like a skinhead to keep people away even though you're not even racist. You love animals. You used to leave food out for the stray cats in Little Five Points, and you took care of Peg's German shepherd every day after school.

You also took my virginity on my ex-boyfriend's bed, which became your bed when he moved out. Handcuffs and honey were involved. Because you're kinky as shit.

You're also an amazing tattoo artist and body piercer. You pierced all my private places and tattooed a knight on the inside of my finger. You wouldn't do it on the outside, like I wanted, because you didn't want it to be permanent. You didn't want us to be permanent. You thought I deserved better.

But you were wrong.

And now here we are.

Be safe, Knight. I'll write again soon.

Love,

BB

P.S. Instead of trying to hang on to who you used to be, maybe try to figure out who you are now. *Because that guy I just told you about...you didn't like him very much. And he didn't fucking like anything.*

DECEMBER 17, 1998

DEAR BB,
    HE LIKED YOU.

                    LOVE,
                    KNIGHT

P.S. MERRY CHRISTMAS.

Knight's note was written on a scrap of brown paper inside of a small cardboard box that looked like it had been hit by a Hummer in transit. When I lifted the note out of the box, I found more brown paper underneath, wadded into a ball.

The fuck?

Pulling it out, I unraveled the baseball-sized hunk of parchment and stared at the contents. My eyes filled with tears, but I didn't blink. I didn't want to take my eyes off it for a second.

Knight had sent me a skinny silver bracelet, coiled to look like a delicate snake wrapping around the wearer's arm. Arabic characters, boats, palm trees, and even a tiny reptilian face had been painstakingly etched onto the surface and painted black.

Although the bracelet's story was written in a language that my mind didn't understand, my heart read every word fluently. The snake was on a journey. Its serpentine head had reached its final destination, but the rest of its body stretched across the ocean, bridging the gap to another time and place.

I slid the bracelet onto my spindly arm and held it under the lamp next to my bed, committing every etching and imperfection to memory. I used to think of Knight as a rattlesnake. Lethal. Irrational. Ready to strike at the first snap of a twig. And he was—with everyone else. But looking at the length of Iraqi silver coiling up my arm, I realized that Knight was an entirely different breed of snake where I was concerned. He wasn't going to kill me with his fangs—his guns, his knives, his baseball bat. He was going to wrap himself around my heart and squeeze until it simply couldn't beat anymore.

Knight was a boa constrictor who'd fallen in love with a mouse.

I took the brown paper the bracelet had been wrapped in and smoothed it out on my bed. Christmas was less than a week away, but maybe, if I paid for expedited shipping, I could get a gift to him in time. It didn't matter how much it cost. The idea of Knight spending Christmas in a war zone without a single fucking present to open made my chest ache. I'd pay anything to make that feeling go away.

The year before, I'd had Knight over to my house for Christmas. I hadn't been ready to introduce him to my parents yet, but what could I do? His stepfather had a restraining order against him, and I couldn't let him sit at Peg's house all alone while she visited relatives. Knight had shown up with his jeans unrolled and a Lonsdale hoodie covering his braces, which I appreciated, and he'd stayed on his best behavior the whole day. I don't think he dropped a single F-bomb, which is more than I can say for myself.

My mom remembered Knight from when she was his art teacher. It had been sweet to watch him squirm as she gushed about his talent. I think I even caught him smiling once or twice. When he left, Knight had told me that it was the best Christmas of his life.

I tore through my drawers until I found what I was looking for—a framed picture of two teenagers standing in front of a puny fake Christmas tree. Both had freckled faces. Both had shaved heads—one with bangs. And both wore matching half-assed smiles. It was the first picture that had ever been taken of us together—one of the only pictures of us in existence. So much of our time together had been spent alone. There was never anyone around to say, *Smile, you two!*

I might not have been able to display it anymore, but I would be forever grateful to my mom for taking that photo.

Placing the frame on top of the brown paper, I wrapped it diligently, making sure to pad the glass side the most, then I flipped it over and wrote on the back.

Dear Knight,
    She liked you too.
    Merry Christmas.
    Love,
    BB

GEORGIA
CHAPTER 28
19 PEACH STATE 99

Seeing that picture again for the first time in months sent my guilty conscience into a tailspin. Not only because it forced me to admit that I was carrying on some kind of long-distance relationship with my ex-boyfriend, but also because it reminded me that I still hadn't introduced Harley to my parents. We'd been dating for six months. *Six months.* That's like six decades in teenage-relationship years. My mom knew I had a boyfriend—mostly from the errant hickey here and there and the fact that I was never home—but I didn't talk about him much. What would I even say?

Sure, Harley got kicked out of high school at seventeen, but he's super resourceful. He even spent a few years squatting in Little Five Points with a band of homeless gutter punks! You gotta be pretty smart to live rent-free, am I right?

Harley might be a mechanic, but look! He drives a hundred-thousand-dollar car! Just don't open the trunk, okay?

Harley is old enough to buy me cigarettes and alcohol! Isn't that great? Now I don't have to steal yours!

You like art. Harley's covered in it!

But if I could bring a skinhead home for Christmas, whose knuckles were still bloody from beating his stepdad's face in the night before, I could bring Harley home. Right? At least Harley was charming. And that face. And that *hair*. What wasn't to love?

When the doorbell rang I bounced down the stairs, skipping the last three steps altogether, and tore open the front door. My eyes went straight to Harley's outfit, hoping he'd at least worn something that covered up his tattoos. He had on a long-sleeved white thermal Henley that hugged his hard chest and disappeared into his dark gray Dickies, which were held up with a studded belt. My mouth watered. Sliding my eyes up to his smirking face, I noticed that he hadn't taken out his lip ring, which was fine. I guess. I mean, it wasn't like I'd asked him to.

Then I noticed his hair.

Or lack thereof.

Harley hadn't just *cut* his hair. He hadn't just buzzed it off, like Knight's. Harley was bald.

Bic fucking bald.

I hadn't seen him in a week—the longest we'd been apart since we started dating—because I was grounded for breaking curfew again. What the fuck had happened while I was gone?

Harley didn't look *bad* with a shaved head, just…different. More sinister. He'd gone from looking like James Dean to looking like a James Bond villain.

I didn't have time to ask what had happened because my mom was already standing beside me, gesturing for Harley to come in. I stood in my parents' modest foyer with my mouth slightly agape as she ushered him straight back into the kitchen where she had a cheese ball and some Triscuits set out to look fancy.

As I followed several feet behind, I watched in horror as Harley took a seat at the kitchen island, revealing the reason why his beautiful sunny-blond sex hair was missing.

He had a tattoo, on the top of his head, the size of a fucking salad plate.

Time slowed to a crawl. I couldn't feel my socked feet as they moved across the linoleum floor. It was as if I were floating above the entire situation. From my vantage point, I could see Harley's tattoo perfectly. It looked like the top of his skull had been removed like the lid of a cookie jar, revealing a network of tubes and gears and pistons inside instead of brains.

I get it. You're a motorhead. Real clever, asshole.

I remembered Harley saying something about having a tattoo on his head when we'd first started dating, but this work looked fresh. The ink was jet-black, and the skin around it was red and raised. That motherfucker had gotten his head tattooed, or re-tattooed, right before coming to meet my parents. If he had at least warned me I would have told him to just stay home, made up some excuse. Now I had a grown-ass man with a facial piercing, a head tattoo, a trunk full of guns, and zero high school diplomas sitting at my kitchen table, eating my mama's cheeseball.

That wasn't *my* problem though. Because I wasn't there. Sure, my body was there. But my consciousness was watching with detached amusement from the other side of the room, wearing 3D glasses and munching on a bowl of popcorn like, *Oh, shit, girl! Your mom looks mad as hell! Did you see that look she just gave you? Just wait until your dad sees. He's probably gonna make you start wearing a chastity belt. You are so fucked!*

"Am I on peyote, or is there a '69 Boss 429 in my driveway?"

My dad's voice was coming from the living room, which was next to the kitchen and behind the garage.

I'd assumed he just hadn't bothered to get up and come say hello, but evidently, he'd snuck outside to scope out Harley's car.

Weirdo.

Harley's mouth pulled to one side in a cocky smirk as he got up to greet my dad. He loved nothing more than showing off that damn car. I wanted to follow him but not badly enough to risk reentering my body. Even my mom's hippie pacifism had its limits, and I did *not* want to be there when she finally lost it and smacked me in the mouth.

Making direct, searing eye contact with me, my mom downed her third glass of merlot, then set the empty stemware on the counter with more force than was necessary. I winced as she stalked toward me, then sighed in relief as she passed, gripping the handle on the refrigerator door instead of my neck.

Pulling a massive honey-baked ham out of the fridge, my mom set it on the counter and said, "Set the table," without looking at me. Then, she turned and walked out of the room.

Shit.

I got my ass in gear. We only used our tiny formal dining room three times a year, but when we did, it was always my job to set the table. Probably because I was the only one who knew how to do it correctly. I'd learned how in Girl Scouts, right before I dropped out at the age of eight. As I arranged the silverware, I looked out the window to my left and saw my dad climbing out of Harley's passenger seat with a giant, stupid grin on his face. Then I looked out the kitchen window and saw my mom puffing on a joint on the back porch.

Maybe it's going to be okay, my dumbass optimism suggested. *Maybe they're not going to put you up for adoption.*

When everyone came in for dinner they were all in chipper moods, except for me. My nerves were fucking shot. My mom giggled at things that weren't jokes and ate with her eyes almost completely closed. My dad and Harley spoke in some car-guy language that was barely passable as English. And I remained silent, pushing my food around on my plate and hoping that nobody noticed it wasn't going into my mouth. I hated holiday meals because I felt so much pressure to eat. I would always end up binging just to avoid the scrutiny, which meant I'd have to spend the rest of the night hovering over a toilet with my finger down my throat to undo the damage. Not a great way to end Christmas. But with Harley there, nobody even noticed me.

Maybe having him over wasn't such a bad idea after all.

Of course, as soon as I got used to the idea of having him in my house, he wasn't. Harley dipped out right after dinner, giving me nothing more than a quick peck on the cheek at the door. As I closed it behind him, I realized that we hadn't exchanged presents. We hadn't gotten a picture in front of the Christmas tree. I don't know if he'd even seen my Christmas tree. It was ugly, but my mom and I had made all the ornaments ourselves when I was a kid.

Just as I was about to turn and sprint up the stairs to go smoke and overanalyze his behavior in my room, I felt a small, firm hand squeeze my shoulder.

"Punkin," my mom slurred, tightening her grip almost painfully, "I hope you're using protection with that man. He looks like he's been to prison."

Truer words had never been spoken.

January 1999

Ninety-eight pounds. That's fine. That's totally fine. It's still double digits. So what if you gained a few pounds over the holidays? That's norm—

"BB!" my mom bellowed from downstairs. "You got a package!"

Shit!

I hopped off my bathroom scale and shut off the water in the shower. Wrapping a towel around myself, I flew down the stairs. My mother was waiting at the bottom with her arms folded over her chest and a manila envelope in one hand. I'd been so good about checking the mail before my mom got home from work every day, but Saturdays were tricky.

I don't know why I cared, but I hadn't wanted my mom to know that I was still talking to Knight. Probably because I hadn't wanted *anyone* to know that I was still talking to Knight. Probably because I shouldn't have been talking to Knight at all.

My mom arched a suspicious eyebrow at me as I snatched the envelope from her hand and turned to run back up the stairs.

"It's from Knight," she said, her voice dropping an octave at the end. She said it the way you would say *The president's been shot* or *The test results came back positive*. Like there was grave danger afoot.

"M'kay, thanks!" I yelled, turning the corner at the top of the staircase without looking back.

Dashing into my room, I slammed the door shut behind me and tore into the package. Whatever was in there felt thick, like a magazine. I pulled out a stack of white paper and began unfolding and unfolding and unfolding until I was holding a life-size outline of a human body before me. The center of the paper man's chest was riddled with bullet holes—in the shape of a perfectly symmetrical heart.

That sweet fucking psycho.

I wonder if they can tell I'm not twenty-one.

I giggled, out loud and to no one, then took another sip of the Cuervo 1800 shot Harley had ordered for me before he split to handle some kind of "business" outside. I couldn't drink it all at once. Shit tasted like hellfire and tarnation. Harley had no problem with it though, judging from the three empty shot glasses sitting next to mine.

BB, you're sixteen and boobless. Everyone in here knows you're not twenty-one.

It's fine. It's totally fine. I mean, they let Knight work here bussing tables when he was like, seventeen, right?

I shuddered, remembering the stories Knight had told me about his time working at Spirit of Sixty-Nine—the skinhead/rockabilly bar down the street from Terminus City Tattoo. How the only girls he'd ever been with before me were skin chicks he went home with after the bar closed—one-night stands that usually ended in bloodshed.

Knight.

I took another sip and grimaced.

I hope he's okay. That target he sent last week didn't come with a letter, and the letter he'd sent last month was, like, two sentences long. That's a bad sign. Knight always writes to me. Even when we went to school together, I think he wrote me more notes than we had actual conversations. If he's not writing, that means he's not talking about the shit he's going through to anyone. At all.

I should write him back.

What would I even say though?

"Hey, *if you're reading this, that means you probably haven't gotten blown up yet. Good job. How's the weather in Iraq? Still deserty? It's cold as shit here. Not much else to report. I love my psychology classes, and I'm still dating that guy who pistol-whipped you. He shaved his head and got kind of mean since he started doing coke all the time, but I secretly like it because it reminds me of you.*

M'kay, bye!

Love,

BB"

"Oh my God! BB! What are you doin' here, hon?"

I swiveled on my barstool and saw Miss July and a rockabilly guy named Jason, whom I recognized from the track, walking over to me. Tracey had Jason's black leather jacket wrapped around her shoulders, and her usually perfect blonde victory rolls were sopping wet.

"It's fuckin' pouring out there," she said, handing Jason his jacket as she plopped down on the barstool next to me.

He gave me a little nod and took the seat next to her. Guess he was still embarrassed about betting against me all those months ago.

Good. Asshole.

Tracey pulled a red bandana out of her purse, and in two

seconds flat, she had it tied around her head like Rosie the Riveter. That bitch couldn't be uncool if she tried.

"Where's Harley?" Tracey said, looking around. "I know you didn't drink all these shots by yourself." Her mouth was split wide in a calendar-girl smile, but her eyes were questioning. *No, seriously. Where's Harley? You shouldn't be in here by yourself, sugar pie.*

"Oh, um, he had to run outside and get something real fast. He'll be right back."

"He ran outside in *this* bullshit?" Tracey gestured to her soaking wet 1950s-style dress and fluffed the tulle under her skirt, exposing her tattoo.

"You still haven't gotten your thigh piece finished, huh?" My voice came out sounding sadder than I'd intended. Like I was consoling her.

"No," Tracey said with a sigh, accepting a froufrou-looking pink martini from Jason. "I called the shop and asked Bobbi if she'd do it, like you said, but she said that Knight's 'punk ass' needs to do it himself." Tracey made finger quotes around the words *punk ass.* "She promised that she'd make him do it for free when he gets home in May, if I can just wait that long."

May.

Knight will be home in May.

"BB?"

"Huh? Oh, sorry. That's awesome. Free tattoo! Bobbi will make him do it, too. Even Knight is scared of her."

"Who's scared of who?" Harley's voice rumbled behind me, making me jump.

I swiveled on my retro vinyl barstool from Tracey on my right to Harley on my left. He was standing against the bar with streams of rainwater cascading down his black leather jacket, over the pistol-shaped bulge in his pocket, and onto the concrete floor. His wet hair, which had grown back maybe an eighth of an inch, looked darker than usual. And the two-inch scar running down the side of his head that I'd never noticed until he shaved it stood out like a sore thumb.

"Oh my God, you're soaked!" I exclaimed, changing the subject. "What took you so long?"

"Yeah, what took you so long?" Tracey asked, leaning around me with her spokesmodel smile. "Jason and I were startin' to get sick of chasing all the guys away."

"Oh really?" Harley smiled back, but his grin was anything but warm and playful. It sent shivers down my spine. "Well, I guess I just need to let them know who the fuck she belongs to then. Don't I?" Harley downed what was left of my shot of tequila and reached for Tracey's half-empty martini glass. Standing up straight, Harley tapped the side of it with a knife from the bar so hard I thought the damn thing was going to break.

The rabble of the rowdy patrons fell away as every skinhead, rockabilly, metal head, and biker in the joint craned their necks to look at my boyfriend.

Oh shit. Shit, shit, shit, shit.

"Everybody, shut the fuck up," Harley commanded. "I got something to ask this little lady."

No! Damn it, Harley! What are you doing? Not here!

Harley made direct eye contact with me as he pulled something out of his pocket and slowly sank to one knee. His gaze was harder than usual. Threatening. Harley usually looked delightfully amused during his bullshit proposals, like he enjoyed putting me on the spot. But there was nothing teasing about his narrowed eyes, dilated pupils, grinding jaw, or that tattoo on the top of his head, which I could still see through his super-short hair.

"BB"—Harley held up two fingers, the ring pinched between them—"will you marry me?"

Without turning my head, I scanned the faces in the bar with my eyes, all of which were gawking at us, before returning my gaze to Harley's challenging stare.

Then I erupted into a fit of nervous laughter.

Grabbing Harley's wrist, I pulled him to a standing position and wrapped my arms around his waist. I pressed my cheek into his sopping-wet jacket, making sure to face Tracey instead of the confused crowd.

She held her palms up and shrugged, mouthing the words, *What did you say?*

I grimaced and shook my head a little bit.

Then Tracey grimaced too.

The dickhead bartender with the goatee who'd been eyeballing me all night came over and said, "Well, what'd she say?" loud enough for everyone in the whole damn place to hear.

"She said, *Hell no*," Jason replied, just as loud.

The entire place erupted into hysterics. I glared at Jason, who was sipping his Pabst Blue Ribbon next to Tracey with a smirk. I didn't even know that bastard could talk. He'd probably been waiting for an opportunity to bust Harley's balls after all the times he'd taken him for his hard-earned cash at the track.

Not that Harley would normally even care. That was his superpower—not caring. Harley was untouchable that way. You couldn't hurt him. You couldn't break him. You couldn't rile him up. Harley was rubber, and everyone else was glue.

That was why I was so surprised when he grabbed me by the arm and dragged me through the tables of laughing tattooed misfits and into a hallway in the back corner of the bar.

"What the fuck was that?" Harley growled, releasing me so that I could turn to face him.

"What the fuck was what?" I said, genuinely confused.

"You made me look like a fuckin' bitch out there!"

Why are you being such an asshole?

"Harley," I said, putting my hands up, "I didn't do anything."

"You laughed in my fucking face!"

Okay, this is definitely Cuervo-and-cocaine Harley. Guess I know at least part of what he was doing in the parking lot. His trunk is probably a few Uzis and sawed-off shotguns lighter, too.

"I wasn't laughing at you," I said, trying to keep my voice calm. "I was just nervous. I don't know any of these people."

"I heard you talking about him." Harley's nostrils flared. He couldn't even say his name.

Shit. Think, BB. Think.

"So? He did Tracey's thigh tattoo. She was just trying to fig-ure out how to get it finished now that he's overseas."

Remember? He's overseas. As in far, far away. As in you can stop being crazy now.

Harley took a step closer to me, and I took a step deeper into the shadows of the smoky hallway. "If that jarhead mother-fucker had been here tonight and *he'd* asked you to marry him, what would you have said?"

Um . . . well . . .

"You can't even answer the fucking question!" Harley pounded the wall closest to us with his fist, causing me to jump.

It also caused me to snap, "I wouldn't have said anything because Knight wouldn't have asked me to marry him in a fucking bar!"

Harley's eyes flared at the mention of his name.

Shit.

I dropped my voice an octave and took another step backward. "Sorry. I don't know why we're even talking about this. Harley, you don't want to marry me. This is just a game we play. You ask me to marry you in front of big groups of people because you love to embarrass me, and I always say no. Remember? I don't understand why you're so mad that I rejected you this time."

Harley's face contorted into something wicked as he advanced toward me. I went to take another step backward but stopped when my heel met the wall.

"Oh, you *rejected* me?" He said the word as if it were in a foreign language that he hadn't practiced, as if he'd never said it in his life. "You. *Rejected* me?"

Harley caged me in with his palms on either side of my head, his face a backlit shadow. I could smell the tequila on his breath and feel the adrenaline in my veins.

"Do it again then," Harley said, grabbing the backs of my thighs and hoisting me up so that my back was against the wall, my legs were around his waist, and his bulging erection was against my crotch. "*Reject* me."

I didn't reject him. I did something even worse.

I poured gasoline on the fire.

I kissed him.

As soon as my tongue grazed his, Harley crashed into me—kissing me so hard my head hit the wall behind me, grinding into me until I thought he was going to bruise my clit. He didn't give two motherfucks that we were in a hallway in a crowded bar. And honestly, I didn't either.

Until he let go of me with one hand and began unbuckling his belt.

Shit!

"Harley," I whispered-yelled over the Social Distortion blasting through the bar, "we can't . . . not here."

I had to hold my own weight up completely as Harley used both of his hands to work on my studded belt and zipper.

"Why the fuck not?"

Um . . . because we're in public. Because my purse full of condoms is back at the bar. Because your gun is digging into my thigh. Because I'm way too fucking sober for this shit.

"Because my pants are too tight."

My eyes darted around the hallway as I tried to come up with a solution. I didn't want to "reject" Harley again, but I also didn't want to get arrested for public indecency. Just then a skinhead came out of the men's room, zipping up his fly.

Lowering my legs back down to the cement floor, I pushed Harley away far enough to wriggle free and tugged him toward the vacated men's room. "In here," I whispered.

As soon as we were inside, I locked the door behind us, relieved that it was a single-toilet-sink situation and not a bustling five-stall operation. Too bad it smelled—no, reeked of piss. Not that Harley cared. Before I could even turn back around, he was behind me, yanking my already-unfastened jeans down to my knees.

I braced myself against the door as hot pulsing flesh pressed against my ass. Harley bit down on my earlobe, his breath warm and ragged on my oversensitive skin. I wanted to push back against him. I wanted to let him fuck me, right there against the restroom door. I wanted to pretend like he was Knight, and I was one of the little skin chicks he used to pick up at the bar. I wanted him to pull a butterfly knife out of his pocket and make me bleed.

But I couldn't. Because my responsible, sober brain chose that moment to blurt out the word, "Condom?"

Harley slid his cock between my thighs, wetting it against my slippery sex. My knees buckled a little at the contact, which only increased the pressure. God, it felt good.

Harley placed his right hand on the door to brace his weight and snaked his left around my rib cage, pulling my back into his chest like a vise. He didn't answer my question. And, judging by the way he was dragging the head of his cock over my seam, he wasn't going to.

I was at war with myself. I could either push him away and risk pissing off Hulk Harley—or whoever it was that he became when he'd had too much blow and booze—or I could give in and risk contracting God knows what from a man who couldn't even tell me how many people he'd slept with.

As much as it turned me on whenever Harley got rough, in that moment, I knew that he wasn't like Knight at all. Knight would never have put me at risk. Knight hadn't fucked me without a condom until he personally took me to the doctor to get on the pill and made sure that he was clean. And even then it had been my suggestion. This person . . . this person didn't even know I was on the pill.

Because I hadn't told him.

As Harley's cock pressed against my entrance and his grip around my ribs tightened, panic seized the lungs they were sworn to protect.

No!

I clamped my thighs shut and wriggled around until I was facing Harley. Well, I was facing his neck. I couldn't bring myself to look up at him. Instead, I kissed his pounding pulse point as my hands found their way to his cock, which throbbed to the same beat.

I'd gone down on him before but never to completion. The few times I'd let Knight come in my mouth, I'd thought I was going to drown—it wasn't exactly something I wanted to relive—but making Harley come was my ticket out of that piss-soaked hellhole. So I took a deep breath...and I sank to my knees.

Harley fisted my shaggy bleach-blonde hair as I struggled with his size. I couldn't take him very deep before I gagged, so I tried to make up for it by wrapping my bony fingers around his length. Harley tightened his grip on my hair and guided my movements until he finally went stiff as a rod in my hands.

Memories of Knight coming down my throat hijacked my control center, causing me to pull my face away suddenly—just as Harley blew his load. With his hands gripping my head, I couldn't get out of the way fast enough, and Harley's first spurt of cum narrowly missed my eye. It grazed my cheekbone and landed in my hair. His second spurt hit the back of the door. And his third dribbled down his cock and onto my hands.

But at least I hadn't drowned.

Wiping my mouth and cheek on the sleeve of my cropped

leopard-print sweater, I stood up and looked into the heavy-lidded, smiling eyes of someone I recognized.

"Damn, woman. You been holdin' out on me," Harley mumbled on unsteady feet.

Relief washed over me. "Don't get used to it," I teased, patting him on the shoulder as I stepped around him and made my way to the grimiest sink in America. "You almost put my eye out."

I heard Harley chuckle as I turned on the faucet, and I watched his reflection as I washed my hands. I could see his profile, smiling as he buckled his pants. With his scar and tattoo temporarily hidden from my view, he almost looked like the Harley I remembered. Playful yet powerful. Baby-faced but no longer blond.

I lowered my head to wash the cum out of my hair and felt two arms wrap around my torso. Fear shot through me in an instant but left just as quickly as the warmth of Harley's embrace sank in. These arms weren't viselike; they were tender. Appreciative. Almost loving.

Almost.

FEBRUARY 2, 1999

DEAR BB,

SHIT HAS CALMED DOWN A LOT
AROUND HERE SINCE WE BOMBED
THE EVER-LOVING FUCK OUT OF
THE IRAQI MILITARY LAST MONTH.
EVEN THE LOCAL MILITIAS HAVE
BACKED OFF.

YOU'D THINK THAT WOULD BE A
GOOD THING, BUT I FUCKING HATE
IT. I'M GOING OUT OF MY MIND. I'M
FUCKING STUCK HERE, IN THIS
CARDBOARD BOX, ON FUCKING
MARS, AND ALL I DO IS THINK ABOUT

YOU AND WONDER IF YOU EVEN
REMEMBER THAT I EXIST.

MAYBE I DON'T. MAYBE THE ME THAT
YOU KNEW DOESN'T EXIST ANYMORE.
I KEEP LOOKING AT THAT PICTURE
YOU SENT ME, AND IT FEELS LIKE IT
HAPPENED TO SOMEBODY ELSE. IS
THAT WHY YOU HAVEN'T WRITTEN ME
BACK? BECAUSE I'M GONE? BECAUSE
I'M SOMEBODY ELSE NOW?

PLEASE TELL ME. EVEN IF YOU'RE
DONE WITH ME, JUST FUCKING TELL
ME. YOU'RE ALL I FUCKING THINK
ABOUT.

I LOVE YOU.

                                    KNIGHT

My teeth chattered and my fingers shook as I finally lit my cigarette on the third attempt. I was huddled in the recessed entryway of the Humanities building, trying to hide from the wind.
But it found me. It *always* found me.

Fuck you, winter, I thought. *I get it. You're cold. You don't have
to beat me over the head with it. Fucking show-off.*

I watched as Juliet and Goth Girl ran-walked over from the
Math and Science building, ducking their heads and pulling
their collars up. We weren't able to get the same classes during
our second semester because I needed to take some specific
advanced placement classes to graduate early. So Juliet and Goth
Girl wound up together most of the day, and I wound up sitting
in the back row of my classes alone, writing letters that I knew I
would just toss in the garbage on my way out the door.

At least I got to hang out with Goth Girl after school sometimes. She liked coming with me to Harley's house when we
were both off work, mostly so that she could disappear into
Dave's room and do God only knows what. But they weren't
officially dating or anything. It was weird.

Just like the new strappy, swing-like apparatus hanging in the corner of his room.

Freaks.

Juliet had brought Romeo over after school *once*. Within ten minutes he'd managed to knock over a water bong and shove a fistful of cigarette butts into his mouth. Now I pretty much only saw her at school between classes.

"Will you bitches hurry up? It's fucking freezing." Juliet breathed into her cupped hands as Goth Girl lit up.

Juliet had quit smoking, *very reluctantly*, while she was pregnant with Romeo, and she always gave us a hard time about it.

"Oh, fuck it. If I have to stand out here you better give me one, too."

And...she always caved.

"Okay, *Mom*," Goth Girl deadpanned as she fished a second cigarette out of her pack.

Juliet fucking hated it when she called her that.

"You working today, BB?" Goth Girl asked, trying to sound nonchalant, which was easy for her. She had the emotional range of an oyster.

"Y-y-y-yeah," I stuttered through my chattering teeth. "I'm off-f-f-f tomorrow though. You should c-c-come over."

Goth Girl rolled her big black doll eyes. "Yeah, maybe."

"Hey, g-g-guys, I gotta go talk to my teacher before class. I'll see you at lunch, ok-k-k-kay?" I stamped out my cigarette beneath my boot.

Juliet just nodded—she was too busy orgasming over her cigarette to care what I'd said—and Goth Girl gave me a little two-fingered salute.

I dashed inside and up the central staircase to the second

floor—my forty-pound backpack bouncing on my bony back like a horse jockey the entire way—and burst into my Psychology II class ten minutes early. My teacher, Dr. Raines, was standing at the whiteboard, jotting down vocabulary words and homework assignments. He was an older gentleman, short and round, and his wardrobe consisted of approximately three tweed blazers and two pairs of shapeless khakis.

"Good morning, Miss Bradley," he said without turning away from the whiteboard. "You're in early. Think maybe you'll join us in the front row today?"

"Um, sure," I said, dropping my backpack on the desk closest to the door. "Dr. Raines, can I talk to you for a minute? Before everybody gets here?"

Putting down his marker, Dr. Raines turned and looked at me over the top of his bifocals. "Everything okay, Miss Bradley?"

"Yeah, it's just…" I really wished I had decided to sit. Standing felt awkward. "My ex-boyfriend…he joined the Marines, and he's stationed in Iraq. He, um, writes me letters sometimes, and he says things about, like, not knowing who he is anymore. In his last one, he said he felt like he was 'gone.' I think he's seen and done some really bad sh—*stuff* over there. I was just wondering if you had any suggestions on ways to, like, help him. I need to write him back, but I don't know what to say."

Dr. Raines took off his glasses and pinched the bridge of his nose. "PTSD," he muttered under his breath, shaking his head. Looking up at me with sad eyes, Dr. Raines said, "I know what your friend is going through quite personally, I'm afraid. I was drafted during the Vietnam War."

Oh, shit.

"The official diagnostic term is post-traumatic stress disorder, or PTSD, although we didn't know that back then. When the surviving members of my platoon and I came home, we all had...difficulties." Dr. Raines pulled a hankie from his pocket and rubbed the lenses of his glasses with it as he spoke. "Identity integration issues, insomnia, increased irritability and aggression, flashbacks, panic attacks, suicidal thoughts and behaviors." Putting his bifocals back on, he continued, "It's actually the reason why I pursued a career in psychology. I wanted to understand what was happening to us."

I sputtered, "I...I'm so sorry. I had no idea."

"That's quite all right, Miss Bradley," Dr. Raines said with a small smile. "These things can break us, or they can inspire us to help others, correct?"

I nodded. And swallowed. And cleared my throat. "So, what can I do...to help?"

"Something I found quite therapeutic while I was recovering was doing things I'd enjoyed as a child. Figuring out how to integrate my newly formed soldier identity with my newly formed young man identity was difficult, but the identity I'd formed as a child was very crystallized. If I was feeling on edge, I would simply sit down and build a model airplane. It always made me feel more like *myself*."

"He liked to draw as a kid," I said. "He's really talented. He's actually a tattoo artist. Or...he was."

"That's wonderful. You could encourage this young man to draw whenever he's feeling...out of sorts."

"I will. Thank you."

"I have a few other strategies that might prove to be helpful, but unfortunately, class is about to begin. If you would like to come by before class again, I'll put together a list for you."

"Oh my God. That would be amazing. Thank you."

Dr. Raines smiled. "Anything to help out a fellow vet. He's very lucky to have someone like you looking out for him."

Guilt slithered up my spine. Knight didn't have me. Not anymore.

"Dr. Raines, can I ask you one more thing?"

"Certainly."

"Can you get PTSD from other things, besides combat? Like...like a really, really, *really* bad fight? Or seeing somebody get killed? Or having your friend commit suicide?"

Or all of the above in the same month?

"Absolutely. Any situation in which you feel extremely threatened or frightened or upset can cause symptoms of post-traumatic stress."

"Like flashbacks? And panic attacks?"

Dr. Raines looked at me over the top of his glasses, as if he had X-ray vision and was snooping around inside my brain. "Miss Bradley, are you sure everything is okay? I could set you up with our counseling department if—"

"Nope. Fine. Thanks!" I chirped, grabbing my backpack and running to the safety of the back row.

As the rest of my classmates trickled in, I took out my note-book and began to write. It wasn't any different from what I did every other day, but this time, the fruits of my labor weren't going to end up in the garbage can on my way out the door.

February 10, 1999

Dear Knight,
   I'm sorry I haven't written you back until now.
Actually, I did write you back. A lot. I just didn't
send any of it. Nothing I wrote felt right. If I just
talked about myself I felt shitty, but when I tried
to write about what you must be going through
I was afraid I would upset you. I didn't want to
bring up the past because that didn't seem helpful.
So, what does that leave for us to talk about? The
future? That seems depressing, too. I mean, what's
going to happen to my Mustang when everybody starts
driving flying cars?
I don't even want to think about it.
   So I got an idea. What if we talk about the past-
past? Like shit from when we were kids. I know
you didn't have a great childhood, so just tell me the
good stuff. What were you like when you were little?
What did you like to do? What were your favorite
cartoons? What did you want to be when you grew
up?
   I was a fucking nightmare. My mom couldn't
make me do shit. I refused to wear anything she'd
laid out for me, and I basically walked around
looking like Pippi Longstocking every day. Red hair.
Freckles. Nothing matched. I wore tutus and grass
hula skirts over my jeans, and I was always trying
to cut my own hair. (Still am.) I was obsessed with
my She-Ra Princess of Power Crystal Castle, mostly

because of the way it smelled. They must have put lead in the paint or something. That shit got me high. My favorite color was "rainbow," and I wanted to be a "jet pilot-architect" when I grew up. Oh, and my favorite things to do were pretend to write very important notes in my notebook (just squiggles), draw with sidewalk chalk on the driveway, and drag all my mom's pots and pans into the backyard and make mud pies.

Your turn.

Love,

BB

P.S. Be safe.

"BB, you are basically *in* the fire," Juliet said.

"Okay, *M-M-M-Mom*," I said, shivering, as I rolled my eyes, doing my very worst frozen Goth Girl impersonation.

Juliet laughed and stood next to me, sweeping her long braids over one shoulder to keep them from burning in the raging bonfire behind us. "I can't believe all these people come out here to race in the middle of fucking winter," she said, scanning the crowd of bodies and trucks and cars and kegs gathered around us.

"I kn-n-n-ow, right?" The warmth was finally starting to creep into my bones, which were only separated from the flames by a burgundy flight jacket, the thin cotton of my band T-shirt, and an even thinner layer of translucent skin. "At least there's beer," I said, holding up my red plastic cup.

Juliet crashed her matching cup into the side of mine. "I'll drink to that."

As she took a sip, a faint smile played on the corner of her mouth. That little bitch was having fun.

I wrapped my arm around Juliet's elbow and dropped my cheek on her shoulder. "I'm so happy you came out," I said.

"Me, too," she answered wistfully. "Now, get the fuck off me before all these cute boys get the wrong idea."

I laughed. "Oh, don't worry. They know I'm here with Harley. He's used me to hustle money out of most of them."

Used. Did I just say used?

"Where is he, by the way?" Juliet asked, looking around. "I don't even see his—oh my fucking God." Juliet gripped my arm with one hand and almost pulverized her flimsy cup with the other. "BB. Is that who I fucking think it is?"

I squinted and looked in the direction she was looking, but all I could see was just a shitload of people. "Who? Where?"

"The girl hanging out with the ride-or-die crew over there. Purple LA Lakers coat. Long black hair."

What little warmth I'd gleaned from the fire froze to solid ice inside my veins. I didn't want to look, but I had to. For my own protection.

The last time I'd seen Angel Alvarez, she'd been flying out of Knight's truck, running toward me and screaming like a fucking banshee. She would have beaten my ass right there in Trevor Walcott's driveway—in front of everybody at his graduation party—if she hadn't tripped over the curb and landed at my feet instead.

I didn't think I'd get that lucky twice.

I followed Juliet's line of sight and found a sea of violet. Angel's older brother, Carlos Alvarez, was some high-ranking asshole in a Latin gang where everybody wore purple—mostly in the form of bandanas and LA Lakers gear. And they all rode crotch rockets like they thought they were DMX and the Ruff

Ryders. I'd seen guys dressed like that at the track before, but it never occurred to me that Angel might be with them.

I finally spotted the girl Juliet was talking about. Her long, straight hair was dark instead of brassy blonde, but everything else about her fit—height, weight, hourglass figure, Lakers jacket and baggy jeans. Her ability to strike fear into me without even looking in my direction.

Thankfully, she and her crew were a good sixty feet away from us, but still, being sixty feet away from a tiger was still sixty feet too close even if it did have its back turned.

"What the fuck is she doing here?" I whisper-yelled over the steady roar of the fire, crowd, music, and engines.

"Hell if I know. You haven't seen her here before?"

"Fuck no!"

As Juliet and I studied the apparition before us, Harley walked up with a giant smile on his boyish face. His lip ring hugged his plump bottom lip, and the light from the fire made the surface of his flame-blue eyes sparkle.

"Hey, pretty ladies. Are y'all watchin' this shit? Bubba's smokin' all the other rednecks! I dropped a new big block in his truck last week, and those assholes don't know what the fuck just—" Harley waved his hand in front of our faces. "Y'all okay?"

Juliet looked at Harley and said, "We won't be if Angel fucking Alvarez looks over here."

Harley's smile disappeared. "Who?" He growled the word.

"That girl, over there with the gangbangers. She tried to steal BB's boyfriend last year *and then* tried to beat her ass. She's fucking psycho."

I looked at Harley, suddenly more afraid of his reaction to

Juliet's mention of Knight than I was of Angel. His eyes were hard and his jaw was clenched.

Shit. Here we go.

"I'll be back," Harley snarled, stomping off in the direction of the cholos. Briefly turning around, he pointed at the ground in front of us and barked, "Stay here."

Wait. What? Harley was mad at *Angel*?

I'd thought he'd be mad at Juliet for bringing up The Ex Who Shall Not Be Named. Harley didn't even know Angel. Did he?

Just before Harley reached the sea of amethyst-colored assholes, I panicked and pulled Juliet away from the fire by the arm. Ducking down behind one of JR's enormous tires, we watched as Harley exchanged words with my one sworn enemy—Angel Alvarez.

"What the fuck is he saying to her?" I whispered.

"I don't know, but it looks like he's chewing her ass out."

"Is he fucking crazy? Doesn't he know who her brother is?" I was flattered that Harley wanted to defend me, but stomping into the middle of a gang meeting to start shit with the leader's little sister was one of the stupidest things I'd ever seen him do.

"I don't see Carlos over there," Juliet whispered.

Thank God.

"But his boys don't look too happy."

I peeked around the tire again and saw two thick, neckless dudes standing next to Angel with their chests puffed out. Their plaid flannel shirts were buttoned only at the collar, and purple bandanas were tied around their bald heads. They didn't try to interfere though. Maybe they had some kind of respect for Harley since they raced their crotch rockets on his track.

As I tried to wrap my head around what was happening, a

shrill, scrappy voice rose over even the loudest engines and ste-
reos. I couldn't make out every syllable, but *where*, *fuck*, and *she*
rang out clear as a bell. Those words hijacked my brain right
through my ears and pressed play on memories I'd been trying
to bury for months.

Angel and her hood-rat friends heckling me in the hallway.
Boxing me in at my locker. Posturing to fight in the parking lot.
About to jump me in Trevor's driveway.

"Knight told me you can't suck cock for shit."

"Knight loves me now, bitch."

"I might be pregnant."

Angel had been completely full of shit back then—I knew
that now—but that didn't exactly keep me from hyperventilating behind JR's truck at the sight of her. My whole body was
shaking—and not because of the cold.

"BB...BB!" Juliet shook my shoulder. "Angel's leaving. And
Harley's coming back over here! Act cool!"

Cool...cool. What's that? Uh...

I spotted the nearest keg and ran over to it with Juliet close
behind, ducking to keep from being spotted. Once we got there,
we stood up and refilled our crumpled plastic cups, pretending
to be engrossed in some hilarious conversation. I watched Harley enter the clearing where the bonfire was out of the corner of
my eye and reveled in the five seconds that it took him to realize
that I wasn't there before he spotted me in the crowd.

When our eyes locked, a grin I wasn't expecting spread across
my face. Warmth bloomed in my chest and unfurled into my
extremities. Heat trickled up my neck and stained my cheeks.
My lungs stopped working, but my heart beat double-time.

Harley James might have been on the wrong side of the

law, but he was still my fucking hero. Not only had he gone toe-to-toe with Knight for me—a feat no mortal had ever even considered before him—but he'd also just stomped into a cluster of gun-carrying gangbangers to chase off my archnemesis—Angel Alvarez.

I wanted to kiss him. I wanted to cry. And when Harley walked over on those long legs with that sexy swagger and pulled a tiny ring out of his pocket with a twinkle in his eye, I really, really, really wanted to just say *yes*.

MARCH 5, 1999

DEAR BB,

YOU REALIZE I'VE SPENT MOST OF MY LIFE TRYING NOT TO THINK ABOUT MY CHILDHOOD, RIGHT?

FUCK IT. YOU SAID JUST THE GOOD STUFF, SO THIS SHOULD BE QUICK.

MY FAVORITE CARTOON WAS TEENAGE MUTANT NINJA TURTLES. I WATCHED THAT SHIT EVERY MORNING BEFORE THE BUS CAME. RAPHAEL WAS MY FAVORITE. HE WORE THE RED MASK AND WAS A FUCKING ASSHOLE.

I LIKED BASEBALL. I WOULD'VE HIT SHIT WITH A BAT ALL DAY, EVERY DAY, IF I HAD THE CHANCE. MY FRIEND'S MOM SIGNED ME UP TO PLAY AND EVEN CAME AND PICKED ME UP FOR EVERY GAME SINCE MY MOM WAS USUALLY TOO FUCKED UP TO TAKE ME. I WANTED TO BE A PROFESSIONAL BASEBALL PLAYER WHEN I GREW UP.

I WANTED TO BE A VETERINARIAN TOO. I HAD ALL THESE LITTLE JARS AND SHIT ON MY WINDOWSILL WHEN I WAS A KID WHERE I KEPT BUGS AND LIZARDS AND TADPOLES. I REALLY WANTED A DOG, BUT OF COURSE CANDI COULDN'T BE FUCKING BOTHERED, SO I CAUGHT MY OWN PETS.

I LIKED TO DRAW, BUT I STOPPED FOR A WHILE BECAUSE ALL THE DRAWINGS I GAVE TO CANDI USUALLY ENDED UP IN THE TRASH. THEN I GOT THIS BADASS ART TEACHER IN THIRD GRADE NAMED MRS. BRADLEY. SHE LET ME SIT BY MYSELF AND HUNG ALL MY DRAWINGS UP ON HER

BULLETIN BOARD, RIGHT NEXT TO
HER DAUGHTER'S.

HER DAUGHTER DREW ALL
THIS GIRLIE SHIT, RAINBOWS
AND FLOWERS AND SUNS WITH
GODDAMN SMILEY FACES ON THEM.
I WONDERED IF I WOULD BE THAT
HAPPY IF I HAD MRS. BRADLEY AS A
MOM TOO. I DIDN'T EVEN KNOW YOU,
BUT LOOKING AT YOUR PICTURES
MADE ME HATE YOU. IT WASN'T
FUCKING FAIR.

THEN I SAW YOU. YOU CAME
INTO MY ART CLASS ONE DAY AND
INTERRUPTED YOUR MOM WHILE SHE
WAS TEACHING. YOU WERE FUCKING
TINY, BUT YOU BURST IN LIKE YOU
OWNED THE PLACE WEARING A HOT
PINK T-SHIRT WITH GREEN SHORTS.
YOUR HAIR WAS THE COLOR OF A
PENNY, JUST LIKE MRS. BRADLEY'S,
AND I KNEW IT WAS YOU. THE HAPPY
LITTLE BITCH WITH THE NICE MOM
WHO HAD DRAWN ALL THOSE SMILEY
FUCKING RAINBOWS.

YOU SAID YOU NEEDED LUNCH MONEY AND WALKED OVER TO YOUR MOM'S DESK TO GET IT OUT OF HER PURSE YOURSELF. MY DESK WAS RIGHT NEXT TO HERS, AND I GAVE YOU MY WORST EAT-SHIT LOOK, BUT YOU JUST FUCKING SMILED AT ME. YOU WERE PROBABLY LIKE SIX, AND WHEN YOU SMILED YOU WERE MISSING YOUR TWO FRONT TEETH. YOU WERE THE CUTEST FUCKING THING I'D EVER SEEN.

THEN YOU LOOKED AT THE DRAWING ON MY DESK AND SAID, "I LIKE DAT DWAGON."

FOR THAT SPLIT SECOND THAT YOU SMILED AT ME AND SAID YOU LIKED MY DRAGON, I FELT FUCKING HAPPY. I WANTED TO FUCKING STEAL YOU. SO I STOLE ONE OF YOUR DRAWINGS OFF THE BULLETIN BOARD INSTEAD.

I DON'T REMEMBER FEELING HAPPY AGAIN UNTIL THE NIGHT I FOUND YOU PUKING IN THE FUCKING ALLEY OUTSIDE OF MY WORK. YOU WERE SO

FUCKED UP, BUT YOU SMILED AT ME AND YOU ASKED TO SEE MY TATTOO DRAWINGS AND YOU SAID YOU LIKED THEM.

YOU NEVER STOOD A FUCKING CHANCE, PUNK. YOU WERE ALWAYS GOING TO BE MINE. YOU JUST DIDN'T KNOW IT.

I LOVE YOU.

KNIGHT

P.S. YOU'RE THE ONLY FUCKING PERSON ON FUCKING EARTH WHO'S EVER GOTTEN ME TO TALK ABOUT MY CHILDHOOD BEFORE. YOU REALLY ARE GOING TO BE A GOOD SHRINK.

———————

March 19, 1999

Dear Knight,

I can't believe you remember all that! You know, you're pretty sweet for an asshole. Don't worry, I won't tell anyone.

Do you ever draw dragons anymore? I'll trade you a smiley sun AND a rainbow for a badass fire-breathing dragon.

Hope you're okay. Be safe.
Love,
BB

P.S. Michelangelo was my favorite Ninja Turtle. He was a smart-ass who loved pizza.

GEORGIA

CHAPTER 35

19_PEACH STATE_99

APRIL 2, 1999

DEAR BB,

   I KNOW WHAT YOU'RE TRYING
TO FUCKING DO. NICE TRY, BUT
PRETENDING LIKE I'M A FUCKING KID
AGAIN ISN'T GOING TO JUST MAGICALLY
MAKE SHIT BETTER. MAYBE FOR YOU.
MAYBE FOR SOMEBODY WHO HAD
A MOMMY AND A DADDY WHO TOLD
THEM THEY WERE SPECIAL AND
WIPED THEIR ASS AND PUT THEIR
PICTURES UP ON A BULLETIN BOARD
WHETHER OR NOT THEY WERE
ANY FUCKING GOOD. BUT GOING

BACK TO WHEN I WAS A KID ISN'T
A FUCKING OPTION BECAUSE THAT
MOTHERFUCKER DIDN'T SURVIVE.
KNIGHT IS ALL THAT'S LEFT, AND
HE DOESN'T FEEL LIKE DRAWING
FUCKING DRAGONS.
   I LOVE YOU.

                            KNIGHT

Just pee and go home, BB. Pee and go the fuck home.

Maybe I could have just one little beer.

No! The movie's over. You addressed all your graduation invitations. And it's nine forty-five. If you start pounding beers, you're gonna end up banging Harley, and if you bang Harley, you're gonna get home late, and if you get home late one more fucking time, you're gonna lose your car for a month, and if you lose your car, life as you know it will cease to exist.

You're right. I'm just gonna go out there, tell Harley bye, grab my invitations, and go home.

No beers?

No beers.

No weed?

No weed.

No sex?

Nope. No way. Not on my watch.

"Hey, lady." Harley's voice rumbled through the thin bathroom door. "You wanna do some shots?"

"Sure!" I yelled back, standing to button my skintight black jeans.

What? I snapped at myself. *You didn't say no tequila.*

I turned to flush the toilet but stopped dead in my tracks when a fucking black tarantula in the corner of the shower caught my eye. I choked on a scream and was about to beat it to death with the trash can when I realized that it wasn't alive. At least, not anymore. Creeping closer, I realized that the hairy black nightmare was actually just . . . hair.

Long.

Black.

Hair.

Blood rushed to my cheeks and ears, fast and hot. My skin was ablaze, and my heart felt like it was doing jumping jacks in my fucking chest.

A woman. Who is obviously not me. Has been naked. In that shower.

Jesus, BB. Get a grip. It was probably one of their sisters. Don't they have, like, four of them? Or a neighbor with a busted water pipe. Or a long-haired dude from work for all you know. What is your problem?

As I stared in the mirror, talking myself down from Cloud Crazy Bitch and waiting for my blotchy pink face to return to normal, I saw exactly what the fuck my problem was.

Clutching cold, hard evidence in both of my shaking hands, I stomped down the warpath and into the living room. "What the fuck is this?" I screeched at Harley, who was lounging on the couch, shirtless, pointing the remote at the TV and drinking Cuervo straight from the bottle. There was a shot glass on the coffee table overflowing with amber liquid—presumably for me.

"What the fuck is what?" he asked, finally muting the TV and pulling his eyes away from the giant glowing screen.

"This!" I hissed, thrusting both fists out in front of me—one containing a few sad strands of black hair, the other clutching a purple toothbrush.

I couldn't read Harley's expression in the strangely lit room. The wall of neon signs lit him from behind, and the enormous television set in front of him overexposed him from the front. Harley lowered the remote and bottle to his lap and turned his head toward me. Every millisecond that I had to wait for his response brought me one heart palpitation closer to full-blown cardiac arrest.

"It's a toothbrush." His voice was teasing and sarcastic, and I didn't fucking appreciate it.

"Yeah, I know what the fuck it is. Does it belong to the same girl who lost half of her weave in your shower?"

"Yeah," he said, completely devoid of sarcasm that time, "it does."

I felt like the floor had been pulled out from under me and I couldn't tell if I was floating or falling. My hands dropped back down to my sides, my heart dropped into my stomach, my stomach dropped into my bowels, and my bowels felt like they were about to drop out of me completely.

I should say words.

I swallowed, testing out my tightening larynx, and croaked out, "Who?"

Okay, that was only one word.

Harley leaned forward, setting the liquor bottle on the table, and rested both forearms on his knees. "You know who."

I fucking know her?

As I stared, unseeing, at a neon Budweiser sign on the opposite wall, waiting for my broken, grief-stricken brain to solve the riddle, a projectile sailed across the room and hit me square in the face.

I blinked in shock as one of my skull pillows bounced off of me and landed on the floor a few feet away, knocking over the stack of graduation invitations I'd just addressed. The sound of deep, rumbling laughter brought my attention back to Harley just as he tossed another pillow at me like a Chinese star. That one ricocheted off my bicep.

"It's fucking Victoria's! What the fuck, woman? Who else would it belong to?"

Victoria... Victoria... wait. Oh my God.

"You're fucking Goth Girl?"

Harley laughed again, harder that time, as he walked across the room to where I was standing in a confused state of suspended animation. Grabbing me by the shoulders, Harley shook me gently. He spoke slowly and with great amusement. "Your friend Victoria is fucking my brother, Davidson. Remember?"

A wave of relief, followed by a tsunami of embarrassment, washed over me.

"Oh my God!" I cringed, burying my face in his bare chest.

Harley's skin was rough and hot against my cheek, and laughter vibrated beneath. Thick, colorful arms wrapped around me and squeezed.

"It's okay, lady," Harley said. "I accept apologies in the form of cash, grass, and ass."

Ass?

"Harley, I have to go!"

Harley's grip around my waist only tightened. "Not until you apologize," he teased.

"I'm sorry!" I brought my arms up and squeezed him back, the hair and toothbrush still clutched in my fists. "I'm so sorry! I don't know what I was thinking."

"Mmm...nope. Not good enough."

I looked up to find Harley smirking down at me, the light from the TV painting a kaleidoscope of colors on the left side of his face. "Harley, I promise, I'll apologize any way you want tomorrow—cash, grass, ass, fuckin' sassafras—but right now, I gotta go. My dad said he's gonna take my keys for a *month* the next time I'm late. A fucking month!"

Harley sighed and released me. I darted around him and began picking up the envelopes that had been scattered all over the floor. Harley picked a few up too, but he didn't hand them to me. He just stood there, inspecting the calligraphied addresses on the front.

"These are really fuckin' good," he said. "Your mom teach you how to write like this?"

"Yeah," I said, looking over at him from where I was crouched on the floor. "She taught me calligraphy when I was a kid so that I could help her address our Christmas cards"—I gestured toward the scattered white rectangles all around me—"and now I'm her bitch."

Harley crouched down next to me and handed over his stack of envelopes. "No. You're *my* bitch," he said with a grin.

Being that close to him, feeling the heat coming off his shirt-less, tattooed body, hearing the warmth behind his words—it was all making it really fucking hard for me to remember why I was in such a hurry to leave.

"You think you could draw a tattoo for me?" Harley asked,

sitting on the floor with his back against the side of the couch and stretching his long legs out in front of himself.

"Really?" I asked, perking up.

Me? Draw a tattoo? To like, go on your body forever? Because you love me and want to take a piece of me with you wherever you go?

"I mean, yeah. Totally. I can do that. What do you want?"

"Somethin' in Old English. Across my knuckles," Harley said, offering me his right hand with an arched brow and a coy little smile. "Surprise me."

Now I was the one sporting a devilish smile.

Challenge accepted, motherfucker.

I found my calligraphy pen among the debris on the floor, yanked the cap off with my teeth, and went to work, penning my best Old English across Harley's knuckles.

When I finally released his hand, Harley turned it around so he could admire the four-letter word I'd scrawled upon his knuckles. "*Lady,*" he read aloud.

Harley's eyes met mine and morphed from curious to wicked in an instant. Opening his inked fist, Harley closed it again around a handful of my T-shirt and pulled me onto his lap.

"I'm never gonna wash this hand again," he said so close that every syllable vibrated through me, thrumming like a fucking tuning fork between my legs.

Without realizing it, I hummed out loud in response.

"Mmm?" Harley replied, mocking the noise I'd just made. "You like to hum, lady?" He ran the silver hoop containing his plump bottom lip slowly across the seam of my parted mouth. "So do I."

I prayed for him to kiss me—to stop teasing me and crash

those perfect, pillow-like lips into mine—but unfortunately for my time-management issues, Harley was in the mood to play.

Pulling away from my desperate mouth, Harley slipped my T-shirt off over my head—the one with the cover of The Cure's *Kiss Me, Kiss Me, Kiss Me* album on it.

How fitting.

As soon as my shirt and water bra were added to the pile of invitations, calligraphy pens, black hair, and purple tooth-brushes on the carpet, I leaned back in for that goddamn kiss. Harley threaded his inked-up knuckles into my shaggy blonde waves, but instead of pulling me toward him, he closed his fist in my hair and tilted my head backward, denying me what I wanted yet again.

I grumbled out of frustration, but the sound dissolved into a purr as the coolness of Harley's lip ring mixed with the heat of his breath on my neck. My nipples hardened in anticipation as Harley dragged his mouth down my throat, humming along the way. His thick, oil-stained hands wrapped around my pale, protruding rib cage as he continued his descent.

I ran my nails along Harley's buzzed head, encouraging him to go faster, and was unpleasantly surprised when I realized that it wasn't soft, like Knight's. Not even a little bit. Harley's scalp felt like beard stubble under my fingertips—a fact that I pushed out of my mind as soon as the seam of his mouth slid across the surface of my pierced, pink flesh. Between the vibration from his humming and the way his lip ring tugged against my nipple ring with every pass, I was practically whimpering in frustration.

I felt Harley smile against my skin at the sound of my agony.

I was just about to call him an asshole when his hands slid from my ribs, down over my waist, and around to my belt buckle.

Oh, thank God.

I took over the job, shimmying out of my jeans and panties in three seconds flat, but Harley didn't move. He didn't get naked. He simply watched me undress with that fucking smirk on his gorgeous, evil face.

What part of I will lose my car for thirty fucking days if I am late again *does he not understand?*

When I straddled him and went after his belt buckle, trying to help speed things along, Harley simply chuckled and grabbed my ass with both hands, encouraging me to stand.

"Nuh-uh. Not yet. Get your pussy up here, woman."

While my mind and libido were engaged in a bare-knuckle brawl over who would get to take control of my body, Harley swooped in and took over, maneuvering me so that my right foot was planted firmly on the carpet next to his hip and my left shin was propped up on the armrest next to his head. I was spread before him and had to hold on to the back of the couch to keep from falling over. Flashing me a look that said I'd better hold on even tighter, Harley leaned forward and bit down on the end of the steel barbell between my legs. Then, he wrapped his lips around my overly-sensitive flesh and hummed.

My knee buckled, causing me to grip the back of the couch even harder.

Holy shit. So this *is a hummer,* I thought as Harley continued his vibrational assault.

I guess my libido won the battle because my thoughts suddenly changed from worrying about my curfew to worrying about humping Harley's face too hard.

When I heard Harley unfasten the buckle on his leather belt, I sighed in relief. Harley's teasing was killing me. When I heard his zipper go down, I practically fell onto my knees, straddling his length and pillaging his lips for the kiss he'd been withholding from me. Harley gave me no resistance when I tried to kiss him that time, just like how my slick flesh gave him no resistance when he pushed his way inside.

"Mmm..." I groaned, involuntarily.

"Mmm?" Harley answered back, smiling against my mouth.

Capturing his earlobe between my lips, I hummed, "Mmhmm," as he grabbed my hips with both hands and did what he did best—made me forget.

When I awoke, sore and sated, I was adrift on a scattered sea of envelopes. The two thick and thoroughly tattooed arms clamped down around my waist were the only things keeping me from floating away on a foggy cloud of bliss. Flickering, colorful lights danced over the surface of our naked bodies. When I glanced at the TV, I expected to find a beautiful underwater ocean scene or a blue sky filled with hot air balloons and rainbows.

I had not expected to see Miss fucking Cleo.

Miss Cleo's psychic hotline infomercials were famous for two things—Miss Cleo's incredibly fake Jamaican accent and the fact that they never, *ever* came on before midnight.

As soon as I saw *that* face with *that* 1-800 number flashing below, I didn't need a psychic to tell me that I was completely and utterly fucked.

It was a motherfucking fact.

I wriggled out of Harley's unconscious embrace and darted around the room, gathering my belongings and snatching and swatting at the square pieces of paper that were stuck all over my naked body. It was like they'd been glued to me. My dread over what would happen when I got home was suddenly over-shadowed by horror as I realized what had already happened.

Harley had just fucked me without a condom.

It's fine, I immediately tried to reassure myself. *It's totally fine. You're on the pill, and judging by your stickiness, he obviously didn't come inside you. No harm, no foul.*

But I felt harmed. Way down deep where I put the things that I didn't want to feel, I felt it. Violated. It felt like coming home to a house that had been left with the door ajar. Everything appeared to be as it should. Nothing was broken. Nothing was missing. Yet I couldn't shake the eerie sense that an invasion had just taken place.

So I quickly found a different feeling to focus on, a safer one—remorse.

I rolled Harley's massive, snoring body over so that I could retrieve the last of my invitations. That easygoing motherfucker just snorted and curled up around one of the skull pillows he'd thrown at me earlier like it was a teddy bear. Taking a mental picture of Harley's sleeping baby face and hard, hot-rod-covered arms, I choked back a sob, turned on my unlaced boot heel, and drove the ever-loving shit out of my beloved Mustang one last time before turning the keys over to my father, who was waiting for me on the front porch when I got home.

Neither of us spoke a word during the exchange.

May 1999

Mailbox, mailbox, mailbox, light post. Mailbox, mailbox, mailbox, light post. Mailbox, mailbox…damn it. Street sign.

Maybe I could check real quick. I mean, what if I accidentally turned my phone off and missed his call?

When have you ever turned your phone off?

Accidents happen, BB! You do dumb shit all the time!

Just call him again.

No fucking way! I've called at least thirty-seven times since I've been grounded, and Harley's only picked up, like, twice. He knows my number! That motherfucker can call me!

Yeah, he can. He just isn't.

Fuck you.

You know my theory—Harley only wanted you because of your car. No car…oh look. No Harley.

Maybe he just got really busy at work. Maybe he got mono and has been sleeping, like, eighteen hours a day. Maybe he was in some kind of a freak accident and got amnesia and doesn't even know I exist!

BB?

What?

You're doing it again.

Damn it! Why is this so hard?

It's okay. Just try again. This time, let's see if you can go for five whole minutes without thinking about him, okay? Ready? Go!

Mailbox, mailbox, mailbox, light post. Mailbox, mailbox, mail—

"BB?"

"Huh?" I snapped my head over to Goth Girl, who was behind the wheel of her old Buick, mercifully giving me a ride to school for the third week in a row.

Rolling her eyes, she repeated herself, as if she were doing me a personal favor. "*I asked* if you've started writing your graduation speech yet."

"Uh . . . no. But keep asking me until I say I did, okay?"

"I can't believe they're making you give a speech. I can't believe you're not even nervous. That shit is exactly why I'm not graduating early," she said, staring straight ahead at the road.

I laughed. "Oh, is *that* why?"

"Yes," she deadpanned. "My two-point-oh GPA has nothing to do with it."

"God, I guess I've been so busy obsessing over fucking Harley that I haven't even thought about graduation."

"Still haven't heard from him, huh?"

"No!" I cried, seizing her invitation to talk about Harley with both hands. "Hey, you go over there. Have you seen Harley lately? Has he asked about me? Is he okay? Does he have a terminal case of amoebic dysentery and he doesn't want me to see him in his final days because he wants me to remember him the way he was?"

Goth Girl shrugged. "Well, Dave has *never* called me, so...
maybe he's just rubbing off on Harley."

"Never?" I squealed. "How is that even possible? How does
he invite you over?"

Goth Girl snorted. "He doesn't. Why do you think I'm
always trying to get you to invite me over?"

"So that asshole twists you into a sex pretzel as soon as you
walk into the house, but then he never even calls afterward?"

Goth Girl gave me a look that said, *Don't rub it in.*

"But you have a toothbrush over there. That has to mean
something," I said, trying to comfort her.

"No, I don't."

"Yes, you do—a purple one. Harley said it was yours."

Goth Girl stopped at the next traffic signal and turned to face
me. I couldn't tell if her porcelain cheeks were red from the glow
of the stoplight in front of us or because she wanted to stab a
voodoo doll made in one of the James brothers' likenesses, but
either way, I knew that look. It was the same one I'd seen in the
mirror the night I found that damn toothbrush.

"That wasn't your toothbrush...was it?"

Goth Girl shook her head from side to side.

"So, I guess that wasn't your hair I found in the shower
either."

The light turned green, and Goth Girl stomped on the accelerator a little harder than necessary. "It probably belonged to
some stripper that Dave brought home. Whatever. I don't even
care. I'm going to the Marilyn Manson concert tonight, and I'm
gonna find me a new..."

I tuned out everything Goth Girl said after that head shake.
He'd lied. Harley had looked me in the fucking eye, laughed at

me, and lied about who had been leaving her shit in his bath-room. And then he'd fucked me.

In more ways than one.

I felt nauseous. I felt like a fucking fool. And, evidently, I felt like running an errand because, just as we were about to pass the post office, I grabbed the wheel of Goth Girl's hand-me-down Buick LeSabre and yanked it to the right.

Tires squealed and horns blared as we careened over the curb and into the United States Postal Service parking lot.

"What the fuck?" Goth Girl yelled, slamming on the brakes as we slid sideways into a thankfully empty parking space. "Are you trying to kill us?"

"I'm sorry! I don't know! I just..." I rambled as I ripped open my backpack, pulling out an envelope that had been tucked away between the pages of my psychology textbook for way, way too long. "I just really need to mail something!"

April 13, 1999

Dear Ronald,
    It's okay if Knight is all that's left.
    I love that asshole.
    BB

You can do this, BB. You're just gonna march up there, knock on the door, and tell that motherfucker he can go to hell.

And then kick him in the nuts!

Yeah! That too! You ready?

Uh... I changed my mind. This was a bad idea. I should have called first. What if Purple Toothbrush Girl is in there?

Then you can kick her in the nuts too!

I think I'm gonna puke.

Don't do it in here! You've been waiting a month to drive this damn car again. Save it for Harley's carpet!

Okay. But wait. What am I gonna say to him? I should have prepared something!

Nah. You're just gonna march up there and say, Motherfucker, you can take that purple toothbrush, and you can stick it up your—

My car door suddenly flew open, revealing a tall, tattooed, baby-faced Harley James, smiling down at me like he'd just won the lottery.

"Get the fuck out here, woman! I missed you!"

He what?

I hesitated for a moment, out of shock, then I took a deep breath and unbuckled my seat belt. I swung my spindly pale legs out of the car and planted my black steel-toed combat boots firmly in the overgrown grass next to Harley's feet. Standing before him and squaring my shoulders, I tried my best to stay pissed.

"There's my pretty lady," he said, pulling me in for a hug. When I didn't reciprocate, Harley held me at arm's length and searched my face with his crystal-blue eyes. "What's up?"

I swallowed, trying to keep the bile rising up from my churning stomach at bay, and did my best to channel my inner J.Lo. Pursing my lips and raising my eyebrows, I said with all the attitude I could muster, "I know that wasn't Victoria's toothbrush."

Harley's face remained impassive. Meanwhile, I had to fold my arms across my chest to hide how badly my hands were shaking.

"You fucking lied to me. Right to my face!" I seethed. "Who the fuck is she, Harley?"

Did you fuck her without a condom too?

I couldn't bring myself to say that last part out loud. I didn't want to remind him of the power he'd taken from me. That I'd given to him.

"BB," Harley said, holding up his hands in a show of surrender, "it's not what you think."

"Oh, really? Well, what the fuck is it then?"

Harley cranked up the puppy-dog eyes and took a step closer to me. "Dave is seeing someone else."

"Bullshit," I spat, rolling my eyes and turning my face away from him. I had to resist. I had to stay strong.

"No, it's true. I didn't tell you because Victoria is your girl. If I told you and you told Victoria, Dave would be fuckin' pissed."

"So you lied to my face because of some kind of bro code?" I hissed.

Harley just shrugged. Of course he did. He and Dave were practically Siamese twins. I wasn't done with my line of questioning though. Something was still off.

Still facing away from him, I snapped, "If they're serious enough for her to leave a toothbrush, then why haven't I met her?"

"She's a stripper. She only comes over in the middle of the night—after her shift."

Well, isn't that convenient?

"What's her name?"

"Staci."

"What's her stripper name?"

"Sapphire...Starfish...*S* something."

I made the mistake of glancing back into Harley's begging blue eyes.

"Sapphire Starfish?" I repeated with every ounce of sass I possessed.

Harley smiled. "I dunno. Maybe she has a sparkly blue asshole."

That shit made me crack. Harley and I both started laughing, but I quickly reined mine in and pulled my bitch face back on. Just as I was about to resume my interrogation, Harley leaned forward and scooped me up into his arms.

"Harley, put me down!" I commanded, trying to sound serious, but it's pretty fucking hard to get someone to take you seriously while you're being cradled like a baby.

"Hmm..." Harley scrunched up his nose like he was really thinking about it. "No."

"Put me down, goddamn it!" I yelled, smacking him on the chest a few futile times.

Harley just chuckled. "What's the magic word?"

I wanted to say *Sapphire Starfish* and have a good laugh, but I wasn't quite ready to play nice yet. So instead, I reached for Harley's right hand, which was wrapped around my left thigh. I had every intention of pulling his little finger backward until it broke off or he let go—whichever one came first—until I saw what was scrawled across his knuckles.

"*Lady*," I whispered.

"Nope. Sorry. Try again. I'll give you a hint; it rhymes with *funnilingus*."

"Harley," I squealed. "Your hand! It still says *LADY*. How is that even...when did you...oh my fucking God!"

Setting me back down on my feet, Harley held his right hand up with his knuckles facing me and grinned. "Now, when I jerk off, it's like you're right there with me."

"You seriously got it tattooed on?"

"Fuck yeah. I love it," he said, turning his hand around so that he could admire the Old English.

I love it...

Love it...

Love.

Now, *that* was the magic word.

Standing there, in the golden light of spring, smiling and joking and using words like *love*, Harley James had me right back under his spell. His sweetness, playfulness, his hard body, his beautiful, boyish face—they were smoke and mirrors, designed to enchant. To make me forget. My traumas, my guilt, his transgressions, my responsibilities—Harley made them all go away.

I couldn't even remember what I'd been so mad about. Hell, I couldn't even remember my own name. The only name that existed anymore was the one tattooed across my hunky boyfriend's knuckles.

Swoon!

And, as if his looks, swagger, and silly Southern charm weren't enough to disarm me, Harley had one more trick up his sleeve. Well, technically, it was in his pocket. And it was more of a potion than a trick.

Somewhere, somehow, Harley had acquired an entire vial of liquid LSD.

———

I remember the exact moment I realized I was fucked up.

I was sitting on a barstool in the corner of a pool hall that I'd never been to before, smoking a bright pink cigarette with a gold filter and clutching an entire quart of orange juice to my chest—the kind that comes in a tall cardboard box with a screw-off cap. The cold, wet condensation had soaked through my Joan Jett tank top and cutoff jean shorts, but the air was so thick and hot in the bar that it was a welcome sensation.

As I stared at the swirling cloud of cigarette smoke before me, the collective spirals and puffs began to resemble a scene from Sodom and Gomorrah. It was like a wispy gray orgy undulating above our heads. I took a swig from the orange juice container, which was missing the cap, and glanced at my foreign cigarette, which had a solid two inches of ash hanging off the end of it. It was as if I had fallen asleep sober and had woken up in the middle of someone else's acid trip.

The parts of my brain that were still capable of forming

coherent thoughts began rattling off questions that the other parts of my brain were in no position to answer. Questions like, *Where am I? How did I get here? Who keeps playing David Allan Coe songs on the jukebox? Where is Harley? What's with all the OJ?* And, *Why is my cigarette the color of a pig's asshole?*

Their answers floated in and out of my murky consciousness like a jigsaw puzzle that had been dumped into a swamp. The images surfaced first—Harley holding an eyedropper over my outstretched tongue; Harley using a hundred-dollar bill to pay for a carton of OJ, a bottle of tequila, and a pack of rainbow-colored cigarettes at the liquor store; a neon sign that read *Empty Pockets Billiards* with at least three letters burned out; and Dave holding a pool cue and smiling in front of a life-sized poster of Bill Murray.

The audio clips surfaced next.

"Here. Drink this. The vitamin C will make the trip smoother."

"Holy shit! Harley! They sell those colored cigarettes that Lori Petty smokes in Tank Girl! *Will you buy me some? Pleeeease."*

"Change of plans. We gotta swing by the pool hall on our way home."

"Dude, I love pool! My dad has a pool table in our garage that I play on all the time."

"This is more of a business meeting, but shit, if you're any good maybe we can make a couple of bucks while we're there."

"Y'all play without me. I'm just gonna find the restroom. This OJ is going straight through me."

I suddenly became aware of the pressure in my bladder and looked around to find a few women to my left, standing outside of a door marked with a female silhouette.

I sat down on a barstool while I was waiting in line for the restroom! Ding, ding, ding, ding, ding!

A laugh percolated out of my effervescent body at the victory of figuring out what the fuck was going on.

Standing, I stamped my cigarette out into the Astroturf-like carpet, set my orange juice down on a nearby table, adjusted my purse strap, and joined the line of full-bladdered women with my head held high. Most people have an act-casual pose but not me. For some reason, whenever I didn't want people to know I was fucked up, I donned an act-like-you-own-the-place pose instead.

I successfully negotiated the restroom process, even in my compromised state, and strutted back through the pool hall like my name was Kate Moss. Eventually, I found the James brothers and a handful of scrappy-looking rednecks hovering around a pool table near the front door.

Dave saw me first. He immediately grabbed me and pulled me aside.

"Are you okay?" he asked, sounding genuinely concerned.

"I just went to the restroom. Relax," I said, staring him in the face. I was aware that my eyes were open too wide—I could feel it—but I was powerless to do anything about it.

"Yeah," Dave said, reaching down toward my crotch. I was just about to slap his hand away when he grasped the waistband of my cutoff shorts and buttoned my fly. Then he untucked and smoothed my disheveled tank top. "I can see that."

Oops.

"Your pupils are the size of dimes, girl. How much did Harley give you?"

"Just a couple drops," I said, feeling suddenly super self-conscious.

"A couple!" Dave exclaimed.

"Dude, you're kinda freaking me out right now," I said, my eyes darting over his shoulder, around the bar, looking for a friendly face. One that wouldn't make me feel like a freak show. I could almost feel myself growing horns as we spoke.

"Here," Dave said, handing me his can of Natural Ice. I took it in confusion as he pulled a little orange prescription bottle out of the pocket of his jeans. Shaking a skinny white tablet into his palm, Dave recapped the bottle and said, "Take this. It's a benzo. It'll bring you down."

A what?

I held out my hand, and Dave dropped a pill with the letters XANAX stamped on it.

"Oh, Xanax!" I giggled in relief. Finally, something familiar. I chirped, "My mom gives me this stuff all the time!" Then, I whispered, "Especially when I have PMS." I popped the pill into my mouth and washed it down with a swig of Dave's beer.

"It'll take a little while to kick in, so just try to stay close until then, okay?" Dave clapped his hand down on my shoulder and gave me a reassuring smile.

Damn, he has a lot of eyelashes. How many eyelashes is normal? Like a hundred? A thousand? I wonder how many Dave has. Let's see . . . one, two, three, four—

"BB?"

"Huh?"

"You sure you're—"

Dave's question was interrupted by chaos as a cacophony of gunshots, screaming, and squealing tires crashed over our conversation. Dave pulled me to the floor behind the pool table, then jumped up and sprinted for the front door.

"Dave!" I called after him, peeking out from behind one of the table legs.

But the screaming was so loud that he couldn't hear me. Or he simply had bigger things to worry about.

Looking around, I saw clusters of grown men and women huddled on the floor under other pool tables.

This shit is really happening.

I'm alone, on fucking acid, and some asshole outside has a gun.

And where the fuck is—

"Harley!"

I could hear yelling outside but no more screaming or gunfire, so I Army-crawled toward the front door. I wasn't afraid of being shot. I was afraid of finding out who or what had been shot.

Please let Harley be okay. Please let Harley be okay.

Please don't let me see a dead body. I am way too fucked up to see a dead body.

Before I could reach the entrance, the door swung open and a familiar pair of black boots stomped inside. A hand with my nickname tattooed on it reached down and grabbed me by the arm.

"We have to go. Now!"

I stumbled, trying to gain my footing, as Harley dragged me out into the poorly lit parking lot. I didn't like it out there. The wind whipped through the parking lot and lifted my shirt, chilling my condensation-soaked stomach. The inky-black sky churned with unusually light-colored clouds, looking like something out of the movie *Ghostbusters*. Like some supernatural portal was about to open and fry us all with a laser beam shot straight through the open gates of hell. I also didn't like the way Harley's hand felt on my arm. It wasn't that it hurt or was too tight. It was like my skin didn't like the feel of his skin. The energy coming off of it felt bad. Mean. Everything out there felt bad.

Mean.

It didn't make sense, but I dug in my heels and resisted. I should have been relieved to see Harley. I should have wanted him to take me away from the place where the people were screaming and hiding under billiard tables, but the drugs were telling me to go back into the building.

"What the fuck are you doing?" Harley asked, yanking on my arm.

When he turned around, the face I saw scared me worse than any other threat that might have been lurking out there. Harley's eyes were two black holes. His teeth gnashed. Veins bulged in his neck and temple. And the scar along the side of his head resembled the seam of a second angry mouth. He looked inhuman. Demonic. Deadly.

I screamed in shock and clamped my free hand over my eyes.

Fuck, fuck, fuck, fuck, fuck.

"Get in the fucking car!"

I refused to look at him. I simply shook my head with my eyes still covered.

"What the fuck is wrong with you?" he snarled, giving my arm a shake.

"I'm fucked up!" I yelled. "I'm fucked up and I'm freaking out and I'm not going anywhere until you tell me what the fuck is going on!"

"I'll tell you what the fuck is goin' on!" Dave shouted from somewhere behind Harley. "Motherfuckers shot up Harley's ride, and they're gettin' away! Now, either you're comin' or you ain't!"

They what?

I opened my eyes and looked beyond Harley's heaving, snarling, raging presence to find a half-dozen silvery bullet holes peppering the Boss's driver's side door. My hands flew to cover my gaping mouth as my eyes met Dave's. He was standing next to the open passenger door, looking only slightly less murderous than his brother.

"They're gettin' away, goddamn it!" Dave yelled, slapping the roof of the car.

The demon that had possessed Harley's body released me with a shove and shouted, "Fine! Stay the fuck here then!" He turned and sprinted toward the Boss, holding his low-slung Dickies up with one hand. As he bent forward to climb into the driver's seat, his T-shirt lifted up in the back—just enough to reveal the handle of his 9mm tucked away underneath.

Even the Boss sounded demonic as it roared to life and peeled out of there, leaving me in its dust.

I stood, blinking into the void left by my boyfriend's sudden departure, and winced into the wind as it lashed my face with my own hair.

He left me.

He fucking left.

I didn't even know where I was. Looking back at the pool hall in the hopes that its facade would trigger a memory, I saw that a small crowd of people had gathered outside to watch the spectacle.

Shit.

I looked down at myself and tried to wring every last drop of logic out of my fucked-up, freaked-out, malfunctioning brain.

Maybe I can leave. Can I do that? Will the universe even allow it, or am I stuck in this purgatory forever?

Looking down, I realized I still had my purse—the long strap slung diagonally across my body—and looking up, I realized that my car was sitting in the parking spot next to the one Harley had parked in.

That's right! We drove separately because of my curfew!

I found more breadcrumbs to help me get home inside my purse—keys, cigarettes, a lighter, a cell phone.

Oh my God. I can. I can just go home. I can go home and pull the covers over my head and pretend like none of this ever happened.

A loud crack of thunder tore through the atmosphere, startling me and setting my feet in motion.

Maybe it's not the gates of hell, I tried to reassure myself as I speed walked to my car. *Maybe this is just the rapture. Maybe I'm just gonna get raptured up. I'm a good person. I mean, I don't go to church or anything, but my mom got me baptized. That has to count for something, right?*

Another clap of thunder boomed—that time, so close it made my ears ring. I dived inside my car not a moment too soon. It wasn't the rapture.

It was a fucking monsoon.

I got the car started and rolling on muscle memory, but things like turning on headlights and windshield wipers required a lot of cognitive effort. As did figuring out which way to go. I didn't have the faintest idea where I was. I'd never been to that pool hall before, I didn't even recognize the shopping center, and the entire drive over was a blur.

Right, a voice in my head said. *Right means the same thing as correct, so you should probably go right.*

Solid advice. I took it.

And drove right over the curb.

Whatever. I was out of the parking lot and onto the road. As my speed increased, however, my grip on reality began to deteriorate faster. The acid was causing me to see trails, so every raindrop that whizzed past my windshield appeared to be pulling a streak of light behind it. I wasn't driving a Mustang anymore. I was piloting a spaceship at warp speed through a field of stars. They created a beautiful tunnel of light around me as they zoomed past but not all of them. Some stars splattered on my windshield. I felt bad for them. The casualties of my space travel.

Off in the distance, a fuzzy red orb of light appeared.

Interesting, I thought. *It's getting closer. Oh, look. It's going to fly right over—*

The sound of horns blaring and tires squealing brought me back down to earth like the snap of a rubber band. I had just run a fucking red light, in the pouring rain, going God only knows how fast, while on an acid trip across the Milky Way. My heart pounded in my chest and thrummed in my ears at the realization of how close a call I'd just had. I could have gotten myself killed.

Or worse.

I could have killed someone else.

I had to get off the road. I rolled down my window so that I could see the lines on the road better, and at the first break in the curb, I cut the wheel to the left, pulling into an eerily familiar parking lot. The rain was so heavy that I couldn't see three feet in front of my car, but something about the terrain, the texture of the crumbling asphalt, or the way the tiny hairs on my tiny arms stood on end told me that I'd been there before.

I parked in the first thing resembling a parking space that I could detect through the downpour and killed the engine. Taking a deep breath, I sat with my eyes closed and let the rain blowing in through my window and the Xanax flowing through my bloodstream calm my nerves. Then I crossed myself like I'd seen my Irish-Catholic mother do a thousand times and said the only prayer I knew.

Our Father, who art in heaven, hallowed be thy name.

Thy kingdom come. Thy will be done, on Earth as it is in heaven.

Give us this day our daily bread.

And forgive us our trespasses, as we forgive those who trespass against us.

And lead us not into temptation, but—

Doodleoodleoodleoodleoo.

A digitized scale of notes came pouring out of my purse.

Doodleoodleoodleoodleoo.

Grabbing my bag off the passenger seat, I dug around inside until I found the blinking, vibrating menace.

Doodleoodleoodleoodleoo, it cried in my hand.

I looked at the caller ID and felt a fresh wave of panic trying to fight through the Xanax as a number I didn't recognize flashed on the screen. I was in no condition to deal with the unknown.

Doodleoodleoodleoodleoo.

Oh, fuck it.

Holding my breath, I jammed my thumb into the talk button.

"Hello?"

If someone was there, I couldn't hear them over the sound of the rain assaulting my metal roof and crashing like waves outside my open window.

"Hello!"

Dial tone.

I hung up and stared at the screen, trying to jog my memory for clues as to where I might have seen that number before. My mind went blank, but my nose... my nose was picking up notes of warm, cinnamony cologne and cigarette smoke on the breeze. I inhaled as deeply as I could, trying to grab that hallucination and hold on to it for dear life. God, that smell. I wanted to wrap it around my body like a blanket. Or a straitjacket. How long had it been? It was May, and I hadn't seen Knight since—

Oh my God.

It's fucking May!

GEORGIA
CHAPTER 39
19 PEACH STATE 99

The moment my fingers grazed the black plastic handle, my car door flew out of my grasp with a force that made me think a tornado had hit. But when rough hands reached in and pulled me out of the vehicle, I knew I was dealing with a very different force of nature.

My senses were on high alert. Rain awakened every exposed inch of my skin. My inner ears rattled at the sound of my car door being kicked shut. My legs locked as I was planted back down on my feet, my back pressed against the door and open window. My lungs expanded, filling with warm, familiar aromas that they refused to let go of.

And the instant my eyes opened, they filled with tears.

He found me.

"You found me." Knight's voice was deep and clear.

His brow was raised in a pained expression of disbelief. I'd seen that look before—on his eighteenth birthday, when I'd stolen a chicken sandwich for him from the school cafeteria. He looked every bit as lost as he had the day I gave him what might have been the first gift he'd ever received. And it broke my heart all over again.

My hands instinctively wrapped around the sides of Knight's head. Even soaking wet, his blond buzz cut was softer than velvet. I hadn't realized how much I'd missed that. His smell. His touch. His zombie-gray eyes, swallowing me like I was his last meal.

I don't know who initiated the kiss, maybe both of us, but as soon as Knight's tongue was in my mouth, I realized how much I'd missed his taste as well. At school, Knight had tasted like Winterfresh gum. After school, he'd tasted like cheap beer and Camel Lights. But that night, he tasted like Southern Comfort. My favorite flavor of him. It reminded me of all those nights we'd spent alone, curled up on the couch in the Terminus City Tattoo break room, drunk on whiskey and first love.

This kiss wasn't like those kisses though. This kiss was a ravaging, desperate, needy thing that started at our mouths and spread until our whole bodies were under its control. Hands gripped and held and tore at clothing. Hips thrust. Feet fought for purchase against the flooded asphalt.

The rain beating down on my bare arms and legs was freezing, but for once, I didn't shiver. Knight was enough to keep me warm.

Knight was enough.

Picking me up, Knight set my ass down on the ledge of my open car window and continued to assault my mouth as I fumbled to unbutton his camouflage pants. As soon as my fingertips slid down his length, Knight yanked the crotch of my loose cutoff shorts and panties to one side and pressed against me. He didn't enter though. He fought the inferno of pheromones swirling around us just long enough to look me in the eye and silently ask for my consent.

Not wanting Knight to see my pupils, I squeezed my eyelids shut and pulled him in for another kiss. Wrapping my legs around his waist, I pressed my muddy combat boots against his ass, giving him the invitation he sought.

Knight was as hot against my flesh as the rain was cold, and the paradox of sensations set me on fire. I clawed at his black T-shirt, dug my heels in harder, and nipped at his tongue as he filled me. With every inch, I felt him erasing the mark Harley had left behind the last time we were together. Knight was the only one I trusted enough to be with like that.

And he was finally home.

Wrapping my arms around his neck, I buried my face in his shoulder and cried. That night had gone from upsetting to terrifying to life-threatening to magical in the span of a few short hours, and my emotions simply couldn't keep up. I might not have known where I was or what was happening, but Knight was there, and his arms kept me grounded. Tethered to reality. Safe. I inhaled his scent and held my breath and prayed to the universe to let him be real.

As Knight's thrusts became more erratic, my silent tears were replaced with audible gasps and moans. Ducking his head, Knight found my mouth with his. Thick fingers pulled at my sopping-wet hair. Teeth nipped at my bottom lip, my tongue. Knight swelled inside me, and a growl tore from his soul as he released everything he'd been holding back for the last nine months into my body. His muscles relaxed. His forehead dropped to my shoulder, and I cradled his fuzzy blond head as he shuddered the last of his release.

When I opened my eyes, still running my nails through Knight's wet buzz cut, I realized that the rain had let up. I also realized where I was. Like a moth to a flame, I had pulled into the parking lot behind Terminus City Tattoo.

"Inside. Now," Knight said, his words vibrating against my collarbone.

Noticing all the cars driving by, I nodded. Inside was good.

I rolled up my window and grabbed my purse. Then I practically sprinted, hand in hand with Knight, across the parking lot and into the alley separating Sin from Terminus City. I held my breath and waited for the flashbacks. I had so many horrible memories from that alley—puking on all fours next to the dumpster, bloody baseball bats splintering against walls, shouting matches, shoving matches—but as we entered the graffitied corridor, a completely different set of memories flashed before my eyes. Memories of Knight lighting my cigarettes, smiling when I cracked a joke, telling me he loved me for the first time. As we walked up the fire escape steps, I saw that he had put out fresh bowls of food for the neighborhood strays, like he used to, and I also saw a cordless phone lying in pieces on the landing, its batteries scattered across the concrete.

"What happened?" I asked, bending over to pick up the components as Knight pulled open the back door to Terminus City.

"*You* happened," he said, holding the door open for me.

In the dark of the alley, his pale gray eyes almost glowed. It made my insides go all tingly.

"You're the one who called me?" I asked, crossing over the threshold.

A sense of calm washed over me instantly as I took in the familiar surroundings. The long hallway with doors lining one side. The opening at the end that led out into the tattoo parlor. The black-and-white tiled floor and faint smell of antiseptic.

We were home.

The heavy metal door closed behind me with a metallic boom.

"Yeah," Knight said, turning my body with bossy hands and pressing my back against the cool surface of the door.

Taking the receiver and batteries from me, Knight tossed them down the hallway without looking. The sound of cracking plastic bounced and echoed off the candy-red walls.

"Bobbi's gonna be pissed." I giggled, dropping my purse to the ground so that I could help Knight pull my sopping-wet tank top off over my head.

"I'll buy her a new one," he growled.

My shirt landed with a wet splat next to the phone. Followed by my bra.

"You put the hearts back in," Knight said in reverence as his thumbs grazed my breasts. He'd given me that jewelry for Valentine's Day the year before. The barbells looked like arrows, and they each held a silver heart in place that went around my nipple.

"Mmhmm," I moaned, letting my head fall back against the door as Knight bent over and flicked my puckered pink flesh with his tongue.

Pulling my nipple into his mouth, Knight cupped a possessive hand over my pussy, his fingertips exploring the mess we'd just made.

"How did you know"—I panted, unable to quiet my curious mind despite the pleasure—"where I was?"

Knight pressed his forehead to mine as he unbuttoned my shorts. "I didn't. I went outside to smoke a cigarette under the awning, and when I finally got the balls to call you, I heard your annoying-ass ringtone coming from the parking lot."

Knight slid my rain-soaked shorts and panties down my thighs, and I hopped around, trying to pull them off over my combat boots. Knight smirked, watching me struggle.

"Guess I set the phone down a little too hard when I came to find your ass."

"Ya think?" I teased, tossing the rest of my clothes down the hall.

As Knight reached back and peeled off his black Terminus City T-shirt, I watched without shame as the light from the red Exit sign illuminated every ripple and plane of his chiseled chest and abs. I noticed that Knight had gotten a new tattoo since I saw him last, on his chest. It looked like the U.S. Marine Corps logo I'd seen on his grandfather's flask.

I swallowed my drool and whispered, "I'm glad you found me."

Knight dropped his T-shirt and stared down at me like I was in trouble. "We're gonna talk about why the fuck you were out there in the pouring rain with your window down later. But right now, you're gonna shut the fuck up and come."

My mouth snapped shut and anticipation exploded through my veins, as Knight sank to the ground, hitched both of my knees over his shoulders, then stood back up, sliding my naked, spindly body up the door as he rose. I screamed and grabbed on to his head in shock, planting my right combat boot against the opposite wall for support. Needing more stability, I pulled my left knee up to my chest and planted my left boot on Knight's shoulder.

The view alone had me close to orgasm. Knight's muscular upper body holding me five feet off the ground, his fuzzy blond head buried between my legs, and his ghastly gray eyes staring into mine as he flicked the piercing he'd given me with his tongue. As my inner walls began to contract around nothing, I felt Knight's cum trickle out of me. A sick part of me wanted to watch him lap it up.

And he did.

The moment Knight's tongue filled me, I dug my nails into the sides of his head and cried out, coming so hard that I saw stars and fireworks and hearts and arrows all exploding behind my lids.

And every spark left a trail of light behind.

Guess the acid wasn't done with me yet.

I *knew* it wasn't done with me when Knight set me back down on my feet, and I opened my eyes. He was smiling at me—that gorgeous, boyish smile I used to bend over backward just to get a glimpse of—only instead of pearly white, Knight's teeth and lips were painted red. With those zombie eyes and blood-streaked mouth, he looked even more demonic than Harley had.

I shrieked and squeezed my eyes shut, trying to rid myself of the image.

Fuck! Was that real? Did I just start my period? Am I even due? Am I dying? Did the rapture reject me and now I'm stuck here on earth with these floods and lightning storms and demons wearing the skin of my lovers?

"Punk?"

I didn't answer.

"What the fuck? Look at me."

"No!"

I felt Knight's thick, mean fingers wrap around my tiny biceps. "Open your fucking eyes, or I swear to God, I will pull them open myself."

Exhaling all my fear, I inhaled his cinnamony aroma and told myself to trust. I peeked out from slits at first, and when I didn't see any devil horns or blood, I opened my eyes the rest of the way. Knight's face looked totally normal—well, pissed off, but that was normal for him. The only difference was the red light from the Exit sign illuminating the bottom half of his face.

Oh, thank God, I thought, exhaling the breath I'd been holding.

"You're fucked up!" Knight roared, pointing at my temple with two fingers like a gun.

Oh shit! I slammed my eyes shut again and buried my face in my hands. *Shit, shit, shit.*

"Have you *seen* your pupils? What the fuck are you on?"

"It's just dark in here," I blurted out.

"Look at me and tell me you're not fucked up!" Knight yelled, squeezing my arm tighter.

I shook my head from side to side.

"What did he give you? Where the fuck is he?" Knight shook me, hard.

"I don't know!" I yelled, shoving his bare chest with both hands. He didn't budge, but he at least stopped shaking me. "It's fine! I'm totally fine, okay? It's almost worn off."

"Like fuck it has!"

I shoved him again, feeling overcome by defensiveness and outrage.

"You don't get to do this!" I yelled, jabbing my finger into his new tattoo. "You don't get to show up out of the blue and act like you fucking own me!"

Knight's face morphed from angry to sinister. "Oh, but I do," he said, pulling his sharp lips to one side in an amused smirk. "I do fucking own you. I told you before, Punk—you're mine until I say you're not." He stalked closer to me until our faces were practically touching. The whiskey on his breath mingling with the orange juice on mine. "Now call your fucking mom and tell her you're spending the night with Juliet because there is no fucking way I'm letting you drive home like this."

My curfew! Fuck!

I dived into my purse and yanked out my phone. The clock on the screen read 10:51. Ten fifty-fucking-one! I was all the way downtown, and I was supposed to be home in nine minutes! What the fuck was wrong with me?

My fingers flew as I called my house.

As soon as my mom picked up, Knight mouthed the words, *Tell her it's raining too hard.*

I stammered and told my mom that I was at Juliet's house, and I hadn't left yet because the weather was too bad. I was afraid she'd be pissed, but my mom said there'd been reports of roads flooding nearby, and she'd been worried sick about me trying to drive home "in that mess." She told me to just spend the night at Juliet's. She said she was proud of me for staying safe.

If she only fucking knew.

But that was it.

As soon as I pressed the red End button, tears of relief filled my eyes. Knight was a fucking asshole, but he'd single-handedly just saved me from losing my car for the entire summer—or wrapping myself around a tree, trying to race home and beat the clock. Harley never worried about putting me in harm's way or getting me in trouble. He got me to do whatever the fuck he wanted, then he disappeared when it was time to pay the consequences.

Looking into Knight's cold, hard steely-gray eyes, the words, "I love you," fell from my mouth.

I hadn't meant to say it out loud, but I meant it. I loved that motherfucker down to the core—in spite of his shitty disposition and possessive psychosis and violent tendencies. I loved him because, underneath all that armor, Knight was the softest thing I'd ever felt. He was a lover *and* a fighter. A killer and a savior. And he was the only one out there on the front lines, trying to rescue me from myself.

"I know," Knight said with a small smile. "I got your letter."

I smiled back. At least we still had that. I might not have been able to say that Knight was the only person I'd slept with anymore, but in that moment, I knew that he was the only boy I'd ever loved. I'd wanted to call what I felt for Harley love so many times, but it wasn't. It was gratitude. I'd been grateful for the distraction, for the exhilaration, for the attention. I loved the way Harley made me feel, but I didn't love the man he was deep down.

That motherfucker could suck my dick.

Knight picked me up and wrapped my bare legs around his bare waist. "I love you, too," he said, planting a small, lingering kiss on my surprised lips.

"I know," I murmured against his mouth. "I got your letters."

————————

About two hours and fourteen orgasms later, Knight and I finally got around to having an actual conversation that didn't get interrupted by someone's body part being inserted into someone else's mouth. I'd gotten cold—shocker, I know—and my clothes were still sopping wet, so Knight grabbed an extra-large Terminus City Tattoo T-shirt from the front counter for me to wear. It was identical to the one he'd had on earlier. Luckily, he wasn't wearing it anymore—or anything for that matter. Otherwise, we would have been all matchy-matchy, and that's just embarrassing.

Knight was reclined in his tattoo chair, and I was lying on top of him with my back to his front. I wondered if we were both staring at the same water stain on the ceiling. I wondered how much antiseptic spray it was going to take to sterilize his chair after what we'd just done to it. I wondered how long it had taken for Knight to call me.

"How long have you been back?" I asked, trying to sound nonchalant.

"Since yesterday," Knight replied, absentmindedly running his fingertips up and down my ladderlike ribs. "Peg picked me up at the airport and brought me home, but as soon as I walked into her place...I don't know. I just...I had to get the fuck out of there. Bobbi had said that I needed to finish a tattoo for some chick ASAP because she wouldn't shut the fuck up about it, so I crashed here last night and did the piece today."

I laughed. "Tracey."

"Yeah, Tracey." I could hear Knight smile through his voice. "She said she knew you. Actually, she said that I needed to call you, and if I didn't, she was gonna come back here and shove a tattoo gun up my ass."

I laughed harder. "That sounds about right."

"She's cool. Her boyfriend, too. Since I wouldn't take their money, they bought me a drink—"

"At Spirit of Sixty-Nine?" I interrupted. Jesus. The way my voice sounded, you would have thought they'd taken him to a brothel.

Even if he had gone there looking to get laid, that was none of my business. Knight wasn't even my boyfriend.

Was anyone? I hadn't officially broken up with Harley, but in my head we were as good as over. Lying about who'd been spending the night at his house was bad. Disappearing for a month was worse. But drugging me and leaving me at a pool hall I'd never been to before in the aftermath of a drive-by? That shit felt like grounds for a breakup to me. He wasn't even worth the phone call. Evidently, all I had to do to get rid of Harley was . . . nothing.

"Yeah, at Spirit." Knight's deep, clipped tone sent shivers down my spine despite the blaze of body heat radiating off of him.

Sitting up between his legs, I turned and looked at him. The open area of the tattoo parlor was dark, but the streetlights and headlights and business signs glowing just beyond the front windows made it easier to see than it had been in the hallway.

"What happened?" I asked, searching his face.

Knight looked exactly the same as I'd remembered him but older somehow. Weathered.

"Earlier, you said you had a rough night."

"Fuck if I know." Knight sat up too, so I swung my legs over the side of the chair. He did the same, sitting next to me. Facing straight ahead, Knight said, "I just had a couple of SoCo shots, but the next thing I knew, Tracey's boyfriend and all three fucking bartenders were dragging me out the back door by my arms and legs. They said I broke a bottle on the edge of the bar and lunged at some motherfucker for no reason."

Hopping off the chair, Knight picked his pants up off the ground and stepped into them. "I didn't believe them, but when I looked down, I still had the motherfuckin' bottle neck in my hand, so..."

Knight shrugged, then dug around in his pockets until he found his cigarettes. He was trying to act like it was no big deal, but I knew him. Knight was a control freak. He had an inferno of rage churning inside him, but he prided himself on keeping that shit in check. Even when he did get into a fight, which had been often before he joined the military, Knight's actions were always eerily calm and calculated.

But when he did lose control, it was like taking the lid off Pandora's box. I could only imagine what the scene at Spirit of Sixty-Nine must have looked like earlier.

"You blacked out," I said, stating the obvious.

Popping a cigarette into his mouth, Knight said, "Yeah, I guess." Then, he gestured toward the hallway. "You comin'?"

I hopped off the chair and followed him back down the hallway we'd just christened and out onto the fire escape landing.

"Do you ever have flashbacks or, like, panic attacks?" I asked, pulling a cigarette from the pack of Camel Lights Knight had extended to me.

Knight lit my smoke, then his own. "Yeah, I guess. I mean, certain shit will trigger memories sometimes, but that's fuckin' life, right?"

"I think it might be post-traumatic stress disorder," I said, trying to sound as casual about it as possible. "I talked to my psychology professor, and that's what he thinks. He had it too, after Vietnam. He gave me some strategies that might help, if you ever feel like talking about it."

Knight rolled his eyes and exhaled a slow stream of smoke. I expected him to shut me out completely at that point, like he usually did, but instead, Knight said, "Yeah, that's what the VA doctor said, too."

My eyebrows shot up. "You talked to a doctor?"

"Yeah. They made me after I got all claustrophobic inside of a tank and flipped the fuck out."

Oh Jesus.

I wanted to grimace, to react, but I did what Dr. Raines had said and just listened. No judgment. No interrupting.

Exhaling, Knight said, "You know what the doc said? He said it wasn't PTSD from combat. It was PTSD from being locked inside of small places when I was a kid."

Being what inside of what?

I felt nauseous. I felt murderous. I felt...

Don't react. Don't react. Don't react. Just smoke and nod. Smoke. And nod.

I took another drag, but I didn't fucking nod.

Knight stared down the alley toward the parking lot, seemingly lost in thought. I was just about to clear my throat or run for the hills before he flipped out again when he continued, "Candi used to hang out at these fucking biker bars all the time, trying to score some dope or find a new boyfriend—I don't fuckin' know. All I know is that she used to leave me locked outside in the car for hours instead of forking up the money for a babysitter. Once I got old enough to figure out how to open the doors, she started making up all this scary shit that would happen to me if I got out of the car."

Knight took another drag, smoking on autopilot, as he stared out into the abyss. The humidity from all the rain caused his smoke to hang heavy in the air. It clung to him like all those horrible memories that he just couldn't shake.

"When I got old enough to figure out that she was full of shit and started running away, my mo—" He stopped himself. "*Candi* started leaving me locked inside whatever piece-of-shit trailer or apartment we were living in at the time."

I almost reached out and touched him, but Knight had turned away from me. It was as if he was in some kind of daze, and the last thing I wanted was to snap him out of it at the wrong moment.

"One time, when I was, like, seven, I got hungry and tried to make myself some macaroni and cheese, only I got bored waiting for the water to boil and started watching cartoons. I didn't even realize there was a fire until half of the kitchen was up in flames."

"Oh my God," I blurted out, then immediately cupped my hands over my mouth.

Knight didn't acknowledge my outburst though. He was so wrapped up in his own mind that I didn't know if he could even hear me.

"I couldn't get out," he continued, devoid of emotion. "And the only phone in the house was in the kitchen."

"What did you do?" I asked—that time, on purpose. I couldn't just stand there and not talk to him.

Knight's hands dangled by his sides. The ash on the end of his cigarette grew longer. His body had been completely abandoned. I knew how that felt. I wondered if he was watching himself talking to me from somewhere else.

"I tried all the windows," he said, sounding like a robot, "but I couldn't get them to open, so I used a broom handle to knock the phone off the wall in the kitchen and dragged it as far as the cord would stretch to call 911. I'd learned about 911 at school. The fire department came and got me out. I thought it was cool, riding in the fire truck, but then they wouldn't let me go home, even after Candi finally came to get me. No one would tell me what the fuck was going on. They put me in this institution-type place until Candi could get her shit together enough to get custody back, but that whole time, I thought I was in jail for starting a fire. I thought I'd been taken away from my mom for being bad."

I stood there, impotent, as Knight's untouched cigarette fell from his lifeless fingers to the concrete. He was gone. He'd left his body behind, reciting a prerecorded story, but the rest of him—his heart and soul—had just vanished. It broke my heart to see him like that, but what shattered it completely were the words that came out of his mouth next.

"That's when she started locking me in the closet."

I flicked my cigarette butt into the flooded alleyway and launched myself at him. Wrapping my arms around Knight's waist, I pressed my cheek into his bare back and squeezed my love into him. But it was no use. Knight's strong, tall, tattooed body had been evacuated. Knight might have gotten that Mc-Knight coat of arms inked across his back under the guise of family pride, but I knew the truth. Knight had no family—he'd just needed a shield.

I'd pieced together from things he'd said before that Candi's boyfriends had been verbally and physically abusive. I knew his mom had a history of drug and alcohol addiction. But I never knew just *how* traumatic his childhood had been. No wonder he hadn't wanted to draw me a fucking dragon.

Knights don't draw dragons. They slay them.

The thought gave me an idea. A risky, stupid, don't-try-this-at-home idea.

"Come with me," I said, taking Knight by the hand.

He didn't fight me or ask any questions. Whatever self-protective state of hypnosis he'd entered while he told me his story was definitely still in full effect.

Leading him back into the building, I didn't stop until we were both facing Knight's black vinyl dentist-style tattoo chair. It was identical to the seven other black chairs in the open room, bolted to the floor, four chairs on one side of the shop and four on the other. Each station came equipped with a red metal tool chest to hold supplies and a large mirror. Knight's was in the far back corner, and the only thing that differentiated it from all the others was the framed picture of two teenagers with shaved heads standing in front of a tacky fake Christmas tree.

"Knight"—I looked at his glassy eyes and locked-jaw expression—"I want you to try something that I think will make you feel better. Okay?" I spoke loudly and slowly, as if his consciousness had a hearing impairment and just needed me to enunciate a little better.

Knight didn't respond.

"It's a therapy technique called The Empty Chair," I continued, holding his lifeless hand. "I want you to pretend like your mom is sitting in this chair. Then, I want you to say whatever the fuck you've always wanted to say to her. You can call her a whore. You can tell her you hate her. You can tell her you love her. Hell, you can punch her right in her invisible face if you want. You can get all that shit off your chest here, in a safe place, without hurting anyone."

Knight didn't respond.

"I'll, uh, I'll give you some space," I said, backing away.

Heading down the hall, I stopped and pulled a cigarette out of my purse—a bright green one this time—and stepped back out onto the fire escape. As I stood and smoked, wearing nothing but an extra-large T-shirt in the middle of the night in the middle of Little Five Points, it began to sink in just how broken Knight really was.

God, I'm a fucking idiot, I thought. *I can't fix him. So far tonight he's blacked out, tried to stab someone with a broken beer bottle, and now he's gone completely fucking catatonic. Maybe I should take him to a hospital. I feel pretty sober now. I could probably get us there in one—*

A loud, metallic crash scattered my thoughts and sent my feet flying back into the shop. I skidded to a halt as soon as I saw what had made the sound. Knight had ripped his tattoo chair out of the floor, thrown it into the center of the shop, and was kneeling over it, hacking it to ribbons with the butterfly knife he kept in his pocket. His back and shoulder muscles flexed and glistened as he stabbed and slashed at the innocent chair.

Suddenly, the blade glinted in the air as Knight flipped it shut with a flourish of twists and flicks of his wrist. When he shoved it back into his pocket, I breathed a sigh of relief, then gasped it all back in as Knight began ripping fistfuls of vinyl and foam away from the metal frame with his bare hands. I could hear him muttering under his breath. Words like *whore* and *fucking* and *worthless* rose above the others as Knight took the chair's life.

I stood in stunned silence as a chasm of heartache and fear opened in my chest, threatening to swallow me whole. I didn't know what to do. Or how to undo what I'd already done. I'd just unleashed the very thing that Knight had been afraid of his entire life. The thing he'd kept buried beneath all others. His secret wish. His sickest desire.

Knight wanted to kill his own mother.

With his bare fucking hands.

I had to figure out a way to put that monster back in its cage—or better yet, set it free—without having it turn on me. Or worse, turn on Knight. I closed my eyes as the piles of foam on the ground grew and visualized my psychology textbook. Flipping through the pages, I finally found what I'd been looking for.

When I opened my eyes, the destruction had stopped. Knight's glistening, shirtless body loomed over the wreckage, heaving like he'd just run a marathon.

With hesitant steps, I walked over to him and placed a shaking hand on his hunched shoulder. Taking a deep breath, I mustered all the courage, all the acceptance, all the false confidence my voice was capable of portraying and said, "Now, let's go bury her."

Without another word, Knight and I picked up the pieces of his tattoo chair, walked them outside, and laid them in the dumpster in the alleyway. When every last spring and chunk of foam had been tossed inside, I bowed my head, said the only prayer I knew, and then gently closed the lid.

Turning around, I looked at Knight and was relieved to see him looking back. He was in there, watching me. And his icy-gray eyes appeared to be melting.

Shit.

"Hey," I said, taking a step toward him. "I'm sorry. I'm so fucking sor—"

"Shut up." Those were the first words Knight had uttered since going catatonic on me.

But I couldn't shut up. "I shouldn't have...I don't know what I'm doing. Tell Bobbi I'll pay for—"

"Shut the fuck up!" Knight stomped forward and grabbed me by the shoulders. "Shut the fuck up, Punk!"

I wanted to slam my eyes shut, but I couldn't look away from the errant tear clinging to his feathery blond eyelashes. Whatever Knight was about to do to me, say to me, I deserved it.

"What you did back there"—Knight let go of me with one hand and shoved his finger in the direction of the building behind him—"you don't fucking apologize for that. Do you understand me?"

I blinked away my own threatening tears and stared back in confusion.

"Something fucking happened"—Knight turned his finger on himself, jabbing it into his chest—"*inside* me. I just got nineteen years of anger and fucking hatred and...and goddamn *poison* out of my system, and the only person who got hurt was a fucking chair. How the fuck did you do that?"

"*You* did that," I said, sniffling to keep my emotions at bay. "You made *yourself* feel better, Knight. You're the one who told me what happened. You didn't have to do that. And you even told your mom how you felt—well, before you killed her..."

And there it was. The smile that I would have moved heaven and earth to see, elicited by my stupid little joke. Knight's chiseled lips split in half, revealing a row of perfect white teeth. His pale gray-blue eyes twinkled like colorless diamonds in the light emanating from the parking lot. And his laugh, deep yet boyish, put me at ease.

It told me that everything was going to be okay.

That *we* were going to be okay.

It fucking lied.

The next morning, I woke up in my happy place—draped over Knight's chest on the black leather couch in the Terminus City Tattoo break room. Although I'd woken up like that dozens of times, it never got old. There is a divinity to feeling someone else's body humming and beating and breathing in perfect concert with yours—an ancient kind of magic. I lay there and soaked it up until my limbs began to tingle and my bladder began to scream.

The clock on the microwave—the only light source in the room—read *8:52*. Ugh. Why was I awake so early?

The shop didn't open until noon on Sunday, but I decided to go ahead and get up. I didn't want to be within a five-mile radius when Bobbi got there and saw that Knight's entire tattoo chair had been ripped out of the floor.

When I peeled my naked body off of Knight's naked body and stood up, the world suddenly took a nosedive to the right. I managed to grab on to the armrest of the couch before I went down with the ship. Thank God. Sliding to the floor, I sat with my back against the couch and waited for the dizziness to stop.

I should probably eat today. Not that I have a choice. Knight's going to force me to eat breakfast as soon as he wakes up anyway— just like he always does. Bossy asshole.

I thought about all the times he'd forced me to eat in front of him. I'd fucking hated him for it at the time—I used to cry and pout—but I understood now. That was his way of loving me. Knight was the only one who'd ever noticed my eating disorder. Even my mom and I had been shocked when the nurse at the hospital told us my diagnosis the year before—anorexia nervosa. But Knight had known all along. And more than that, he'd fucking cared.

Harley never said shit about my weight. He didn't care if I ate or not. Probably because he didn't care about anything. Including me.

Harley. I grimaced just thinking about him.

I tried again to stand up—that time slower and more successfully. Walking over to the right side of the room where I knew the counter and cabinets were, I reached above the microwave and quietly took out a small box. Even after nine months, Bobbi hadn't gotten rid of it. The thought made me smile.

I carried Knight's box of toiletries down the hall to the restroom where I peed and brushed my teeth with his toothbrush. When I caught my reflection in the mirror, I almost screamed. I looked as cracked out as a human could look, minus the track marks. All of my black eye makeup had run down my face in the rain. My shaggy, wavy bleach-blonde hair had air-dried into some Robert Smith-style Afro. My reddish-brown roots were close to two inches long. I had a scabbed-over bite mark on my shoulder where Knight had gone fucking vampire on me the night before. And my body looked like an anatomy class skeleton that had been shrink-wrapped in translucent, freckled skin.

Jesus Christ.

How was *that* girl graduating in two weeks, a year early, with honors? I was the world's most functional fuckup.

I grabbed my purse and clothes out of the hallway and went to work, putting myself somewhat back together. My tank top was still pretty wet, so I just pulled the extra-large Terminus City T-shirt I'd been wearing the night before back on, rolled up the sleeves, and tied the bottom in a knot. I washed my face, shoved a handful of bobby pins into my hair, and threw on the only makeup I had in my bag—lipstick, blush, and concealer. It wasn't a masterpiece, but it was better than looking like an extra on *Night of the Living Dead.*

I took the box back into the break room and gave Knight's shoulder a little nudge. He was out cold. Looking at the clock again, I decided to just let him sleep. He'd had a long night. Fuck. He'd had a long nineteen years.

Grabbing my purse and shoving my feet into my boots, I decided to hit up a drive-through and surprise Knight with breakfast. I propped the back door open with the chunk of cement we always used, and checked my phone as I walked through pond-sized puddles out to my car. I couldn't believe the damn thing hadn't died yet. I also couldn't believe that I had three recent missed calls from Harley. I had just assumed I was never going to hear from him again. Maybe my annoying-ass ringtone was what woke me—

"There's my little whore."

My feet froze at the sound of his rough voice. It was grittier than ever, like he'd been up all night smoking glass shards and gargling gasoline. I looked up slowly and saw Harley leaning against his driver's side door, facing me. He'd parked right next to my car—which, in the light of day, I could see was parked right next to Knight's truck.

"You wanna tell me why the fuck your five-oh and that jacked-up redneck mobile are parked side by motherfuckin' side right now?"

Um…

"I told you to stay the fuck there!" Harley spat, shoving a finger in my direction. "And what do you do? What *the fuck* do you do? You come *here*? To get fucked by that psycho skinhead?"

I wanted to turn and run back inside. I wanted to scream at him for being a piece-of-shit boyfriend. But I pussied out on both impulses and tried using my brain to smooth things over instead.

"Harley," I said, keeping my voice calm despite the alarm bells blaring inside my head, "you're not making any sense. The pool hall is closed, baby. It's nine in the morning. You're tired. You just need to go home and get some—"

Harley's oil-stained hand gripped me by the chin and lifted my face. His beautiful puppy-dog eyes were unrecognizable. That bright twinkly blue had been eclipsed by two soulless black pupils. The whites were marred and slashed with red. Their expression was demanding, not begging, not playful. Cruel.

Cruel and crazed.

"Don't fuck with me!" Harley yelled, squeezing my jaw. "You think you're smarter than me because you go to some fancy fucking college, and I'm just a stupid dropout? Well I know shit too, lady. I know you're fuckin' lying."

Harley leaned in closer, so close that I could smell the alcohol on his breath and see the white powder crusted around his left nostril. I squeezed my eyes shut and tried to pull my face away, but he snapped my head right back.

"You like gettin' cut, lady? Is that what this is about? Because I'll be more than fuckin' happy to—"

Before he could finish his threat, Harley's hand was knocked away from my face by a force so powerful that the impact spun me halfway around. I turned back to find a shirtless Knight straddling Harley on the ground, raining punches down on him with both fists.

Fuck! No, Knight, no! Harley probably has a—

A deafening blast rang out, echoing through the parking lot and reverberating through my soul, just before I realized that I was falling.

In slow motion.

Oh my God, I thought. *Did I just get shot? Somebody fired a gun, and now I'm falling, sooo...I probably got shot. Why doesn't it hurt? I don't feel anything. Well, except for someone's hand yanking on my wrist. Wait a fucking minute! I'm not falling. I'm being pulled!*

I braced myself for impact, expecting to hit the cracked cement of the parking lot. I landed on something warm and yielding instead.

A body.

I screamed as dread oozed through my veins, spreading to my extremities and squeezing my lungs.

No. No, no, no. Please God, no.

I opened my eyes, prepared to find Knight covered in blood, gasping for air like a guppy out of water beneath me, but instead, I found him kneeling before me, very much alive. His nostrils flared with every heave of his chest. His zombie-gray eyes burned white-hot. And his jaw was clenched shut tighter than a bear trap. I'd seen that expression before—the first time Knight had killed someone in my defense.

Images from the previous May flooded my mind—a junkyard dog lapping up its master's blood. A crimson-covered baseball bat. A scarlet-splashed hoodie. I couldn't bring myself to look down at the body below me, but when Knight's murderous eyes darted to something over my shoulder and his hands shot up in surrender, I didn't have to. I knew in that moment that Harley was alive.

And when the searing hot barrel of his Glock pressed against my temple, I knew *I* was fucked.

GEORGIA
CHAPTER 41
19 PEACH STATE 99

They say that your life flashes before your eyes when you have a near-death experience. Well, that's bullshit. At least, it was for me. Maybe my angels are just slackers, but there was no cute little slideshow of all my greatest memories and achievements cued up and ready to go. All those bitches did was hit the pause button. On my whole life.

Pause.

Oh, look. We're upside down.

Where did all of this glass come from?

Is that a dump truck?

Who is screaming?

Oh, my bad. It's me.

I can't believe the Boss is about to get totaled. Goddamn, I love this car.

I can't believe Harley put a fucking gun to my head and made me leave with him.

I hope he lives so that I can haunt him forever.

But if he lives, then Knight will kill him, and then Knight will have to spend the rest of his life in military jail, so maybe we should just die together.

That would be fitting, wouldn't it? We fucking deserve each other.

I wonder if this is gonna hurt.

I wonder if the coroner is gonna tell my parents about all my piercings.

I wonder if my parents will be okay.

I wonder if I'll be able to hang out with my mom still—not in, like, a scary, haunty way, but more like an I-know-you-can't-hear-me-or-see-me-but-let's-just-sit-on-the-couch-and-watch-Seinfeld-reruns-together kind of way.

My poor mom.

Man, did I fuck up or what?

I blame Knight. If he hadn't left for the Marines we'd still be together and none of this would have ever happened.

Okay, let's be honest. While Knight and I were together shit like this used to happen on, like, a monthly basis so . . . maybe let's just go back to blaming Harley.

Yeah. Fuck that guy.

Oh my God. Is that a light? You have got to be kidding me.

This is it.

This is all I get.

A moment of reflection and a goddamn light to walk toward.

As soon as I find out who my spirit guide is, that motherfucker is so fired.

"Miss Bradley? Miss Bradley, can you hear me? Can you tell me what hurts?"

My ego—after that lame-ass production y'all just put on. I didn't even get any harp music? What the fuck?

"Miss Bradley, wake up. I need you to tell me what hurts."

The light I'd been moving toward suddenly blinded me as my eyes fluttered open. I immediately snapped them shut again. Wherever I was, it was way too damn bright. I winced and tried to suck in a breath as a sharp, stabbing pain registered in my side.

I reached across my body with my left hand, but the voice put my hand back down and told me not to move.

"My...side," I gasped.

"Miss Bradley, do you know where you are?" a sweet Southern voice asked.

I shook my head, unable and unwilling to open my eyes to see for myself.

"You're in an ambulance, honey. You and your boyfriend were just in a car accident."

"Where...he?" I choked out.

"He's in another ambulance. Don't worry. He's gonna be fine—just a broken arm and a few broken teeth from that hard little head of yours."

As soon as she said that, a spot on the left side of my head began to throb. I lifted my hand to touch it.

"Don't touch. You gotta pretty good goose egg over there," the nice lady said. "Now, Miss Bradley, I'm real sorry, but I'm gonna have to cut your clothes off. Okay?"

I nodded, but I wasn't happy about it.

I was gonna miss those damn shorts.

And that Terminus City T-shirt.

As soon as the nice lady cut my bra open, she gasped. "Oh my goodness! Look at those titty rings!"

I went to laugh, but the pain in my side shut that shit right down.

"Miss Bradley, I'm gonna have to take these out...if I can figure out how they work." She giggled.

"Don't...lose them," I begged.

"Don't worry, honey. I won't. You got any other jewelry I should know about?"

That time, I laughed right through the pain. I couldn't wait to hear what she had to say about my *other* jewelry.

GEORGIA
CHAPTER 42
19 PEACH STATE 99

I flirted with consciousness for the next twenty-four hours, but it was always just beyond my reach. I'd hear a few words here, a few words there, but I didn't fully open my eyes and take in my surroundings until the next afternoon. When I did, I was in a hospital bed with so many tubes and wires coming out of me, I looked like an emaciated jellyfish.

One of the tubes—a clear one the size of a garden hose—emerged from between two protruding ribs on my right side. Well, it had been clear at one point. Now the inside was smeared and dotted with chunks of red.

A skinnier clear tube snaked out from between my legs. And even more tubing tethered my wrists and elbows to bags hanging next to my bed. A dull pain throbbed on the left side of my head, and a sharper one stabbed at my right side.

My mom, who was sitting in a chair by the window reading a magazine, noticed the movement when I lifted my sheet to assess the damage and came over to my bedside.

"Hi, baby," she said in a sympathetic tone. She looked tired. So, so tired. "How do you feel?"

"Sore," I said, winded after just that one little word.

My mom went to sit on the edge of my bed, then stopped herself. Throwing the sheet back, she checked to make sure she wasn't about to crush that nasty blood-and-gore-filled tube.

"What's...that?" I gasped, pointing at the horror coming out of my body.

"They call it a chest tube," she said, moving it closer to the foot of the bed so that she could sit next to me. "You have some broken ribs and a punctured lung, sweetie. That tube is draining the blood out of your deflated lung."

I winced at her description of my injuries. *Jesus.*

"What...happened?"

"All they said was that Harley lost control of the car and spun out right in front of a dump truck. It hit on your side, baby. The paramedics said you're lucky to be alive."

Reaching over and clasping my hand, my Irish-Catholic mother kissed the top of my head and said, "Your guardian angel was watching over you yesterday."

The emotion in her voice made my throat tighten and my eyes burn. I squeezed my mom's hand back, and when she looked down at me, I gave her a small smile.

She smiled back, then cocked her head to the side and said, "Oh, and the paramedic I was talking to gave me a baggie with all your *jewelry* in it."

I felt my face heat with the fire of a thousand suns.

Then she added, "I put it in your purse...right next to your *birth control pills.*"

Oh my God!

"Uh...thanks," I rasped, wanting to pull the covers over my head and hide. Or die all over again.

Then she laughed and said, "Can you imagine if they had given all that to your father? He would have had a heart attack right on the spot! They would have had to wheel him in here right behind you!" Then she laughed even harder.

I couldn't laugh with her because it hurt too much, but I could smile. I smiled and smiled and closed my eyes and gripped her hand and silently thanked my slacker guardian angel for letting me hear that woman laugh again.

And silently apologized for almost firing him the day before.

My mom left a little while later to go pick up some fast food for dinner—and probably smoke a doobie in her car—when there was a knock at my door. A female police officer walked in. She had a short Afro to match her short stature, and what I assumed was an even shorter temper based on her scowl.

"Miss Bradley, my name is Officer Hoover, and I'd like to ask you some questions about the accident you were in yesterday."

Fuck. Me.

"I, uh... is that allowed? I'm only sixteen. Don't I need to have a lawyer present or a parent or something?"

Real smooth, BB. That didn't sound guilty at all.

Officer Hoover raised an eyebrow at me and said, "No, ma'am. You haven't been arrested, and your drug test came back negative. I'm simply asking for your cooperation while we investigate the dealings of Mr. James."

My what? I was drug-tested? And it came back negative?

"Um... okay."

"Miss Bradley, Mr. James was found unconscious at the scene with a blood alcohol level of point fifteen. That's almost double the legal limit."

Jesus.

"He was also under the influence of cocaine and marijuana."

I guess their drug tests don't pick up LSD.

Officer Hoover sat on the rolling stool the nurses used, which, for some reason, put me at ease a little bit.

"Normally, in a DUI arrest, Mr. James would post bail and appear before a judge; however, he was already out on parole for grand theft auto, so he will be held without bail until his court date. At the scene of the accident, Mr. James was also found to be in possession of several illegally obtained weapons as well as a vial of liquid lysergic acid diethylamide with enough hits to charge him with intent to distribute."

Holy.

Fucking.

Shit.

Pinching the bridge of her nose, Officer Hoover took a deep breath and leveled with me. "Miss Bradley, Harley James needs to be taken off the streets of Atlanta. He is a danger to himself and others. Now, we spoke to an eyewitness who claims that you were forced into that car at gunpoint. If we add a kidnapping charge, I believe it will be enough to put Mr. James away for a very, very long time. Possibly life."

Kidnapping?

Kidnapping!

Kidnapping.

"Miss Bradley?"

"Huh?"

"Did Mr. James force you to leave with him against your will?"

"I…" *Don't know what the fuck to do!*

"I…" *Don't want him to go to prison for life, do I?*

"I…" *Wonder if Knight was the witness she talked to. Did he come up here to see me? Was he at the scene?*

"I…would like to talk to my lawyer."

Officer Hoover scowled at me and opened her mouth to speak when another officer knocked on the open door and poked his head into my room.

"He's been discharged. We're heading out," he said.

Standing right outside my door, next to the male officer, was baby-faced Harley James. The one I remembered. The one with the puppy-dog eyes and the pouty bottom lip. His lip ring was gone—probably in a baggie somewhere—and his expression was pitiful. My heart skipped a beat, then sputtered back to life with a vengeance when I remembered what he'd done. If I'd been wearing a heart monitor the damn thing would have exploded.

Harley's left arm was in a cast from his shoulder to his wrist, and his hands were cuffed in front of him.

A sad, silent exchange passed between us, and in that space, I thought we'd said everything we needed to say. Harley's eyes whispered apologies, confessed his shame, and pleaded for mercy.

Mine whispered, *Go fuck yourself.*

As Officer Hoover rose to join them, she reached into her pocket and produced a card with her contact information on it. Extending it to me, she said, "Miss Bradley, we'll be in touch." Then, she turned and left.

The trio was gone just long enough for me to exhale the breath I'd been holding and to replay most of that fucked-up conversation when I heard the male officer shout, "Hey! Stop him!"

Two seconds later, Harley was at my bedside. The last time

he'd been that close to me he'd held a gun to my head, so I didn't know what the fuck he was about to do now that he had nothing left to lose. I tried to gasp or scream or sit up, but my lungs and ribs were so fucked that all I could do was wince in pain and brace for impact. Reaching into his front pocket with his hands cuffed together and the cops right on his heels, Harley pulled out a tiny diamond ring.

"I want you to have this," he said, sincerity pouring over that pouty bottom lip. "For what it's worth I wasn't kidding when I asked you to marry me. I really do love you, lady." With a flick of his thumb, Harley tossed the ring to me.

Then, he turned and held his hands up as high as his cast would allow just in time to be tackled by Officer Hoover.

I picked up the delicate trinket and examined it as they hauled him away. It really was pretty.

I couldn't wait to pawn it.

GEORGIA
CHAPTER 43
19 PEACH STATE 99

I spent the next few days in the hospital, sleeping, picking at the bland cafeteria food they'd insisted on bringing me, and waiting for Knight to show up. He came by every afternoon to take me on my daily walk up and down the hallway, but he seemed different. Distant. I couldn't figure out why. Knight should have been over the moon. Harley was in jail, and probably would be forever. I was fine, relatively speaking. Knight had gotten all that shit off his chest about his mom. And we were back together.

Weren't we?

I told myself that he was probably just beating himself up about the wreck. I knew how self-deprecating Knight could be. He'd probably concocted some way to blame himself for what had happened. Or maybe he just felt awkward, being around my parents. One of them was at the hospital at all times, and he knew they kind of hated him. They hated Harley more, but I doubt that made him feel any better.

Whatever the reason, I still got butterflies whenever he walked in. I didn't care that I had no makeup on and hadn't bathed in almost a week. The way Knight looked at me, the way he helped me out of bed and made sure I didn't snag any of the tubes coming out of me, the way he held my hand on our walks, the way he whispered "I love you" in my ear before he left every night—that shit made me feel beautiful.

On day six, I finally did it. I blew into that goddamn tube hard enough to make the needle go all the way up to the top. The nurses made me do it every day to test my lung capacity. They'd said that once I could make the needle go past a certain point, I would be ready to go home. I was beyond ready, in every sense of the word. Ready to sleep in my own bed. Ready to take a shower. And ready to test out my newly inflated lung with a much-needed Camel Light.

I gingerly put on the clothes my mom had brought for me, wincing with every movement, and walked out to the parking lot with her. My beloved Mustang was waiting for me, right in front.

"Knight and his friend from work brought your car up here so that you wouldn't have to go get it." Her tone was sharp.

I guess it was pretty obvious that I'd lied about where I spent the night before the accident since Knight was the one returning my car.

"Typically, you'd be grounded right now, but I think your broken ribs are punishment enough."

I nodded, feeling my cheeks turn scarlet with shame, and gave my mom a painful, grateful sideways hug. "I'm just gonna stop by work and pick up my check on the way home, okay?"

My mom said, "Okay," and reminded me not to do too much. She wanted me home by dinner.

I shuffled over to my beloved and spent five minutes trying to figure out how to climb inside without it feeling like I was being stabbed in the side with an ice pick. As I flailed, my purse began to sing.

Doodleoodleoodleoodleoo.

I landed in the driver's seat with a yelp, then dug my phone out of my bag. The caller ID showed Harley's home phone number.

What the…

I answered on the second ring, "Hello?"

" 'Sup, BB?"

"Dave?"

"The one and only. Hey, whatcha doin' right now?"

"Uh…nothing? Why?"

"I was wonderin' if you wanted to come over here and help me throw Angel's shit out on the lawn. I'm kickin' her crazy ass out."

I knew that I was on painkillers and had had a rough couple of days, but Dave wasn't making a goddamn bit of sense.

"Wait. What? Start over. You're kicking somebody out, and you want my help? Dave, I got in a car accident with your brother. You know that, right? I literally haven't even left the hospital yet."

"Yeah, I know. That's why I thought you'd want to come help me kick out the bitch who's been livin' with him."

I stared out my windshield for a solid five seconds, waiting for a thought or a feeling to surface. I had nothing. I was one hundred percent unable to process that sentence. I just blinked at it, admiring the way the syllables sounded in my ears.

"BB?"

"I'm sorry. What did you say her name was?"

"Angel, but the bitch acts more like a ghetto swamp demon if you ask me."

"I'll be there in twenty minutes."

———————

Dave answered the door in a surprisingly good mood for a guy whose brother might be going to jail for life. He was wearing a white wifebeater, tight Wranglers, and had that navy-blue baseball cap with the fishing hook in the bill pulled down over his pretty eyes.

"Good to see you, girl. Get in here." Dave went to give me a hug but stopped when I put my hands up defensively. "Oh, right. I forgot. You doin' okay?"

I nodded and tried to return his smile despite the acidic ocean of dread churning in my gut. "Thanks for calling."

Dave stepped aside to let me in. "I miss havin' you around, girl. You're way fuckin' cooler than that other bitch. I figured she'd leave once Harley got locked up, but she just keeps showin' up. Last night she even tried to fuck *me* to let her stay. Now, I'm not one to turn down free ass, but ass don't pay my rent."

"How long has she been living here?" I asked, looking around for some evidence I might have missed.

How have I been so blind?

"I dunno. She kinda came and went for a while, but she's been livin' here full-time ever since you stopped coming around. I just figured you musta found out about her and broke up with Harley. But then when I saw you with him at Empty Pockets, I knew that motherfucker was playin' you."

Dave pulled two beers out of the fridge, popped the tabs on

both cans, and handed one to me. I knew I shouldn't mix alcohol and painkillers, but fuck it, I needed a drink. Bad.

"Thanks," I said, accepting the beer with a small smile and wandering aimlessly into the living room.

I thought about the last time I'd seen Angel—at the track. How weird I'd thought it was that she was there. How weird it was the way that Harley had yelled at her. How weird it was that her brother's gangster friends had just stood by like they were on Harley's side.

It all made sense now. She was his fucking side chick, and everybody had known it but me.

"Sorry, B," Dave said, following me into the living room. "I love him, but Harley's a motherfucker. Always has been."

Turning around, I took three long steps toward Dave and wrapped my arms around his waist. He lifted his hands, afraid to touch me at first, then gently held me while I gritted my teeth and tried not to cry.

"Thank you for telling me," I murmured into his tank top. "I feel so fucking stupid."

"I know what'll make you feel better," Dave said, humping me a little.

"Not that." I giggled.

"Damn it," Dave said with a chuckle. "Well, how 'bout we throw this bitch's shit out on the lawn instead?"

"Deal," I said, making a beeline for the bathroom. I might not have been able to lift much in my injured condition, but I could throw a purple toothbrush like nobody's business.

Once all of Angel's clothes and toiletries were scattered in Dave's front yard, we sat in the lawn chairs under his oak tree and admired our work. The kiddie pool was full of mildew, and the inflatable palm tree had long since blown away, but it still felt good to sit and have a beer with my pervy friend Dave. The painkillers were nice, too.

"So what happened?" I asked. "At the pool hall?"

"Fuckin' Smoke got paroled, that's what happened." Dave spat on the ground. "Smoke had the gun market on lockdown 'til he got busted on some bullshit possession charge last year. While he was out of the picture, a few entrepreneurs—like m'self—saw an opportunity to make a few bucks. Supply and demand, you know?"

I didn't know. I didn't even nod like I knew.

"Well, as soon as he got out he went around deliverin' messages to everybody sellin' on his turf. That drive-by was just Smoke's way of lettin' us know that he'll be takin' his business back now." Dave rolled his eyes and took a swig from his beer.

"You're not worried?"

He shrugged. "I guess I was 'bout ready to retire anyway." A glimmer of sadness crept into his voice.

"Are you worried about Harley?" I asked, studying Dave's profile.

"Harley?" Dave snapped, looking over at me. "Fuck no. That asshole lives like a king in jail. On the outside you gotta have a job and shit, but on the inside, hustlin's your job. And there ain't no better hustler than Harley."

"Jesus." I choked on my beer. "How many times has he been to jail?"

Dave snorted. "Prob'ly more times than you got fingers and toes to count 'em on. This was actually the longest he's been out since he was a kid. Used to get busted for boostin' cars all the damn time."

Oh my God, I'm such a fucking idiot! That's it!

"Is that how Harley got the Boss?"

I knew I should shut up. I was asking way too many questions about shit I had no business being involved in, but that question had been plaguing me since the day I met Harley James—the twenty-one-year-old mechanic with the hundred-thousand-dollar car. I could have just come out and asked him how he got it, but I was afraid. Afraid that he would lie to me.

Afraid that he would tell me the truth.

"Actually"—Dave's face fell—"Harley rebuilt that damn thing from the ground up. Our old man wasn't really a part of our lives, but when he died Harley and I each inherited one of the old rust buckets they found in his garage. We weren't even old enough to drive yet, but Mama let us keep 'em in a shed out behind her house. I got the truck. Harley got the Boss."

I didn't even know what to say. I just sat there with my mouth hanging open. How did I not know that? How had I been in a relationship with a man for almost a year without finding out that his father had passed away? It's not like he wouldn't have told me.

I never found out because I never bothered to ask.

Dave took a sip from his can and gazed off into the woods. "Harley was obsessed with fixin' up those damn cars. Fucker even started skippin' school so that he could go steal car parts from the junkyard and teach himself how they worked. By the time he turned sixteen, he had both vehicles up and runnin'. Course, he'd also been to juvie at least three times by then too.

Even after Mama kicked his ass out, she let him keep the Boss in her shed because she knew how much it meant to him."

Well, I sure felt like a giant asshole.

"Damn, Dave. I'm so sorry. I had no idea—"

"It's all right," Dave interrupted. "Like I said, we weren't real close."

Somehow, I got the sense that that wasn't true.

Not knowing what else to say, Dave and I sat in an awkward silence for the next few minutes, finishing off our beers and admiring the sea of purple bullshit scattered about us on the lawn. Maybe it was the mixture of Vicodin and cheap beer, but I felt...numb. I knew on an intellectual level that I should feel enraged about being cheated on, sad about Dave losing his dad and now his brother, conflicted about Harley going back to jail, worried about Knight's weird, distant behavior, and freaked out about the final exams and graduation speech I needed to prepare for, but...I didn't. I didn't feel anything.

Until a beat-up, off-white, Buick Regal lowrider pulled into the driveway, that is. Then I felt all of it at once, doused in fear and lit with a match called jealousy.

Dave clapped his hands and stood up to greet our unwelcome guest. "Ha! Here's the bitch now!"

Adrenaline shot out to my extremities, preparing them to flee or fight, but with three broken ribs I couldn't do either one. I thought about standing up next to Dave to look like a unified front, but I decided to just stay sitting in my lawn chair. Partly because I knew standing up was going to hurt like hell, partly because if I didn't stand up she couldn't knock me down, and partly because I thought it would look more badass. Of course, it's kind of hard to look badass when you have no makeup on, haven't bathed in a week, have hair like a troll doll, weigh ninety-eight pounds, and are wearing the *I ♥ New York* T-shirt your mom brought you to wear home from the hospital.

As Angel threw the car in park, I braced myself for her wrath. I couldn't believe I was right back where I'd been a year ago—about to get attacked by the bitch who was trying to steal *my* boyfriend. And it was the *same* bitch!

"What the fuck is this shit?!" Angel screamed as she came around the front of what I assumed was a hand-me-down hoop-tie from her brother.

She was wearing baggy Dickies that looked like they might have been Harley's and a white cropped tank top that barely contained her massive tits. Her long, scraggly black hair spilled out from under a backwards LA Lakers ball cap and reached almost down to her elbows. I felt my cheeks burn and my pulse speed up as I pictured the way that hair had looked dangling from my fist when I'd confronted Harley about it. If I had known I was holding Angel fucking Alvarez's hair I probably would have wrapped it around his neck and tried to strangle him with it.

Fucking asshole.

"Sorry, sugar," Dave said with a shrug. "Looks like you just got evicted." I couldn't see his face from where he was standing, but I could hear the smugness in his voice.

Angel's eyes flared as she looked at all of her shit strewn out across the overgrown lawn. Then they landed on me.

"You!" she screamed, pointing a long French-manicured finger-nail directly at me. "This is all your fucking fault!" Angel's voice took on a shrill pitch at the end, signifying that she was about to lose her shit.

Dave took a protective step in front of me and said, "Home

girl, you got five minutes to get your shit and go 'fore I start burnin' Kobe Bryant jerseys."

Angel didn't even hear him. Her dark brown eyes were trained on me and me alone. "Why do you keep doin' this to me?" she shrieked. "It's not fuckin' fair! You don't need them! You don't need fucking anything!"

"What have I ever done to *you*?!" I snapped back.

Oh shit. I just poked the bear.

Angel cackled and rolled her eyes. "Your life is so *fuckin'* perfect. You don't need nobody protectin' you. Ain't nobody pimpin' you out to gangstas and dealers at your house. Ain't nobody smackin' you in the mouth when you try to say *no*. I need a man who ain't afraid to throw down for me, and every fuckin' time I find one, yo ass got there first!"

Dave pretended to yawn and looked at his wrist. "Four minutes, bitch."

"Angel," I said, using the slow, soothing voice that usually, kind of, sometimes worked on Knight. "I'm sorry your home life is fucked up. I am. But lots of people have fucked-up home lives, and they're not out trying to fuck all my boyfriends!"

Welp, so much for soothing.

"Fuck you, bitch! Let's do this!" Angel spread her arms wide and lunged forward, tits first, like she wanted to fight.

Dave blocked her advance with his body, then looked over his shoulder at me and said, "BB, be a doll and go grab my shotgun. It appears as though we got ourselves a trespasser."

I knew what Dave was doing—he was getting me the fuck out of there, and I loved him for it. I stood up, trying not to let Angel see me wince in pain or shake in fear, gave her a little smirk, and sauntered back into the house with her cursing and lunging at me from behind Dave's protective stance.

As soon as the door was shut firmly behind me, I leaned against it and burst into tears. My hands were trembling from the adrenaline. My newly-inflated lung burned with every gasp and hiccup. I was so fucking mad, and felt so fucking weak. I hated that I couldn't just stick up for myself and pummel her face in. If Dave hadn't been there, I don't know what would have happened. Angel said I didn't need a man to protect me, but I did.

From *her*.

I peeked out from between the yellowed plastic blinds on the window next to the front door and watched Angel stomping around the front yard picking up armfuls of her belongings, cursing at Dave the entire time. He just stood there with a smartass smile on his face, pointing out things she'd missed. I could hear every snide little comment he made through those thin walls.

"Don't forget your toothbrush. Looks like it landed over there in that pile of dog shit. Crazy, right? I mean, we don't even have a dog."

"You call yourself a Lakers fan and you don't have a single Shaquille O'Neal jersey? What the hell? You think you're too cool for the Shaq Attack?"

"No, I will not run away with you and be your new lover. Gah! Stop askin', all right. It's gettin' embarrassin'."

By the time Angel shoved the last of her belongings into her trunk and peeled out of there my ribs hurt from laughing instead of crying.

Dave gave her a middle-finger salute, then sauntered back

toward the house like Captain Big Dick, his chest all puffed up and proud.

I wiped my eyes on my ugly-ass souvenir T-shirt and greeted Dave with a smile as soon as he walked through the door.

"Well," Dave said, clapping his hands together once for effect. "Looks like I'm in the market for a roommate. You in?"

I smiled. "Not after seeing what happened to the last two."

After Dave and I said our good-byes, I drove away a little stronger, a little braver, and with a lot more baggage. *Literally.* I had a wooden chair with skeleton upholstery riding shotgun and a jackalope wearing a purple bandana buckled into the backseat.

Looking out over the audience, I picked at the corner of my notecard and scanned the bleachers for familiar faces. Luckily, so few high school students graduated through East Atlanta College that my entire graduating class was able to fit on a portable stage in the middle of the basketball gym. If I'd graduated from Peach State High, I'd be giving a speech to a football stadium filled with people. The thought made me a little less nervous. It could have been so much worse.

I spotted Juliet and Goth Girl immediately. They were sitting all the way in the back—too cool, as usual—but they were holding up homemade signs that read *Vote for BB* and *BB for President*. They were the world's least enthusiastic cheerleaders, and I fucking loved them for it.

My parents had arrived late as shit—per their usual—so they were in the back as well.

I continued to scan the audience, desperately searching for a pair of scowling gray zombie eyes, but I knew he wasn't coming. In fact, I had the letter to prove it—tucked away in the center console of my car, right where I'd found it.

I had just begun rereading the note from memory when my psychology professor, Dr. Raines, introduced me. He regaled the crowd with tales of my dedication—how I had come to class early every week to learn advanced therapeutic techniques and aced all of my final exams despite missing the last two weeks of school due to a car accident. What he didn't tell them—because he didn't know—was that I'd cheated my ass off during those make-up exams. I was pretty sure I would have done fine on my own, but why risk it? Four-point-oh grade point averages don't grow on trees.

As I stepped up to the podium, I felt it. A crackle in the air. Notes of warm cinnamon just beyond the edges of my awareness. It was enough to give me hope.

Glancing down at the notecard in my hand, I took a deep breath and looked at my parents.

"When I came to East Atlanta College," I said, wincing slightly at the sound of my own voice booming over the loudspeakers, "I had one goal in mind—to get my six credits and get the hell out of here."

That got a laugh from the crowd and even one from me when I saw my mom cover her face in embarrassment.

"But I got so much more than that…" I said, looking at Juliet and Goth Girl.

They shouted a lackluster, "Woohoo," and held their signs up.

"I got an education." I looked over at Dr. Raines, who smiled and pushed his glasses up his sweaty nose.

"Not just a list of names and dates to regurgitate for a test. Not just a few algebraic formulas that I will literally never use in my adult life. *Ever.*"

That got another chuckle from the crowd.

"See? Y'all know what I'm talking about." I smiled at my dad, who seemed to agree with me the most. "No, I got a *real* education. I learned things that weren't on the syllabus. That would never appear on any pop quiz. I learned about *life*."

And near-death experiences. And dumpster burial techniques for imaginary death experiences.

"I learned about *love*."

I glanced at my parents and thought about them rotating shifts to stay by my side the entire time I was at the hospital. I glanced at Juliet's bored face and pictured the way it would soften whenever she held Romeo. And I thought about Knight. Always.

"And I learned about *people*. I learned that sometimes the strongest, bravest members of our society are the ones who could crumble at any minute. And sometimes the tiniest and frailest among us... turn out to be tough as nails. I learned about *humanity* here—mine, and yours. I guess that's why they call it the Humanities department. I finally figured that out, too."

While the crowd cheered and laughed graciously at my stupid attempt at a joke, my gaze landed on a pair of pale gray eyes, off to the side of the gym by one of the exits. I realized immediately why I hadn't recognized them sooner.

They were smiling.

I congratulated the graduating class of 1999, and with the dean's nod of approval, my classmates and I tossed our caps into the air. Then we ducked for cover as their pointy corners rained down on us.

Diploma in hand, I smiled and hugged and nodded and thanked my way toward the door, desperate to catch the only person in that gym who *didn't* want to talk to me. I thought I was home free as soon as that hot, humid late-May air blasted my face, but before I could sprint through the parking lot in search of a certain white monster truck, a familiar voice called out my name.

I turned and saw my parents standing with Juliet and Goth Girl against the brick wall of the gym. My mom was the only one in the group holding a tissue to her nose, which made me smile. That woman laughed when everyone else cried and cried when everyone else laughed.

By the time I accepted my mom's hug, my dad's pat on the back, and my friends' monotone congratulations, I had also accepted the fact that Knight was gone. Again.

I plastered a fake smile onto my face and agreed to meet everyone at my favorite Italian restaurant right around the corner, then let it fall as I turned and walked toward my car.

Don't think about him, I told myself. *Don't. Stop it. You just graduated from high school, bitch. You're happy. Be happy. Hey, let's see if you can make it all the way to the car without thinking about him. Ready? Go!*

Honda, Nissan, Mazda, Honda, Honda, BMW, Chevy…

I named the make and sometimes model of every car I passed all the way to the little black Mustang hatchback parked in the center of the lot. Then I forgot what I was doing completely. Forgot to blink. Forgot to breathe. Because tucked underneath my windshield wiper was a delicate paper rose, folded from a mint-green graduation program.

I clutched the paper flower to my nose, trying to extract the last few hints of cigarette smoke and cinnamon from it, as I sat behind the wheel. Staring out the windshield, I fought the urge as long as I could.

Just one more time, I finally decided. *I'll read the damn thing one more time, but that's it.*

MAY 21, 1999

DEAR PUNK,

I'M SORRY I HAVEN'T BEEN AROUND MUCH SINCE THE WRECK. I NEED TO TELL YOU SOMETHING, AND I'VE BEEN TOO FUCKING CHICKENSHIT TO DO IT IN PERSON. I MEANT TO. I FUCKING TRIED. BUT EVERY TIME I CAME BY YOU ACTED SO FUCKING HAPPY TO SEE ME THAT I COULDN'T PULL THE TRIGGER. NOBODY'S EVER BEEN HAPPY TO SEE ME IN MY WHOLE FUCKING LIFE. NOBODY BUT YOU.

HOW WAS I SUPPOSED TO LOOK AT YOUR SMILING FACE AND YOUR BROKEN BODY AND TELL YOU THAT I'M THE ONE WHO DID IT TO YOU?

HOW WAS I SUPPOSED TO HOLD YOUR HAND AND HELP YOU WALK, THEN TELL YOU THAT I BLACKED OUT AGAIN AFTER HARLEY TOOK YOU? THAT THE ONLY THING I REMEMBER

IS RUNNING INTO THE WOODS AND SEEING HARLEY'S CAR PINNED AGAINST A TREE. THAT I SCREAMED AT YOU TO WAKE UP, BUT YOU WOULDN'T. THAT I WATCHED THE PARAMEDICS PRY YOUR LIFELESS BODY OUT OF THE CAR. HOW WAS I SUPPOSED TO LOOK YOU IN THE FACE AND TELL YOU THAT WHEN I WALKED BACK TO MY TRUCK IT HAD MATTE BLACK PAINT ALL OVER THE FRONT BUMPER?

I CAUSED THAT WRECK, PUNK. I FUCKING KNOW I DID.

JUST LIKE I ALMOST STABBED THAT GUY AT THE BAR.

JUST LIKE I DESTROYED BOBBI'S PHONE AND TATTOO CHAIR WITHOUT EVEN MEANING TO.

I HAVE NO FUCKING CONTROL ANYMORE. I USED TO KNOW HOW TO CONTROL IT, BUT FOR THE LAST NINE MONTHS I'VE BEEN TRAINED TO DO THE OPPOSITE. NOW I CAN'T FUCKING TURN IT OFF.

SO, I SIGNED UP FOR ANOTHER TOUR IN IRAQ.

I'M SO SORRY, PUNK. I'M SO FUCKING SORRY. BELIEVE ME WHEN I SAY THAT I WANT NOTHING MORE THAN TO STAY HERE AND PLAY FUCKING HOUSE WITH YOU AND WAKE UP WITH YOUR SKINNY LITTLE ARMS AND LEGS WRAPPED AROUND ME AND PRETEND LIKE I DON'T DESTROY EVERY FUCKING THING I TOUCH. BUT I CAN'T.

BECAUSE THIS TIME, I ALMOST DESTROYED YOU.

I CAN'T BE A CIVILIAN ANYMORE. I WAS FUCKING MISERABLE IN IRAQ, BUT AT LEAST THERE I HAD A PURPOSE. I COULD CHANNEL ALL MY HATE AND RAGE INTO SOMETHING USEFUL. HERE IT HAS NOWHERE TO GO. IT JUST BUILDS UP AND BUILDS UP UNTIL I SNAP OR BLACK OUT. THERE I COULD HELP PROTECT OUR ENTIRE COUNTRY. HERE I CAN'T EVEN PROTECT THE ONE PERSON I LOVE FROM MYSELF. AS MUCH AS I

FUCKING HATE TO ADMIT IT, I KNOW
THAT'S WHERE I BELONG.

AND THIS IS WHERE YOU BELONG.

I'M SO FUCKING PROUD OF YOU FOR
GRADUATING EARLY. YOU'RE GOING
TO BE AN AMAZING PSYCHOLOGIST,
PUNK. YOU ALREADY ARE. I KNOW
IT DOESN'T SEEM LIKE IT, BUT YOU
HELPED ME WORK SOME SHIT OUT
THAT I'D BEEN CARRYING AROUND
WITH ME SINCE I WAS A KID. YOU'RE
THE ONE WHO MADE ME WANT TO DO
SOMETHING GOOD WITH MY LIFE. AND
YOU'RE THE ONE I'LL BE FIGHTING FOR
WHEN I GO BACK OVERSEAS.

I LOVE YOU. PLEASE DON'T HATE ME.

KNIGHT

I allowed myself to read his letter one more time, then I neatly refolded it, sliding my bony fingers along the seams that Knight's thick fingers had made. I could feel his remorse and resignation radiating off the page. I tried to pull those feelings in through my pores. Take them on as my own.

I shook a cigarette from my pack and placed it between my lips, then sparked the flint of my lighter. Staring at the flame, I felt the resignation work its way into my chest and blanket my heart like a quilt too heavy for the summer heat. Even though the weight of it is stifling, throwing it off would leave you vulnerable to monsters.

For too long I'd left my heart vulnerable to monsters. I'd let them take and take and take. My innocence, my devotion, my freedom, my control. I would have given one of them my whole future, if he'd asked. But he didn't. He left instead. He was always leaving. For a year I'd been mourning him, even when he was right in front of me. I'd worked my way from the pits of despair, to the highs of false hope, through the battlefields of anger, and had finally arrived at acceptance. I took Knight's resignation on as my own.

But the remorse never came.

Not even when I held the flame under Knight's confession and lit my cigarette with his blazing apology.

GEORGIA

EPILOGUE

19 PEACH STATE 99

The summer of 1999 looked a lot like the summer of 1998. I celebrated my seventeenth birthday by blowing out a match instead of a candle on a lopsided, overbaked cake. I spent my days sleeping and smoking and watching daytime TV. Knight was gone. And, once again, I was dying.

Only this time it was from sheer fucking boredom.

Other than graduation, my parents had basically kept me under house arrest for six weeks after the accident because that's how long the doctors had estimated it would take for me to fully heal. I'd wanted to start taking classes at Georgia State that summer, but *noooo*. No school. No work. No fucking life.

So when Goth Girl called and invited me to a Fourth of July kegger at her new boyfriend's house, I sprinted to the calendar to do the math.

"Seven weeks, motherfucker! I'm there!"

Goth Girl had met—and made out with—this guy at a Marilyn Manson concert about two months before, and they'd been inseparable ever since. His name was Steven, but I called him Goth Guy—in my head at least. I hadn't met him yet, but the fact that he owned his own house and used it to throw keg parties for teenagers made me like him instantly. It was going to be a total rager too, with a band and everything. I mean, not a band anyone had actually heard of—just some local act called Phantom Limb—but still, a band!

Shit.

I wet a cotton swab in my mouth and tried to fix my fuckup. Again.

How does someone just forget *how to put on liquid eyeliner?*

Shut up. I haven't had to do it in, like, a month.

Excuses, excuses.

Great, now the line on the right is thicker.

Here we go again.

Maybe I'll just go heavier on the left to even it out.

That's what you said about the right side.

Applying one more swoop of black, I forced myself to put down the eyeliner pen and look for something else to obsess about. It wasn't hard. I hadn't been out of the house in weeks, and it showed. My jeans were all too tight to button, my makeup application skills were rusty as hell, and my hair...

Oh God, my hair.

It had been over a year since I'd shaved it last. My bangs grazed my jawline, my two longer side pieces dusted my collarbones, and my buzz cut had grown into a riot of shaggy, bushy, unkempt waves. I hadn't even noticed how long it had gotten. I'd just been sweeping it to the side and shoving handfuls of barrettes into it.

I couldn't walk outside with that mess on my head. Once the humidity got to it, it might literally suffocate me. Or someone else.

The voice inside my head—the one that didn't give a fuck what anybody thought, the one that had been utterly mute ever since Lance Hightower told me I looked like a little boy— whispered to me again for the first time in ages. It said, "Get your scissors, bitch."

———————

I could hear the band a block before Goth Guy's house was even in view. With my windows rolled up. *And* my stereo on. The noise was coming from inside a cute little yellow one-story in a family-friendly neighborhood out in the suburbs. Not exactly what I'd expected for a single twenty-something-year-old Marilyn Manson fan. Maybe he needed the extra space to hide all the bodies.

"Your hair looks rad!" Goth Girl yelled as soon as she opened the door. "I love that pixie cut! You look like Drew Barrymore back when she chopped all her hair off!"

She was decked out in full gothy glory—black baby-doll dress, chunky black platform Mary Janes, makeup that looked like a creepy porcelain doll. I suddenly questioned my cut-up, safety-pinned Black Flag crop top, but hey, at least my pants were pleather. Glancing around the room, that seemed to be part of the uniform.

I walked through the open door and into a darkened living room full of trippy, pulsing lights and blaring heavy metal. The furniture had all been pushed against the walls, and dozens of silhouettes bounced and headbanged in front of a four-piece band playing in the corner of the room. As my eyes adjusted, Goth Girl waved someone over.

"Steven!" she yelled.

A thin man with shoulder-length black hair and a pointy black goatee emerged from the crowd, wearing a black mesh shirt and vinyl pants that were too baggy. He reminded me of Lord Licorice from Candyland.

Once he was within earshot, Goth Girl leaned toward him and shouted, "This is BB! Doesn't she look just like Drew Barrymore?" Then she smiled at me and tugged on a lock of my inch-and-a-half-long, bottle-blonde DIY pixie cut.

Goth Guy looked me up and down in a way that made me feel small and shouted back, "Maybe if she had some tits."

Yeah, so Goth Guy could go eat a bag of dicks. *Asshole.*

Goth Girl pretended to slap him across the face, then giggled and linked arms with him, disappearing back into the crowd.

Awesome.

I needed a drink. And I needed to go hide some perishables around Goth Guy's house. Maybe he had some eggs in the fridge. Those would rot nicely in a few days.

As I made my way through the sweaty, unfamiliar crowd and toward what I assumed was the entrance to the kitchen, the thrashing subsided and morphed into a sultry, whispery song that I recognized. And actually liked. I turned and watched the lead singer of Phantom Limb—a wiry little thing with a black bowl cut parted right down the middle—growl the lyrics to "Sanctified" by Nine Inch Nails into the microphone. For such a tiny guy, he exuded a disconcerting amount of confidence.

The lead guitar player was a short, stocky guy who tried to hide behind both the lead singer and his own greasy chin-length hair. The drummer all but disappeared behind his elaborate set of drums and symbols and electronic pads. But the bass player was a goddamn giant. The fact that his band consisted of wee folk only made him seem taller.

I found myself watching him instead of the lead singer even though he didn't call any attention to himself whatsoever. The song had a heavy bass riff, and he seemed completely adrift on it. I liked watching people who didn't know they were being watched, and this guy acted like he didn't even know other people were in the room.

When the song was over, they switched to another thrashy number that I didn't recognize, effectively breaking the spell. I wandered into the kitchen and stood in line at the keg, behind some chick with blonde pigtails wearing an oversize Korn T-shirt. Unfortunately for me, Korn Girl wanted to do a keg stand. People trickled in to watch the spectacle, and suddenly, I wasn't next in line anymore.

Fantastic.

By the time I fought my way back to the keg, the live music had been replaced with prerecorded techno, and the entire crowd seemed to have pushed its way into the kitchen. I filled my Solo cup with piss-colored beer and spun around, careening face-first into an unyielding wall of hot muscle and sweat.

Stumbling backward, I watched in horror as half of my beer landed with a dramatic splash on the floor, just missing one of the human barricade's massive black Adidas. Luckily, the giant grabbed my upper arms to steady me before I completely busted my ass on the linoleum.

As my eyes made the long journey from his boatlike shoes up to his face, I took a quick mental appraisal. *Baggy black pin-striped slacks, chain wallet, slightly damp wifebeater plastered to a seriously bulbous set of six-pack abs, obviously tall as shit, seeing as how I haven't even made it up to his face yet—*

Oh my God! The fucking bass player!

Hoping he was a friendly giant, I donned my best please-don't-hurt-me-mister smile as I continued to crane my neck the rest of the way back, finally taking in his looming face. This dude could have gotten a walk-on role as one of the German bad guys in a *Die Hard* movie, no problem. His features were severe—jet-black hair violently headbanged into a mop of stabby, sweaty little spears, heavy brow impaled with a silver barbell on one side, prominent nose. But his playful gray-blue eyes and kind mouth, which was upturned into an adorably dimpled smile, fought hard to betray his otherwise villainous appearance.

Just looking at him made me feel as though I were standing under a streetlight on a hot summer night. While he was imposingly tall and slender and dark and hard, the glow he cast down on me was nothing short of sunshine.

"Hey, Tinker Bell. Going somewhere?"

I managed to squeak out an apology, but when I went to scoot around him to get out of his way, the giant simply snickered and tucked me under his arm. Holding me firmly to his side, he wrapped his long, strong, callused fingers around my shoulder and steered me back into the living room. It was a bizarre move, but for some reason, I was helpless to stop the forward progression of my steel-covered toes. It was as if I had been sucked into his cool, unassuming aura, suspended in a magical fairyland where strange men don't take advantage of drunk teenage girls at parties. Plus, with our height difference, my head fit perfectly under his big tattooed arm.

Mmm…

The raven-haired rocker guided me toward Goth Guy's black leather sofa, but rather than release me to sit, he effortlessly flopped onto the couch, twisting me on the way down so that we both landed side by side, his arm never leaving my shoulders. During our descent, he also managed to maneuver me so that my legs landed across his lap, his free hand coming to rest on my thigh.

Holy shit. This fucker is good.

"So, what's your name, Tinker Bell?"

As the dimple-cheeked devil beamed at me, I became aware that he was also nonchalantly rubbing a slow circle on my thigh with his thumb. All I could process was heat and rhythm—heat in my face, heat where his massive hand was absentmindedly kneading my body, stoking a virtual fire in my belly, and the tempo of his fingers strumming my thigh, which seemed to be in perfect concert with the blood thrumming between my legs just inches away.

When my brain finally registered that the expectant look on his face meant I was supposed to be answering a question, I frantically searched my recent memory for whatever the fuck it was that he'd asked me.

Something, something, Tinker Bell. Something…

Shit.

Taking a lucky guess, I blurted out, "BB." I swallowed and tried again, forcing myself to meet his gunmetal-blue gaze. "I'm BB…hi."

Jesus, real smooth.

"So, *Bumblebee*, why were you in there getting your own

beer? Don't you know pretty girls aren't allowed to get their own drinks? You're lucky I found you."

He could say that again.

It was a cheesy pick-up line, but the tattooed mystery man had delivered it with such a flirty playfulness that I felt myself relax.

I smiled and rolled my eyes. "Well, who else was gonna get it for—"

"Me," he interrupted with a grin. "I think I'm gonna be getting *all* your drinks from now on, Bumblebee."

He wasn't being arrogant, and I didn't get the sense that he thought I was a sure thing. It was more like he was just stating a fact. Like *we* were a sure thing.

I scoffed, trying to keep my cool, and said, "I don't even know who you are."

Mr. Tall, Dark, and Tattooed beamed at me. White teeth glistened. Dimples deepened. My heart rate skyrocketed, and my palms got sweaty.

"I'm Hans," he said without a shred of ego. "I'm the bass player."

BB and Hans's story continues in *Star*.
Available now.

GEORGIA
PLAYLIST
19 PEACH STATE 99

The following list of modern and '90s-throwback tracks revolves around fast cars, open roads, and reckless love. These songs provided me with hours of *Speed*spiration, and I am eternally grateful to each and every one of the brilliant artists who created them. You can stream the playlist for free on Spotify here:
   https://open.spotify.com/user/bbeaston/playlists.

"14 Faces" by Lewis Del Mar
"Army of Me" by Björk
"Bad Habit" by The Kooks
"Bad Things" by K. Flay
"Beat-Up Car" by Taking Back Sunday
"Break the Rules" by Charli XCX
"Breaking Free" by Night Riots
"Drive" by Halsey
"Drive" by Miley Cyrus
"Driving Fast in My Car" by Paramore
"Glitches" by Flint Eastwood

"Go with the Flow" by Queens of the Stone Age
"Green Light" by Lorde
"Highway" by Bleeker
"Joke" by Chastity Belt
"Lurk" by The Neighbourhood
"Messin' with My Head" by K. Flay
"Midnight City" by M83
"Muthafucka" by Beware of Darkness
"Next in Line" by Walk the Moon
"Slow It Down" by The Lumineers
"The Getaway" by Red Hot Chili Peppers
"The Sharp Hint of New Tears" by Dashboard Confessional
"Title and Registration" by Death Cab for Cutie
"West End Kids" by New Politics
"You're Mine" by Phantogram

GEORGIA
ACKNOWLEDGMENTS
19 PEACH STATE 99

Mom—Thank you for volunteering to watch my kids so that I could finish this book on time. You didn't even care what I was writing about. I could have been toiling away on an article about the latest cat fashions in Indonesia or penning some manifesto about how the government is implanting tracking devices in our skin through tiny robotic mosquitoes; it wouldn't have mattered. If it's important to me, it's important to you. Thank you for being the best mommy in the whole world. I love you.

Ken—You truly are my better half. You're the better-looking half. You're the more responsible half. You're definitely the soberer half. You're the half who does the taxes, the dishes, the grocery shopping, the laundry, the yard work, the couponing, the car maintenance, and the breakfasts when I'm too tired from pulling another all-nighter. Thank you for excelling where I fail. You are the left brain to my right, the blue sky to my rainbow, the tether to my balloon. I love you.

Ken's Mom—Mrs. Easton, thank you so much for stepping up to watch my children overnight while I gallivanted all over the country, promoting books that you are never, ever, *ever* allowed to read. I love you.

Staci Hart—Your unconditional love, sweet vulnerability, fearless pursuit of your best life, lady-boss levels of determination, ability to write both literary prose and one hundred and one sexy math jokes, and your superhuman tequila tolerance inspire me every day. Thank you for all of your brilliant advice and for forgiving my stubborn ass when I refused to listen to it. I love you, Kevin.

My Editors, Jovana Shirley and Ellie McLove—Thank you from the bottom of my heart for always giving me your best. You women are awe-inspiring, and I'm so lucky to have you on my team. I love you.

Larry Robins and J. Miles Dale—Thanks to you, these stories are no longer confined to my head and these pages. They will be immortalized on screen by actors far cooler and prettier than any of us deserve. If you need me, I'll be over here pinching myself forever.

My Team at Hachette Book Group and my agents at Bookcase Literary Agency—Because of you brilliant, talented, driven women, these unconventional, genre-blending books are now sitting on bookstore shelves all over the world. Thank you for not only embracing my weirdness, but thinking outside the box in order to preserve it. I couldn't ask for a better team.

My Beta Readers and Proofreaders (in alphabetical order: April, Leigh, Mary, Sara Snow, Staci, and Sunny)—You girls are my bottom bitches. I'd go to jail for any one of you. But, like, overnight jail, not like prison jail. Basically, I'd get arrested for you and then let you bail me out, and then I'd let you pay for my defense attorney. But I'd totally take the rap for you. All day, erry day. Thank you for helping take this book from good to great. I love you!

Colleen Hoover—Stop flirting with my husband. Oh, whatever. Go ahead. We can be sister wives. It's fine.

All My Author Friends—In a society that teaches us to compete, compete, compete, you ladies choose to share instead. You share with me your time, your advice, your encouragement, your resources, and often, your platforms to help me succeed in an oversaturated market where so very few do. Thank you for letting this pink-haired, foul-mouthed new kid sit with you. I love you!

My Reader Group, #TeamBB—You guys have literally brought me to tears with your support and enthusiasm—not only for me, but also for each other. I grovel at your collective feet. You make me laugh. You share my announcements. You make me teasers. SO many teasers. You make me blush with some of the reviews you post, and you keep my ass in gear. Thank you for *everything*. If any of you ever need a kidney, I'm your girl.

Harley—We had some good times, man. Wherever you are, I hope nobody has made you their bitch.

GEORGIA

ABOUT THE AUTHOR

19 PEACH STATE 99

BB Easton lives in the suburbs of Atlanta, Georgia, with her long-suffering husband, Ken, and two adorable children. She recently quit her job as a school psychologist to write books about her punk rock past and deviant sexual history full-time. Ken is suuuper excited about that.

BB's memoir, *Sex/Life: 44 Chapters About 4 Men*, and the spinoff Sex/Life novels are the inspiration for Netflix's steamy, female-centered dramedy series of the same name.

The Rain Trilogy is her first work of fiction. Or at least, that's what she thought until 2020 hit and her dystopian plot started coming true.

You can find BB procrastinating in all the following places:
Email: authorbbeaston@gmail.com
Website: www.authorbbeaston.com
Facebook: www.facebook.com/bbeaston
Instagram: www.instagram.com/author.bb.easton
Twitter: www.twitter.com/bb_easton
Pinterest: www.pinterest.com/artbyeaston
Amazon: author.to/bbeaston

Goodreads: https://goo.gl/4hiwiR

BookBub: https://www.bookbub.com/authors/bb-easton

Spotify: https://open.spotify.com/user/bbeaston

Etsy: www.etsy.com/shop/artbyeaston

#TeamBBFacebookgroup: www.facebook.com/groups/BBEaston

And giving away a free e-book from one of her author friends each month in her newsletter: www.artbyeaston.com/subscribe.